The Smoke of her Burning

M J LOGUE

Copyright © 2015 M J Logue
All rights reserved.
ISBN: 1518889328
ISBN-13:9781518889325

DEDICATION

For my boys, as ever, the big one and the little one.
For Claire, for her assistance with Tyburn and Doubting Thomas.
Services rendered by Alan, Pixie and Geoff, Laura, David, Jacquie, the Wardour Garrison and the Fairfax Battalia, Charles, Anna, Adrian, Francine, Jess, Cryssa, Mark, Jemahl, and the rest of the Little Commonwealth. And Debby and the crew at Abbots Staith, for geography and general Yorkshireness.

FOREWORD

"The Smoke of Her Burning" is the book that should never have been...

It's a funny one, Selby. It seems such a quiet town, now, but in 1644 it was key to the North of England, being not only the gateway to the York road, where the King was based, but also then a vital shipping port on the Ouse for bringing in supplies. And yet it's such a little-known battle.

Abbot's Staith is a real place, and you can go there. In fact, I recommend that you do! (And while you're about it, pop in to Selby Library, because they're lovely.) The rebel rabble, as ever, are fictional, for which the reputation of the Army of Parliament must be grateful. However, Thomas Fairfax, Black Tom, that most honourable and overlooked of commanders of the Civil War period, is a very real man. (Read Rosemary Sutcliffe's "The Rider on the White Horse". And then you could read "Command the Raven", in which Hollie is first detached to Fairfax's company in Yorkshire.)

The Earl of Newcastle's retreat from Hull and its fall into the hands of Parliament, and the loss of Gainsborough, had completely changed the situation in the Midlands. Brereton, Parliament's commander in Cheshire, was joined by the younger Fairfax from Lincolnshire, and the Royalists were severely defeated for a second time at Nantwich on 25 January. As at Alton, the majority of the prisoners (amongst them, Colonel George Monck) took the Covenant and entered the Parliamentary army. In Lancashire, as in Cheshire, Staffordshire, Nottinghamshire, and Lincolnshire, the cause of Parliament was in the ascendant. Resistance revived in the West Riding towns, Lord Fairfax was again in the field in the East Riding of Yorkshire, and even Newark was closely besieged by Sir John Meldrum.

Sir Thomas Fairfax, advancing from Lancashire through the West Riding, joined his father. Selby was stormed on 11 April and thereupon, Newcastle, who had been manoeuvring against the Scots in Durham, hastily drew back. He sent his cavalry away, and shut himself up with his foot in York. Two days later, the Scottish general, Alexander Leslie, Lord Leven, joined the Fairfaxes and prepared to invest that city.

Which gives you an idea, of course, that very shortly Rosie Babbitt and the rebel rabble will be at Marston Moor.

But first, they've got to get through Selby....

1

A WHITED SEPULCHRE

London
October 1643

Thankful Russell stood in the darkest corner of the parlour, the scarred side of his face turned to the wall, and closed his fingers around the fragile stem of the wine-glass on the cold white plaster mantel. Not, quite, hard enough to break it. Not this time, at least.

He'd been good to look on, once. Before. He'd known women – had known a good many, until a year ago – they'd taken delight in his company, once. Had tried to catch his eye, in a room full of people. Had whispered shocking things into his ear in the hope of eliciting a startled laugh, or at the very least, a smile. And then this – he would have put a hand on his puckered skin, but he wasn't sure he could bear the touch of it.

Stitched and patched like a joint of meat, and he doubted anyone in their right mind would *choose* to see his twisted smile, now. (He looked up at the smug, beefy painted face of his host, hanging in a pompous gilt frame over the fireplace. An arrogant whoreson – and not much better in the flesh, either.)

He'd gone home, after the battle at Edgehill, this twelve months past. No, he had gone back to lodge under his sister's godly roof, which was no home at all. There had been a girl, once, back there in Buckinghamshire, and now there was not. Margaret. Meggie. Her family's lands marched next to his own. He hadn't loved her, not in any grand and passionate way, but they had dealt well together and they would have been happy, in a small and contented way, for their allotted span. Of that he had been sure. It had been one of the surest things in his life, that he would have settled, one day, like a bird to its roost.

It had been a small tragedy, out of the wreckage of Edgehill. A very small thing, to receive a letter from Meggie's father, to say that they should not, after all, suit. It had not broken his heart, because his heart and his pride were already broken, but it had been one more tiny humiliation. And so he'd turned again, quartering to and fro like a masterless hound, grovelling for crumbs of preferment. He'd been a lieutenant in John Hampden's famous Greencoat regiment of infantry at Edgehill — and now he was not, turned loose, unfit for such service. Hampden had found him a place, in pity — a sober, respectable place, away from life and fire and action, in the personal service of the Earl of Essex, Commander-in-Chief of the Army of Parliament. It was a safe, snug post, with little more to do than write letters and keep records, and see to it that the Earl's shirts were laundered. It paid well. He loathed it, utterly.

And then in the spring he had by chance fallen into company with a two-yard high, raw-boned, North Country captain of horse with too much untidy russet hair worn unfashionably long, and a lamentably prominent nose, and a Dissenting turn of humour. Hadn't meant to like him. Hadn't meant to like anyone, actually, if he could help it, but had somehow persuaded himself that it would be an act of cold charity to abet Captain Hollie Babbitt's clumsy courtship. And whilst it had remained just that, an act of charity, he had been fine. Numb, but that was enough.

Russell's shadow fell long and thin and spiderlike on the wall behind him, and he turned his eyes away from that, even, with a shiver. From the right, he was still himself. His barley-pale hair was still thick and straight and almost as unfashionably long as Babbitt's, now, since he'd stopped caring. He still had the same dark eyes — dark grey eyes, slate grey, storm grey: some of the more articulate ladies in society had told him so, when he was still beautiful. So unusual, those dark eyes against his fair skin and his pale hair: so striking. Almost as striking as the great purple puckered starburst where a splintered Royalist pike had burst his cheek open as effectively as a mortar shell. If it had been a whole pike instead of the shattered butt, it would have killed him. He wished it had. Anything was better than this – bitter and useless, dependent on a great man's charity for his bread.

Well, he spat on charity. (He spat on most things, when he was drunk. It was about as distasteful as everything else to do with his marred face.) He didn't want pity. He wanted to be dead. He wanted not to hurt any more, but the wind was in the east, and all the bones in his head hurt, and he leaned his elbow on the overmantel and looked at the company assembling and disregarded Essex's disgusted expression, taking another pull at his wine. It wasn't very nice. He had a suspicion that Master Jonathan Harris was perhaps not the most discriminating of buyers. Not that Russell cared. It was anaesthetic, even if it tasted like horse's piss.

"Well, sir, you are scowling most ferociously, and I am sore afraid. Are we perhaps not a serious enough company for your taste?"

"No," he said flatly, resolutely looking away from Mistress Harris. Who had kissed him, once, a lifetime ago, when she was plain Meggie Corder of Buckinghamshire. It had meant nothing, at the time, sweethearted by the romance and chivalry of the beginning of the war. She was probably forty years younger than her new husband, and vivid, and not entirely pretty, and she laughed like a little chiming bell. Meggie had lively, irregular features: brown eyes that crinkled at the corners when she laughed, and a wide mouth, and thick, horse-brown hair. She was sweet, and innocent, and not very bright, but she was uncomplicated and loving. Or she had been, a year ago.

He had walked in behind Essex, this frosty autumn night, expecting no more than the customary brittle social thrust and parry, of flirting and flattering rich Jonathan Harris into throwing his massive personal and financial bulk behind the cause of Parliament. A company of some importance, with Master Harris already supplying and outfitting his own men, at his own expense. Russell wasn't feeling anything by then, not anxious, not awkward, because with the better part of a pint of brandy in his belly before they had even left London he found he did not care if they stared at his marred face or not. Could stare all they liked, actually, because he was in an untouchable place of his own by then, safe inside his own head. Someone had put a glass into his hand, something warm and spiced and he assumed it was supposed to be welcoming, on a cold night in almost-winter. The house smelt of cooking and warmth and spice. Russell almost gagged at the thought of food, and Essex had glared at him again, and then the mistress of the house had scampered in. And he knew her, even in her new silks and her pearls. Her eyes had widened, in pity and horror and recognition.

And knowing that – knowing that his old almost-sweetheart still recognised him, even like this – his hand had jerked closed around the stem of his glass, shattering it, staining his cuff with blood and wine mingled. He had managed. Had not been alive, not properly alive, not since Edgehill, but – he was managing. He functioned. But things had started to unravel in his head, when he'd begun to see Hollie Babbitt as *real*. Not a logistical problem to be solved, or a chess piece, but a feeling, thinking fellow man, sheepishly in love and awkward with it. And over a rather frighteningly short space of time, Russell had come to want everything to turn out for the good, because sooner or later, for *someone*, the Lord had to show some favour. Because otherwise it wasn't right. It wasn't *fair*. And that was heresy, and he was sorry for it, and the arrogance of it made him feel a little sick when he thought about it too much, but of late, Thankful Russell had come to believe in fair. That actually, God *did* punish sinners, and reward good people, eventually. That if you had had everything you believed in, everything that mattered to you, taken away, it would come right for you, in the end, if you only held fast, and had faith. It was a test, a trial, to see if you might be worthy, like Job. And so he had wanted things to come right for Hollie Babbitt, with the big russet-haired captain's unconventional courtship, because that would be a sign, that one day all would be well. In the end. One day. There would be someone, somewhere, who could love Russell, in all his marred, mad misery, and then he would be happy, and at peace. For the first time in nineteen stormy years, he would have a place to belong, and everything would be all right, forever.

And then it wasn't just Babbitt, it was all of them, all the man's wretched ruffianly troop. The whole lot of them, to a man, had been kind. Had treated him as if he was one of their own, as if he mattered. They had made a place for him, and he had tasted belonging. And it had been good.

And he wasn't sure he could bear it, having known what it might be like to have a place in the world, and to have lost it again. He knew it for what it was. It was pure, black, jealousy. It was a vile sin. He knew that. He couldn't stop it, though.

They were not perfect, they were not beautiful, they were not worthy or even especially godly. And yet square, freckled Venning had his Alice, out in Norfolk, and his square, freckled children. Babbitt had his Het, who looked at that big-nosed, judas-haired tempest of a man as if he were the only man in the world worth the looking at. (And Babbitt looked back, in his unguarded moments. It went both ways.) Even Luce, who claimed to be heartbroken after his first love had married someone else – his heart might be broken, but the rest of his romantic anatomy was in perfect working order, so gossip would have it. It was not impossible that someone might look on even such as Thankful Russell with kindness – not if there were women in the world who could see something loveable in this rag-tag rabble. She didn't have to bed him, this imaginary she. He was a man, not a beast. He asked only a little: that someone might be kind to him, and love him a little, and hold him, when he woke up whimpering. He didn't scream in his nightmares, not any more. He wasn't quite nineteen. He was – his marred face excepted – hale. Forever was a long time to be frightened, and hurt, and lonely.

"There, you see. You're scowling at me. I think you must disapprove of me very thoroughly these days, sir. I was never counted too gay for your company previously." Meggie dimpled at him prettily, and he favoured her with the closest he could manage to a grin, these days, knowing it looked feral. Her dark eyes flared sympathy. "Oh, I'm sorry. I meant only to amuse –"

He closed both eyes, which was somewhat unsettling as the room shifted behind his eyelids, and dipped his head till his forehead hit the cool, moulded plaster above the fire. "Mish –" he shook his head, was sorry he'd done it, put his fingers to his cheek furiously, "*tired*," he said through gritted teeth, "will not answer."

When he was tired the rags of stitched muscle would not always answer, and his voice grew slurred and mushy. That was all he meant. She blinked at him, uncomprehending, and he wanted to cry. She was still so young. She wasn't, he suspected, very worldly, yet, and he was frightening her. Which made him ashamed as well as sad. He had been frightened and uncomprehending, in another life, and he had *hated* it. He took a deep breath, and another mouthful of wine, and the warm sting of it eased his cheek a little. He touched his fingertips to the scars, and smiled at her with his eyes. "Hurts," he said, as clearly as he could manage. "I'm sorry."

And she understood *that*. Had looked at him, with those big soft brown eyes, a sort of wood-brown, like the gaze of a patient horse or a good dog. "It must have hurt," she said, and she put her hand on his face, wonderingly, and he had forgotten just how good it felt to have someone touch him in kindness. "When it happened," she said, as if he might not understand, and he looked at her and still said nothing because it was a fairly witless remark, after all. Well-meant but witless, and he was growing accustomed to it, after the better part of twelve months, but it still –

"You must have been fairly in the thick of it, Thankful. You must have been very brave."

He shrugged. Didn't want to talk about it. Wasn't sure that he could, had he wanted to. Inclined his head with what remained of his old feline grace, and looked away. "Oh, I am sorry," she said, "I did not mean to *pry*, but –" She looked at him, at the plain, decent, black suit that didn't quite fit him since he'd been hurt, at the slightly-crumpled lace to his collar. "You do seem to have had something of a hard time, though," she said, and he couldn't help it, he was quite drunk enough and it was a daft enough thing to say to make him laugh out loud, and she looked at him as if he was mad. Though he wasn't sure that he wasn't, and he hadn't laughed out loud in months, and it felt rather nice.

And she looked at him uncomprehendingly and then she laughed, too, and that felt even nicer, to be making a girl laugh again. "But you are scarcely changed, madam," he said, and her eyes crinkled again, and he bowed over her hand because he could still do that much, and she giggled. After that she decided he was harmless. Not, perhaps, entirely in his right wits, but harmless, and entertaining, and she put him at her elbow at table, smiling at the stout and severe middle-aged military men around them because, she said, she and my lord Essex's secretary were of a like age, and they could be children together whilst their elders talked of weightier matters. And everyone laughed, and Russell said precisely nothing, not feeling particularly childlike, but sufficiently numb that Meggie could talk of old times at his side and he could stare at unfocussed nothing. She dimpled prettily. "He won't mind, Thankful. I doubt he'll notice. Look at them, talking of battles." She smiled at her fat old husband, and then glanced back at Russell. "Are you married, yet?"

"Only to my duty," he said dryly. "You – no, sorry. Of course."

Russell propped his chin on his hand, disregarding the sharp kick in the shin from his patron at such rudeness at table, and scrutinised the girl. "You happy?"

She had a way of flickering her eyelashes when he said something she didn't understand. She *was* pretty, he'd never noticed it when she could have been his, she was pretty like a tree or a sunset, a natural thing, not a thing of artifice, and he could have wept for what he'd not known he had. "Happy?" she said blankly, as if he might have said something in a foreign language.

"Happy. You know. Joy cometh in the morning. Does he –" he jerked his head at fat, bullish Jonathan Harris, holding court at the head of the table in his fashionably martial buffcoat with the impractical glittering sleeves that had never been near a battlefield – "he make you happy?"

And she licked her red lips, glistening with wine and supper, and her tiny pearly teeth showed just a little, and she glanced at Russell under her eyelashes. Touched the pearls at her throat. "What do you think, Master Russell?"

He gave her the courtesy of consideration. And then he said, "No," very firmly, and very definitely, because she didn't look happy, she looked like a little bird in a gilded cage. A little wild bird, a lark or a linnet, all mewed up behind her silks and her pearls. All tied up in propriety.

And Meggie Harris was not happy. And that was sad. All dressed up like an expensive doll, but not happy. Poor Meggie. Poor Russell. He put his hand on hers, and ignored the black, glittering eyes of the Earl of Essex warning him across the frigid expanse of tablecloth that he was going too far. "It's all right," he said, patting her, clumsily. "All will be well. And. All manner of things shall be well. Dame Julian of Norwich said that, you know." He forgot himself and smiled at her, properly, not his careful company-smile. "Stupid wench, what did she know?"

The supper laboured to a close. He thought he hadn't spilled too much, made too much of a show of himself. Flung his head up defiantly at Essex's simmering disapproval – he'd done nothing wrong, but keep a pretty girl amused while his superiors talked of tactics and politics. Something touched his knee under the table, and he put his hand down in idle curiosity, thinking it was perhaps a lapdog or a pet slipped into the hall.

Found her knee instead. She gasped as if he was doing something outrageous, and he looked at her quickly, ready to apologise, to explain –

"I *am* rather warm," she said, and her eyelashes flickered again, and Russell sat with his mouth open, feeling his throat go dry. Had she – she couldn't have – she wasn't – *was* she? He took another mouthful of wine to cover his astonishment, and then felt her knee press against his again, under the table. *Deliberately*.

"Would – would you care to walk on the terrace, mis – Meggie?" He was all but an adulterer. She was offering herself to him, quite blatantly, with her husband barely an arm's length away, and there were any number of things that he could hear his sister's harsh voice whispering in his ear about adulterers and the sins of lewd women. Most of them involved hellfire. He closed one eye and squinted at the dancing candle flames. Hellfire tomorrow – but perhaps a little ease, tonight.

"That's right, my Margaret, you go out and enjoy the moonlight, there's a good girl." Harris grinned across the table, showing all his square, yellowing teeth. "My little pearl without price, gentlemen. Is she not lovely?"

There was a murmur of agreement. "She is yet young," Essex said, with a hint of warning in his voice.

"Romance is best kept for the young," one of the other officers at table said, sounding rueful. "When you've the bills to pay, and a houseful of squalling brats –"

And moonlight, and romance, was consigned to the ashes, while those dull, responsible middle-aged men shook their heads and talked of headstrong youth and the expense of stabling horses in the City. Meggie looked sad again, and lonely, standing in a square of silver light from the window with her skirts billowing pale and stiff around her.

Russell pushed his chair back, stood up – he was remarkably steady on his feet, he was proud of that – bowed his leave to the company, and took her arm. She smiled up at him. "Don't stay out too long, Meg," Harris called to her. He sounded suddenly protective. "Think of your health, gal. The night air –"

"I will trust to Master Russell's judgement," she said softly, and he felt like the worst of leprous sinners, briefly, and then her little hand closed round his and he was lost again.

They did not go too far. They stood on the terrace, and the top of her head barely came to his shoulder, and she pointed out the new rose that her husband had sent for from France before the wars, and did he think it would take in good English soil?

– It looked like a dry stick to Russell, but he thought it might be rude to say as much, so he said something non-committal and trailed after her hushing skirts like a dog on a silken leash, pacing the silver flagstones and looking onto the silvered garden.

And then, in the soft shadows of the arbour, she whirled suddenly and said, "Oh, Thankful, you were *always* my hero!" And having no idea what she was talking about, he could only look quizzical, and she went on to elaborate at some length about his bravery in a noble cause, and his sacrifice, and how it was like a romance out of the olden days, the tragedy of no lady to wear his knightly favour – "You see?" she said fiercely, and in the half-light he couldn't see her face but it sounded as if she might be crying. "Even now, you say nothing – so humble, and yet so brave!"

And while he was still wondering what the hell she was on about, she pressed her body against his, and her trembling mouth against his, and she kissed him.

She was eager, and she was clumsy, as if she did not know what it was she wanted of him but would have it anyway, and somehow the clumsiness roused him more than the eagerness. There was something defiant about her innocence. Her mouth was soft and fierce and she tasted of wine and cream. Suddenly his awkwardness was swept away and he was kissing her back, kissing her as if he was himself again, the deft, practised boy who'd learned how to make a girl sing out in pleasure. Her hands were flat on his back, her fingers suddenly splayed wide, and he didn't know if she was pulling him closer or pushing him away – and he didn't, actually, care. One hand at her waist, the stiff silk of her skirts crumpling under his fingers, and the other where the cool smoothness of fine linen gave way to the feverish smoothness of Meggie Harris's breast, cupping the softness of it against the cruel stiffness of her bodice. She had gone stiff in his arms, her little body struggling, all fragile and bird-boned – so fragile he could have put both his hands round her small, stiffly-boned waist and picked her up without an effort and laid her on the moonlit grass –

– and she was panting, her plump breasts rising and falling wildly under that elaborate lace as if she had been running, and she had one hand tangled in his loose hair and the other was flat against his chest pushing him away, and by now Russell was most thoroughly confused, she wanted him, she didn't want him, what the hell? Not the bloodless dream-knight in shining armour she thought he was, for sure, but a flesh and blood man, and surely that was what she wanted, she had *said* she wanted –

And then she gave a gasp that was almost a sob, wrenching herself free of him, and her dark hair was all fallen down from its pins, and he would have gone to help her, comfort her – find out what the bloody hell he was supposed to have done – had Jonathan Harris not said, three yards behind them, in a voice of absolute outrage, "Madam, you *whore!*"

She wept. She looked every bit the whore he called her, with her hair all unbound and her collar loose, the brooch gone, and her mouth swollen with kisses. And that was all his doing – this innocent, sweet girl, brought low with his vile acquaintance –

He lifted his head. "She is not to blame, sir. She is innocent. *I* am at fault."

"You?" Harris squawked, "*you*, you scar-faced whelp?"

"This is my doing," he said coolly, and Meggie raised her tearstreaked face and wailed, "I'm sorry, baba!"

She called him baba. That fat, blustering old man, who spoke to her like a child. And she called him baba. "I tempted her," Russell went on.

Paused. "My fault." The muscle of his cheek was beginning to stiffen again, and soon it would twitch, and he would be yet more shamed. A light, rosemary-scented breeze blew his loose hair across his eyes, and he put a hand up absently to brush it away. Harris was looking from one to the other, his eyes darting bright in the silver light. He wanted to believe Russell. He wanted to think that his pearl without price was foolish, perhaps, misguided – but not unfaithful. Russell dropped his gaze. "I tried. To. Dish." Ah, God, he sounded more drunk than he was. "*Diss*. Honour her."

And then looked up again, and loosed the strings of his collar, and unfastened the top buttons of his doublet, tugged his shirt open to expose his bare chest. The cool air stirred the hairs on his chest, raised goosebumps, but that was all right. "Kill me," he said flatly.

Harris looked at him, cocked his bullish head to one side, shifted his weight, and punched Russell in the face.

He wasn't sure, afterwards, what had happened. God knows he thought he wanted to be dead, but evidently his stupid damaged body had reflexive ideas of its own. He remembered tasting blood – it didn't hurt, which was odd – he remembered the sudden smell of soil as the force of Harris's blow knocked him off his feet, remembered rolling over in the wet grass with the spiky rosemary branches scratching his face and tangling in his hair.

He had an odd recollection that couldn't possibly be true, of coming up on his feet like a cat, hissing through bared teeth, with the hilt of his sword warm and solid and absolutely right in his hand, and the familiar ringing hiss as it started to come clear of its scabbard. Could not, possibly, remember Meggie Harris screaming as if he'd drawn steel on *her*. He could not have heard a yammer of outraged voices, because he could not have done those things. He could not have lunged for Harris in the wild confusion, could not have run him through the thigh. Could not gone down fighting like a wild animal until he was disarmed and bloody, and then carried on fighting with fists and heels and teeth, despite four of them bringing him down, trying to overpower him.

He didn't remember any of it, except what they told him, afterwards. How much he had hurt her, and shamed her. Of bruised flesh and torn silks; of blood and tears in the moonlight. It was only afterwards, with his wrists bound before him, wanting to touch the great tender bruise on the back of his head where some malcontent had knocked him on the head with the hilt of his own sword to quiet him – with his mouth bruised and split, and feeling as if most of his ribs were broken where the household of Master Harris had put one or two well-placed boots in – it was really only then that he began to be cold, and afraid, and to shiver with the knowledge of what he was, and what he might do, loose in the world.

And to start to pick at the frayed edge of the blanket they'd left with him, hoping to find a weak spot and tear it to a makeshift noose, because the stout frame of the high window looked sufficiently sturdy that it might hold his worthless carcass.

He could see the street, if he stood on the edge of the bed. Hear the hawkers calling their wares, the sentry downstairs on the door laughing with a passing girl. Someone singing. A dog barking. On the tiles above his head, a pigeon, its wings clapping as it lifted in flight.

Despair was a mortal sin, they said, but he thought it was perhaps a worse sin to leave something like him, alive. He was afraid. Had been more afraid, at Edgehill. That was fine. It would only be for a little time, God willing.

No, he retained some faith, yet. A faith that his God was not his sister's God – might yet find a little forgiveness for a frightened, unhappy man, who had been a frightened, unhappy little boy, once.

He swallowed, hard. Felt the torn edge of the twisted blanket move against his throat, and thought that for once, he might have done something right.

Trust in God, Thankful. And –

Let go.

2

LIKE ARROWS IN THE HAND OF A WARRIOR

Essex
November 1643

Hollie Babbitt didn't know quite how he felt, actually.

There was part of him that was strutting-proud, because he had a son on the way. (Son, daughter, it was of no account, so long as Het was happy.) He'd gone respectable, at last. A pretty wife, and a solid house, and a babe in the cradle, and three weeks' back pay tucked safe inside his coat. It made him feel properly smug about life, that did, being able to go home to his girl with a bit put by, to provide for her over the winter.

There was another bit of him that was scared witless, it having been ten years and more since he'd been anything like respectably married, and he had little moments of panic when he wondered if he'd forgot the niceties of it. Margriete had had a real bee in her bonnet about Hollie leaving his sword propped against the wall by the bed. (He still did it. It had saved his sorry arse on more than one occasion.) This chamber is for sleeping, she'd say to him sternly, if you are of a mind to brawl take it outside. He'd been twenty then, and sleeping had been the last thing on his mind most of the time. But Het – well, he just didn't know. He'd been married to her for almost eight months, and he'd spent no more than a week of it in her company, and the rest of it sloping at Thomas Fairfax's heels bringing up a rag-tag cavalry troop in the Army of Parliament.

(Did she mind? he wondered, rather wildly. Would she rather have him a proper officer, with a chain of command and shiny armour, instead of a slightly ragged captain in a stained buffcoat, with one junior officer to do his bidding?)

How would they fare, together? He'd lain with her – twice? Three times? – he remembered every soft, clean, freckled curve of her, the soft swell of her belly under his hand, the sturdy breadth of her hips. The weight of her uncorseted breasts. He had a dark suspicion she might not be flattered, that perhaps he ought to call her frail and delicate as an early snowdrop, but that was getting into Lucey Pettitt's poetic territory, even if it wasn't an out and out thumping lie. The softness and the cleanliness and the solid comforting sturdiness of her was always in his head, had been in his head under the guns at the siege at Hull, on the battlefield at Winceby in Lincolnshire in the autumn, in the thick of the fray: that if anything was worth the fighting for, it wasn't a distant moral principle. It was Het Babbitt's right to order, if he was fighting for anything. Her right to live at peace, and to bring up her – their – children as she saw fit, in the faith she saw fit, and the faith of her fathers. By God, he trusted to his wife's honour more than he trusted to the King's, after this last twelvemonth.

And that was the thing, that was the bit that rubbed at him, like ill-fitted harness. He trusted Het with his life. He was made like that: once he was won, he stayed won, with a degree of bloody-minded resolution that bordered on stupidity. He'd known her – in the strictest Biblical sense – less times than you could count on the fingers of one hand. He'd not lived with her, not slept in the same bed, not shared her board: not as her husband. Living under the same roof counted for nothing. He'd been nothing to her, then, no more than her nephew's slightly-broken commanding officer and a thing of pity. And now he was coming home, and she might be disappointed in the scruffy russet reality of him. He just didn't know.

Still, he was bringing her beloved baby nephew with him, safe and unharmed and as daft and dreamy as ever. Luce was five yards behind, umpty-umpetty-ing in the incomprehensible and profoundly irritating way he had of counting out his versifying syllables. God knows who it was this time. Luce had a habit of finding his rural Philomenas no matter what scant rations you put him on: and the bugger of it was, they looked back. No, Hollie had no idea what to expect when he got home, and he didn't much care. He didn't even mind his father's dour and devout presence ten yards behind them, sullen as a raincloud. He didn't object to Luce's happy prattle – though the thought crossed his mind that he'd have to get used to a continual meaningless stream of chatter, if he was going to have a son of his own by the spring.

Other than that, she was going to have to take him as she found him. He'd left the Army's winter quarters at Hull a fortnight ago feeling quite stubbornly proud of his scruffiness: he was a plain fighting officer, as worn and straightforward as his plain standard-issue backsword, and Het had married him exactly as he stood up in front of her. It was funny how every mile that passed that brought him nearer to home, made him more aware of his own shortcomings. He wasn't vain. He'd never been vain.

Two yards high and plain as a pikestaff – plain and awkward and lanky, with the sort of colouring that was both conspicuous and unfashionable –

Drew Venning called him a lolloping great mawkin and that was exactly what he was, a great raking scarecrow of an individual with no graces and no looks to speak of –

"Hollie," Luce said kindly, kicking his red mare up alongside Hollie's equally raking black Friesland stallion, "did you pick up a flea at that last inn?"

"What?" He'd grown fond of his young cornet, over the last eighteen months. It didn't mean he had a clue what was going on in the little bugger's head, most of the time. "Where the bloody hell did *that* come from, Luce?"

"You're wriggling," the brat said. "Just wondered. Auntie Het will murder you if you come in the house lousy."

"I am not lousy! And I am *not* wriggling! I was thinking!"

"If you look like that when you're thinking, you ought not to do it. It's clearly not good for you. What's amiss?"

"Nothing!" Like he was going to tell a twenty-year-old lad what was bothering him – especially a twenty-year-old lad with delusions of knight-errantry. Bloody Luce never looked like he'd been dragged through a hedge backwards. Bloody Luce had the sort of smooth, straight hair that looked neat from dawn to dusk, and even when it didn't look neat he looked elegantly dishevelled and not like he should be under a hedge begging his bread. Bloody *Luce* didn't have something unmentionable splattered down the skirts of his buffcoat, which Hollie knew for a fact was nothing worse than last night's supper, though it looked it. Bloody Luce –

"You're doing it again," the brat said, sounding amused, and Hollie turned in his saddle and gave him a wordless snarl.

"What ails the lad?"

"I am not a lad, I am your bloody commanding officer, you old bastard, and don't you –" Hollie stopped, because both Luce and his father were conspicuously not looking at the absence of plate and officer's sash.

Captain Holofernes Babbitt had reverted to being plain civilian Hollie about a week and a half ago, when he'd left Hull for his home leave. These two might be serving under his command while he was with Fairfax in the North, but when he was at home in Essex it was a happy coincidence. Or, in the case of his father's company, just plain coincidence. "Nothing. Whatever. Ails. Me," he said through gritted teeth.

"Tha looks feverish, boy."

From someone who'd spent Hollie's boyhood trying to beat the Lord's grace into him with the buckle-end of a stirrup leather, Elijah Babbitt's paternal concerns didn't cut much ice with his firstborn. "Then we'd best crack on and not stand here in the pissing rain passing remarks on the state of my health. Hadn't we?"

Luce dropped back a length, eyes downcast, and since his father showed no signs of having the wit to do likewise, Hollie snarled again and belted his awkward horse down the shoulder with the flat of his hand – feeling the need to take his temper out on somebody, and black Tyburn in one of his more unhelpful moods was an ideal candidate. The big horse gave an affronted snort and took off through the hock-deep mud at a racketing canter, splattering Hollie with an additional cosmetic enhancement of wet black Essex slurry. After a hundred yards or so, he'd run out of sweariness and the horse had run out of devilment, so they halted in the lane while Tyburn churned the track to a bog and

Hollie fought to hold him still. "Well, what are you two waiting for – Judgment Day?" he snapped, glared at the pair of them, and then turned the black horse straight at the nearest hedge and let him go.

It was messy. Tyburn was not a horse built for athletics, being as clumsy and rawboned as his master and having the cussed temperament to match, but when the stallion was in the mood for compliance there wasn't a mount to touch him in the Army of Parliament. Today he wasn't in the mood, so he went crashing through the hedge instead of over it, stopped partway across a ploughed field and started to buck like an unbroken yearling.

Luce and Elijah waited patiently in the thin December drizzle, watching the mist roll in off the river. "Never proper broke to bridle, that one," Elijah grunted disapprovingly, and Luce – who wasn't entirely sure to which party that cryptic comment referred – made a non-committal noise.

"Not for want of discipline, mind," the old man added thoughtfully, which clarified matters somewhat, although it didn't make Luce any the more comfortable.

The swearing from the field had stopped. "Prob'ly broke his stubborn neck. Pride goeth before destruction, and a haughty spirit before a fall."

"Indeed, sir. Although I am at a loss as to how exactly we might explain that one to my aunt."

"Aye. Well. I imagine that lass has got plenty spirit of her own, lad, or she'd never have took up with my boy in't first place." Elijah glanced sideways at Luce and then pulled out a spotlessly-clean, if ragged, handkerchief. The old man was wheezing like a leaking bellows, close to, and no matter what he might have done in the past Luce did not like the sound of his rattling chest.

"No doubt. Sir. Um – it will be dark in a while, sir, would you be so good as to make some haste –"

"Lad," the old man creaked, "will tha, in all charity, use my name. It pains me to see thee tie thisself in knots trying to work out how to call me." He gave a breathy laugh. "Miscall me, more like, if tha listens to my boy."

"Quite. Elijah. Sir. Would you – my aunt will be expecting us."

Well, *someone* must have told Auntie Het that her little nephew had turned in off the Braintree road, in the company of some great raking red-haired ruffian on a black horse. And possibly, in the fading grey light, Elijah's sandy-grey hair looked as russet as his son's, and a wet bay horse could pass for black, but even so, it was almost comical to see her come barrelling out of the parlour and across the hall. Auntie Het was wearing an old-fashioned fur-lined cassock coat but even without the additional bulk of the fur that lady was the size and shape of the Great Bed of Ware, and Luce was stunned into silence.

She looked at the pair of them with the eagerness fading from her face. "Lucifer," she said accusingly, as if he might have concealed Hollie about his person somewhere. "That is not –"

Elijah stepped forward and bowed, with considerably more dignity than Luce had ever expected from that quarter. "Thee is my daughter, mistress. Tha's not a daughter I'd ever thought to see, neither, but the lad did well for hisself."

"Indeed, sir. I – I bid you welcome to my – to our house. Lucifer, I want a word with you. Now." She gave her new father-in-law a brittle smile, and then took her nephew in a grip like a horse-bite just above the elbow. "Do make yourself at home, sir," she called over her shoulder. "Just a tiny bit of family business – Lucifer what the – how *dare* you bring *that man* to our house?"

"I didn't –" Luce began, but this was evidently a flood that was not going to be stopped. He had a suspicion most of it wasn't aimed at him, either, but you had to allow breeding women these fancies. So they said.

"Six months, sir, and not a word from you! You *are* literate, I assume? You can write? How dare you! Just turn up out of nowhere without a word – you might have been dead for all I knew! And to bring *him* with you! Lucifer, do you have any idea how much my husband *loathed* that man? Do you? And – Lucifer what the – what in the name of the Lord is the dratted man doing *now*?"

To the open-mouthed astonishment of most of the household at Fox Barton, Elijah Babbitt was standing in the middle of the hall, still in all his travelling dirt, hat in his hands, eyes piously upturned to heaven, and was grimly offering his thanksgiving to the Lord for his safe deliverance. Loudly, and at some length, with specific reference to the state of the highways of Essex, the inclement weather, and the intemperate ways of the malignant soldiery of Charles Stuart. Auntie Het stood and watched him with her mouth slightly open for a while. "He *looks* quite a bit like Hollie, doesn't he?" she said faintly.

"I think the captain is quieter," Luce said, and his aunt turned the same dumbfounded look on him as she'd been training on her father-in-aw, where he stood still dripping on the stone flags and still bending the Lord's ear at full belt.

"You said 'is', Lucifer?"

"Well, yes, I – auntie, you didn't think – " She did, though. She was very upright and very stern and very dignified and her freckled, capable hands were white on the edges of her coat where she was gripping the sleeves. "Auntie, he'll be here any minute. He's fine. He was just a little delayed –"

– at which point he braced himself to take the full weight of his Auntie Het in a most expansive and interesting condition, which had never been lightweight and in an advanced state of pregnancy was nothing short of leviathan. Hysterical, too, he thought. He patted her back awkwardly and she carried on howling into his shoulder. At least Elijah had stopped bothering God and was now scowling at Luce in disapproving silence, although precious little could be heard above the sound of Auntie Het's noisy tears.

"Er. Luce. Not being funny, brat, but what the hell d'you think you're doing?"

Het's tears stopped as effectively as if someone had choked her.

Her head came up from Luce's shoulder and she stepped away from him, paced across the hall with steady deliberation, and looked up at her errant husband as the door slammed behind him on a gust of bitter wind. All two scruffy mud-splattered yards of him, wet and windblown and filthy and with an expression of mild bemusement on his face. "Husband," Het said sweetly. "*So* good of you to let me know of your intentions to return with company."

What Hollie may or may not have said in excuse was lost to posterity, but he started to say *something*, and his dignified, respectable little wife simply hauled off and smacked him flat-handed across the cheek with her full weight behind it. It was not a love-tap. She meant it.

There was an awkward moment of silence. "By Christ, lass, tha's got a good right arm," Hollie said indistinctly, one hand to his scarlet cheek, and then that suddenly-shameless little madam he'd got himself married to stood on tiptoe, wound both her hands in his hair, and kissed him with enthusiasm.

"I think all is well," Luce said, just in case anyone hadn't noticed.

That was perhaps an overconfident statement. Even after Luce had given his farewells and fled to his mother's house, five miles away in Witham – even after Hollie had explained that he couldn't in all conscience have left his poor old Lancastrian father alone and friendless at winter quarters in, of all places, Yorkshire – even after Het had recovered herself sufficiently to bespeak hot buttered ale and cakes to be brought through to the snug confines of the winter parlour – it wasn't, precisely, comfortable.

Hollie had positioned himself on the floor in front of the fire with his back against his wife's skirts. He wasn't saying much, looking into the fire with a faint smile on his face. Not paying anyone any attention, unless Het gave his ponytail a sharp tug, and even then it took him a while to come back from whatever daydream he was in and talk sense. Het said, in a fierce whisper, that she thought it was a most undignified place to sit and it made her feel positively awkward, having her husband sitting on the floor leaning against her like an old dog, but on the other hand he thought it was comforting her to have his solid presence there, and not just the thought of him. Since the letters he'd been writing this last six months seemed to have vanished like smoke – she'd not had a one of them. And Elijah plainly didn't know what to make of either of them – whether his new daughter was wholly wanton, or merely afflicted with the fancies of a breeding woman, and whether or not she was dangerously violent towards all and sundry or just Hollie. "Tha looks tired, lass," Hollie said, ignoring his father and looking up at his girl with a contented grin on his face. "Bed, I reckon."

She glanced at him quickly. He looked back with his most innocent expression –which she evidently found endearing, but unconvincing.

"Husband?"

"Oh, I'm proper worn out, me."

"We have *guests*, Holofernes," she said sternly, and he gave her a sideways look that made his opinion of those guests, and his intentions, more than amply clear.

"Give you time to get the bed warm, then, won't it?" he murmured, without batting an eyelash. She stood up hastily, and her closeness to the warmth of the fire may have explained the colour of her cheeks. "I will bid you a good night, sir. Husband." She didn't order him to behave. Didn't have to. They hadn't been married that long but Hollie knew that tone of voice already.

He was half-inclined to give Het's – admittedly rather tempting – backside a possessive squeeze as she passed, just to annoy his father, but the lass had that glint in her eye and she'd already belted him once tonight: he wasn't wholly a glutton for punishment.

The door closed quietly behind her, and Hollie took a deep breath and set his shoulders and braced himself because he was bloody *sure* Elijah was winding himself up for a tirade. It had been twenty years since he'd spent a civilian night under the same roof as the old bastard, since he'd run away from home, after that final stand-off. He'd been sixteen then, and as lanky as he was now. And Elijah weighed half as much again, probably, as his rawboned firstborn, but in that last row Hollie had thought he'd killed the old man. And he'd fled to the Low Countries, with nothing but a sword to make his way in the world, and the two of them hadn't set eyes on each other from that day to the day Hollie had turned up with the troop in Bolton in the autumn, drawn back to the family farm like a magnet to true north.

Wanting to prove a point, to rub the old bastard's nose in his temporal glory, if no more. Proved nothing, except that the old bastard was as perverse as ever. Well, he still knew the signs and they still sent a cold ripple down his spine, and that made him bloody furious at the same time as he was afraid. No. No, he was not afraid of the old man. He was bigger than Elijah now, and thirty-odd years younger, and he was fitter, and –

And he was still, at heart, the same scared boy that he had been all that time ago, and he leaned a casual elbow on the mantel so the way his hands were shaking wasn't too apparent.

"So," Elijah said. "This is where thee has been hiding out all this time, boy, is it? '*If a man have a stubborn and rebellious son, which will not obey the voice of his father, or the voice of his mother, and when they have chastened him, will not hearken unto them: Then shall his father and his mother lay hold on him, and bring him out unto the elders of his city, and unto the gate of his place.'"*

"Had a bloody good go, didn't you?"

"At what, Holofernes? At correcting thy wickedness? And what would thee have had me do? *Withhold not correction from the child: for if thou beatest him with the rod, he shall not die. Thou shalt beat him with the rod, and shalt deliver his soul from hell.* Book of Proverbs, lad, as tha well knows, for I do know thee knows the Lord's words better than thee claims to. Thee was ever an unruly boy –"

"And *thee* has been in my house five minutes," Hollie snarled, "and tha's fighting me already!"

"Aye, and I am still thy father, Holofernes, and thee owes me a duty!"

"I owe you *nothing*, you old bastard."

He was still quick, for an old bastard. "Keep thy voice down, boy. Has thee no respect for thy wife, that she needs to hear thy intemperate squalling all over t'house, with her breeding?"

"*Me?*"

"Aye, thee. Still ungovernable as ever – still arrogant, and wilful – I see my lord Fairfax ent took none of that out of thee, boy –"

"Aye, and I'm still thy commanding officer, on the authority of my lord Fairfax. So think on that, and mind thy mithering tongue, owd mon!"

Elijah spat into the fire. "*That* for temporal glory, boy. Put not thy trust in princes –"

"Any more o' that talk, and you are out on your arse at first light."

"What? Thee is Fairfax's dog, to follow him without thought where he bids?"

The funny thing was, there was a bit of him that was Fairfax's dog, and would do exactly as he was bid. There wasn't a lot, because Elijah had seen to that when he'd beaten all the unquestioning obedience out of Hollie twenty years ago. Even so. It had been meant to raise Hollie's hackles, that remark, and instead it made him smile. "Aye. Aye, I reckon so far as I'm anyone's I am Black Tom's hound, to follow at his heel."

And it was worth it, just to see the old man's jaw drop. "Thee, boy? *Thee* take governance from another?"

"Just because you never managed it – *father* – don't mean it's not possible. Just that happen Fairfax is a better man than thee. And he's never raised a hand to me, neither." For the first time in his life, Hollie had got the old bastard on the run, and he liked it. "Looking a bit peaky, owd mon. Lass left a bit o' buttered ale, I reckon it's still good." He hefted the jug out of the embers – considered belting the old sod with it for the sheer joy of it, as he seemed to consider a lot these days – and then decided against it. The look on Elijah's face at his firstborn's sudden domestication was much more satisfying. Hollie poured the old man another mug of warm ale and gave him his sweetest smile. "Now, sit thee down. Shall I move up and let thee have this space hard by t'fire, in respect for thy years?"

"I'll punce thee in t'head, boy, if tha doesn't –"

"Now, father, have a bit o'respect for my wife, as is breeding and wants a bit o' quiet. As tha's at such pains to remind me. Can tha manage the stairs, or shall I see if Catterall can get a pallet for thee down here?"

"Tha pushes thy luck too far, Holofernes!"

"Ah, now, if tha wasn't so frail and dothery I'd never have brought thee with me in t'first place. I'd have left thee in Hull to rot, as thee deserved. Now drink your god-damned ale." Hollie was poking the old bastard about being in his dotage because it was so clearly vexing him.

Even so. Elijah's bony hands were veined and spotted with age –

"Thee never wore a wedding ring, before?" Hollie said warily.

"And how should you know, boy? *Thee* doesn't."

"I'd have felt it. *Wouldn't* I?"

To which Elijah had no answer except to drop his mad yellow eyes reluctantly. "Aye. Well. It was –" He stopped there, and twisted the plain gold band from his finger. "Happen it's your wife's, by right."

"What – it was my lady mother's, then? Touching. She must have been a fair old size, for it to fit thee." Hollie held it up to the firelight, peering at the worn inscription on the inside. "What in the name of God is *that* supposed to mean?"

Two crudely drawn hands around a lopsided heart, well, that was obvious enough. And they said Hollie's mother had been tall – tall and slender and graceful, they said, for which she must have been turning in her grave, because her son had the height and the build but before God he had inherited none of the grace. It crossed Hollie's mind that the flesh must have come off the old bastard like melting candle-grease, for him to be able to wear that ring. Elijah had never been fat, God knows, but his fingers were like bone, now. "That won't go near Het," he said, handing it back. "Lass has got her own, anyway. She don't want none o' your gimcrack baubles."

"Thee has a vicious tongue, boy."

"Only because I am mindful of my filial duty, father. Were I not related to thee by blood I'd not have the least hesitation in cutting thy miserable throat."

"Aye." Elijah looked up, quite calmly. "Believe me, I am sensible of that."

No, Hollie didn't wear a wedding ring. Had always had it dinged into him that a good Puritan boy didn't hold with such fripperies and vanity, and it had sort of stuck. He'd stood up with Het in front of a distinctly non-conformist Army chaplain last year and he'd put a ring on her finger then, though he considered himself just as bound without any such outward show. (And had known men lose fingers on the battlefield, for their rings. Though he wasn't going to tell her that.) On the other hand, he did wear one of her hair ribbons about his wrist, under his shirt, and Luce reckoned Hollie had acquired a trick of rubbing his wrist when he was tired, or unhappy, like he was comforting himself with the touch of a thing she'd had in her hand. He realised he was doing it now, all unconscious of it, his right hand up under the cuff of his left sleeve, absently rubbing the faded silk, and the lass was only up a flight of stairs from him. And she would hate what he was doing. Hate it? She'd probably forbid him her bed for all eternity.

He took a deep breath. "Aye. Well. I shouldn't have said that. It's –" Christ, the words nearly choked him, but Het would have it so – "it's not true, anyway. Luce – some of the lads – I'm a bugger for saying things I don't always mean, just in badness. Known for it."

"What is thee saying, boy?"

"I'm saying I might not like thee, but I'm not going to murder thee in thy bed, neither."

And to his absolute astonishment, Elijah laughed. The old bastard sounded like a creaking door, but it was a recognisable laugh. "I never thought tha would. Thee is too much thy mother's son for that."

"Is there any chance one day tha'll stop making mysterious remarks like that and actually *tell* me what she was bloody like?"

Elijah snorted. "Like? Look in a mirror, Holofernes, and that's what she was like. Though somewhat bonnier. Not much mistaking my side o't' family in thy face. And –" he was tugging at that ring again – "considerably sweeter of temperament, I reckon. But then, that girl o'thine might yet be the making of you, for I don't reckon she'll put up wi' none of your peevishness."

"Thee is looking tired, owd mon. No –" as Elijah went to protest, "I'm not asking, I'm telling thee, it's time tha saw thy bed or I might yet reconsider that decision not to offer thee violence."

Those mad bird of prey yellow eyes flicked to Hollie's face for a second – not frightened, just considering. Then Elijah cocked his head, looking even more like an ageing hawk. "Thee is in jest, boy. Thee did ever have a perverse humour."

Well, that wasn't a family trait, for sure. "Does tha need help?" Hollie said abruptly, and for the first time in his life, he meant it. He hadn't been entirely joking about the old bastard looking done in, either. The soft amber light of the fire forgave a multitude of sins, but what was mostly holding Elijah Babbitt upright was pride and sheer bloody-minded will, and Hollie knew *that* look when he saw it. "I do not," his father said stiffly, and Hollie put his hand under the old man's elbow anyway.

First time he'd ever laid a hand on the old bastard without the intention to hurt, too, and it shocked him how frail he was, under the shell of linen and wool. How warm and human and *alive* he was – a fragile, ageing man, not a leathery fiend from the pit. Trembling slightly under Hollie's hand, with the ropes of muscle in his arm tensing as he levered himself out of his chair. Thinking of his father as a fellow man, and not a demon? Getting soft in your old age, Holofernes. "Is thee sickening for summat, owd – father?" he said warily, and Elijah turned his head and looked his lanky son full in the face. Age hadn't stooped him that much, then.

"Nowt a night's sleep won't cure, boy. Nowt for thee to fret over." The corner of his mouth lifted in a wry grin, which was disconcerting, because Hollie knew for a sure and certain fact he had the very same mannerism himself. "I won't die on thee, lad. I won't show thee up in front of thy wife."

3

A LITTLE COMMONWEALTH

There was a wicked easterly wind whipping up off of the Fen Country, bringing with it a chill that left Hollie flexing his crooked wrist, wincing. He couldn't say he took much to the climate in Essex. Not like home – like Lancashire, not home, this was his home, and he gave himself a mental shake – it got bloody cold in Lancashire, but at least in Bolton they had something between them and the sea. Even if it was only Yorkshire. He perched awkwardly on the edge of the clothes press at the foot of the bed, trying to undress quietly so as not to wake Het. (As if he was going to get his boots off without a struggle, but a man had to show willing.)

She snored like a little hedgehog, all curled up and snuffly, and he stood there watching her sleep, loving her so much it hurt him. Sounded like her bloody nephew: it drove Hollie mental sharing quarters with Luce and his dignified purring snores, though he thought it was adorable coming from Het. He wrestled the quilts off her. Dear little lass, she had them quilts pulled up to her chin and she wasn't letting go for nothing and no one. She gave a cross, sleepy little murmur and settled against him, wriggling her flannel-covered backside in his lap. Which was nice. He put his arm about her middle, carefully, somewhat astonished by how warm and *solid* she was. He'd expected that – prominence, put it tactfully – in the front to be as soft and pillowy and comfortable as the rest of her and it assuredly was not. It was quite frighteningly solid. And it *wriggled*. Which was fine, as the wriggling of his wife's precious cargo was presently reducing him to silent giggles.

He was being kicked by *his own son*. Little bugger was a Babbitt, right enough, restless even in his mother's belly.

"Hollie?" she said drowsily. "You have cold hands, husband."

"Now *there's* a surprise. Is he always this lively?"

"Indeed *she* is." She was definitely awake now, heaving herself over in bed so she could rest her head on his shoulder. "Jane Pettitt thinks definitely a girl. She says I'm too well for it to be a boy. Boys take it out of you – she says."

Hollie thought of the boy in question – couldn't imagine Luce being so unmannerly as to take it out of anyone, but presumably the brat's mother knew best. "Don't care, lass, so long as you and – she – are well." He patted Het's belly awkwardly. "You listening in there, wriggler?"

She settled with a great sigh – he felt her frown, as her hand strayed to his loose hair and discovered the acorn-sized tangle just behind his ear, and then she proceeded to worry at it with her fingertips. "Holofernes," she said crossly, and he wasn't sure whether she was referring to his ungroomed state, or his perfectly reasonable curiosity as to the extent of her expansion.

"Hmm?"

"*You*, sir, are incorrigible – with your father in the next room, of all things –"

"That's all right, love, he's not like to come in and make helpful suggestions."

"Yes, but – "

"Het?" She looked up, her eyes bright in the moonlight, and he tugged the quilt up over her shoulders. "You know I've been in this house four hours, lass, and tha's not kissed me once?"

"Now that is no way to greet a husband who has been away these six months and more, is it?" she said wickedly.

Afterwards, lying curled like spoons with her hair tickling his nose and his hand idly exploring the rest of Het's interestingly-expanded person, he thought he could get used to this being married. Warm, and dry, and sleepy, in bed listening to that bitter wind rattling the roof tiles, with his lawful wife's warm bare backside snuggled against him: Yorkshire could be a thousand miles away, Newcastle and his half-arsed doings a distant memory –

"Husband," she said, sounding far too awake for his liking, "why did you bring him with you?"

Which he didn't have an answer to, because he wasn't sure. Pity? Duty? Spite? "Lost his house, lass. Bloody Malignants took it over when they took Bolton." He sighed. "I couldn't hardly leave him in Hull on his own, Het. Bloody ars- horrible place, is Hull. We spent long enough there for me to know it's permanently bloody raining, it stinks of rotten fish, and it's full of bloody Yorkshiremen. He can't go back ho- to Bolton, because he's got nowt to go back to. And because I imagine since the silly bugger took to trailing round the countryside after me, my lord Newcastle'd think it was a smart idea to catch him up and try using the old bas- feller to shift me out of quarters. Which it wouldn't," he added, consideringly. "But I'll not have the old bas- feller used as a bargaining tool."

"Because he is your own flesh and blood after all? Oh, Hollie." He wasn't sure, but it sounded frighteningly as if she had a catch in her voice. "Oh –" definitely a little quiver there, and she heaved herself over and hugged him so hard he thought his ribs were creaking. "Oh husband you are so good – you have such a loving heart –"

"Mmm," Hollie said non-committally. Actually, it was because Thomas Fairfax would personally tear his head off if the Babbitt family loose ends got caught up by the Royalists and used to unravel the Parliamentarian cause in the North, and it was something he could see happening all too easily with that evil-natured old gobshite. Could also see the old bastard mouthing off at any Royalist who was daft enough to lay hands to him. Oddly flattering to think that for once in his life Hollie had done something the old bastard approved of – even if not for the right reasons.

Het gave an admiring little sigh, which he greatly approved of. Lass seemed to think he was a much finer being than he thought he was himself, and it wasn't his place to disillusion her. "Oh, Hollie," she said again. "Oh my dear love. Why can't all men be as decent – and, and honourable – and *Christian* as you are?"

"Steady on, gal!" They reckoned women got funny notions when they were breeding, but even so.

"Well, if all men had your forgiving nature, we wouldn't be at war, would we?"

In his younger days, Hollie had been described as a lad who could take exception to the company in an empty room – by Sergeant Cullis, as it happened, and he should know – so being told he had a forgiving nature came as something of a shock. "It's a bit more complicated than that, Het," he said carefully, before she had him down as peace envoy to the Army of Parliament.

"Well, why can't you just make the King promise not to do it again? I'm sure he's a very honourable man – Hollie, are you *laughing* at me?"

"Me? No, no. Far from it." Apart from the description of that shifty-eyed little bugger as honourable, given that in his experience of the King, what you mostly got was piecrust promises – easily made, and just as easily broken. Sneaking behind Parliament's back. Conniving with the bloody poisonous little French baggage he was married to, encouraging Popery in Newcastle's forces in the North because he thought the Papists might do his fighting for him. By all means cease hostilities, gentlemen, but only for as long as I say so and on my terms. The man had more faces than the Town Hall clock, and the longer the war went on, the more Hollie disliked him. Mind you, that said, the Earl of Essex, that gormless overbred pillock, had spent most of this summer bleating for a cessation of hostilities, claiming that the Army of Parliament was inadequate, whereas in the opinion of Hollie and every other officer who'd had the misfortune to be commanded by the dilatory bastard, it was the Earl of Essex who was inadequate. Should've accepted the bastard's resignation when it was offered in June, in Hollie's opinion, instead of patting him on the head and telling him it was all a bit of a mistake and everybody loved him really. "Be lovely if it worked like that, though, Het."

"I am very sure that the Lord's will, will prevail," she said primly.

"Ah," said Hollie, whose private opinion was that the Lord's favour was less important than superior firepower and a supreme commander who wasn't a tosspot with his thumb up his arse. "Tha's not frightened, lass – I mean, I'll be close to home, if tha needs –"

"To *home*? You're not going back?"

"Colonel Cromwell's asked us to join the Eastern Association, lass. I'm going no further than Essex. Can come home every night, if tha can stand t'sight of me –" She gave a little wail that he hoped was one of joy, and his firstborn jiggled and kicked against his flank in a most disconcerting fashion. "I wasn't frightened," she said with a sniff, and he hadn't realised she'd been crying till she looked up with silver snail-tracks on her cheeks, "but I shall be so glad to have you with me. They say – well, you know the sort of things they say, in the streets. This time next year we'll all be starving, presuming that we're not all murdered in our beds." She snuggled again. "It will be nice to see to your linen," she said musingly. "I don't know what kind of wife people must think you have, with the state of some of your shirts. Hollie."

"Mm?" He liked her snuggling. He even liked being treated as her own personal warming-pan. It was a novelty he could grow accustomed to. "Yes, lass?"

"I thought – I was afraid you didn't like me any more," she said shyly. "When I had no word. I – I knew you couldn't have been hurt, because Lucifer was with you, so Jane would have said –"

"Lass, I wrote to you every day. That's God's honest truth, Het, any one of the lads will tell you. I had to put bloody Eliot on latrine duty for a week, he was taking the pi- rip that much. I used to put 'em in wi' Fairfax's dispatches – Russell said he'd see to it, if you remember –"

"I haven't seen a one of them, Hollie. Russell is the nice boy with the scarred face that brought me home after our wedding? No – I haven't seen him, either, not in months."

4

A CHILD OF HIS OLD AGE

On campaign, Hollie was invariably awake before dawn and prowling his horse lines, kicking sentries awake and checking on mounts and kit with a detail that bordered on the fanatic. At home, God help him, he didn't even wake up till it was full daylight, or as full as you could expect in bleak midwinter Essex, and Het was up and dressed and he'd missed the glorious sight of his girl wrestling with her stays. He didn't even know where he was for a few minutes, lay flat on his back looking at the embroidered hangings round the bed and trying to remember where he'd seen them before.

Oh, but she was lovely, sitting on the end of the bed all bright-eyed and neat and tidy, with a plate of new-baked bread and a pot of honey in her hand. "Awake, I see," she said sweetly, and he wasn't entirely sure he was, or if he was still dreaming. He sat up.

"I really must add a nightshirt to your wardrobe," she said thoughtfully, looking straight at the unlovely purple puckered hole in his shoulder from Reading, and then looked up into his face with a glint in her eye that made him slightly breathless. "Or perhaps not, husband."

He thought there must be worse ways to start a day. And then it got better, because when he made it downstairs, there was no sign of his father, and Catterall informed him – with a relish that was perhaps a little bit uncalled-for – that the old man was abed with a feverish cold and Het wouldn't let him get up. At which point Hollie rolled his shirt sleeves up and set off whistling, considering himself a happy man. Even when it started to rain, partway through the morning while he was trying to clear the culvert, knee deep in rotten leaves and murky water, didn't bother him at all. He thought he might just be having a little ride out to see Thankful Russell at some point, though, the treacherous little snake. (Wherever the little bastard was. Somewhere cold and wet, hopefully. Dead in a ditch, even better.)

It set a pleasant pattern for his days of idleness, thumping inaccurate nails in to pieces of the farm buildings by day, and watching his wife expand like rising dough by night. Reckoned he could almost see her doing it, and she grew fat and sleek and contented. He was even there when the mare Yaffingale dropped her colt – the first foal that he knew of, of Tyburn's siring – in the middle of a howling sleet-storm in the middle of December. Looked as leggy and frail as a harvestman spider, and was as stubborn and solid as his massive black father. Het wanted to call him Harvestman. Hollie favoured something plainer, but – well, she was his girl, she got what she wanted. Elijah suggested Jehu, but then as Elijah was still confined to his bed with an inflammation of the lungs that showed no signs of improving, he hadn't seen the colt and his opinion counted for nothing.

The house glistened like frost, all hung about with green – great swathes of rosemary branches and flourishing bay trees: every room was golden and the air was permanently scented with honeyed beeswax. All new to the Puritan-born Hollie, and he couldn't quite shake himself of the impression that at any point this winter garden of earthly delights would vanish into the bitter darkness. Het laughed at him for it. She reckoned he was like a little boy, all eyes, poking warily into wonders that didn't concern him. And he was inclined to agree, if not to argue about it. He was banished from the kitchen during this week of wonders, which teased him mightily, it being his favourite part of the house. His lovely girl relented sufficiently to occasionally pass him a handful of sugar-plums, though she still spent most of her time in there with the door very firmly closed, and the smell of spices and sweetness curling out like temptation through the wood.

Banished from the kitchens, too wet and too cold to work on the farm, he found himself occasionally passing the time of day with Elijah, propped up on his pillows with the breath whistling in his chest, hacking up great lumps of yellow phlegm into a basin. Fully expecting the old bastard to be calling down hellfire and brimstone on the pagan celebrations being prepared under his very nose, and instead finding that the old man was too weak to be angry. "Read," Elijah wheezed, pointing at his Bible.

"Where?" Hollie said warily.

"Start. The beginning."

Got as far as the forty-fourth chapter of the Book of Genesis. "*'And we said unto my lord, We have a father, an old man, and a child of his old age, a little one; and his brother is dead, and he alone is left of his mother, and his father loveth him'* –" before Elijah's gaunt hand closed on his wrist, and Hollie dropped the book with a yelp.

"Thee has a father, and thee alone is left of thy mother."

"Reckon I left summat on the fire downstairs –"

"No, boy. Stay. I'd –" he began to cough, and Hollie winced, because it was a horrible, wet, tearing noise, and it seemed to go on and on. "'Tis the time of Christ's birth, Hollie." The old bastard had never called him Hollie before either. Always the full version – or "boy", which he particularly hated – he knew the old man just didn't have the breath in his sodden lungs for more, but it fairly laid him flat. "Start – again?"

"No," Hollie said flatly, because he couldn't, and he would not: not while the yellow-eyed bastard was still drawing breath would Hollie forgive him. Not for fifteen years of trying to break his spirit: like breaking a colt to bridle with a curb bit and spurs –

"I loved thy mother. Boy." He turned his head on the pillow, and in the grey afternoon light his silver-stubbled cheek was wet. "Thee. I did not."

"Old news," Hollie said bitterly.

"Wanted thee to be – Ruth. Thee looks so like, boy. So like." Elijah laughed. "And is not. Thy mother's eyes. And the worst – of my temperament." Didn't laugh, though his shoulders moved, under the old-fashioned heavy nightshirt that Het had found in a chest somewhere, that had belonged to her late husband. "How should me and thee get on, boy? Too much alike in temper."

"Bit late to be telling me this, isn't it?"

"Stubborn. As a bloody rock. Boy. Sit down. Not finished. Would have loved thee if –" he struggled to sit up, wheezing, amber eyes blazing in his wax-pale face –"thee had been a girl. Thee is not. Never loved thee as a boy. *Never*. Wanted thee to be summat thee could not be –" he took a great shuddering breath, "I would have chosen Ruth's life over thine ten times over if the Lord had offered me the choice but I was stuck with thee, Hollie. Now you listen. Fought with thee – watched thy back – stood with thee on the field six months and more." He settled back on his pillows with an expression of grim satisfaction. "Given thy siring – thee has turned out decent enough."

"In spite of everything you could do," Hollie said, unmoved, and his father's mouth twitched.

"Aye. That."

"So birthing me killed my mother, you wanted a daughter anyway, and you never cared for me?"

"More or less."

"Honest," Hollie agreed, and walked out.

5

THE SINS OF THE FATHERS

All he could think of at first was to get out – out of the house, out of sight of that man, out of the bloody county for preference – saddle Tyburn and just bloody well go and never come back, keep riding till he ran out of daylight, find himself some dirty dark tavern and get wholly pissed and break things –

And it might have been what he'd done when he was a stupid boy with no more sense, but he was a grown man with a wife and a – wriggler – depending on him now, and more than that, he was buggered if he was going to let the vicious old bastard who'd sired him, run him off his own god-damned turf. Which didn't stop him being in almost as filthy a temper as a big horse who'd been hauled from his warm stable into a howling storm, tacked up, and ridden at intemperate speed into the freezing dark. Tyburn was seething. His ears were flat, his tail was clamped between his legs, and he'd bitten Hollie twice already. He was a mile past the church in White Notley before he realised the sleet was turning to snow, fat white flakes nestling in Tyburn's shaggy mane. He could turn round and go home. It was his home. It was Christmas Eve, it was a time of peace and joy and celebration, and that old fucker had chased him out of his own bloody house –

But he couldn't, he could not force himself to swallow his temper that far and go home, and so he hauled the black's head round and belted him round the backside with the buckle end of the reins, and then when he'd picked himself out of the ditch at the side of the road and caught the horse he thought they'd try that again and get it right this time. (Tyburn bit him for the third time, but by this time they were reaching a point of mutual disfavour and Hollie wasn't in the mood for playing silly buggers.)

By the time he finally dismounted it was near dark, and his boots were squelching, but he'd made a sort of inner peace with himself, the horse was blown, and since he appeared to have arrived on Luce Pettitt's doorstep without any conscious thought on his part he thought he might as well call and pass the time of day. Regretted it, mind, as soon as the door was opened and he found himself knee-deep in what appeared to be most of Witham, all laughing and chattering all at once, and Jane Pettitt in an understated and probably hugely expensive deep-red wool gown with fine lace at her collar and cuffs, smiling in welcome at him. "My dear Captain Babbitt," she called above the hubbub, and he wasn't sure when he'd become her dear, or what in God's name Het had been telling her sister-in-law –

"My son's commanding officer," she said proudly, to whoever it was at her elbow. "The captain is *very* well thought of by Sir Thomas Fairfax, you know –"

"And looks," Luce said at his elbow, "like a sack of –"

"Thank you, Lucifer," Hollie said through gritted teeth, catching the words "most well-connected" and "apparently something of a hero earlier in the war, they say" and wanting to sink through the well-polished floorboards and die. The white-haired old date at Jane Pettitt's left was now craning her neck to get a better look at Hollie, squinting in a deeply unappetising fashion. She looked less than impressed with her well-connected war hero, and since Hollie had been digging out culverts in the clothes he was wearing now, he could see why he might be a disappointment. "You're wet," Luce said thoughtfully. A small girl suddenly appeared from between the legs of the multitude, tugged on the skirts of Luce's doublet, scowled at Hollie, and whispered something to Luce. "This is Bab," he said resignedly. "Baby sister. She says I promised to play blind man's buff in the parlour with them. Mother's knee-deep in guests – they always have open house on Christmas Eve. Father's customers, mostly –" he nodded politely to a middle-aged gentleman with a ruddy complexion and too many ribbons attached to his person.

"Don't mention bloody fathers to me," Hollie snarled, and then some kind soul put a mug of mulled cider into his hand, and he downed it in one irritable swallow. "Christ, I – sorry, brat. I, um, that was most welcome, sir." He gave the fair-haired man hovering at his shoulder a stiff bow. "Master Pettitt. Your servant. sir –"

"On the contrary, captain, it is myself who is indebted to you," Gabriel Pettitt said smoothly, and you could see where Luce got the manners from. "Not only do you fight for my Cause, but you keep my son in hand. A difficult task, I imagine."

"What, *Lucey*?" He remembered too late he was talking to the brat's father and tried to make it sound like he'd just been clearing his throat. "No trouble at all. A lovely lad. He's a credit to you."

"And I never had to pay him a penny for that testimony," Luce said, shaking his head.

"How fares my sister?" Gabriel said, taking Hollie most earnestly by the elbow. "She is well, I hope? And – " he coughed nervously, "– you know?"

"What, the bump? Fine – coming along nicely – Het's well, aye, thriving." The older man's face relaxed, as if he'd expected bad news. "No – no, just thought I'd – you know – Christmas, and all – friends –" And Hollie had managed to come out with a whole sentence that said precisely nowt, but sounded reassuring. He was congratulating himself with a second mug of cider, and a sigh of relief at having escaped his brother-in-law's interrogation so easily, when someone poked him in the small of the back.

"Might ha' known *you'd* turn up, Rosie. Like a bad penny, 'ee is."

He dropped the mug, and then in the ensuing commotion and hastening to the kitchens to mop up the debris he stood like a mooncalf and stared blankly at Drew Venning. Drew in company with a fine-boned, stunningly beautiful lady that he could probably have picked up in one hand.

"Our Alice," Venning said smugly. "Has that effect on all the boys, don't 'ee, gal?"

"Only in your imagination, Andrew," she said, and he grinned.

"She got a smart tongue on her as well, my girl. Alice, this is Captain Babbitt, what was serving with me at Caversham Bridge. Lolloping big lad I told you about – decided to take on half the King's Army by hisself on the bridge, the daft gret –"

"*Andrew*," she said warningly, and the big freckled captain wriggled like a naughty puppy.

"Not keen on cursing, our Alice. Anyway. Rosie – for the hair, gal, thass why we call him Rosie –"

"No, that's why *you* call me Rosie, and I wish to God you'd stop!"

"*Rosie*," Alice Venning said, in exactly the same forbidding tone she used to stop her husband mid-swear, and the two younger officers giggled.

"Hol–"

"–lie." Before Venning gave his full, humiliatingly zealous name away. "Hollie Babbitt."

"Short for Holofernes," that unregenerate ruffian finished, refusing to be diverted. "Married to Luce's auntie, out at White Notley, five miles hence. And you come out here to wish the lad the compliments of the season, in this weather? You have to be off your head."

"I am acting in the capacity of a pander," Luce said sweetly, appearing at Hollie's elbow with a fresh mug of mulled cider.

"Thass right, bor, me and Alice have been having assignations for the last fortnight." He grinned, and put his arm about his tiny wife's waist, and squeezed her most familiarly. "I'm quartered in London with m'lord Essex, and she'm out at Diss, and Luce reckoned that'd be about half-way house. And here I be!"

"Thass right," Alice said, sounding briefly as countrified as her husband. "Left our lil' jasper with his nurse overnight, he's good as gold."

He missed Het, suddenly, so much it hurt him. She should be standing here with him, talking about babies with Alice Venning, and poking him in the ribs to stop him swearing. Standing on her tiptoes to hiss into his ear that there were *other guests*, Holofernes, and did he not see food at home. "Here," Venning said, dropping his voice to a conspiratorial roar, "d'ee hear about that scarred lad, that mate of yours? Funny lad, thought he was a bit of a cut above, as was at your wedding?"

"Still alive, is he?" Hollie said, unable to stop himself from sounding as if that might not be a situation likely to continue.

"Oh aye! Here, Alice, did you not say you was going to write down that receipt for gingerbread for Mistress Pettitt?"

"That was subtle," Luce said wryly. Alice evidently agreed, because with one final look over her shoulder that promised later retribution she strolled off to monopolise her hostess.

"Ah. Well. I wouldn't like to say, in front of our Alice. He went a bit odd, did that Russell. Drink. On the ale from sun-up to sun-down, they reckon. Never hardly saw him sober. And then –" Venning glanced behind him furtively like a six-foot gossiping goodwife –" he was at a supper with m'lord Essex – feller who'd raised one of the trained bands in London, chap called Harris, rich as Croesus?"

Hollie raised his eyebrows with polite disinterest.

"Russell only tried to rape his wife, they're saying."

"Christ." And that came from Luce, who wasn't given to such things. "*Russell?*"

"Thass right. It was all over London. Tore her dress off her, got into a hell of a brawl with Harris, nearly killed him, they say. Took half of Harris's lads to bring him down. Harris wants him hanging, o' course, and they say Essex ent so sure, or whether he just wants him broke or indentured – well, 's all immaterial, anyway, Essex has had him banged up this last six weeks, thinking what to do with him. Prob'ly die of a gaol fever before he decides, and weasel out of his deserts that way. Filthy little scut," Venning added disapprovingly, "I'd ha' caught him with his marred little paws on any gal in *my* company I'd have broke his bloody neck for him."

"Dirty little bastard," Hollie agreed, and Luce, being Luce, shook his head.

"No. No, not Russell. No. He's too particular."

"He weren't particular that night, Lucey, I can tell 'ee that, and I had it from a man who had it from someone as was *there*. Too drunk to stand, more or less, and pawing her at the table and all – you know what they say, the quiet ones are always the worst."

"I do not believe it," Luce said again, more firmly. "I *will not* believe it. Not from second-hand gossip, Drew. I *liked* Russell."

"Ah, well, so did Margaret Harris, till he tried to have his dirty little way with her, in front of everyone."

"Wants hanging, if that's true," Hollie said. "I knew there was summat. I *knew* it. Not one single one of my letters home, did he pass on. Not a one. Het's been worried sick. And I cannot abide a man who breaks his word. Hanging's too good for that scar-faced whelp. If he laid a hand on my girl he'd have been wearing his balls as ear-bobs –"

"Would you care for another cup of cider....sir?" Luce said, very firmly, and once again Hollie could only admire the little bugger's diplomatic skills. Venning laughed, and said Luce was fierce when he was roused, and to mind him, and said he was going out for a smoke after all that ferocity. He did not say no to the cider, however. Although Hollie thought he probably ought to be mindful. He had been caught by the local brew before, himself. Was, possibly, married as a result of the local brew, actually. As Luce well knew, having been smugly present at that momentous, marvellous occasion – dear God, was it a year back, that he'd sat at table at White Notley for the first time, that first time Hollie had set eyes on his girl, and the first time he'd tasted Essex cider?

Well, regardless, he was being careful. Was under his brother-in-law's roof, and had already managed to acquire himself a reputation of carthorse-like dexterity, the last thing he needed was the impression of intemperacy as well. Luce was prattling at his elbow. Something else the brat was good at, that bright social inconsequential babble. That was not an insult. The day you got Hollie Babbitt to stand in a room full of strangers and sweet-talk fat middle-aged wenches with hairy moles, would be a cold day in hell. "That's better," Luce said smugly, and Hollie returned to the here and now and said, "What?"

"You don't look quite so intimidating when you're not scowling fit to crack a glass."

"You sound like my wife."

"Well, she is my auntie, sir. It's not inconceivable." He gave Hollie a bright, social smile, and said, "Look happy. Mother's on the prowl. If she thinks you're not enjoying yourself she'll start introducing you to people."

– like the old bat with the hairy mole. Hollie stiffened. "I'm off out for a smoke with Venning. If anybody wants me."

"But Hollie, you don't smoke!"

"I know," he said over his shoulder. "But it's better than the alternative."

6

COMPLIMENTS OF THE SEASON

Luce shook his head. "Coward," he said, to no one in particular. Smiled politely at Mistress Canning, a ruddy-faced lady from the town whose jowls rested on her old-fashioned ruff and who seemed to get through a phenomenal number of gloves. Her eyes seemed to gleam with a strange fervour. Since to his knowledge the lady had not been reborn in the Lord's grace, Luce had the dreadful suspicion that she might have news of another grandchild, and that he might be the last man in Witham not to have heard tales of this infant prodigy.

There were advantages to his position in the Army of Parliament. Mostly the ability to be somewhere else, when there was the possibility of tired local gossip. Out of the corner of his eye, he saw the tablecloth ripple, briefly, and the tail of a skirt disappear beneath it. He checked the table automatically. There had, indeed, a rather imposing marchpane centrepiece of a gliding swan, magnificently gilded and bedecked with rosemary branches. It had a somewhat lopsided look, as if person or persons unknown may have recently removed one wing and a number of tail feathers. (Bab. Under the table. With marchpane. A lot of marchpane. That could only mean one thing.)

"Oh, God," he muttered, and fled.

It was raining, but it didn't seem to be bothering Venning, who was leaning cheerfully up against the backhouse wall trying to keep his pipe alight. "Dunno why's I bother," he announced. "Reckon I must just be a glutton for punishment, eh? I could be enjoying the company of my wife and a good supper, and here I be, outside in the tipping rain. Filthy habit."

"Bloody dear habit," Hollie muttered alongside him, looking more like a moulting bird of prey than ever in the downpour.

Luce just looked at the pair of them. "There is, I assume, a reason why you two are out here. Plotting Caesar's assassination?"

"Beware the Ides of March," Hollie said darkly. "Bit bloody early, brat, or d'you reckon we're that useless it'll take us three months to sort it out?"

"He didn't do it," Luce said, one more time, "he couldn't have," and Hollie narrowed his eyes. "Since I assume we're not talking about Caesar now, Luce, I don't care. He's not my problem. Leave it."

"But –"

"Lucey. I'm not going to talk about it any more. Not my problem. Your Uncle Essex's problem."

"Shirking," Luce muttered, evidently recognising defeat. "That's what you're doing. Shirking."

"Aye. Truanting. For myself, I'm thinking I've stood out here long enough to look like a drowned rat, and that it might be time to make my apologies and get off home. Tactical, you see, gentlemen. Been here long enough to be sociable –"

"And wait till the cheese was finished," Luce added, and Hollie shot him a dirty look.

"Nowt to do with the cheese. With respect to your lady mother, but her ember tart's not a patch on the tart as comes out of our kitchens at home." He sniffed. "You will observe, gentlemen, I am wet enough to be an object of sympathy. So I'm going to bugger off home and get it."

"Good for you," Venning said, taking another satisfied pull on his pipe. "Mind, your good lady's probably thinking you're running some secret errand. I done that with our Alice." He grinned. "She thinks I gone running out to get her suffen for Christmas. Bless the gal, she reckons I'd forget my head if it wasn't screwed on. What she don't knowis I got her a bolt o'silk round about quarter-day and it been stowedaway in my quarters ever since. Rosie, what's 'ee looking like that for,like a lad just swallowed a caterpillar in his sallet?"

"I don't think Ro-um, Captain Babbitt has a deal of experience with the festival aspectsof the season," Luce said delicately, and Hollie snorted.

"Aye, summat like. What the brat means, Venning, is that the old feller didn't hold with celebrating Christmas, and I never had much practice, and I don't think the lass is going to take that as an excuse since I've not considered myself one of the Lord's Elect this twenty years and more. So by your leave, gentlemen, and if you don't see me in the spring it's because our Het's buried me under the knot-garden."

He was trying to look nonchalant and worldly about it. It was rather comical, actually. The house door shut to behind him with a bang, and Venning turned to Luce, grinning again. "Well, well, well. Reckon our Rosie's scared of suffen after all, then. Under the cat's foot, is he?"

And there were a number of things Luce could have said. That of all things, Hollie Babbitt was most afraid of losing what he had: what other men took for granted, a hearth and a home and a place in the world and his own people in it. That there had been little between Hollie and the blackness before now but Luce, and a friendship that had not yet been tried, then.

That Hollie might like to give an impression of caring for nothing, but he did, with a silent ferocity. That he might like to be seen as a rebel and a reckless outcast, but he was the most conventional of men, under that scratchy outward seeming: a man who preferred enduring home comforts to fleeting grand passions.

It wasn't Luce's place to say, of course, and so he said nothing. He might not be the greatest soldier in the Army, but he flattered himself that he was, also, a friend.

He was also Drew Venning's friend, and he smiled, as if it was so unlikely as to be humorous, and not true. "You have not yet met my Auntie Het," he said, and Venning chuckled.

"There, 'ee is a poet even when 'ee don't mean to be, bor!"

7

THE PRODIGAL SON

It had stopped raining, though Tyburn was making it clear that he thought Hollie was finally and totally off his head, as did most of the Pettitt family and the great and the good of Witham.

The annoying thing was he'd been caught like this before. Even bloody Drew Venning, who was a bloody turnip from the Fen country, knew it was bloody Christmas. Something else to hold Elijah *bloody* Babbitt responsible for, then, that even Venning was capable of remembering that Christmas was not always a time of fasting and prayer, thank you very much – whereas bloody Hollie, dragged up dour in a house where the nearest you got to festival was a clean shirt on the Sabbath, just took it as another day in the year. He shook himself irritably, and so did Tyburn.

Ah, God, it annoyed the hell out of him that once again he was bloody different. Feeling fifteen again, the tallest lad in the room by a good hand's width, and trying to stoop to look like everyone else, and instead drawing every eye in the place with his clumsiness. This time every eye in the place was on his *bloody* stupidity, and he might as well be wearing a placard round his neck that said "Brought Up Puritan" because once again, he didn't know how to behave in decent company. Once again, the world was full of cheerful, ordinary, small celebration, and once again, Hollie *bloody* Babbitt was half-shocked by the wickedness of the secular world, like he hadn't had twenty years out in it to get used to the idea.

He hadn't brought a gift for his wife. They'd not even been married a twelvemonth, and he'd not brought so much as a handkerchief for Het, and he knew bloody well she'd done something nice for him. He'd done nothing for her, save bring that horrible old man into her house. *Nothing*.

– He'd done nothing for Margriete, either, that first year he'd been married to her. He'd been so piss-broke he'd had to sell his god-damn sword, the only decent thing he'd ever owned, to buy her a trinket. And the memory of that made him more furious than ever, because he was rising thirty-six, and he still had no more sense than he had then, at eighteen. So irritated that he hit himself in the side of the head, hard, with the heel of his hand, and Tyburn picked up his pace to a skittery canter.

He hoped to God there was no one still up in the house, and that he could slide into bed and pretend he'd just gone and sat at the bottom of the garden and sulked for an hour or two, instead of thumping around Essex in the dead of night. It was cold, but not bitter, and Tyburn hated being kept shut in, so he turned the big horse loose in the river meadow and stalked across the yard. Considered dumping filthy tack and leaving one of the farm lads to clean it. Thought of that younger version of himself again, and exactly what his estimable sire would say of any man who thought he was too good to take care of his own horse's harness. (And what his estimable sire had done, on a number of occasions, to ensure that the young Hollie had looked to his own horse's comfort before his own. And what, if he was honest, he did to his own troopers, in like case. Dear God, he was admitting the old bastard might have had a point – the end of the world must be indeed nigh.)

There was nothing he could do about the state of himself. He was as cold and wet as a puddock, and she'd probably give him hell on, knowing his girl, but it was that or sleep elsewhere and he was not going to give up the pleasure of her bed for the sake of a bit of water. He could take his boots off downstairs, and kick them under the table out of the way, and hope he hadn't left too much of a trail of mud across the hall, and dump his coat over the stairs and hope it'd be dry enough in the morning not to pass comment –

"Boy."

The raven's croak that came from the back parlour sounded like a voice from the tomb and it startled him so much he dropped his coat, whirled round, and nearly tripped over the bottom stair.

"What?" he hissed furiously. It was dark. No one needed to know his hands were shaking. "What the hell are you still doing up?"

The old man laughed, or coughed, one of the two. It was a horrible wet noise, anyway. "Waiting for thee, boy. One of us had to stay up. Thy wife was fretting for thee. I sent her to her bed. Thee is a bloody fool, betimes. Get in here."

And he went, though he hated himself for it. He *would not* bow the knee to that old bastard. "What?"

"You know what. She would not tell thee to thy face thee is acting like a spoiled brat, boy, so I will. Leaving that lass so near her time, sulking off wi'out so much as a by your leave! And where hast' tha been, eh? Till near enough dawn –"

"None of your business!" Hollie snarled, and then pulled himself up because he didn't need to account to the old man. "What d'you mean, she's been fretting? She's all right, isn't she?"

"Not for any effort on your part, bloody shiftless whelp. What kind of husband does tha think thyself to be?"

"The hell business of yours is that? I –"

"Walked out on her, Holofernes. Thee is not a bachelor now, boy, thee has a wife to think on –" the old man hawked, and spat contemptuously into the glowing ashes of the fire. "That is not the act of a good man. That's the act of the same stupid heedless boy I tried to train some sense into, and thee wouldn't have it then. I'm not going to hold thy hand, boy. Thee has a wife. Thee is supposed to be a man grown, not a child, to require governance, and yet thee has not the sense to at least tell that lass that God hath given you as a helpmeet – not even tell her where tha was going? She was worried sick, boy!"

"It is no business of yours, old man!"

"It is *every* business of mine, you mannerless puppy! That lass is my daughter!"

"She's nowt to do with you!"

Elijah got to his feet, slowly. He was stooped with age, but he was still tall enough to look Hollie in the eye, and he was still intimidating enough for Hollie to back up a step till the overmantel of the hearth dug into his back, just below his shoulderblades. "She is everything to do with me, Holofernes. She is the mother of thy child, and thee should have the wit to know that, and if thee does not, it falls to me to either correct thy manners till thee does know it, or to remedy that lack myself."

"Oh, aye, and I should take thee as a pattern-card for domestic harmony, should I?" The little sensible part of his mind was urging him be wary – in fact, hold his tongue altogether, for this was a conversation that could only end one way. Had only ever ended one way, and one day would end one way forever, for neither of 'em could back down. "How should I know how a father should act? I never bloody had one!"

"I haven't had a wife for nigh on forty years, whelp, but I know what a husband's duties are!"

He wanted to run again. And yet, he did not: didn't know what way to go, and stood, with his head flung up, jerking like a curbed horse. Realised his hands had crept clasped in front of him again, damn it all, the way they always had, when he was a fearful child again in his head – pulled his fingers apart with an effort. "Aye. Well. What I know, I didn't learn from you," he said. "You taught me *nothing*. I've not even a gift for her, for the morrow, and that's your teaching, straight down the line, you joyless, godly *bastard*."

Elijah gaped at him, his bony face illuminated by the soft amber light so that he looked like nothing so much as a demon from the pit. "Christmas is yet celebrated in this house," Hollie went on. "*Celebrated*. That lass would have it a time of peace and happiness. I have ballsed it up sufficient already. I'll not let you cock it up any further. You can hold your tongue and be civil in my – in her house, old man, or you can fuck off back up north, and I hope the King's Army stands aside for you. She would hold the season of Christ's nativity as a festival, and if that's what my wife wants it's what she will have, for before God I gave little thought to a better gift for her, thanks to your schooling."

The old man closed his mouth. And looked ashamed. Which, under different stars, might have given Hollie some pause for consideration, that his father was capable of shame. He said nothing, though his jaw clenched and unclenched briefly. "I would not give her any hurt," he muttered stiffly, and then looked up. "*She*, I would not. She is a good woman. A sight better than thee deserves: shameless, intemperate whelp." His eyes dropped again. "Thee has a gift. If thee would have it."

"Me? It's Christmas Eve. I have nothing, nor the –"

Elijah's hand shot out, quick and hard as a kicking horse, and grabbed Hollie's wrist and forced his fingers open. Stuffed something into his hand, and then ground his fingers closed over it.

Something small, and warm, and hard.

"Thee has thy mother's wedding ring, boy."

And actually, the feel of it – the thought that it had been put on the finger of a woman who'd been dead for as long as he'd been alive, and worn thin and warmed by the flesh and bone of his appalling father – it made all the hairs stand up on the back of his neck, as if someone had thrust a snake into his hand, and he couldn't help that he yelped and hurled the thing from him, into the heart of the fire.

And wished, then, that he had not, though he felt as sick and shaky from it as a man new come from a battlefield, because he thought for a minute that he had finally gone too far. Hollie stopped, staring at his father, tense and waiting for that final blow.

Which did not come.

Elijah nodded, just the once.

"Aye," he said, as if it had confirmed a thing he had long suspected. "Aye. I can't blame thee."

He brushed past Hollie, and walked out of the parlour, into the dark. He didn't look old, or frail, or pitiful. He looked like a stubborn, greying, wretched old bastard, and if he'd been any other man Hollie might have felt sorry for him, in his hurt and his dignity.

As it was, he waited for the sound of footsteps to die away, on the stairs. Listened for the creak of the loose floorboard on the landing, in the angle of the stairs. For the door to close, because you had to give the door of that chamber a right good tug, where it had swelled in the damp – been Hollie's room, when he'd stayed here, that first winter, before he was married.

He left it a while after that, for the old bastard to say his prayers, and to fold his meagre belongings neatly on the coffer at the end of the bed.

Hollie could almost say the prayers along with him. Elijah had probably made the same prayers for the last forty years, and would probably make them for forty more. The immortal soul of Ruth Elizabeth Babbitt, now with the saints in Christ's bosom. That his prodigal son might be brought again to the Lord's grace.

Waiting. Waiting. Because Hollie felt as if what he was about to do was somehow shameful.

The house was still. Only the rain in the gutters again, and the sound of the wind in the trees in the river meadow, and the fire finally falling to ash, and the sound of Hollie's own breathing. The sound of his heartbeat, eventually, steadying down. With a sigh, he took up the poker, and pulled the sleeve of his doublet down over his fingers.

That ring was going to be bloody *hot*, when he found it.

8

AFTER THE WAR WAS OVER

It felt like such a little thing, though it had his heart with it. And he was ashamed to give her that ring in front of them all, tomorrow – such a tiny, insignificant thing, and so he folded his clothes neatly and set them on the press at the foot of the bed, and slid between the blankets, and very gingerly snuggled up to his sleeping wife.

"Your hands are freezing, husband," she said tartly, and she had not been so asleep after all, then. She followed it up shortly afterwards with, "As are your feet, dear. What on earth have you been doing? Swimming?"

"Went over to wish Lucey – um, Lucifer – and his family a peaceful Christmas," he lied. "It suddenly occurred to me that I had not done so."

"I'm sure we should have seen them very shortly," she said, "without the need to catch your death of cold. Come here."

– Not something he needed to be asked twice, and she put her feet on top of his and rubbed his fingers and told him off for his lack of care for himself and did he want to see this babe come into the world without a father. And then she told him off again, saying he only ever thought of the one thing when he was at home, and he might have argued with that, since he thought of meals as well. But she seemed to like ticking him off, and he rather liked the way the new expanse of Het bounced and shifted as she was doing it, and so he decided to say nothing but lie quiet and enjoy it.

She curled herself up around him, and he put one arm round as much of her as he could reach, and she heaved a gusty sigh into his armpit. (Which was brave of her, considering how much thumping about the countryside he had been doing this night.) "Oh, husband," she said, and she sounded as if she was dropping off to sleep, this time. "I so wish you would be here for good and all. I do miss you."

He was just getting settled himself, and he wasn't expecting her to pat his backside in a most affectionate manner. With intent, he realised, with astonishment. Approvingly. "What do you think we shall do?" she said drowsily. "When you are home for always? When it's all settled?"

"Nothing," he said. "For as long a time as possible. And then... you know what? Funny thing with being a cavalry man. One thing we lack, here." He yawned. "Good horses. Decent ones. I wouldn't use half this lot for kennel-meat, lass." Briefly distracted from the comfortable domestic bliss of his wife's well-padded backside in his lap and his hands linked over her belly, he gave a happy sigh. "Breed from my Tibs, for size and speed. Maybe not for temper. Me and old Noll Cromwell was talking about this, only a few weeks back, when he asked me to come over to the Eastern. That's what's needed, my lass. Not for military service, but for – you know. Good solid riding horses. That's where the money is, Het. Going to be short of decent stock after this is all over. And it won't be long, sure of it. Long enough for me to come home and bring Tib and we can start to build up a – Henrietta, are you *listening* to me?"

She wasn't, of course. Lulled by his warmth and presumably, as he had been told on a number of occasions, that he was a dull bugger on the subject of horses, she had fallen asleep with her head nestled on his shoulder. He was going to wake up tomorrow – later today – with a hell of a stiff neck, then. He shifted experimentally and she muttered in her sleep, her breath warm on his skin. It tickled, not unpleasantly. Hollie sighed and settled himself as comfortably as he could against the pillow, tugging the quilts up over her shoulders one-handed.

His mother's wedding ring felt odd, on his own hand, and he kept wanting to scratch underneath it, but it was as safe a place as any, till the morning. Thinking of scratching, there was another itch, just under his nose, and he couldn't reach to scratch it for the limp breathing weight of her on his arm, but that was all right. There'd been many a long night, this last few months, when he'd have given his hope of heaven for the solidness of this lass in his bed. Pins and needles in his fingers seemed a small price to pay for that pleasure.

And there – the words were out there, now, and saying them made it almost real. When the war was over. When he was just plain civilian Hollie Babbitt again. They could do it. He knew they could make a go of it.

The farm kept itself, barely, but with that bit of extra money from breeding Tyburn, he could start to put a bit by, for his sons. (Daughters. Whichever.)

The new colt, Harvestman, if he was anything like his promise, and if all Tib's foals were as pretty and sweet-natured as the little dappled colt, they could all but name their price for such horses.

They could have the old barn put right, the roof re-tiled, bring it back into use. Decent fences. Pearls, for Het. Them big ones, like robin's eggs. He could take her to bed wearing nothing but pearls, like some kind of barbaric princess. (That thought merited further consideration.) Decent schooling for his sons – daughters – he wasn't fussy, he'd have his daughters literate, they weren't cotter's brats.

A decent marriage, maybe, for his daughters. Lucey's boy, maybe, by then? No, he could look higher than any son of Luce Pettitt's for his daughters, when he bred the finest horses in Essex. Always assuming Luce had finally stopped sowing his profligate wild oats by then, the relentless little bugger.

Maybe a desert-bred mare, or a Barb. Not for riding, but for the simple joy of it, the pleasure of seeing a thing of fire and beauty and knowing it was yours. He was fairly sure Tyburn wouldn't complain about it, either. He'd seen the big black stallion flirt with Luce's red mare on a number of occasions. Which was a possibility in its own right, if you didn't mind that the resulting offspring might be speedy, gorgeous, temperamental, and almost entirely feather-witted. Aye. Well. He knew any number of young gentlemen who'd pay silly money for that kind of fiery steed.

Most of all, though, he wanted peace: to settle, like a stone in the mud. Peace, and a sufficient comfort to enjoy it. "Oh, lass," he said, very quietly, into the sleeping silence. "Oh, my dear lass. God grant us a good few years, yet."

9

ARMED TRUCE

A week after Christmas, and Venning was soaked, shivering, and splattered with mud, and if he wasn't on duty now he had been very shortly, because he was still wearing plate and officer's sash. "Mistress Babbitt," he said politely, ducking his head to Het in a bow that was just short of curt, and she smiled up at him, struggling up out of her chair.

"Drew! What a lovely surprise! You look wet through, dear. I'll just pop down to the kitchens and bespeak some buttered ale – oh, do take your coat off, you'll catch your death. We don't stand on ceremony in this house, Andrew."

Drew smiled and nodded as if he was listening, and didn't fool anybody, but Het still bustled past him. Ponderously, like an overladen baggage wagon – which wasn't the kindest comparison, but she was coming to the end of her time, and as Luce had put it all those weeks ago, she was the size of the Great Bed of Ware.

Hollie watched her go with a contented sigh, and then turned back to Drew with raised eyebrows. "So, then. What's to do?"

Drew gulped. "Rosie, I need a word with 'ee, lad."

He bit off the end of his thread and gave an experimental tug on the stitching of the noseband he had in his hand. "Well, now. Do you, now, Andrew?"

"Must be a big 'un, to come out all this way, in this," Elijah muttered from the shadows beside the fire, and Venning stopped, mouth ajar.

"Rosie, there's – you – what's *he*?"

"Can't you tell?" Hollie said dryly. "Captain Venning – Trooper Babbitt. Troop chaplain, he is."

Elijah nodded grimly, which did not help Drew's discomfiture. "T'lad has a care for the souls of his troop as well as their bodies, captain."

"What – I thought – you – you and him –"

"Call it an armed truce, Drew. Cessation of hostilities, you know like His Majesty keeps doing? On my terms, and for as long as I say so. Now. What?"

"Russell."

"You come all this way to talk to me about that sodden little weasel? Don't want to hear it, Venning. How's it going in London these days?"

"*Russell*," Drew said determinedly, and Hollie put his mending down and folded his arms and looked into the fire. "Not interested. He can go to hell for me. He had his chance wi' me and he blew it."

"Whited sepulchre," Elijah croaked from the shadows, and Hollie sniffed.

"Aye, well, not often I agree wi' him but – that's it exactly."

"Aye, well, thass what I thought, bor. Bothered me for about a fortnight, it has, how come he'd had us all took in. Including the Earl of Essex, and he din't come down wi' the last shower, Rosie, he been around the block a score o' years and more."

"Because Russell's a two-faced, slinking, duplicitous little shit who deserves to be shot on sight?" Hollie suggested, perfectly cheerfully.

"No. Because he *ain't*."

Hollie dropped the poker, burned his fingers, and swore indistinctly. "What the hell you mean he's not?" he said. "You know it – I know it – *everybody* knows it – *Christ*, that's hot –"

"Not as hot as the flames of hellfire, boy, reserved for deceivers and sodomites," Elijah muttered, and Drew looked at him blankly.

"He like this all the time?"

"When he's not asleep."

"Bloody hell, Hollie, how come you haven't –"

"I've thought about it," Hollie said, before Drew even finished that sentence. "Don't you think I haven't. What d'you mean about Russell?"

"Lad ain't a deceiver, bor – more in the line o' deceived, you might say. And he certainly ain't no sodomite. That poor lass they was putting it about he – um – he tried to – you know? Nothing of the kind. Old flame of his, poor lass, she was flirting with him, thinking no harm. Boy and girl stuff, when they was children together. She reckoned he was still a boy, and he wasn't, though she'd been sweet on him the one time but – well, you know how lads are, and he never. Not when they were growing up together. Never set a hand on her."

"And adulterers. They'll burn for all eternity, an' all," Elijah went on with a degree of grisly satisfaction. "Be like when tha roasts a joint o' pork, and the fat melts, and the hair singes, and –"

"All right, all right, I get the idea – give over!" Hollie shook his head. "Go on."

"Nawthen else to say. That dinner – well, I got told by one o' the other lads as was actually there, *she* took *him* out on the terrace. Might ha' been a little bit of light – you know – he might ha' took it the wrong way, let's say. She takes him outside for a quick kiss and a cuddle, thinking all is moonlight and roses, you know, childish stuff, and he's maybe a bit more, uh, enthusiastic than what she recalls from back then. Which was bloody stupid of Russell, and most lasses might have give him a knee in the cods and told him to keep his hands to himself. So then her husband come out and starts giving it mouth, saying she's a most shameless whore and that, and Russell starts getting shouty right back at him, and next thing you know we got a full-on brawl in the shrubbery. Wish I'd a seen it, like. You know who the gal is, don't you?"

Hollie nodded warily, and Elijah looked blank.

"Jonathan Harris's missis – you know, fat feller, looks like a bull in a fancy buffcoat? Got his own lil' troop in the London Trained Bands, hell of a nice kit they got, all bought and paid for by…. Want a guess?"

"Master Harris?" Elijah guessed.

"The same as. So you can see, bloody Russell rattling his missis on the terrace in full view o' the assembled masses, it didn't go down so well, like. Sort o' took it as an affront on his dignity, if you get me. To the extent where he said he might well think to taking his money elsewhere, if that was the sort o' lads Essex encouraged in his household. Mind you, being pinked in the arse by Russell – oh, hell, bor, I'd ha' paid money to watch that fight, bloody Harris lumbering about like a chained bear and Russell swiping at God knows what:

thank the Lord Russell only poked him in the ass, and God knows there's enough of it he couldn't miss – Harris yawping about defending her honour, and half the party saying she ent got none, and the other half wanting Russell strung up by the cods for bringing the Army into disrepute –"

"So what the hell – aye, all right, it was stupid. If he was in my troop I'd have kicked his sorry arse from here to bloody Scotland. He was stupid, but – you said *Essex* was going to hang him? The hell for?"

"Losing him the better part of two troop of infantry, bor, is what, not to say showing him up in company. And you know how m'lord Essex feels about adultery, given as how he's worn horns himself on more than the one occasion. You might say as he hates bedsprawlers like he hates the Devil. Oh, this week he wants to hang him, last week he just wanted him cashiered, next week it be, I dunno, bloody Jamaica or suffen. And it's not Russell he wants to hang, if you ask me, it's the feller who was keeping Essex's bed warm, that time. Well, you know what Essex is. He changes with the weather." Drew shook his head disapprovingly. "Thass a bit o' no good, for a commander, you ask me. Should make his mind up and keep to it. Well, thass the other thing, you keep Russell banged up for weeks on end, keep telling him to make his peace with his Maker this week, pack his bags next week, see where I'm going with this? Specially Russell who's been pissed 'most every hour God sends since you left in the spring. Then shut him up on bread and water? That'll help," Drew said darkly. "'Ee thought he was high-strung before, Rosie, I tell 'ee, won't hardly recognise the lad now. Trooper Babbitt, sir, would 'ee leave the room, or not listen, or suffen?"

"Close as an oyster, lad," Elijah said, and Drew stooped to Hollie and whispered, "Tried to hang himself on Monday just past."

Hollie's mouth went quite abruptly dry, and he eased his own collar with his unburnt hand. "Russell? Tried to hang himself?"

Drew nodded, clearly uncomfortable.

"We're talking about the same lad – *Hapless* Russell, like, prissy feller, owt like that and you're going to burn forever, sort o' lad? You *sure*?"

"Bloody right I'm sure. It's been all over London, Rosie. Can't keep suffen like that quiet, no matter how much Essex wants people not to know. Don't look too good on him, had the lad locked up nigh on three months while he makes his mind up if he's like to throw him to the wolves or not."

There'd been a time when Hollie had seriously considered finding his way in front of the Royalist artillery at Edgehill, accidentally-on-purpose. He had a good idea what that particular black hole felt like. And he had ten years on Russell. A bloody nineteen-year-old lad, in possession of all his limbs and a full set of marbles, pretty from the right side – he shouldn't be that desperate. Desperate enough to throw your soul away, as well as your life? That was no bloody good. Drew was looking at him.

Bloody *Elijah* was looking at him.

Like the pair of them was expecting him to sort this mess out.

He put his bit of mending down. "I'll get my coat," he said, with resignation.

10

FOR SALE TO THE HIGHEST BIDDER

London
January 1644

"Captain Babbitt. Sir." The Earl of Essex's patrician nostrils twitched, involuntarily. "I see you have ridden to seek audience with all, hmm, dispatch." Implying, perfectly correctly, that Hollie hadn't washed since dismounting, and possibly not for some time previous. "What news have you, captain?"

"News? What – oh, no, no news, no, been at winter quarters, sir, nothing of note – Not since Winceby, any road. Well, that's all the news there is, so far as I know. I come on personal business, my lord –" Hollie remembered his manners, belatedly. Remembered on what errand he was in Essex's elegant family home in the Strand, and what favour he had to ask. Straightened his shoulders and looked humbly at the floor and muttered his petition like a small boy reciting his Bible verses. *Exactly* like a small boy reciting his Bible verses, he thought furiously, jerking his linked hands apart. What with his father and Oliver bloody Cromwell, he'd got into the habit of doing it again.

"I didn't hear a word of that, captain. You will have to speak up."

Essex was doing it on purpose to make him squirm, he was sure of it.

"I would – most humbly – beg that you spare a prisoner you have in your custody as is condemned to death, sir," he said through gritted teeth. "Thankful Russell."

"*Russell?* That vicious animal? No."

Straight out, flat as that. No. Which made Hollie the more determined to have him. "He's a man. Not a beast. My lord."

"No, captain, he is worse than a beast, for he is a feeling, reasoning being and yet he has made a choice to turn his face against God and wallow in his sin."

And Essex couldn't have picked language better placed to put Hollie into fighting mettle, than this judgmental talk of sin and unreason. "That – *boy* – is nineteen years old. He is a little younger than your nephew. And you'd have him murdered, for what? Being hot at hand? Have you spoken to him, then, sir, before making your judgment?"

"I have not had the opportunity, captain. I witnessed for myself the – the *disgusting* spectacle of his unwelcome advances towards Colonel Harris's good lady – the man's periodic debauches, his ungovernable fury, his violence towards godly men, his – his – he has no shame, sir, he feels no remorse!"

"Well, that's a fiction, for a start!" Hollie snapped, briefly forgetting where he was and who he was talking to. "The lad tried to hang himself last week. With his own blankets, they said. Sounds pretty damn' remorseful to me!"

Essex paled to a pallid olive. "Hang himself? But –"

"But you'd know all about that, like, because obviously you wouldn't have just left the lad out there locked up in a stinking garret in Cheapside and forgot about him, would you? But like I say, that wouldn't be a most Christian thing to do, so I'm sure you wouldn't have done it."

"And on what misinformation would you base this calumny, sir?" Essex said coldly, and Hollie shrugged.

"Captain Venning's, as has been going out to see him for the last fortnight and usually don't get to, but passes the time o'day with the lad through the window. Even the most godly has to go for a piss, my lord. Not that Captain Venning would see to it that the Lord's Elect is kept well supplied with ale to facilitate same. No, he's not *seen* Russell. Talked to him through t'window, and says he sounds like death. But not, from what Captain Venning says, what you might call dangerous. Unless you're frightened of daddy-long-legses, since by all accounts the lad's like a picked rib, what wi' one thing and another. A most desperate villain, that one, oh aye. Half mad and frightened out of his wits."

"So you *condone* his behaviour, do you?"

"Don't rightly know what his behaviour was, sir," Hollie said primly. Looked up. Met Essex's startled gaze. "And neither do you, my lord, do you? Because you weren't there either. You were still inside with the rest of the party. There was only two people on that terrace knows the truth of it, and one of 'em had the wits kicked out of him shortly afterwards, and the other's keeping a tactfully closed mouth. I'm not wholly daft, sir. I have asked round a bit before I come asking for him to be let off. Is the cause actually that hard up you need to hang him for the sake of keeping Master Harris's bankroll?"

Essex reared up, eyes darting into every which corner of the room, his mouth working wordlessly. "Captain Babbitt, you have no idea of – I would not expect such as *you* to understand – the man is a filthy and most shameless adulterer, and I will not have a man of such blemished reputation on my staff!"

"Bloody hell, he had you convinced he was a nice godly boy for a few months, then, didn't he? You could just dismiss him, you know. He doesn't say much at the best of times. You don't *have* to have him murdered just to keep your secrets."

"You presume too far, Captain Babbitt!"

"No doubt. I often do. But I ain't your problem any more, my lord. Be a bugger of a thing if I brought my lot back up here with the Eastern Association, though, wouldn't it? Just think. You'd have the pleasure of my company every other day, sir. Getting under your feet, cluttering up your nice tidy headquarters. I mean, obviously I wouldn't just want to leave Russell to rot, what with him being such a particular friend of your nephew's, I'd have an eye to his care, wouldn't I? And – " he snapped his fingers – "there *was* a bit o' news I forgot. Colonel Cromwell's asked me to take up with his lot – very keen, he is, proper impressed with us. Bit of a power in the land, our Noll, from what I hear. Quite the coming man, isn't he, Colonel Cromwell? Proper fell on my feet there, with the colonel taking such an interest in us."

"Are you trying to *threaten* me, Captain Babbitt?"

Threaten him? God forbid. "Me?" Hollie gave the commander of the Army of Parliament his sweetest, most innocent smile, because it was that or lean across the table and choke the life out of the intransigent judgmental bastard, and he thought that might not be a good career choice. "Hardly, sir."

"I am pleased to hear it, captain, because I will not be swayed on this head. Russell is a deceiver and a foul lecher, and I intend his execution with immediate dispatch, and as little ceremony as may be decently undertaken. Colonel Harris will be satisfied with no less than the harshest penalty for Russell's outrageous breaches of regulation, and I will not subject the good name of Mistress Harris to the kind of filthy slander that a public trial would expose her to. I was undecided, sir, but if men of *your* calibre would speak up for him, I see my decision is made."

Which was something of a slap in the face, to be sure. "Quick decision, I'm sure, my lord," Hollie said through shut teeth. "So you're going to hang that lad because I've asked you not to."

"My decision, captain. As you say. And the more you try to sway me, the more I am convinced of Russell's guilt. If only by association."

"With the likes of me?"

Essex inclined his head coldly. "As you say, captain. With the likes of you. A useful creature, to be sure, but not, I think, a fit and proper man to make any moral judgment." He paused. "You fought under Wallenstein, did you not? In the wars in Europe – for the Holy Roman Emperor?"

" I did. I was seventeen. I learned my trade under Wallenstein – under Colonel Butler, since you ask. There wasn't many taking on apprentices in them days," he said sarcastically, "but you might consider Butler to have trained me up."

"Indeed. Trained by a Irishman – against your own countrymen – for a Papist cause, I believe. And then, I understand, you fought for the Swedish Army, turning against your *previous* employer. Perhaps all done with the noblest of intentions, captain. However. I should not choose to scrutinise your loyalties too closely, nor, I think, to trust to them. I think perhaps at heart you are yet for sale to the highest bidder."

Hollie didn't bother with the civilities of farewell. He stood up without acknowledging the sheer bloody *rudeness* of that last remark, his elegantly-appointed chair scraping across the polished wood boards and, he hoped, leaving permanent and indelible scrapes of fury.

He did, however, make sure that his scabbard brushed every paper off Essex's neat desk as he turned to go, and managed to walk across a good half of them. Then he stopped at the door. "Then I thank God, *sir*, that you do not have sufficient gold to command my conscience. "

11

A COMFORT IN THY ADVERSITY

Venning looked uncomfortable. "Look, Luce, I ent sure you ought to come in, bor. I know he's your mate and all, but – oh, hell, lad, if it was me I wouldn't like my mates to see me like that."

Luce raised an eyebrow. It managed to encompass the whole of Cheapside – the hawkers shouting, the stinking refuse, the shabby houses in the alley, and the stench of rotting meat from the shambles a quarter of a mile away, all in one neat arch. "I'm sure," he said.

"You're not listening, are you?"

"I'm listening. But I'm not taking any notice." He rapped on the door, sharply, with the hilt of his sword. The hollow sound startled a nearby rat, which went scuttling away through the cess. "And they call this Honey Lane, by God."

"Luce, they're not going to let you in. I've been trying for weeks to get in and talk to him. They won't let you."

"Not let the Earl of Essex's nephew in, captain? They bloody well will."

The door jerked open. Luce expected to see some shabby, down-at-heel, black-toothed villain. Instead he was being glowered at by a very neat trooper, fully armed, fully armoured, and very, very clean. "Bloody hell," he said involuntarily.

"Sir?"

"I'm here to see the prisoner."

"You can't. My lord Essex's orders."

"I'm my lord Essex's nephew," Luce said, truthfully, and left it at that.

"I've had no orders to allow anyone –"

"Mate," Venning said, looming up out of the shadows, "we won't tell if you won't. And if you want, you can pat us – him – down for poison, ropes, and sharp objects – leave your weapons wi' the boys, won't you, Luce? – Jesus Christ, man, look at us. Either one of us could snap the poor bugger like a twig. Now let us in, in all charity."

"I *am* Essex's nephew," Luce said again, looking innocent. "My uncle would wish to reassure himself of the prisoner's well-being, in all Christian charity –" at which point Venning went off into a paroxysm of coughing and Luce could have willingly shot him.

"Straight up the stairs," the trooper said, deciding quickly. "Ten minutes, and you're out. And I haven't seen you. Understood?"

"Thank you." Luce inclined his head and then edged up the narrow stairs. The plaster that brushed against his shoulder was crumbling, and as he approached the top of the stairs the scabbard of his sword caught the wall and a whole chunk dropped away, exposing mouldering laths.

"*Nice*," Venning said sarcastically, from the front door.

Luce tapped at the latched door. Not padlocked, not bolted, not triple-barred. Simply latched. "Thankful, are you in – Sorry. That is a stupid question, even by my standards. Where else would you be?"

"Indeed."

What was shocking was that Russell still sounded like Russell – dry, slightly mocking, coolly polite. "I regret a certain indisposition prevents me from getting up to greet you, Cornet, so you may have to let yourself in," he said, and Luce lifted the latch.

And stopped, blinking. He had expected filth, squalor. Russell was sitting on the edge of a narrow, bare mattress. No sheets, no pillows, no blankets. There was an empty bowl at his feet, that had contained, by the look of it, some kind of thin gruel. A small leather bottle and a small leather jack beside it. The scarred young man looked up and smiled wanly.

"As you see, Lucifer." He lifted his hand, and Luce realized that his wrist was tied to the bed by a length of rope. "Chained up like a bandog in a yard, I fear. I can walk as far as the window, but no further. Presumably for fear that there may be no end to my invention and I may seek to hurl both myself and this bed to my destruction."

"Oh, for goodness' sakes, Thankful –"

"Must I be so dramatic? Seemingly so, Luce. I'm evidently considered dangerous, for a –" he broke off, coughing, unable to speak.

Luce forgot that Russell was supposed to be a murderous lunatic and he was across the room in a stride, offering his handkerchief – less than impeccable – and sloshing whatever was in the bottle into the jack.

"Water," Russell wheezed. "They don't trust me with anything stronger, though God knows I've lost my taste for spirits since – since then, Lucifer – that I might, I might – I would not have hurt her, not for all the world, not in my right wits!"

"Didn't think for one minute you would," Luce said. Sat down on the edge of the bed, and then suddenly Russell was in his arms, sobbing like a child. Smelling of stale sweat and unwashed hair and faintly of vomit, the fastidious young man was an unlovely object, with the bones of his back standing out against the coarse linen of his shirt. "All will be well, and all manner of things shall be well," Luce said awkwardly, smoothing his palm up and down his friend's heaving back and wishing to God he knew what to say, while Russell – cool, self-contained, distant Russell – burrowed against him with increasingly wild tears.

Not the time to mention that in ten minutes' time he'd be summoned hence. Unless Hollie Babbitt appeared, bearing a signed and sealed pardon. "They're going to hang me," Russell said in a shaking voice. "Harris will have nothing less. And I *deserve* it."

"Don't be ridiculous, Thankful, they couldn't do that. My uncle wouldn't do that, not without some sort of trial – some kind of justice!"

"Oh, they have sufficient charge. Rape. Insubordination. Drunkenness. Striking a superior officer, although God knows there's enough flesh on Colonel Harris's arse that I barely pinked him – Lucifer, it's not funny!"

"At least you're guilty of one of them, though," Luce said helplessly, and Russell straightened up – looked him with wide, reproachful eyes – hiccupped – and finally, finally smiled wanly. "Aye. Well. I suppose it is funny, in a way."

"Oh, Russell. How on *earth* did you get yourself into this pickle?"

"Oh, the usual. I might have married her, once, though it never went so far, and her father decided we should not suit, after Edgehill. And who's to blame him, Luce – I can't say as I care for myself, much, right now. And I saw her again, and she was – she was kind. I do know so much. She was kind, and we talked of old times, and – " he shrugged. "More than that, I do not know. Only what they tell me." He laughed bleakly. "Did they tell you I am not often sober, these days? So how far you can trust the word of a most notorious drunk and backslider…" He pushed himself upright, away from Luce. He was shaking, and for the first time Luce saw the livid ring of bruising round his neck. "What could I say in my defence, Luce? What *can* I say? I'm a mess – I'm marred, half-mad at best, I'm useless – I doubt I could even beg my bread with this face – oh, sweet Christ, I wish to God they hadn't cut me down. Though I couldn't even get that right, could I?" He straightened his back. "Well. There you go. Thank you for coming, anyway, Lucifer. I am – " his mouth worked soundlessly, briefly, "– am pleased that I am not forgot by all my former friends, at least. Though I hope my acquaintance doesn't tarnish your career. Give my regards to Captain Venning. He has likewise been most – most – comforting in my adversity. I should prefer you left, now, please." The unscarred side of his face twitched. "I think I have disgraced myself sufficiently, for one day."

"I will not," Luce said stubbornly. "I'll stay till –"

"Till they come for me? I'd rather you didn't. Leave me with some dignity, please. For I am afraid – I am considerably rumpled in spirit," he said, with a sudden wild hilarity, " – bloody terrified, actually. And yet if nothing else I would redeem myself at the last by comporting myself with dignity –"

"Oh, stop it," Luce said impatiently. "You are making a fuss about nothing, and we will come about. I am, after all, my lord Essex's right well-beloved nephew."

"There's nothing you can do — even you – do you not think I have tried, to make my apologies, to explain – they will not listen!"

"Well, have you tried putting your coat on?"

Russell looked, briefly, stupid. Shook his head. "I don't understand –"

"Well. You are currently bound and guarded. Yes? And I am my lord Essex's right –"

"Yes, yes, I understand that much, but I don't see –"

"My dear Master Russell, I can assure you –" Luce pitched his voice to carry down the stairs –" my uncle is most sensible of your previous good conduct. This is all a misunderstanding, I'm sure, and will be dealt with in a civilised manner." Even as he spoke, he was sawing at the rope fetters on Russell's bony wrists – wincing at the raw flesh underneath, where he had twisted in too-tight bonds.

"Now then. Your arm, sir. We leave as gentlemen." He nodded curtly to the trooper on guard duty, who frowned and tried to bar their way, and Luce pushed the man's musket aside with a haughty sneer. "Sir, I am the nephew of the Earl of Essex. How dare you treat me with suspicion – *you*, a common soldier?"

"My lord's orders, sir –"

Luce inclined his head gravely. "Your devotion to your duty is commendable. My uncle, however, knows my direction, should I fail to return his captive within the allotted span. Master Russell stands my friend, still, and I give you my word as a gentleman that I will be responsible for his parole. I give you good day, sir."

12

A LITTLE WINE, FOR THY STOMACH'S SAKE

Back out in the street, with Russell blinking like a mole in the unaccustomed pale wintry sunlight, there didn't seem much to say – and what there was, Russell would say in his own good time. Luce took him firmly by the elbow. The scarred young man was shaking like a wet dog, out in the open air. "Thankful, you're safe with us, do you hear?" he said. "No need to –"

"I'm not –" Russell's appallingly thin shoulders jerked and then set rigid. "Frightened. Not frightened. I think I might be sick, and – Luce, I need a drink very b-badly, but –"

"Not a good idea," Luce said. "I think we need you clear-headed for this, sir. For the one thing, we still have to face up to Captain Babbitt."

Under the rags of lank fair hair, Russell's face turned white. "He doesn't *know*?" And then he squared his shoulders with a pathetic return to his old cool dignity. "Well, they can only hang you the once, I'm sure. At least I get to be – outside – for a while, and –" he rubbed his bruised wrist, where the raw patch showed under his frayed cuff –" at liberty, before the captain has me recalled."

"I think you may be confusing Hollie with someone else," Luce said dryly. "He's gone to talk to my uncle about having you released anyway. I've just – well, I've pre-empted him, that's all. It's *fine*, Thankful. Please don't – don't – um –" he didn't like to draw attention to the tears rolling unheeded down Russell's cheeks, but – "Honestly, it will be fine. The captain's bark is worse than his bite, and – oh, Russell, *stop it*. " He stopped in the middle of the bustling street, jostled by housewives amarketing and hawkers crying their wares, and gave the other man a little shake. "Captain Venning is quartered out at Hampstead, and it's a long walk. Shall we get a pie, to stay us?"

It was a long walk – at least, as Russell pointed out, two pies and an apple's distance, and Luce terrified every step of the way that they'd be found and taken up again before they reached the safety of Hampstead. Not that he was saying as much to the scarred young man, who was frightened enough already. Frightened, and near to collapse with weariness, plodding along in dazed silence as the lanes grew leafier and the houses thinned and the dusk fell. By the time they found the house that Venning had occupied Luce had his hand under Russell's elbow again.

Venning looked up from the fireside and grinned at them both, as at ease as if he were at home, with a half-grown brown and white puppy sprawled on his feet chewing on someone's boot. "Made it back, then, bor," he said cheerfully. "We was just about to send out the search parties. His Nibs is up yonder –" he jerked a thumb upstairs – "though I wouldn't cross him till he's had a lie down and a bit o' sluss. He come in about an hour back and he looks about as done in as 'ee do. 'S what all this galligantin' does for 'ee, gentlemen, and I don't hold with 'en."

"I imagine that was probably English, sir, but I fail to understand a word of it," Russell said with a flash of his old frigid dignity, and Venning's grin widened.

"I see being locked up ent took none of the starch out of 'ee, Russell. Come in and have a warm, bor, pair of you look like what the cat dragged in. Mind the dog. He don't bite but he'll have that pie out of your pocket, Luce, if'n you don't have a sharp eye to him – Tinners! Here!" He snapped his fingers to the dog, catching the wiggling little body between his knees. "Don't mind dogs, do 'ee, Master Russell?"

The pup broke free and came to investigate Luce's outstretched fingers. Russell was looking at the little beast with awe. "I do not," he said stiffly. "I have never made the close acquaintance of one. My sister did not care for beasts in the house. I –" he put his hand down, warily, and Tinners licked him, and he snatched his fingers back with an involuntary giggle.

"He's after your bread and cheese," Venning said firmly.

The little dog wriggled closer to his new friend, panting happily. "What bread and cheese?"

"Any o' you louts in back near the kitchen? Fetch us out a bit o' bread and cheese! And if there's any wine –" Luce glanced, fractionally, at Russell, back at Venning, and shook his head, almost imperceptibly.

Venning wasn't as slow as he liked to make out to be. "Forget that, lads, I do reckon there's a bit of the spiced ale left over, that'll do us. Save a bit for Bennett, when he comes in off his patrol, won't ee?"

Into which unruly feast entered Hollie Babbitt – looking like he'd just woken up, for the first time in almost a year of Luce's acquaintance with him. Usually the redhead looked rumpled but alert, but tonight he looked worn and very, very weary. "The hell is going on down there?" he said, bracing himself against the banister, halfway down the stairs.

Luce stood up. "Sir."

"Oh, it's you. Come up, brat. Got summat to tell you."

"Likewise, sir, and –"

"Aye. Well. Yours'll keep. Come here."

He staggered back up the stairs, and Luce stood up, shrugging, and went after him. Russell's face had gone white again, his eyes almost black in the firelight. Venning stretched lazily in his chair, poking Tinners with his foot. "Seriously, Russell, 'ee never had a dog? He's suffen fierce with the rats, is this lad. Surely. Thick with 'en, it was, yonder barn, when we first come, and –"

And Luce, watching the fair-haired young man's scarred face relax into a wary attention at Venning's random tales of rural pest control, had to admire the big Norfolk captain.

Hollie had collapsed back onto the bed. "And you will excuse the informality, brat, but it's been a long old day and I'm just about done in. So you can please yourself if you sit or stand, I don't rightly care."

"Sir –"

The redhead had his eyes shut. "Luce, I've cocked it up. I thought I could talk Essex into kicking your mate over to us and I can't. I just pissed him off. More I argued with him the more bloody stubborn he got about it. He's determined – which has got to be a bloody first for your uncle – he reckons it's the principle of the thing. More like, Harris isn't for backing down, and two troop of infantry are worth more than one unpredictable little bugger of a secretary. So there we go. Bit shit for Russell, who as you know and I know hasn't done owt worse than letting his prick do the thinking for him, but if your uncle wants to make a tit of himself far be it from me to stand in his way –"

"Hollie –"

"Christ, lad, if your uncle gets into the habit of hanging every man in the Army who's led by his bollocks, he's going to have a pretty bloody small army –"

"Hollie!"

"Me excluded, mind, though I can't see me hanging round here much after the deed's done, not with my girl less than half a day's ride – Luce, will you stop bumping about like a fart in a bottle and tell me what the hell's up with you!"

"Russell's downstairs."

Hollie sat up abruptly. "What?"

"Thankful Russell is downstairs. Captain Venning and I paid a visit to his – lodgings, and Thankful – er, Trooper Russell – we were able to persuade his guards to allow him to leave with us. And here we are. I, um, I gave the impression that we might head to Witham for the night."

Hollie sat up. "You broke Russell out. Without my knowledge. Against your uncle's explicit directions. Brat, I am going to break your bloody neck."

"He has been treated *appallingly*, sir. I gave his parole – he can be equally of good behaviour with us as he can rotting in an attic in Honey Lane, Hollie, he –"

"Hasn't exactly been the flower of sodding virtue himself, Lucifer! What the hell am I supposed to do with him? He's pretty bloody distinctive, if anyone comes looking for him! And the way me and your uncle parted company, he'd like to have me strung up alongside him!"

The boards on the landing creaked, and with a patter of paws Tinners came bouncing onto the bed. "Then, sir, I will return from whence I came," Russell's voice came from the top of the stairs. Cold and flat level and expressionless, as if he did not much care where he was sent.

"Oh, for – get in here. Hell, see if Venning wants to come up as well, why don't I just have everyone – *and his dog* – on my bed. This was supposed to be a private discussion, Russell. About you, not to you.

Now – Jesus, man, what did they do to you?"

"This?" Russell touched the bruising above his collar, stark black against his fair skin in the fading light. "They didn't, captain. I did this to myself. My apologies for any inconvenience you may have been put to, as a result of your cornet's well-meaning activities. I will put you to no further trouble."

Hollie stood up. "Russell, if you're attached to that – that soft-headed lackwit of an officer of mine, you're under my command, and I'll not put up with bloody awkward soldiers in my troop. I *said* what am I going to do with you. I did not say you're going back there. Lucey, fuck off. Me and your mate are going to have words. Possibly, more than words. Get down them stairs. And take that god-damned dog with you."

13

GOD HATH TURNED HIS FACE FROM ME

"Sit. Down. Now."

Russell sat. Even the way he sat set Hollie's teeth on edge – neat, orderly, knees together. "Care to enlighten me on what the hell these last six months have been all about, Russell? No – let me fill it in for myself, I bet you I can. Nice lad from a nice respectable family, gets a nice respectable safe position in Essex's household, decides to piss it all up against a wall after a bit o' stray. Right so far?"

He heard Russell's breath drawn in with a quivering hiss. "Do not, *ever*, refer to Mistress Harris in that way, sir. Not in my hearing."

"Jesus Christ, you and Lucey Pettitt would mar another couple. You don't write poetry as well, do you? – in which case, back you bloody well go and they can hang you with my full approval. We're not in a sodding playhouse, Trooper Russell. You're not the first and you won't be the last to push your luck with somebody else's girl. Boy, if you take a swing at me I will kick you down the bloody stairs. Sit down."

"You don't understand," Russell snarled, but he sat down. Bless him, he was that mimsy and well-brought-up and properly-trained that it hadn't even crossed his mind that if you're sat on a rackety bed and you stand up to go for someone, even in the dark, the bed creaks.

"You're right, I don't. I haven't got a fucking clue. Proper rag-mannered, me. Dragged up in a ditch, that being how come I'm an officer and you're a very well-bred drunk with a rope scar round your neck and a ruined reputation." Hollie leaned forward, with menace. "You broke your word, Russell, and if there's one thing I cannot stand it's a man who will not keep a promise. You said you would deliver my letters to my girl. She went almost six months without a word from me, through that. She stood by me, God love her, but for all she knew I was dead and buried and she still kept her faith with me. *You* did not. Russell?"

There was a long, a very long, silence. And then, "I was ashamed," he said, in a small voice. "I was mortal ashamed that she – she of all people – should see me. So."

"Drunk?"

"Yes." Another long pause. "Often."

"And?"

"Disgusting," Russell said, his hoarse voice vibrating with passion. "The worst of vile sinners. God hath turned his face from me."

"I see. By Christ, boy, you've got a high opinion of yourself."

"I am not obliged to explain myself to you. I should be wasting my breath."

"Least you still got some to waste, lad. Now me, I'm going to shout downstairs to Drew Venning to bring us up a light and summat to eat, because I've been on a horse since first light chasing round London trying to keep your worthless carcass from swinging, and I'm starved. You still hungry?"

"Yes," Russell said sullenly, and Hollie grinned to himself, in the darkness.

"That's yes, *sir*, to you, trooper."

As he lit the last candle, Hollie glanced up at what was left of Essex's prim orderly, and had to look away lest his expression betray him.

His imprisonment had marred the man's looks worse than the scar ever did. It wasn't so much that Russell was thin, though God knows the skin was drum-tight over his prominent bones, and in the candlelight his dark eyes looked like the empty sockets of a skull. It was the look of him, somewhere between desperate and furious. The trick of it with such men was that they never had to know you pitied them. Drive him – though, he suspected, not too hard, at the moment, the lad's will being somewhat stronger than his much-abused flesh – harry him, insult him, and he knew from bitter experience with such that sheer bloody-minded pride would carry him through. Hollie ate his bread and cheese deliberately slowly, averting his eyes as Russell went at his, and half of Hollie's, like a starving wolf. "Leave the bloody pattern on t'plate, lad," he said mildly, and Russell stared at him, black eyes unreadable, before his marred face relaxed into a reluctant smile.

"They called me murderous. They wouldn't give me anything to eat that couldn't be eaten with a spoon," he said – realized what he'd said, stiffened.

Hollie scratched absently at his three-day beard. "Fair enough. It does sort of rule out most puddings, though, don't it, if you've took against spoons?"

"If you feel you can trust me with a knife. Sir."

"I'd trust you with a glass of wine, too, if you want one, lad."

Russell's eyes closed. "I should rather say I need one, sir, rather than want one. And so, I will decline your kind offer."

The lad's hands were shaking with it. Hollie stood up. "Ah, well, I didn't want one, either. No bloody fun drinking on your own. Buttered ale do you, instead?" And without waiting for an answer he ambled downstairs to the kitchen.

He'd known Russell was drinking more than was wise. He'd thought it was habitual. He hadn't known it had gone so far as necessity. That frightened him, a little. The lad would bear careful watching. But, what was done couldn't be undone. "Right, then. You was going to tell me how things got to this pretty pass?"

"You wouldn't understand."

"Which bit?"

"Any of it, captain. I doubt you would understand *any* of it. People like you don't."

"Mmm. I'd be intrigued to know what you reckon counts as people like me – if, God forbid, there's more like me."

"Rag-mannered bastards out of a ditch, with no soul," Russell snarled, his voice shaking with fury. "Now *will you leave me be*, sir!"

And Hollie didn't mean to, he really, really didn't mean to hurt the lad's feelings, but he just burst out laughing. Tried to stifle it and absolutely couldn't. Those dark eyes were wide and bright with indignation and that just made him laugh even harder. "Russell, if you want to go and talk to my father about my lack of birth or breeding, I wish you all joy of it. He'll probably kick your arse, being a bit touchy on the subject of my saintly mother's memory, but – aye, my parents had a full set of marriage lines, and before he took up a career as a professional God-botherer in the Army of Parliament, he was a most respectable gentleman farmer out at Bolton-le-Moors. If I'm feeling like a right bastard, I'll introduce you. He's about forty miles distant, currently, on leave from his position as my bloody troop chaplain. Pair of you'll get on like a house afire."

Surprise was not a flattering expression on Russell's marred face. His wry mouth hung open slightly askew. He knew it, too. Recovered himself quickly. "Well, he disowned *you*, no doubt."

"In a manner of speaking," Hollie said. "Let's say it's a relationship of armed neutrality."

There was a long silence. Then Russell muttered, "I'm sorry, sir. That was – uncalled for."

"And most ungentlemanlike," Hollie said, with just a hint of malice. He didn't care, mind, it tickled the hell out of him – he'd been successfully deceiving half the world that he'd been dragged up in a ditch, for the last twenty years. "Well. We advance, then, lad. Having established that both you and I are of respectable and pious Puritan stock, and probably neither of us welcome at home."

The lad's gaze wavered and dropped, and Hollie was mortified to see tears in Russell's eyes. "On the contrary, captain. I am the last of the Buckinghamshire Russells, sir. The only redeeming aspect of my present humiliation is that my mother is not alive to see it."

Open mouth, Babbitt, insert thumping great foot. One single tear made its wavering way down Russell's cheek. The lad looked resolutely at one of the candle flames. "I am grateful for your concern, captain. However, as you rightly point out –" he lifted one hand and indicated his ragged person, with a horrible ghost of his former dignity –" I am no better than a well-bred drunk with a ruined reputation and a rope scar about my neck. I imagine that the dog downstairs is of more significance than my worthless self. Do not be deceived, Captain Babbitt. I have some degree of manners left to me and that is all I have. No beauty, no virtue, no standing. I am not loved, and nor am I respected. Do not waste your pity. The world would be a better place without my marred face in it."

Hollie listened in silence, and then – "Russell."

The dark eyes lifted again.

"By, lad, tha's an arrogant bastard at times. The world doesn't give a toss about you one way or another."

"And this?" Russell touched his face, gingerly. "Of no significance, is it?"

"We've all got 'em."

"Oh, do we? Don't dare to condescend to me, sir –"

There were words to that. And there was grabbing the self-pitying little bastard by the scruff and shaking him till he screamed, which probably wasn't helpful, but was tempting. "We do, Trooper Russell. Every man in my bloody troop has got scars. It's not a competition. Yours are on your face. So bloody what. You don't look at the mantelpiece when you're poking t'fire."

"Captain *Babbitt*, sir!" But he laughed, even if it was startled out of him, and it was the first time Hollie had seen Russell laugh in – actually, since he'd first set eyes on him. He looked like a perfectly normal young man when he laughed. Bit too thin, in need of a wash and a brush-up, definitely in need of a clean shirt, but no different from the rest of Hollie's rabble. He wondered if he could scrounge one of Venning's remounts for the bugger. God, he was hard work, though. Touchy, self-pitying, moody, arrogant – all words Nat Rackhay had used about someone else not a thousand miles from here, once. And Nat would have done a better job comforting this poor bastard, too. Hollie took a deep breath. Comforting might come later, when he'd stopped being bloody livid with a nineteen year old whelp who thought he was the most important link in the chain of being.

Cracked as a pothouse jug, of course, but possibly not beyond mending. One of these days, Hollie's habit of picking up lame ducks was going to finish him off.

A spatter of sleet hit the window, and Russell's dark eyes slid sideways, quite involuntary, widening as if the lad was afraid. As if whatever had been done to him, this last few months, had left him wary of his own shadow, spooking at sudden noises, his bone-skinny hands shaking.

Hollie sighed. It probably was going to finish him, one of these days, but it wasn't going to be this night. He might not like it. He might wish, most fervently, that of all the officers in the Army of Parliament Luce had dumped this overwrought, underfed object on another. But. There it was.

"Get your traps together, Russell. We ride north. *Tonight*. I'd like to not be anywhere near my lord Essex when he finds out you're in my company, and that his bloody nephew put you there."

14

A STRANGE HAND ON THE BRIDLE

She was almost beginning to worry, heaving herself out of the chair by the fire to peer out of the window at the lacy curtain of sleet blanketing the fields.

He was safe, she knew that. Not even Holofernes was so daft as to ride home in this. He'd have taken shelter for the night somewhere – the Pettitts, possibly, in Witham. He'd be cluttering up their parlour, for once, chattering with Lucifer and quite absently working his way through a plate full of little cakes that was intended for the whole company, the way he always did when he was here: the way that man of hers carried on, you'd think he didn't get fed at home. And no one to give him a brisk poke in the ribs – the remarkably skinny ribs, for someone who ate as much as Holofernes did – and remind him that there were other people present. Well, if that misguided soul thought this was going to set any kind of pattern for the future, he could just think again. She would simply not stand for his benighted military friends turning up unannounced and uninvited, and her husband going jaunting off into the winter dusk for three days without a by-your-leave, with Het about to be brought to bed any day –

He was *fine*. She was being silly, and she gave herself a shake, very deliberately picturing Jane Pettitt's warm parlour where it faced into the street: the big hearth with its herringbone pattern of rose-red bricks, the little curving staircase up to Jane's chamber in the corner of the room – the little alcove beside the chimney breast where she just knew Hollie would have gone to earth with Lucifer and the cakes, talking soldier's talk while the sleet hissed down the chimney. He was fine. No harm would have befallen him. *Nothing.*

"Lass."

She stood up more abruptly than was wise in her condition because for a moment she had thought the lanky figure in the open doorway was her man and it wasn't, and –

"Sir, you should not be downstairs, in your state of health," she said sternly, and slightly breathlessly, and her father-in-law stalked across the room and sat her down in her chair in a most unceremonious fashion.

"Aye, and thee should be a-bed likewise in thine, but I can hear thee pacing from upstairs. What is tha fretting for, lass? A bit o' sleet won't melt the lad."

"Doubtless," she said stiffly, "but I should like to know his direction, nonetheless."

Elijah cocked a shaggy eyebrow at her. "I didn't know his direction for twenty years, mistress, but I didn't go round wringing my hands over it. Still – tha's breeding, it's to be expected. Don't coddle the boy, mistress. He won't thank you for it. He was ever a stubborn colt, that one. Has a habit o' shying off as soon as he feels a strange hand on t'bridle –"

"My husband is not a horse, sir."

"True enough. Reckon he'd have been easier to gentle, if he had been. Lass. If tha plans to sit up till dawn waiting on that shiftless rascal thee is married to, let me bring thee a coverlet or summat. Catch thy death of cold, tha will. And I'll bear thee company, if I must."

"I should prefer not to keep your company, Master Babbitt," she snapped, and the old man grinned at her. "That's better, lass. Rather see thee sparky than drooping. What can I fetch thee?"

He would not go away. He sat in the settle across the hearth from her, and she could hear the creak and wheeze of his laboured breathing as he shifted in the seat, and yet he would not go away. "My – there is an old coat on the door behind you, sir." Hollie was *fine*. The temperature was dropping, the fire settling to grey ash, and she would not go to bed, *would* not. How could she – he might need her, might be cold, or hurt, or – she just needed to see him, to be sure he was safe, and whole, and well. The child kicked vigorously, unaccustomed to these late hours, and Het set her hands to her belly with a stifled squeak.

"Sit down, lass." The old man clicked his tongue chidingly at her. "Thee is doing that babe no good at all, bumping about like a bee in a bottle. Be still, and settle to thy work. Let me fetch –" he caught his breath and then broke off to cough and spit into the fire, and she gave him a wry look.

"I am not sure as to who should be fetching for whom, sir, presently. I will not disturb the servants at this hour of the night, Master Babbitt. They work hard and they deserve their rest. *I* will do the fetching. If you feel the need to make yourself useful, you may serve me by making up the fire."

"Where is thee going to? Lass?"

"To begin with, to the stillroom, sir, for a pot of sage oil, and to see what I might give you for that cough."

Busyness settled her, somewhat, and she was busy with liquorice and honey, and considering whether the old man's rattling chest merited the use of some of her precious store of ginger root, when she heard voices in the hall.

Closing her eyes with relief, and then opening them again quickly because Hollie did not sound like a man who'd enjoyed a contented social call.

"Dear?" she called warily, and he came thumping down the corridor sounding like the wrath of God, coming to a skidding halt in front of her. Scowling most ferociously, with sleet in his hair, and on the shoulders of his coat, and looking most uncharacteristically wearied. "Dear, is – has something happened?"

He caught her by the shoulders and kissed her, hard, and somehow absently, like a man with his mind on other things. "Oh aye something's bloody happened," he snarled, letting her go – leaving her arms tingling, and she thought his fingers might have left a bruise underneath her sleeves. "I won't be at home when the babe comes after all, lass. I'll be in the bloody North. *Again.*"

"But what – when –"

"Now," he said, narrowing his eyes. "I'll see you in the spring, Het. *Probably.*"

"But –"

"This is madness." Luce coming in behind him, looking even more weary and draggled, and ten years older than his true age. "Sir, you can't do this."

"Stop me?"

And Het gave a superstitious little gasp as the forlorn and drooping Thankful Russell drifted into view, bringing up the rear, because with the great ring of bruising round his throat, the young man bore an uncanny resemblance to his own ghost. "It's all my fault," Russell said pathetically, and Hollie turned on him and roared, "I know it's all your bloody fault, Russell, the question is what I'm going to bloody do about it!"

"Leave me to Essex. I deserve it."

"You *deserve* a punch in the head, boy. Lucifer, leave him the *fuck* alone, will you? Yes, Het, we are going to Yorkshire. Now. Not a time or place of my choosing, but someone – Lucifer *fucking* Pettitt – decided it might be a smart idea to defy the Commander in Chief of the Army of Parliament and tag this bloody waste of a good skin along with us!"

"Mind thy language, boy," Elijah croaked from his seat by the fire, and Hollie turned slowly and glared at the old man.

"Oh, *you're* up and about, are you? Well, that puts the fucking tin lid on it, that does. Seems I command a troop of degenerates, do-gooders and itinerant bloody preachers, now. Lucky bloody me. And Russell, unless tha wants do something fucking useful and oblige me by dying of a consumption, I'll thank thee not to hang around my house coughing your guts up. If you're like to die of a well-deserved jail fever, *fuck off outside and do it.*"

Het gave her husband a stern look and took Russell by his sodden sleeve. "Come and sit by the fire, Master Russell. I'm sure this can all be dealt with without you catching your death of cold – see, I've some liquorice tea made already, now you sit down and get warm and –"

"Henrietta, don't you *dare* encourage that god-damned ambulant liability to get his scabby arse comfortable!"

"I will not have that boy's death on my conscience, Holofernes, and I won't have him on yours, either! Now hold your tongue."

"What?" It was unlikely that anyone had ever spoken to Hollie Babbitt in that manner before – or at least, not without hitting him first. He looked perfectly astonished.

His plump, comfortable little wife smiled up at him, perfectly at her ease. "Husband, you're cold, and I doubt very much if any of you have had anything proper to eat since, oh, I'd guess noon by the state of your temper, dear. Well, I'm sure there's something in the kitchens that I can lay a hand to. It might be a little informal, but I'm sure you won't mind, will you?" She tucked her arm confidingly into his, then glanced over her shoulder. "Russell, *sit down,*" she said, and there was a hint, the smallest hint, of the steel beneath the softness. Russell blinked in bewilderment, and sat. "Would you be so good – " Het looked at her father-in-law thoughtfully, then up at her husband – "as to see the young men at ease, father? I should be grateful for a little assistance from my husband in the kitchens. Seeking, as you might say, what he may devour."

Elijah looked about as stunned as Russell, although Hollie was still way out in front in the taken aback stakes. "You don't have a cough as well, do you, Lucifer?" she said sweetly, and Luce shook his head. "Well, perhaps you ought to have some liquorice tea as a preventative anyway, dear. That's a good boy. Now, I imagine the three of you will be wanting to set off early tomorrow –"

"Four," Hollie said, cocking an eyebrow at Elijah.

"Three," Het said, and Hollie opened his mouth, looked at her, and meekly said, "Three."

"Your father is not yet fit to travel, Holofernes. I should prefer that you did not, but – well, dear, you know best. I do hope Russell's cough is better in the morning, poor thing. Otherwise he will be going nowhere, dear, either. I'm sure a good night's sleep will set all to rights. I'm afraid we have no beds aired, gentlemen, but there – I wasn't expecting guests, you see."

"No," Hollie said, sounding, for the first time, utterly defeated. "No. Well. Neither was bloody Byron, the Malignant bastard. But he got 'em. Fairfax, right up the ar– nether parts. I'm consoling myself with the thought that having kicked Byron's, um, breeches seat at Nantwich, my lord Fairfax is somewhat out on a limb in Cheshire. And he could probably do with a troop of horse to turn up out of nowhere, about now, so he's not going to send us back. So. What with harbouring known fugitives, and helping out a mate in trouble, it looks like I'm honour-bound to go, lass."

He forgot Luce, forgot Russell, forgot his father, but took his girl's hands in his own. "You know I'd not go, if I had the choice." He shot a glance of loathing at Russell, who had his eyes closed and did not care. "We are for Cheshire, if we like it or not."

15

A DINNER OF HERBS

Het did not cry, although she looked as if she might, but she took a hurt breath as if he'd kicked her, and her mouth drooped a little at the corners.

And then she straightened her dear shoulders, and ah, Christ, he could have wished for a dozen Henrietta Babbitts under his military command, because she nodded and heaved herself to her feet without a word, and waddled off towards the kitchens, like a woman on a mission.

"Where are you off to?" Luce said, which was a relief – it meant Hollie didn't have to – and she turned at the door. She smiled, and there was possibly only Hollie in the room who knew what it was costing her to carry on smiling.

"Well, dear, if you must leave before dawn, then I must be sure you are all well-provisioned. It is a –" her voice broke, a little, you'd have to know her well to hear it, "– a long way to the North. And cold."

"Give over, lass. We won't melt for a bit of water." And he didn't care who was watching, he got up out of his warm corner – was tempted to kick Russell in the shin as he passed, just to relieve his feelings, though he restrained himself – and put his arm round his sturdy little wife's waist.

Took him a couple of goes to find, in her current interesting and expansive condition, but fondling his girl in the vague region of her lower ribs was a comfort to both of them. His father, the old bastard, gave an approving grunt. "We'll be fine," Hollie muttered into the top of her head, feeling somewhat awkward. Public displays of affection were not his field of expertise, and she was burrowing her face into his coat as if she might be intending to grow there. She wouldn't cry, though. She wouldn't show herself up. "You need your bed, my lass," he said sternly. "Me and Luce are more than capable of coming down on that kitchen like the hosts of Midian, first thing. We won't go short."

"Actually, Auntie Het, you had probably lock up anything you *do* want to keep, or we shall carry off the lot," Luce said. He caught on quick.

"You will leave Master Babbitt and, um, –" her eyes darted at the erstwhile secretary to the Earl of Essex, because she didn't know quite what Russell was, and to be honest, neither did Hollie.

"I will not."

"And I'll not stop," Elijah said grimly. "I'll go wi't' lad. I spent long enough not knowing where thee was, boy, I know thee – tha'll slip off as soon as my back's turned, and I'll not set eyes on thee for another twenty years."

"Are you suggesting I'd abandon my wife, you foul-minded –"

He forgot that Het was no sweet, milky-watery girl. "Husband," she said sweetly, and anyone who spared a casual glance at them would have thought what a loving couple they made, the husband so tall and stern and his meek little wife yielding to him with her hand on his waist in the most devoted way imaginable. In truth, Hollie was standing bolt upright because Het had managed to find a bit – a very little bit – of soft flesh just above his hipbone, and she was nipping him with some asperity. He stifled a yelp. The lass had a grip like a horse-bite.

"Husband, your poor father is not fit to be dragged out into this intemperate weather, dear. It would kill him – and he so recently risen from his bed."

"I'll not," Elijah began stubbornly, and Het turned her head.

"Yes you will," she said, and Hollie stifled a grin. Revenge being a dish best served cold –

"You will," he echoed, and enjoyed it. "You're not coming with me, old man. I've got no use for you."

Because he hated the old bastard. Because now, for the first time, this was his call, and he had something the old man wanted.

Then Elijah's eyes dropped. Hollie looked at his father, at a man who'd used strap and sin to try and break some grace into him. Who'd failed, utterly and absolutely, to mould his boy into the kind of judgmental and pious canting bastard he was himself.

"Ah, Christ, you're more use to me here than there," he muttered. "I'll want someone to see the lass taken care of, when the child comes. I'd not leave you wholly defenceless, Het. He's better than nowt. Though not by much."

Not for his sake. Not for the old bastard's sake, because no matter how lonely he might be, how few the places that might welcome him, Lije Babbitt could die in a ditch so far as his son was concerned. No matter how much he might crave favour, now his boy was apparently in the Lord's good graces sufficient to be a senior officer about His work in the Army of Parliament.

No, it was for the look in Het's eyes, and for her belief that he was a far finer man than he knew himself to be.

16

NOT A MAN, BUT A BEAST

It took three weeks to get back down to Nantwich, and they were the longest, bleakest three weeks of Hollie's life. Thinking of Het every step of the way, and her brave, bright, shaky smile as he'd ridden off, and he'd been so bloody cross he'd not even said his goodbyes proper because he'd still kept thinking it wasn't happening, couldn't be real.

It was real. By the time they skirted Peterborough – cautiously, because that city hadn't yet made its mind up whose side it was on, and it could go either way – the three of them had been forcibly ejected from just about every inn they'd sought accommodation in. It wasn't just down to Luce's unexpectedly ferocious blonde beard, either.

They'd lost Russell a clear half-dozen times. He lied. He fought. (He bit, the little bastard, as well.) He would have stole, if he could have. He'd bolt as soon as your back was turned and he didn't care where he fetched up as long as he got a drink out of it. He had his liberty, and as soon as he was steady enough to have stopped shaking he was not grateful.

He screamed like a snared rabbit in the night, fighting battles in his head when he slept, and when he didn't sleep he sat up with his back against the wall, his eyes glittering like black frost in the moonlight. And Thankful Russell under a full moon, with that rope scar livid round his neck and what little spare flesh there'd been on him burned off by fever and debauchery – ah, God, no, he was the stuff of nightmare, and Hollie was not surprised decent inn-keepers wouldn't have him.

For two pins he'd have turned a blind eye and let the little bastard run. Lucey wouldn't let him, though. And if it was a battle of wills, Hollie was, grudgingly, going to put money on his cornet, because there was something in Luce that was essentially decent. He looked wispy, and he was presently going through a phase of painful heroic couplets, but when you got right down to it he was a good solid merchant's boy from a decent family and he was well aware of the value of a bad penny. He reckoned Russell was worth saving, and so saved he would be. Luce hated waste, and Russell hated – well, Russell hated Russell, and Luce, and Hollie, and being alive, mostly in that order. And so it was a constant battle, day in, day out, with the scar-faced lad either shaking and puking and too sick to go anywhere, or on his feet, drunk, mental and ranting.

Cullis came out into the yard scowling, wondering who was stupid enough to be travelling through hock-deep slush in midwinter, and the expression on his face was almost worthwhile. "What the hell," he started to say, and before Hollie could say a word the benighted Russell had caught his breath with a creaky gasp, and pitched off the horse sideways into the mud.

"God almighty, lad, what you done to him?"

"Done to himself," Hollie snapped, not feeling very charitable.

Luce, that self-appointed medic, knelt in the freezing mud and looked resigned. "Well, we can't in all kindness leave him like this, sir."

"He's your problem, brat. You brought him. You see to him."

Hollie took a deep breath. Cullis was giving him that you're not fooling anybody expression. "He's not catching, if that's what you're wondering."

"What happened to-" Cullis tapped his throat meaningfully.

Luce had the draggled and unlovely object propped against his knees. Well, at least the little bastard hadn't puked, this time. He stank of it.

"*I* happened," Russell said, very faintly, in a flat voice. And then he laughed. "I am cursed, sergeant. I violated someone. No. Not just *someone*. My friend. I shamed her and I hurt her. She meant nothing but kindness."

"What?" Cullis said.

"I would have dis. *Dishonoured*. Her. I thank God I was stopped. They should have killed me. They should have –"

"Oh for Christ's sake, Russell, shut up!" Ah, God, he heard this every night, sober and drunk, the same whining self-loathing, and it grew tiresome.

And Russell came upright in a splatter of slurry, eyes so wide that a ring of white showed all round the black, and both Hollie and Cullis took an involuntary step backwards. "I am a bloody rapist, sir, do you have any idea what it feels like to wake up every morning and know that? And the worst of it is that I know nothing of it – nothing – I can not even apologise, though I'd not blame her if she wanted to put a knife in me. I should welcome it – and I don't even know what I did."

Which rather left Hollie lost for words, because that was more than the usual cupshot maunderings you got from him. It was Essex's tale, but it was coming from Russell with a shaking, bone-deep belief that was frightening. "The hell are you on about, Russell?"

Give him credit, the whelp had balls. His head came up and it didn't matter that every man in the yard was looking at him as if they'd like to kill him, very slowly, for what he'd just admitted to. He swallowed, and he was so thin now that you saw the black scarring on his throat jerk with the movement. "I raped her," he said, with a sort of cold ferocity. "And I don't even remember it. I don't recall any of it. And you – you two – you think my life worth the preserving? You're mad. Both of you. You're madder than I am."

Hollie shook his head again. "You did what? Who the bloody hell told you *that* cock and bull story? You didn't rape *anybody*, you silly bugger."

He remembered the oddest things about that long moment of stillness that followed. That Luce sat with his head cocked to one side like a little dog. That Russell looked like he had something stuck in his throat, and that the scarred lad's mouth hung open slightly askew. "I'm not excusing what you did do, mind," Hollie said quickly, just in case the lad thought it meant he'd got away with it. "But you didn't rape anybody, Russell. Luce here doesn't think you've got it in you. And I'm inclined to agree with him. Where the hell did you get that idea?"

Russell's lopsided mouth worked silently. "But I must have," he said eventually. "I remember – Harris said – I remember her dress –" he took a deep, shaky breath. "Tore. I tore her dress. Her –" he put a hand flat on his own breast – "I wanted to. I know I did."

"Aye. Well. Drew Venning made it his business to know, Russell. You did not. I'd not have took you, if you had. Luce's soft heart or no, you'd have hanged. I'll tolerate much. I'll not tolerate that. You did not. You were stinking drunk, mind, and they gave you more of a beating than I should have said was strictly proportional for what you *did* do. Though you'd have done better to give in with good grace, next time. The which there will not be, boy, or I will hang you myself. *You did not rape her."*

"I *must* have," Russell said stubbornly. "Guards." He was struggling to get the words out of his bruised throat. It sounded painful. "They *said*. They told me. Said I was – was vile, and depraved, and did not deserve God's mercy – "

"I *know* what they said, Russell. What Essex put about. You did not."

"They were decent. Godly. Men. Why should I not believe their words?"

"And you're an adulterous drunk who tried to murder himself." All against his will, Hollie had a tiny tickle of sympathy for the lad. "It's not hardly the sort of behaviour the Lord's Elect approves of, lad."

Russell said nothing, but raised an eyebrow, and it would have broke the heart of a stone to see that old elegant mannerism on the wreckage presently sprawled in the mud of a wintry stableyard on Pepper Street. "I did …nothing? They had me believe I did – this dreadful thing – and I had not?" He looked, actually, as if he might be sick. "I had not hurt Meggie, after all?"

"No." It was a hard thing to say. "You broke one of the Commandments, and you did it in front of an audience. Pretty bloody stupid, but not terminal. Thing is," – how did you put this, exactly? – "if it hadn't been *that* Commandment, and if it hadn't been the wife of the feller who was bankrolling two troop of musketeers to the London Trained Bands, I've no doubt you'd have been given a slap on the wrist and sent on your way. You did not hurt her."

"What. Did. I do, then?"

Luce's hand closed on the lad's shoulder, hard enough to dimple the leather of his buffcoat, with heartfelt sympathy.

"You kissed her. That was all. Well. Not quite all. A bit more than that. But you did not rape her. Captain Venning did a bit of snouting around, and found some of the other lads who was there. He – Russell, it was pretty bloody stupid of you, and aye, well, if you were going to be strict about it, a quick kiss and a cuddle with another feller's wife under his very nose is a bit – well – it's not on. If I ever catch you groping my wife on the terrace, lad, there will be hell to pay and no pitch hot. And, well, I've spoke to the lass myself. You frightened her, Russell, you frightened her badly. She meant to kiss you. But that was all she meant." Ignoring the mud, Hollie got down in the mud beside his cornet, and the poor bastard who'd been silently taking himself apart for the last month for something he hadn't done. He looked into the lad's white, terrified face. Russell looked like one of the minor demons, poor sod, but he wasn't one. He had to understand that. "Russell. You did summat stupid. When a lass takes you outside for a little walk in the moonlight, sometimes, maybe, what she wants is gentlemanly wooing, not a full-on cavalry charge. I know you got two speeds and one of 'em's flat out and the other's backwards, but Jesus, lad! And with somebody else's wife! If I catch you doing anything quite so witless in my troop again, I will personally break your neck!"

Russell did not laugh. He blinked, as if it was taking him a while to understand the words. "I did not force myself on Meggie. I did not." His dark eyes were wide and absolutely blank, absolutely numb. "I have – this." His hand jerked towards his scarred throat, fell back into his lap. "They told me. They said. I – why did they say I had done such a thing? If I had not?"

Because there were a number of men amongst the Army of Parliament who feared joy, and humour, and – aye, adultery, if you wanted to be judgmental about it: a young girl mewed up in a house with a fat old Croesus, wanting a little laughter and a little light-hearted flirtation in her life, and no harm in that – there was a core of men like that, and a lot of them seemed to gather round the Earl of Essex. Men who feared and hated women, and light, and laughter, and loving, and wanted it stamped on, for a black sin. And Meggie Harris, surrounded by them, had blamed Russell for her fall, and no shame to her, because a woman taken in adultery could be put aside, even now. Essex had done it, twice over, before now. But to leave a lad as high-strung as Russell – beaten bloody for defending the lass's honour, leaving him with the wits kicked out of him by a gang of Harris's own bought and paid for bravos – Christ, no, you didn't have to punish him. Drop godly poison into his ear every day for six weeks and you'd drive him to devise worse punishments for his own self than the cruellest commander in Christendom could have dreamed up.

"You are sure?" Russell said again, with a shaking passion. "*Certain-sure*? I did not hurt her?"

"You did not hurt her," Luce said gently, and his fingers tightened again on the scarred young man's shoulder, with sympathy, though he looked up at Hollie with an expression that did not bode well for Uncle Essex, on their next meeting. "You have my word of honour, Thankful."

"Then – why did you not tell me? Why did none of you *say*?"

It was a reasonable question, Hollie supposed, in its way. But then how would you not know – how could a man even think he *might* be capable of such a thing? "But I thought you must know. Didn't you – well, you were there, did you not think – it might not be – you couldn't have?"

"They were good men. Godly men. Better men than I. I trusted them. " The lad's voice had gone slurred and mushy again, and that was a sure sign he was at point of breaking. "Tell a man he is not a man, but an animal, for long enough. And he may believe you. Why should I *not* be capable of it? Why should I not be capable of *anything*? If you tie any brute beast up for long enough, beat it and starve it, it will turn on you." And Hollie would have said something in response, but he found himself looking at Russell – at Russell whose bones showed through his skin, who flinched at sudden noises, or if you moved unexpected, who whimpered and choked in his sleep – and found that actually, he couldn't say anything at all.

"I –"

"I sinned. I know it. But I did nothing that any other man might not have done. It was wrong, and wilful. It was not a mortal sin, captain. I should not have hanged for it. To satisfy Master Harris's honour. And my lord Essex's pride."

He got to his feet, with the rags of his old grace, shrugging Luce's hand from his shoulder. "I did not hurt her. Though I would have had her, if she'd willed it. I wanted to." Finally, he blinked, and his gaze dropped, looking at his hands as if he still did not know what they might be capable of. "I might as well have, in their eyes. I looked on Meggie Harris with lust, and that makes me a –" he swallowed, hard, "a rapist?"

"No," Hollie said helplessly, and then, "no more than any of us, Hapless, just –"

"None of you. Not *one*. None of you thought to tell me I had done nothing to hurt her. Knowing my – my – distress of mind. Not a soul of you thought I deserved even that comfort." He sounded as if he could not breathe, and Luce went to touch him, because Luce was like that – a gentle soul, the brat, and he did not deserve the vicious hiss of indrawn breath and the flinching away he received. "May I not even call my person my own, sir? Must I be pawed and petted when it suits you to ease your goddamned conscience, and ordered hence at your whim when it does not?" It was almost a sob, and Hollie looked at his boots, while the rest of the company ostentatiously busied themselves elsewhere, gawking behind-hand.

"You are a creature of free will," Luce said gently, "you may come and go as you please. At no man's orders."

"Unless you're on duty," Hollie added, and then shut up, realising he'd walked into the middle of one of the brat's metaphysical webs. "Er. Not literally. Obviously."

"May I," Russell said sardonically. "May I, so. Then I would choose to go. With your leave. Captain." He gave a mocking bow, and turned on his heel.

"Go – where?" Hollie was aware that the scarred young man was eyeing him with a sort of weary contempt, as if he was neither convinced by or cared for Hollie's concern.

"I am going to get drunk," Russell said over his shoulder. He wasn't defiant, he wasn't challenging, it just wasn't open to negotiation. He was wet, filthy, he hadn't changed his linen in a month, and God knows when he'd last washed his hair. Even so. He paced across the yard with his head up, looking to neither left nor right. Tripped over a loose cobble and went sprawling headlong in the mud again, to the detriment of the skin on his hands and the knee of his breeches. But nobody laughed. Luce opened his mouth to say something.

"Leave him be," Hollie said, with a sigh. "He has not been well served."

17

MAD AS A MARCH HARE

It was not a comfortable night, that night, with Luce looking as if he might cry, and the pair of them sat in front of a warm fire with a civilised jug of buttered ale in the embers, warm and dry while the cold spring rain sluiced down the gutters outside and a nasty little March wind poked and prodded through the cracks in the shutters and under the doors.

He wasn't going to talk about it, of course. Because yes, the lad was as cracked as a pothouse jug, Hollie had known that much before, but he hadn't got that way by himself. Wondering whether you might come downstairs in the morning and find Russell swinging from the bloody rafters, having decided to make a better job of it this time, or if he'd end up getting himself knifed in some tavern brawl, or if he was just passed out in a bloody ditch somewhere catching his death of cold. Luce took another deep breath, and rattled his pen ostentatiously in the ink-pot that he wasn't using.

"I hope the men's quarters are dry," he said, for the fourth time that night.

"Should be, Luce. Cullis looked 'em over, and Cullis has been seeing to the quartering of my troops since you were in skirts."

"Will there be sufficient –"

"Bread? Yes. Straw? Yes. Blankets? Yes. Cheese, not if that bottomless pit Weston gets his jaws round it, though I imagine his brother will fight him for it. Lucey, if you want to go out and look in every alehouse in Nantwich for him, you may be my guest, though I'd suggest you put your cloak on before you do it, because it's tipping down and I reckon it's set in for the night. Pass us the ale."

He poured himself another mug and sat with his hands linked around it, staring moodily into the fire. "Don't envy that lad," he said at length.

"Russell? No. No, the poor soul, he has a hard row to furrow, and it must be lonely, I'll warrant —"

"*Cullis.* Seeing to the provisioning of that lot of ungrateful arsebites. Bloody hard work for one man, and that not as young as he might have been."

Luce had narrowly escaped being made troop adjutant not so very long ago, and that only by the simple expedient of being able to add a column of figures three times and come to a different conclusion every time. He smiled faintly. "He does a sterling job, mind."

Hollie gave another sigh. "He's right, though."

"Sergeant Cullis?"

"Russell. Christ, brat, keep up!" He shook his head. "How do you go about saying sorry to someone for – that? Sorry your life's turned to ratshit, old son, but that's wars for you? And he's lucky! – Sort of. He still has straight limbs – he can still earn his bread, he's young, he –"

"Is unhappy, and probably younger than I am, and I would imagine, in a deal of pain, a lot of the time," Luce said tartly. "Some consolation, Hollie, I'm sure." He looked sternly over the rim of his mug as he drained it. "Well, there is always someone worse off than you are, as my lady mother says."

"Luce, you've got a dab of butter on the end of your nose."

"It's buttered ale, and don't change the subject. Of course you can't apologise to Russell. – to *Thankful*. You see? We even speak of him like a – a dog, or a servant!"

"That's because he has one of the more inappropriate Christian names of my acquaintance, brat. What that poor bugger has to be Thankful for, I do not know."

"That's not funny."

The windows shook under another onslaught of wild wind, rattling in their casements.

"I hope the men are dry," Luce said again.

"Five," Hollie said, and his friend gave him a hard stare.

"If by this levity you are attempting to prove once and for all that you are a hard man with care for nothing but your own comforts –" he leaned forward with what was clearly intended to be a menacing scowl. "You're fooling no one." He set his mug back down in the hearth, and pushed his chair back. "I'm just going to go and set my mind at ease, about the troop's accommodation. I – well, I may be some time, is all."

Hollie stretched his legs out to the fire, and grinned. Luce was fooling no one, either. "If you happen to be passing by the kitchens, ask 'em to send us up another jug of ale. And I'd not mind someone slipping a warming-pan by the beds, neither. I'm getting too used to my home comforts, that's what it is. Growing soft." He did not mean to smile, but he did, he felt the corners of his mouth turn up, and couldn't help it. "That girl of mine, brat. All her doing. She'll be the lighter of a little 'un by now. Hope she's safe and snug, this night."

"I imagine your father will see to her comfort, Hollie. He is most tender in her care."

"Aye. Aye, well, I owe him that. If nothing else." He looked into the heart if the fire, and smiled, and said nothing for a while. And then, "Leave us your paper out, brat, if you're done versifying for the night. I've a mind to write to the lass."

"In prose, I trust, captain," that poetic reprobate said smartly.

Hollie said nothing, but gave him a thoughtful look, and tapped the end of the pen on his teeth – a habit he had that drove Luce mental, and he knew it. "You happen to come across Hapless," he said eventually, casually, "if he's stuck for quartering, he'd be welcome to come in with us. Seems a bit of a waste, having Essex's secretary with us and not making use of him."

18

A POSTING TO THE AMERICAS

It was almost worth being up to the arse in freezing mud, with a bitter February wind blowing stinging hail straight into your face, stood in a field in benighted Cheshire with your wife two hundred miles away, just for the look on Black Tom Fairfax's face.

Fairfax looked at Hollie. Hollie blinked innocently back at him. He knew his commander stammered. Everybody knew Black Tom had a stutter. He had to be proper flustered for it to come out in company, though. "Captain B-Babbitt," Fairfax said faintly. "What –"

And Hollie's hand went to the back of his neck, that dead giveaway that he was flustered – he heard Luce stifle a snort of laughter. "Uh, bit of a long story, sir."

"I *understood* you to have joined the Eastern Association, captain."

"Aye. Well. In a manner of speaking. And then again, sort of, not."

"I understood Colonel Cromwell to have offered you some advancement, sir. Is that not the case?"

Well, he could spend all day verbally fencing with his commander, slowly freezing to death. On the other hand, he could just come right out with it, and –

"Not bothered about that, sir. Eastern don't need me, the missis don't need me, given that I've left the old ba– the, uh, former troop chaplain back at home."

"And I, presumably, do?"

Hollie took a deep breath and straightened his shoulders. "Aye. Well. It's a bit – well – it's like this. I could do wi' keeping a bit of distance between me and my lord Essex at the moment, you might say. Like, if you've got any postings going to, oh, I don't know, the Americas – kind of thing. I haven't actually done owt, not to speak of, but –"

Luce stepped forward – gave Hollie a rueful sidelong glance – cleared his throat. "It was me this time, Sir Thomas."

"You, cornet? What –"

"It is a really long story. It's a bit –"

"Me," Thankful Russell said, with a sigh, joining the two officers. Technically, Russell wasn't an officer any more, he was more a sort of – well, Hollie suspected technically Russell was a deserter and an escaped prisoner, not to mention a rapist, a dangerous criminal, and a most notorious whited sepulchre. All of which he looked and more at the moment. Fairfax, God bless him, simply looked at this gaunt and ragged spectre, betrayed his surprise only by a tiny twitch of his eyebrows, and cocked his head at Hollie. "I am assuming there is a good explanation for this, captain?"

"No," Hollie said, honestly. "But there *is* an explanation."

Listening to it – sat very upright and trying to look stern and disapproving because he knew damn' well that every word was being silently absorbed for onward dissemination back to the Earl of Essex – it sounded like a good tale. Coming from Hollie it would have sounded like spite and insubordination, but coming from wide-eyed, earnest Lucey Pettitt it sounded like the veriest act of Christian charity. "So you see, I couldn't leave him there," Luce finished, turning those big guileless grey eyes onto each face in turn. "It would have been a shameful thing to desert a comrade in his hour of need – especially a trusted friend like Russell, whose only crime is to be one that loved not wisely, but too well –"

Hollie shaking his head fractionally at his cornet, don't start quoting Shakespeare at a quiverfull of Puritans, brat, it won't do us any favours –

"Russell has served the Cause most faithfully, and it is *unfair* that he should be treated so."

Actually, looking at Russell in his current state, it looked perfectly fair that such a desperate ruffian should be taken up for execution, but the brat didn't seem to agree, and Russell didn't seem to care. He hadn't seemed to care about a lot, since they'd got the hell out of Essex. At first he'd seemed slightly dazed, and now he just seemed sullen-stupid and resentful. "Not to mention the fact that the Earl of Essex would have looked a bit of a – er, it would not have reflected well on his judgment."

"And so you have deserted Colonel Cromwell's ranks?" William Brereton asked silkily, leaning forward to light his pipe at the glowing embers at the edge of the hearth. It was Brereton's own hearth, so he could say what he liked, and Hollie had sufficient good manners not to poke him in the nose for that crack – especially since Brereton was Essex's spymaster in the North, as well as commander of his forces in Cheshire. And as long-nosed, interfering, holier-than-thou a puritanical bastard as you might hope to meet in a long day's ride, at that. Luce looked flustered, Russell looked as bleakly blank as ever, and Hollie took enormous delight in reaching into his doublet and producing a letter of explanation in Colonel Cromwell's own hand. Well – as good as.

"Colonel Cromwell agrees wi' me, sir. What's done is done – *isn't* it, Lucifer – and since I knew nowt about this till my cornet arrived with the, uh, with the prisoner in tow – we reckoned it might be best to, uh, be somewhere else for a while. Like, nowhere near Essex."

"But your duty, sir, is to return the prisoner to legitimate custody," Brereton said, and Hollie gave him a thoughtful look.

"Depends who you reckon my duty is to, sir. If you reckon my duty is to the person of Earl of Essex, then you might be right – or you might argue that my duty is to protect the Earl of Essex from a serious error in his judgment, but that's sort of by the by." He folded his hands in what he hoped was a meek and pious manner. "My duty to the Army, as an officer, is to the care of my men, and – well, look at the state of him, sir, does he *look* like he's been taken care of in his imprisonment?"

He leaned across the settle and tugged Russell's shirt collar away from his discoloured throat. The lad stiffened – his scarred face was utterly expressionless, but he managed to look at Hollie with an expression of utter hatred without moving a muscle. In for a penny, Babbitt, in for a pound. "Lad tried to hang himself, Sir William, due to the kind offices of the gentlemen into whose care he was entrusted. He hadn't done nowt to merit his treatment, other than a particularly ill-advised flirtation with a married lady. Nice lass, Russell here thought he might marry her, one time, but she knocked him back."

Russell gasped. He hadn't thought it was going to be made the subject of public gossip, poor bugger. Well, Hollie had had his own wounds searched before. It hurt, but you couldn't leave them to fester. "Her father reckoned Colonel Harris was the better bet, but it seemed she still had an eye for Russell warming her bed after all," he said, and Luce choked and Fairfax looked mortified.

"Captain *Babbitt*!"

"Um. Sorry." Russell looked, out of the corner of his eye, as if he'd like to kill Hollie, Luce had most of his sleeve in his mouth and was turning purple, Fairfax was mortified and Brereton – well, it was hard to tell with Brereton, if he smiled his face might crack. "I made my own enquiries, sir. Is what I mean. She was a nice lass, and I've no doubt she still is a nice lass, with more hair than wit and about as much worldliness as my horse. My duty as a Christian, gentlemen, is to see the truth told, and there was precious little chance of that going on. And Colonel Cromwell agrees, as you can see from this letter. Given that he went and had a word with Colonel Harris his very own self, to find out the truth of the matter. Reckon he put the fear of God into him, too."

"I hope there will be no repercussions for the lady?" Russell hissed through gritted teeth.

"Not if Colonel Harris proposes to keep his bollocks where the Lord placed them," Hollie said sweetly. "The lass did nowt to merit either blame or punishment – you can take the full blame for that, Russell – and I'd not have her held to account for your, uh, misplaced enthusiasm, shall we say. My lord Essex happens to value two troop of musket rather higher than he values his own staff. And *I* bloody don't."

"The Earl of Essex values Parliament's cause above –" Brereton, the zealous bastard, looked down his nose disapprovingly, "the skin of one dissolute young wastrel? Surely not, sir. So how do you propose to sort out this – tangle?" he said sternly, and that, Hollie had no answer to.

There was a long silence. A log split on the fire, and the wind in the chimney stirred the ashes. Fairfax suddenly laughed out loud. "Choose your officers, *Colonel* Babbitt."

"What?" Brereton said it – and Hollie just thought it.

Fairfax was grinning like a boy. "Choose your officers, sir. I'm promoting you out of harm's way. Indispensable to the command of the

Northern Army – or at least, where I can have an eye to your continued good behaviour. Pettitt I assume you will keep – will he make captain, do you think?"

"This is – this is some game, yes? Let's pretend?"

"Sir Thomas, this is madness," Brereton said.

"Madness, Sir William? The only madness I can see is the captain's – the *colonel's* – insistence on keeping faith with old comrades though it costs him his hope of advancement. Anyway," Black Tom finished, with a stubborn satisfaction, "if I've trusted Colonel Babbitt with the life of my only daughter before now, I think he can be trusted with a command. He saved Colonel Cromwell's life at Winceby –"

"Oh, hardly!" Hollie burst out, unable to bear that particular fabrication, "I lent him my horse."

"In the middle of a battle. As one does. Be quiet, sir. Your modesty does you no favours. Well, Hollie, will you take it, or are you going to sit here and argue with your superiors all night?"

"Officers," Hollie said faintly. "Luce, you reckon you'll make captain?"

"Rather be dead, sir, for the foreseeable future. Let me learn this job first. Here, sir, what'm I supposed to call you now?"

"Hollie," he said. "All the time. Well. If I'm going to be a full colonel, I reckon I'll need a decent adjutant. That'll keep you out of trouble, Russell. You'll be too bloody busy."

The dark eyes lifted, but sparkling, now, alight with a kind of disbelieving joy.

"Trust you as my lieutenant, can I?"

Russell said nothing. He just nodded, slowly.

"Can't hear you, Russell. Or d'you not fancy?"

"I would be honoured, sir."

"What did I just say?"

"I would be honoured. *Hollie*."

"That's better. You mean it, Sir Thomas? Truly? That I – that we can – I could ask you for any officer to command, and you'd –"

Fairfax shrugged. "So far as it's within my gift – yes. It's your own company, Colonel Babbitt. You may staff it as you see fit." He looked thoughtfully at Russell, who had straightened, almost imperceptibly, in his seat. Whose gaze was alert, and direct. Fairfax looked at Russell, and Russell looked straight back with an air of cool enquiry, and Hollie rubbed his nose to hide a grin.

"Drew Venning," Hollie said promptly, and Luce gave a whoop of delight, quickly stifled. "One of Essex's captains, and a particular friend to us – to the troop. He would be a – a valuable asset, sir."

"He'd be a howling bloody menace," Luce said, not quite inaudibly. "For a Fenman, he's all right. He's stood a friend to you two ruffians, anyway. And – um – sir?"

Fairfax raised an eyebrow.

"Um, any chance of –" he hardly liked to ask. All this – and then to ask for more. "Any chance of a decent horse for Russell? We had to scrounge one of Venning's remounts to get him down here, and –" he stopped. "Russell, for Christ's sake. I'm not having you tagging round after me balanced like a pea on a bloody drumhead on that carthorse. It can get back in the bloody baggage train where it come from. I'm not thinking of your comfort, I'm thinking of my dignity. And if you haven't got a clean handkerchief, use your bloody sleeve, and I'll get the missis to send some up when she writes next."

Russell stood up, excused himself with a bow that was a ragged ghost of his former elegant courtliness, and left the room with haste. "Soft bugger," Hollie said, with a sniff. "Crying over nowt."

Brereton was nodding to himself. "I see," he said slowly. "I see."

"Exactly so," Fairfax agreed, and it was on the tip of his tongue to ask what, exactly, he'd just done that was so illuminating, when he realised that even Luce was giving him incomprehensible starry-eyed looks of admiration. It wasn't the done thing to ask the Commander-in-Chief of the Parliamentarian forces in the North West what the hell he was looking at. Even *Hollie* wasn't that stupid.

He could ask Lucey later on, though.

19

THE TENDER MERCIES OF THE WICKED

"Got a surprise for you, Hapless," Hollie said smugly.

Percey had groomed the bay horse till its coat gleamed like a dark conker. He'd even acquired some chalk from God knows where and he'd whitened the gelding's stockings. There were times when you had to wonder about Mattie Percey's previous career in a stable-yard in Essex. Just how honestly he might have come by certain skills. That lad was a better painter than Lely.

What he hadn't done was improved the big horse's temper, and it came out of the line rearing, ears pinned against its skull. Mattie had his hand gripping the bit-ring, trying to keep the horse's head down, and even so the bay nearly had him off his feet.

It was a bloody fine horse, though. Big-built, not one of your lightweight sprinters like Luce Pettitt's spindly witless Rosa: backside like a gable end and a proud arch to its thickly-muscled neck that hinted that someone might have been a little behindhand with the shears to its gelding. That was a beast that'd go all day chasing Malignants and come in at the end of it dancing. It was the sort of mount any junior cavalry officer with any dreams of a future career in the Army might covet, provided a man could train some sense into its thick head. Plenty of staying-power, plenty of fire and dash, though possibly a bit light on good humour. Hollie closed one eye and looked at the bay horse consideringly where it ramped and curvetted like some maniac heraldic emblem.

"What d'you reckon to him, then?" he said, and looked at the scarred lieutenant, expecting to see gratitude and pleasure on that cold, half-lovely face.

Instead the lad was white to the lips, the great scar on his cheek standing out a most unlovely purple, and his eyes were as mad as the bay horse's.

"Is – *thish* – intended to be meant in humour?" he said stiffly, and his voice had that funny slur it had when the ragged muscle in his cheek had gone stiff as wood, like it did when he was tired or ungovernable. Or drunk. That was still always a clear and present possibility.

Hollie shook his head, thinking he must have misheard, or Russell must have misheard, because –

"All right, ain't he?" Percey said happily, still being jerked around like a rag doll by the beast's flinging head, but as cheerfully good-humoured as ever he was even when his arm was being yanked from its socket by an unwanted cavalry remount. "Want to take him out, Hap– uh, Lieutenant Russell? Take a bit of the ginger out of his heels?"

"I. Should. Rather. Be. Dead," Russell said, through gritted teeth. Flung his own head up, looking not unlike the bay horse, and glared fiercely at Hollie, and Hollie would have sworn to it the lieutenant's dark eyes were brimming with wholly incomprehensible tears. *"A righteous man regardeth the life of his beast: but the tender mercies of the wicked are cruel."*

"What?" Hollie said blankly, and Russell snarled at him, actually snarled, baring his teeth like a dog.

"The Book of Proverb. *Ss.*" He bit off the last consonant with a hissing, furious sibilance, and then hit himself in the temple with the heel of his hand. *"Shir."*

And then wheeled about and was gone, shoving Luce rudely out of the way, storming back to the house. "What," Hollie said again, shook himself, "what the bloody hell was that all about?"

"What on earth did you say to him – oh, sir, that was not well done!"

There were times when Luce didn't half remind Hollie of Het. Well, Hollie's wife was his cornet's father's little sister, it wasn't so much of a surprise, but even so. That hurt, shocked, disappointed look was pure Het, an expression she reserved for when he did something completely stupid. What, precisely, he'd done this time, he did not quite know, save that he was still trying to make things all right for a lad who was as tricksy to handle as a barrel of rotten gunpowder, and he didn't know from day's end to day's end what mood he was going to be on the receiving end of. Like walking on eggshells, if eggshells were volatile, suspicious, and prone to soothing their tempers by getting fiercely rat-arsed.

"What wasn't?" he said warily. "What, seriously, sir? You did not mean to be – um – funny?"

"No, of course I bloody didn't!"

Luce gave a great sigh. "Ah, God. So you – you know – did you look at the beast? Other than, um, you know – professionally?"

"What –" With one final jerk of the bit, Mattie had the bay horse with all four feet on the ground. It was still a handsome beast. It was just – odd-looking. Three white feet, and a great lopsided white blaze to its face. One blue eye, and one, slightly manic, brown one.

A perfectly sound, sturdy, fine cavalry mount, who just happened to look both ugly and irregular. It was a bloody good horse, sound in wind and limb, beautifully put together, a mount a man could rely on – could be proud of. But now Luce came to mention it, the brute did look a bit like it had been sewn together from bits of at least two other horses. Good ones, but –.

And that *had* been a coincidence.

"Ah," said Hollie.

20

RESOLUTELY ABSTINENT

March in Cheshire was a god-damned lousy month. When it wasn't raining, it was snowing. There was a persistent drip – and for once these days, he wasn't talking about Thankful Russell – from one of the sodden branches hanging over his head. Hollie was starting to conceive a cordial loathing of Cheshire in the early spring. It was cold and grey and it hadn't stopped raining in the best part of a month. His boots were leaking, his linen was damp – he pushed his draggled hair out of his eyes with the back of his hand, noting with grim relish that he was definitely feverish.

Even the indefatigable Tyburn had taken one look at the perpetual grey clouds of rain gusting across the fields and decided he was incurably lame. The Rabbit was too thick to play that game, so Hollie was mounted on that sluggish, witless, clumsy great beast, an experience which didn't improve his temper either. Sat under a dripping black tree in the passing rain waiting for the back-markers of his bloody lack-witted, purposeless patrol to catch up so that he could give them what for – for the nine hundred and ninety ninth time – for their slowness, their – he was sure they were doing it on purpose. Dragging their heels just so he had to sit here in the bloody rain, and that was bloody insubordination, he was sure of it.

On the other hand, that mad mismatched horse and the mad mismatched lieutenant seemed to have taken to each other like salt to meat, and they were in their overwrought element, crashing about in the slush at what Hollie considered a most unnecessary speed. The troop were bloody chattering like a bunch of bloody goodwives. Not Hollie's fault there wasn't a sniff of a bloody Malignant for miles, and Fairfax had got into the habit of sending them out looking just in case they might have missed Prince Rupert hiding under a bush or some bloody thing. Hollie growled, and then wished he hadn't as it set him off coughing, which hurt.

"I. Am. Going. Home," he snarled at Russell, who always copped for the brunt of Hollie's bad temper at the moment, considering he was the cause of most of it. Russell halted his mount neatly in a large muddy puddle, brushed a splatter of mud from the skirts of his stained buffcoat (neatly, the bastard) and inclined his head. "Very good, sir."

"No it bloody isn't," Hollie snapped. Yanked the Rabbit's head out of the ditch, thumped his heels into the grey's rotund sides, and set off at a humiliatingly sedate walk. He could hear one of the bastards laughing behind him. He suspected Ward. He always suspected Ward. Of everything.

Oh, Christ, Hollie hated the world. He hated Charles Stuart, who could have put an end to the whole god-damned soggy mess by just agreeing to stop trying to squeeze every last brass farthing out of the population. He hated the Earl of Essex, more so now than ever, but that was nothing new. Prince Rupert, he could piss off as well, lurking in Shrewsbury instead of doing the decent thing of coming out and getting shot at like a man. He hated Cheshire. He hated having a streaming cold, which he'd had for the better part of a month and which was starting to seriously annoy him. He really hated the cheerful, rosy-cheeked goodwife at the farm where they were quartered, who seemed to have taken a fancy to Hollie in her husband's absence and who gave him the glad-eye and went all coy and giggly every time he set foot in the house. He hated Lucey bloody god-damned Pettitt, who'd decided rustic pleasures were his new passion in life and spent most of his time chatting up the dairymaid, a fine strapping wench if ever Hollie had seen one. Amazing how many times bloody Pettitt, who was supposed to be Hollie's junior stand-in, found excuses not to go out on patrol with the rest of the lads and turned up mooning about the house batting his eyelashes at the wench. Probably Hollie should mind, but it was also amazing how up to date the paperwork was, and Fairfax got on Hollie's neck something fierce about paperwork.

Russell, on the other hand, who *should* have been doing the paperwork, preferred to be out on patrol looking for trouble, even when there wasn't enemy action for the best part of twenty miles. Oh, the bloody lot of 'em made Hollie's head ache.

The lads had the common sense to keep about ten yards behind him, even at the Rabbit's ponderous speed, and he thumped into the farmyard in sodden isolation. Hock-deep in sucking mud, and he slid off the horse and threw the reins at Percey. "You all right, sir?" Percey said, and he was the first person all bloody day who'd actually sounded like he gave a toss whether Hollie was alive or dead.

"*No*," Hollie said, and wiped his nose on the back of his hand, and then remembered he was wearing an armoured bridle gauntlet. For two pins he could have sat down in the mud and cried. He really did feel that bloody rough. "You want to get inside," Percey said kindly, "out of the wet. I'll see to this 'un."

"Thanks, Mattie." *Het* wouldn't have made him go out in all weathers, half-dead of a cold. Het would have been all sweet and kind and nice about it, and she'd have put him to bed and made a fuss of him and –

"Pettitt, what the *fuck* are you looking at?"

Clean, dry, neat Luce Pettitt, comfortably wrapped up in a thick cloak, raised an eyebrow at Hollie's bedraggled person. "You have a rather elegant moustache, sir. It's very nice, but I'm not sure black's your colour."

"What?" His cornet took a handkerchief from up his sleeve – "Lucey, if you dare spit on that, I am going to skin you and eat you!"

"I was going to lend it to you, sir, in order that you make yourself presentable before you receive company."

"Bollocks –" he sneezed, thought better of the bridle-gauntlet, and used his shoulder instead – "to company. I am going to bed."

"Well, I think you ought to stick your head round the door, at least."

"No." He couldn't even be bothered to think up a smart reply. He just pushed past Luce, glowering, and squelched towards the stairs. "I've asked Mistress Cowper if she could warm a bit of ale for us," Luce said innocently, "and the toasted cheese shouldn't be long..."

"I don't care."

"By God, Rosie, 'ee must be sickening for suffen if 'ee's turning down cheese."

He must be sickening for something. He'd just imagined Drew Venning in Cheshire, as large as life, and twice as filthy: scruffy and unshaven and travel-stained, sat in the kitchen at White Gates Farm with his appalling boots on the fender. "Never heard 'en that quiet, Luce – lad lost his voice or suffen?"

Mistress Cowper pattered up from the buttery, closing the door with a sharp bang behind her. She glanced up at Hollie, doing his best impersonation of a dying duck in a thunderstorm up against the doorpost. This time yesterday, she'd have been all over him like the measle, cooing and fussing. Now – when he reluctantly wouldn't have minded – he'd been relegated to second place behind the rather unglamorous form of Andrew Venning, making himself right at home and hogging the fire.

"Drew –" he still wasn't sure the freckled fenlander wasn't a product of some fevered dream – "what the hell are *you* doing here?"

Venning struggled to his feet, looking embarrassed, and gave Hollie a brisk salute. "Um, congratulations on the promotion, sir, and we come down as fast as we could after 'ee asked. Sorry. Forgot 'ee's not a captain any more, sir, sorry. I took the liberty of sticking my head round the door in Essex – got suffen for you, Luce –" and then he leaned down and thumped on the lid of a box at his side. "And missis sent you this, Rosie. Uh – Rosie, 'ee looks like 'ee's either going to pass out or puke, and I'd take it kindly if 'ee didn't do either in here. Mistress Cowper's just sanded the floor, bor –"

There'd been some to-ings and fro-ings with the Earl of Essex, whose initial response to Fairfax's request for Venning's transfer was that the only thing Hollie Babbitt would be granted was a swift and summary trial by martial justice. Seemed Fairfax had set him straight in two or three short lines. "He never mentioned owt about that other letter, did he?" Hollie said warily, and Luce looked enquiring and said nothing, and Venning grinned.

"Wouldn't of mattered if he had, bor. I told 'en."

"Say what?"

There was a scrabbling sound at the door, and Venning stood up, loped across the parlour, and let his brown-and-white shadow in. "Went and told 'en. I ent daft, Rosie. Caught Old Noll in a good humour and pitched it so's we saved a lil' brand from the burning. Just like you said to say, lad was being stitched up good and proper, and him a decent boy who just made a mistake. So you tell that lad, Rosie, you tell 'en he starts acting up down here and Colonel Cromwell's like to come down and give him hell on, in person. The which I can do without. Me and Old Noll got a bit of past, you might say. He reckoned I was too hot for the Eastern, and I reckoned he was too prosy for me. Anyways, he d'say that if he'd known about it he'd have written that letter for Fairfax hisself. I just saved him the job o' setting pen to paper. I write a neat hand, though I say it as shouldn't."

And then Venning had just hung around London looking solid and conspicuous till they got fed up with him, which, given his appetite, was usually a matter of days. "Suffen like a house wall in a buffcoat," he said comfortably, settling himself back in the chair by the hearth, and Tinners collapsed at his feet with a sigh. "I don' argue back, bor, 'ee knows that. Just stand about the place looking lackwitted till they gets sick o' the sight o' me. Rosie, 'ee's shaking."

"Captain Venning, you – you – you said you had – my – " he linked his hands together in his lap to stop the shaking.

Venning gaped at him, and then slapped himself in the forehead. "Oh, hell, I clean forgot, I thought you knew – your gal's lighter of a daughter, bor. Lovely lil' mawther, she is. All pink and smiley, lil' tuft o' black hair. Looks nawthen lilke 'ee, but thass no bad thing, in a girl. She don't half favour her mother, about the eyes. Het's fine, having a high old time of it, bit tired, but she sends her best love, and bloody 'Lije is like a dog with two – uh, begging your pardon, Mistress Cowper." He took a hefty bite of his toasted cheese. "They're well, Rosie. All of 'em. Promise. Now where's 'ee going?"

Hollie pressed the back of his hand to his mouth, hard. "Bollocks to the Cause," he said shakily. "I want to go home."

"If I didn't know better, I'd reckon that lad was crying," Venning said comfortably after the door had slammed shut, stretching his long legs out in front of him. "And thass not like our Rosie."

"What with one thing and another," Luce said, "I think he's been run a bit ragged, lately. Not sure he's quite got his head round the idea of promotion, yet."

"Ah?"

"Mm. Mother sent cake, Drew. Ooh – clean stockings. D'you know, I shall be twenty in three weeks, and my mother still doesn't think I can arrange to have my own stockings mended? Bless her. Help you to a piece of cake? Save some for the ca– the colonel, though. No, he's not good at the, um, the administrative side of things. You know what Hollie is. No patience."

"Thass true enough. Good cake."

"There are a number of things that can be said about my mother, Captain Venning, but never let it be said she's light-handed with the plums in cake. Ooh, apples, too. How lovely. No, Russell and I deal with the, ah, diplomatic side of things, between us."

"How's he going on?"

"Who – Hollie?"

"Russell, lad. If 'ee trusts him with a proper job, he must have bucked his ideas up?"

Luce shrugged. "No choice, have I? He's fine, unless he gets bored. Not what you call amiable company, Hollie hates him, or at least he says he does, and you can imagine what a jolly little gathering that makes us at supper. Which is fine, because Russell feels much the same about Hollie, and so the pair of them sit there resolutely abstinent and looking daggers at each other." He raised his eyebrows and looked down the length of his nose. "Though neither of *them* have yet taken to forgery, Captain Venning."

Venning snorted. "Give 'em time, lad, I didn't forge nawthen. Colonel Cromwell reckoned it was the best letter he'd never written." He paused, preened, and waited for the praise he didn't get, before shrugging. "What the hell's Russell got against Rosie, anyway? I'd ha' thought he'd be grateful –"

"Really? Then God willing Russell never owes you a debt of gratitude, Drew, because he hates it. He doesn't like owing anybody anything. It might involve him having to speak to other members of the troop in a civil fashion, rather than brushing us off like so many – ah, never mind. I have never met a more stubborn, awkward, bloody-minded –"

"Not took to Russell at close quarters, then?" Venning was grinning, and Luce shook his head.

"I find it almost impossible to take to Russell, captain, and it is entirely his choice. I intend to keep making the effort, mind, because in spite of the way he persists in behaving in company, it fairly wrings my heart to see him lurking on the edges of any social gathering like a stray dog."

"Speaking of stray dogs –" Venning helped himself to another slice of cake, "mate o' yours asked for a transfer to come down wi' me? One o' Noll Cromwell's boys? Reckon he just couldn't keep up wi' the wild social life, poor lad."

"Of *mine*?"

"Mm. Lil' short lad, quite stocky built, fierce temper on him? Thass why I reckon Old Noll was keen to let 'en go, 'ee never sees that lad without a black eye or a fat lip or similar –"

Luce couldn't put a name to that description. "And he says he's a friend of mine? But I don't – what's his name?"

"Gray. Prob'ly got a proper name, but he only ever gets called Gray. Dunno if thass Gray as is short for Graham and he's a Scot, or if it's for the colour of his hair, would of called it more mouse meself, but you know what soldiers are for stupid nicknames. To be honest with 'ee – Lucey – I been that short, what wi' one thing and another, I don't care if he calls hisself Beelzebub Lord of the Flies, so long as he can fire a pistol. Us lot got ordered south to fall in with William Waller's lads in Hampshire, tag along of William Balfour's horse. Tell 'ee what, you was under Willie Balfour at Edgehill, wasn't 'ee – you know him?"

"We were. Best not mention it to Hollie. He's a bit touchy about Edgehill."

"Got no reason to be, so far as I can tell. Lad did hisself proud – did the lot of 'ee proud, Balfour's still talking about it, your lot charging the Malignant guns – anyway. Hacking his way through Hampshire, is Oor Wullie, seeking for whom he may devour, and he's a fierce owd bugger. I'm all for a bit o' decisive action, but Balfour's a bugger for chucking lead at a problem and the hell with the casualties. Can see why he took to our Rosie, he's another bugger for going at it hammer and tongs, ent he? Tell 'ee what, Luce, 'stead of me sat here cackling, why don't 'ee tell me to put a stopper in it and we'll go find your mate?"

21

MOUSE GRAY

"Not a clue who he is," Luce whispered, looking at the small and very upright figure sitting quite alone amongst the milling troop. "Where did you say you found him?"

"One o' Cromwell's boys, and he did come with a personal recommendation from Old Noll hisself – and no, I didn't write it. Well, he didn't say he was glad to see the back of him, reckon thass the same thing. Gray! Trooper! Over here!"

Small and very particular, as he set his plate straight before standing up and saluting. Almost a head shorter than Luce, who was considered tall, though not unreasonably so, Gray was almost entirely inconspicuous – small and slight and narrow-shouldered, mouse-brown hair worn cropped short, eyes of an indeterminate shade of blue-grey – would have passed entirely unremarked in a crowd, had it not been for the blood all down his collar and his puffy lower lip.

"What was it this time, Gray?" Venning said patiently.

"Parker had a greater ration of bread than I did, sir," Gray said. "I passed remark, sir. Parker asked if I was trying to be funny, sir."

"Which presumably you were, Trooper Gray?"

"No, sir, I was pointing out the inequality. Trooper Parker has got an arse the size of Hampshire already, Captain Venning. He was quick to mention that I am, and I quote, a stunted little shit. Just thought if I'm that stunted might be an idea if Trooper Parker was to share his excessive ration with those with less excess flesh. Sir."

Venning coughed and scowled. "It won't do, trooper. What was it last time – stoppages?"

Gray ducked his head. "Three days' pay, sir."

"A week, Gray. And I'll tell 'ee now, if Rosie – uh, if Colonel Babbitt – cops hold of 'ee brawling in his troop, he'll – what will he do, Luce?"

"Promote you, probably," Luce said ruefully, and the freckled Fenlander gave him a narrow-eyed look. "Don't encourage him, bor. Can never tell wi' Rosie what he'll do. I known him take a man out o' the ranks and have him shot, Gray, just like that, just because he didn't like the way the man's horse was turned out –"

It was Luce's turn to look at Venning sideways. He opened his mouth – Venning still slowly shaking his head. "Don't want to get on the wrong side o' Rosie, lad. You listening to me?"

"Sir."

"Now. Cornet Pettitt. Trooper Gray. You know each other, or what?"

Gray raised those indeterminate blue-grey eyes to Luce's face, and Luce had the oddest impression of having just stepped on a stair in the dark that wasn't there. "I – yes. Yes," he said. "Yes, you were at Winceby. You came after the battle, didn't you? I remember you, now."

22

OUT TOWARDS CREWE

They'd done nothing, a flat nothing for three weeks, apart from hear rumours of distant thunder over the county boundary in Shropshire, where they reckoned Rupert was giving it hell on. To which Fairfax's response was do nothing, and sit tight, because he wasn't sure yet what way the cat was going to jump.

Hollie wasn't much of a man for doing nothing and saying less, but he wrote a hell of a lot of letters home, in those couple of weeks. He still had his more or less perpetual cold, which he personally put down to the fact that they were ill-fed and worse-quartered, in a farmhouse that leaked no matter how much time he spent leaning perilously out of the window poking at the immovable bung of sodden moss under the eaves. – Not that the goodwife was grateful, oh no, no, she'd gone all soft on Drew Venning now, and he got the scrapings off the bottom of the dishes these days, the smug freckled bastard. So far as Hollie could tell, Venning's only claim to the goodwife's affections was that dog of his, who was keeping down the rats in the buttery with an air of busy self-satisfaction that properly set Hollie's teeth on edge.

This particular morning he was huddled in his blankets, hoarse and feverish and teasy as a snake, and even Luce had grown tired of his peevish company and sloped off downstairs to flirt with the dairymaid and hog the kitchen fire. "Could be bloody dead up here for all any of you lot would care," he croaked into the dawn silence. Broken by bloody rooks creaking and unmilked cows yelling their heads off, and there were times Hollie would have given his hope of heaven to live in a civilised city, where there were less beasts complaining and more men. If a man pissed you off as much as those infernal clattering birds did, you could just punch him in the head and be done with it –

And then a clattering of hooves on the cobbles, a skidding clattering of hooves, as if someone had ridden into the barton at speed. A single someone, so he wasn't overly worried about it. Shoving his chilblained feet reluctantly into cold, stiff boots, with the wrist he'd broken at Edgehill aching like fire. His shirt, and the sheets, and the whole rotten chamber, had that faint, musty odour of unaired damp, and there was a patch of powdery grey-blue on the brim of his decent felt hat. It did nothing for his temper, nothing at all. Rifling the chest he'd had from home for a clean handkerchief, and realising he was down to his last one, and he felt so bloody rough and miserable the thought of it made him all wobbly. Thank God Lucey was downstairs batting his eyelashes at the domestics, or he'd have been treated to the unedifying sight of his commanding officer having a most unmanly and snotty weep to himself.

He missed her. He'd not even seen his daughter, yet, and he was sat in the middle of the Cheshire plain doing nothing. Every day he was here was a day he could be at home, with his girl – his girls – he didn't know what a child so young did, even. Would she ever have the chance to know who he was, he thought gloomily, or was he like to remain here, indefinitely, in the guise of an ill-wished guard dog between Prince Rupert and the North Country?

He'd have sat there all morning, with that last link to cleanliness and order and kindness crumpled in his hand, if Luce hadn't come thumping up the stairs. Shouting, "Hollie! Hollie! Hollie!" like a bloody four-year-old released untimely from school, and then skidding to a tousled and bright-eyed halt in the doorway panting and grinning. "You want to go back downstairs and come back in like a proper soldier, brat?"

Luce shaking his head, his hair flopping in his eyes. "Gray says –"

"*Trooper* Gray, you mean?"

"Oh Hollie just stop it!" his young cornet said crossly, and then realised he might have gone a little bit too far as Hollie started to stand up, growling. "Um. I mean. Sir. Uh. Yes. Trooper Gray was – yes – he was – "

"Get *on* with it, brat!"

"Gray's sighted a troop about six miles out, and Lieutenant Russell's taken a patrol out to investigate."

Hollie stopped, hoping he didn't look as stupid as he felt. "On whose authority?"

"Um..... Lieutenant Russell's," Luce muttered. "He didn't ask."

"Captain Venning?"

"Still in."

"Who the hell's he took out with him, then?"

Halfway down the stairs with the brat trailing behind him, wrestling his way into a buffcoat that was stiff with damp, and yelling all over the house. The goodwife in the kitchen with her cap all askew and her face puffy and creased with sleep, wanting to know what was happening, what he thought he was doing, rousing the house at this hour –

"Got a choice of me or Prince Rupert, mistress," Hollie said over his shoulder, happier than he'd been in weeks. "Though I'm told he's considerably better-favoured than I am. Cullis! Cullis, you old bastard, where –"

Cullis slit-eyed and dour, unshaven, with a hell of a bruise high up on his cheek, a new one. "Sergeant, can I ask how come you appear to have had a leathering already, and it not much past daybreak?"

"You know bloody well, you judas-haired whelk, " Cullis growled. "Trying to stop that bloody marred nutjob mate o'yours rousing half the troop. The worse half. And God knows when that bloody web-footed frog-fornicator's going to roll out of bed, though the noise –"

But Venning was awake, all right. Venning was furious. Venning had been locked in the buttery. It would appear that Trooper Gray and a select party of like-minded comrades had taken out a little patrol of their own, last night. Gray, Eliot, Ward –

"Oh God," Hollie said faintly –

One of Venning's lads, a squint-eyed Cambridge lad called Lewis, who was a known gambler. They'd gone rattling off into the dark about midnight, and rolled back in about dawn, in extremely high spirits, without Gray. Seemed that Russell, who never seemed to sleep, had been the only one up and prowling at that hour, and his first thought had been to turn about and go straight back out, armed to the teeth and more than half-drunk. He'd tripped over Cullis's boots in the kitchen and there had been a brief, a very brief, scuffle – in which Cullis, astonishingly, had come off the worst. The sergeant looked uncomfortable about that. "Ah. Well."

Ah, well, it seemed Russell had gone straight in for the kill – or, to be more accurate, for the balls, at which just about every man in the troop winced, and Hollie tactfully suggested that Cullis might not want to be mounting up quite so soon after a smack in the cods with a three-legged stool.

"I'm having that bugger," the sergeant said grimly, settling himself gingerly into the saddle.

Venning had endeavoured to intervene, and been bundled into the buttery by Gray and Ward. "Thass insubordination," he said, narrow-eyed. "Laying violent hands on an officer, thass gross insubordination." And he was not going to be mollified. "I want they lot disciplined, Hol – uh, Colonel Babbitt. They want reining in, all five on 'em."

"Which way d'they go?"

"Out towards Crewe, reckon."

Out towards Crewe. With Rupert's headquarters out at Shrewsbury, and the man himself helping out laying siege to Newark, ninety-odd miles away – talk about between the hammer and the anvil. And bloody Russell, mad bloody Russell, who swung between trying to prove himself redeemed and trying to get himself killed, had just gone thundering off into the sunrise with a handful of the most notorious firebrands and reprobates in the Army, with the avowed intent of stirring himself up a little hornet's nest of bother.

"What d'ee reckon, colonel? Leave 'em to it and pretend we didn't know nawthen?"

Hollie pulled Tyburn's head up, and the big black horse grunted his displeasure, skittering heavily in a half-circle. "Oh aye? What, after bloody Russell fetches his own personal war into Cheshire? I'm thinking not, Drew. Come on. Let's go and haul his arse home."

23

NOBODY DRAWS STEEL ON MY OFFICERS

It was a typical enough skirmish, in the end. Hoofbeats and shouting and the clash of steel and thank Christ, no shots, not yet, they hadn't got so far yet, it was at the chance meeting stage, and there was yet time, so Hollie thumped his heels into his black horse quite without thinking and his perverse black stallion suddenly took off from a sedate trot down the sodden lane to a flat gallop. He knew the rest of the lads weren't expecting quite such a speedy response, because he heard Luce's anguished yelp as he copped a faceful of wet black mud. "Pick it up, brat!" he yelled over his shoulder, and someone in the back threw back his head and bayed like a dog, and all of a sudden there was a troop and a half of horse crashing through the hedge, that lovely, heart-singing moment when the whole boiling lot of them were moving as one, like some great leviathan beast with one mind and one purpose.

– Apart from Tyburn, obviously, three yards in front and fighting the rein, wanting to run for the joy of running, and in a moment of sheer wild madness Hollie gave the stallion his head. And even from three yards in front and gaining, even over the black's drumming feet, over the sound of a hundred mounted men suddenly giving chase, he heard Luce's not-quite-stifled, "Hollie in God's name!" and the red mare's startled grunt as the young cornet urged her to greater speed. She had the edge on Tyburn, she was lighter and faster-bred, but on rough ground and downhill there wasn't a mount to touch Hollie's black bastard in the Army of Parliament, and so the two of them arrived in slithering almost unison, smashing into the back-markers of the fight with Venning's lads strung out behind them like the tail of a comet. The black horse was a weapon in his own right, and Hollie had one of the bastards on the ground and another half out of the saddle without ever having drawn blood, and that was even before the flower of Norfolk came blundering in, and then it was every man for himself, in a great melee of clashing steel and shouting men and snorting, squealing horses –

And bloody Russell, you could see it was Russell by the fall of straight white-blonde hair caught in the plates of his helmet at the back, standing up in his stirrups with his sword in one hand – by, the lad was a bonny brawler, for someone who looked as wispy as a dandelion clock, and it was half in Hollie's mind to hang back and just let the little bugger go at it, Russell laying about him yelling the ninety-first psalm at full belt and Gray right behind him mopping up the scraps. Russell had just belted some poor benighted Malignant in the face with the guard of his sword, and he hadn't picked *that* trick up at officer's school, neither, Hollie thought admiringly – that was street-smart, that was. He found himself urging the bugger on, his own hand tightening on the bridle – push the horse in there, go on, get your elbow up under his guard and –

And the Malignant, his face streaming blood, simply slid out of the saddle, between the churning legs of the horses, under Russell's blade, and for a minute Hollie thought he was down but he wasn't, he was just on his own feet and his scrubby horse was crashing out of the melee in a panic, and all of a sudden Russell was gone off his own horse with a yelp that was audible across three counties.

And Luce was at Hollie's elbow yelling something and it took Hollie a minute to come back into his own body, and stop brawling by proxy, and understand the words. He didn't like them, but he understood them.

"Draw off!" he yelled, and since nobody heard him, drew one of his pistols and fired into the air, which had most of the rooks that hadn't been scared witless by Russell, go clattering into the air. "Fall back, damn it! *They're our lot!*"

"Been trying to tell you that," Luce gasped, "this ten minutes and – Gray *will you draw off!*"

Venning was scarlet in the face and belting his own troopers with the flat of his sword, like whipping off hounds. None of them happy; surly, sweat-streaming faces, sulky and almost mutinous, soured by too many weeks of inaction. All they needed then was Captain bloody Chedglow. He had been a thorn in Hollie's side since Edgehill – no, that wasn't true, he'd been more of a splinter under the thumbnail, a minor irritation who pissed Hollie off every time their paths crossed, a zealous, godly, dislikeable wretch of a man, who liked nothing better than to root out sin and hold it up to the light. Bloody horrible man. He saw it as his duty to drop Hollie in the brown and sticky stuff as often as possible, and he had a turn towards the disciplinarian that bordered on the unnatural.

Hollie stared at him blankly, and Penitence Chedglow stared smugly back at him. "What –" he blinked, in the hope that this most unwelcome of apparitions might be some lingering effect of a low fever – "What in God's name are *you* doing here?"

Chedglow's greasy, bland face oozed resentment. "Reinforcements. Colonel Babbitt. Sir. My lord Fairfax sent word to the Commander-in-Chief that you was made up to a full colonel, and to make you up to full strength. *Ye stiffnecked and uncircumcised in heart and ears, ye do always resist the Holy Ghost: as your fathers did, so do ye*. The Acts of the Apostles, sir." He narrowed his eyes. "Me and another officer, who has been assaulted in the commission of his duties by that whited sepulchre yonder," he glowered, and one of the troopers behind shuffled his horse aside.

Russell on a horse in the commission of his own duties, was a fierce little brawler. Russell on his own two feet, still half-drunk and sick as a dog, was an object of pity and scorn. He appeared to have been face-down in the mud, and was presently held upright by his draggled hair, wet and filthy and furious, by the bloody-faced ruffian with the split mouth. It was hard to tell, what with him being fairly expressionless at best, but the scarred lieutenant looked bloody livid – rolled his eyes sideways at his captor and spat a great mouthful of blood. Possibly one of his back teeth.

"Filthy little scut," the bloody-mouthed ruffian snarled, and backhanded Russell across his marred cheek with his bridle gauntlet. Must have stung like hell, because the plate snapped against flesh like a whiplash.

There was a lot Hollie didn't know about Russell, but the one thing he was sure of was that there was so far you could push him and then he'd snap. And when he snapped all bets were off. Hollie might have predicted that if you belted Russell across the scarred side, showed him up in front of nigh on two hundred men, he'd do exactly what he did do, and break himself free though it left a handful of his hair hanging from his assailant's fingers – break free and go for the man like a thing possessed. He would have killed him, if he could. "Captain Webb!" Chedglow yelped in warning, and the mounted trooper kicked his horse into a half-rear, bowling Russell and the battered Webb into a sprawling tangle. Russell did not swear. Webb, who'd just been stepped on by a horse, assuredly did.

Chedglow rolled his eyes at Hollie. "Will you not impose discipline on this troop, colonel!"

"*Me?* They're your bloody lads!"

"They are – that is – Captain Webb commands his own troop, sir!"

Captain Webb had just copped for a knee in the face and he was about as ungovernable with it as Russell, and about twice as big in the shoulders, and if someone didn't stop this shortly it was going to be a fight to the death. Surging to his knees with a roar and hurling the lieutenant over backwards with a splash, with startled horses scattering to left and right – and then someone was dragging Russell half on his feet with his arm up his back, though he was still fighting like a black devil, and Webb was coming up still snarling, his sword screaming from its scabbard –

Right to the point where Hollie smacked him in the face.

It actually probably hurt Hollie more than it hurt Webb, and he felt the jar of it right the way down his badly-set wrist, but he wasn't going to let his new captain see him flinch. Webb came up short, shaking his head like a fly-bothered horse, and drops of blood from his battered mouth spattered on Hollie's cuff. And it did not stop him, not for one second.

He'd have gone in for another go, had Gray not materialised like smoke from between the horses' legs, and rested the muzzle of his cocked pistol against Webb's jaw.

"Nobody," the little trooper said grimly, "*nobody* draws steel on my officers. Nobody. D'you hear me, captain?"

Webb stopped, blinking. There was a droplet of bright blood hanging from his nose, and in the long silence that followed, it lengthened, drooling onto his top lip. Not a bird sang. Not a horse stirred.

"So," Hollie said, and wished to God he'd stayed on his horse and had the advantage of height. Looked at Chedglow. At Webb. At Russell. At Gray. Did not dare look at Luce, who was currently about all that stood between him and anarchy, and Luce was only keeping their lot under tenuous control by the simple expedient of looking as if this kind of wholesale insubordination was nuts and fruit to Colonel Babbitt. He wasn't going to look round at Venning, neither, because he had a suspicion that a man in full control of a situation does not make a habit of craning his neck to see what his subordinates are doing behind his back. Stare 'em down, like dogs. Keep eye contact, and back, slowly, away...

"Trooper Gray," Venning said, very clearly, and very coldly, "you are on a charge, sir. Drawing a weapon on a superior officer."

"As is Lieutenant Russell," Hollie added, equally coldly. "Captain Webb, likewise."

– And the only reason Chedglow wasn't, was that he could find no legitimate reason to discipline the dour bastard other than for the sheer animal pleasure of it.

Hollie pointed at the puddle in front of him, wordlessly, and Gray came like a prisoner, shoulders back and eyes mutinous. "No, not just you. All three of you. Webb. Russell. Now."

It was starting to rain again. He let them stand there until he could see Gray starting to shiver. Gray he knew, and Russell he didn't know well and God knows probably never would, and Chedglow he knew of old. But this Webb feller. Minded him of Venning in that stolid imperturbability, but without the good humour or the sense.

"Who started it?"

Webb said nothing, and Russell wouldn't even look at him.

"If neither of you will speak, then you can both take an equal share of the punishment."

Russell's head lifted and his swollen mouth twitched, but he still said nothing, though his throat worked as if he was afraid, and that was new. Russell – afraid, and showing it?

Webb set his shoulders and said nothing either. It wasn't a nervous nothing. It was a nothing that was daring Hollie to try it and see where it got him.

Gray looked at Hollie defiantly. "I started it. Sir."

"Have them all flogged," Chedglow suggested, a little too enthusiastically for Hollie's liking. "I'd not have such shameless perjury in any troop under my orders. Bad for discipline."

"Having you shot would be very good for morale, though," Luce murmured, just within earshot. He also remembered Captain Chedglow of old, clearly. Captain Chedglow had been almost solely responsible for the despoilment of the beautiful interior of Worcester cathedral, all those months ago. Luce had been barely breeched, then, by Hollie's recollection, but he'd taken exception to the captain anyway, on principle. Wholly independently, bless the boy.

"You can't flog a fellow officer," Webb sneered. "It's not done."

"Surely," Hollie agreed. "Can break you first, though. It most certainly is done to order a flogging for a common trooper."

It was some satisfaction to see the captain's face turn a greyish pale, like uncooked dough. By the Army's rules, though –

"Webb – fined. Three weeks' pay. And that I can do. Gray – a dozen strokes." He took a deep breath. "Same for you. *Trooper* Russell."

24

A ROUND DOZEN

"Mine is the blame," Gray said, very precisely. "I misled Lieutenant Russell. I was wrong, sir, and I should have made the more certain that the troops I saw were enemy soldiers, and I did not. I am at fault."

Hollie looked at the scrawny little trooper, shivering in the fine rain, his eyes enormous and bruised-looking in his pasty face. He had spots, and his mousy hair was wispy and chewed-looking, a fringe sticking out thinly under his helmet. And he nodded.

They'd always told Hollie that if you apologised, admitted, owned up, the punishment was the less.

In Hollie's experience, that was bollocks. "A dozen lashes," he said icily. Behind him, he heard Luce's sharp intake of breath, and shrugged.

"All right. Make it ten. Cornet Pettitt thinks I might break you. Captain Webb. The hell kind of behaviour d'you call this, for an officer? Brawling? In front of the men?"

"It was –" Gray began again, and Hollie swung on that mouthy little wretch, narrowing his eyes. "Reckon you just made it up to a round dozen again, boy. I didn't ask you for your opinion. Hold your tongue, or I'll have you muzzled."

Webb looked up, glowering. He had odd, reddish-brown eyes, and they seemed to glow with a degree of brute malevolence, like a bulldog chained till it lost its wits and thought of nothing but freedom, and the taste of blood and torn muscle. He was half a head shorter than Hollie, and about twice as wide, and he smelt of stale sweat and stale linen. There was nothing at all unnatural, or awe-inspiring, about him. He was, Hollie suspected, a dirty, cruel, disliked officer who had been sent to bolster Babbitt's ill-assorted company in the hope of having his head shot off and removing an unimportant but antisocial problem from the Earl of Essex's immediate area. "I was speaking to you, Captain Webb," he said. "You're beginning to piss me off."

"He –" Webb turned and hunched his shoulders at Russell – "started it."

"I'm sure he did, captain. He often has been somewhat over-zealous in his duties."

Venning snorted.

"Well, the man's drunk. Stinking of it."

Which was also patently untrue. Had been drunk, some hours previously, and was now sober, sorry, and sick. That bird didn't fly. "We were not discussing Trooper Russell's failings, Captain Webb, we were discussing yours. If you believed an officer to be drunk on duty, would it not be your duty to turn him over to his superiors for correction? Rather than to brawl with him in a public thoroughfare, and then have your own men hold him while you drew steel on him? What did you plan to do, captain? Report a skirmish in which the lieutenant had been somewhat unfortunately killed?"

"It. Wass," Russell gagged a little, spat blood again, tried a second time. "It was me. Started it. You know that. Don't you? I deserve it."

"So Gray rattles in off a patrol, yelling about incoming soldiers. Russell, you take a few lads, and go out to see for yourself. Don't look so hopeful, lad, Sergeant Cullis wants your arse skinning for that stunt with the milking stool. And then what?"

"He loosed a shot at me," Webb said. "He challenged me – bloody rudely, the scar-faced whelp, in front of his betters – refused to state his authority, and then he shot at me."

"Good lord," Hollie said mildly, "imagine how dangerous he'd be, sober. This true, Russell?"

"In most particulars."

"Which was it – marred, prissy, or Puritan?"

He'd called Russell a blemished son of a whore. Russell had not shot at him, at all. That was a lie. Russell had simply kicked that mismatched pied horse of his into a furious charge and sliced Captain Webb across the bridge of his nose with the buckle-end of the reins. It had somewhat gone downhill from there. "Ah, the cavalry, lending distinction to what might otherwise be a vulgar brawl," Luce said unhelpfully, rubbing his nose in what was clearly a desire to camouflage a fit of the giggles. So Webb was a liar, and a man who was touchy on his honour but shy of his punishment. Chedglow was a zealot, and a hot one. Welcome to command, Hollie. He was starting to get a headache. "Twelve lashes each," he said firmly. "Both of you. And you've not started well, Webb."

"I will take Russell's punishment," Gray said, sounding very odd indeed. "As well as my own. I began it. It was my fault."

A rumble of assent from someone.

"You can't," Luce hissed, "you'd kill him, sir, look at him! He's no more than a boy!"

Hollie was sick of the lot of them. "All right then, Lucey, if you would spare Trooper Gray his flogging, you take it for him, you're so keen."

25

A KNIFE IN THE SOUL

It was not a day that Hollie was ever, ever going to be proud of. He thought somewhere along the line he'd cocked it up, and he didn't know how to uncock it, and he kept seeing Luce's white, set, terrified face, even with his eyes shut.

Because no one had ever hurt Lucifer Pettitt, not by choice. No one had ever put stripes on his back, with malice aforethought, the way they had Hollie's, and the worst Luce had ever had was a warm bum. And the idea of a public flogging was scaring him witless, and yet Hollie could not un-say it, because it was a worse punishment for Gray than anything even Venning in his most malevolent moments could conceive. That Luce should take Gray's punishment for him was one of the most bloody stupid, uselessly chivalric, decent things Hollie had ever come across, and he wished to God he could un-say it, un-do it, but he could not.

Luce's bare back was pitifully smooth and pale, the rough pebbles of his spine childishly clear under his skin. Hollie swallowed. Almost handed the whip to Cullis, and then – no. If Luce could do this, he could do this. "You can –" he thought he might be sick, actually. Set his jaw. "You can keep your shirt on, brat."

"Would you have let Gray keep his shirt on, sir?" Sounding quite calm about it, damn him.

"I would not."

"Then I shall not, either. I'll not have anyone say he escaped his punishment."

They were looking at each other. That was all Luce was looking at – his eyes fixed on that scrawny little reprobate, unblinking, as he folded his hands on the hitching-post in the yard of their quarters, and an awkward hush fell over the troop. And it was just Hollie's own company. There wasn't anybody else had earned a right to be here, this morning. Not even Venning. Russell was here, upright and shaky and stone-cold sober, looking scared and heartbreakingly young, and even Russell seemed to mark this as an occasion of moment because he was turned out like he was attending a wedding –

Or a funeral. Don't be so bloody witless, Holofernes, the boy's not made of glass.

"Lay on, sir. Or I may lose my nerve and run away."

And he was only half-joking, and that was what broke Gray, and the two of them stood twenty yards apart with the tears and the snot running silently and unchecked down the little trooper's unremarkable face. Not a pretty sight. But somehow the boy's silent, ugly misery wrenched at your heart, more than if he'd cried like a pretty girl, to get a thing he wanted. Sickened and sorry, Holly brought the lash down on his friend's back, harder than he had intended, and Luce's body convulsed, just the once.

He wanted to say he was sorry. He knew that sound – ah, Christ, he knew the sound of leather bruising your back, the criss-cross of fire across the tender parts where the bone lay close to the skin, and how you thought for a second you'd never breathe again, and then you thought it was none so bad, and then you'd move and it was as if someone had poured boiling water over your flesh, burning and tingling so that you could find no rest –

"One," Hollie said, in a voice he didn't recognise as his own. And Luce looked up from where he'd put his head on his folded arms, and he'd bit clean through his lip in his pain, and blood was running down his chin, soaking into his shirt.

"Can we dispense with the conversational accompaniment…sir?"

By twelve the fair skin showing beneath the sheet of blood trickling down the lad's back was mottled purple, despite all Hollie could do to pull the blows, and he threw the whip down and he would have walked away, had Russell not blocked his path.

"You have another. To. Discipline."

He wasn't drunk, though he sounded it, his voice oddly slurred, and then Hollie realised that the lad's teeth were chattering. He was mortal afraid, and yet he was quietly shrugging off his own shirt and folding it, tidily.

Russell straightened his back, and did not touch the post, though he set his good shirt on its top. Luce staggered a little when he let go, and there was only the barest brush of his fingers against the scarred lad's, but it was enough to bring a flush to Russell's face, and a shaky smile to Luce's.

And then Luce went to stand beside Gray, and that was almost enough to break Hollie's heart, the fear that what he had done in the name of duty and discipline might have snapped that cord of liking between them. Gray was looking at him with loathing and that was unimportant. Gray was overdue a flogging of his own. Luce would not always be around to save the stunted little bastard. But not Luce – ah, Christ, that he might have hurt Luce, who was as close as his own conscience – that felt like a knife in the soul.

Bruises and weals would smart, but they'd heal, and the brat be none the worse for it. The bruises on his spirit might be forever, and that Hollie could not bear.

26

NOT A MAN, BUT A BEAST

He thought he should probably pray for his safe deliverance, but somehow the words wouldn't come. He had much to be – ha! – thankful for. He had not pissed himself, though he had thought he might. He had not fainted, nor cried, nor pleaded for clemency, which was more due to the fact that after the first three lashes his cheek had locked rigid and he couldn't have cried for mercy had he wanted to. Could choke a little, and mew, but though it was so silent, in the courtyard, none could hear it. Had not heard it himself, over the sound of the blood thumping in his head and the sound of knotted leather against his bare back.

He'd lost count, in the end. Hadn't bitten through his lip, the way Pettitt had, but that was only because he couldn't bite down on anything, at the present, or he should have possibly bitten through the hitching-post, splinters and all. It was a point of pride that he had not bowed his head to that judas-haired bastard, nor had he asked quarter. He had tried very hard to remember who he was, and what he was, and to hold to that fierce little flame of self, but he hadn't. Had only, at the last, thought of the pain. It might have been a minute, or it might have been a hundred years, before he felt a touch on his folded arms, almost a breath, and raised his head to find that judas-haired bastard eyeing him.

"I'm done," Babbitt said, and dropped his eyes, as if he could not even bear the sight of Russell.

So am I, he thought, and did not say. He did not know how he might stand up straight, but he would, though it finish him. He kept his eyes closed till the world stopped spinning, red and black flashes behind his eyelids, and then he straightened his shoulders. His throat burned with the remains of last night's brandy, but he did not shame himself. Babbitt – the vengeful swine – held his shirt out, indicating that he might dress again, and he did, though raising his arms above his head nearly killed him, and the brush of even that worn linen on his ragged skin was an agony.

Our Lord Jesus Christ put up with worse, Russell, brace up and stop squalling.

He looked neither to left nor right. Why should he? He had no one to look at, and as he passed the troop drew back from him as though he were the worst of abominations. That, possibly, hurt worse than the whipping. No one spoke to him. No one looked at him.

He would have crawled on coals of fire for a drink. He would have given his hope of heaven for a kind word, or a shoulder to hold on to.

He was still upright, though sweat was stinging on his raw back, when he reached the anonymity of the stables. Cold, shivering-cold, but he doubted if he could have got so far as his own bed to lie on.

He had not broken. They had not broken him. Yet. He stumbled, in the warm, breathing darkness, and fell to his hands and knees, and the thump of it left him whimpering and retching, holding onto the wisps of clean straw with both hands as if it might save him from falling. And eventually his back eased enough that he could uncurl, and lie shivering against the cold floor.

In his head, he was at Edgehill again, and the fat widow who'd nursed him through those first bitter weeks was with him, and her square, workworn hand was gentle on his hair. He didn't know what she might say to him. He could not imagine so far as kindness. He smelt bile and blood on himself but she didn't mind. It was more grace than he deserved that she should have come to him. He dragged himself a little to the side and laid his head in her lap. (It felt like piled straw, against his skin, but it wasn't. It was the fat widow's lap. Of course it was. And the softness grazing his shoulder, touching his hair, was her hand, and not the mismatched horse's questing muzzle.)

"Oh, Thankful," she said, in his head, at last, because more than anything else he wanted to hear someone call him by his name again.

To not be Russell, or the lieutenant – some hope of that, he thought bitterly, now – but his own self, such as it was: someone who was of worth, and precious, and not a useless thing of pity and contempt. "Poor lambkin." And stroked his hair again, over and over, until his shivering eased and the pain in his head died and if he kept still, the pain in his back was bearable.

"Poor lambkin," he said aloud, muzzily, and nestled his head into her lap more comfortably, not minding the spiky ends of straw against his aching cheek. It was only the roughness of her skirts, that was all.

He had the oddest dream, when he slept, eventually. He heard Captain Venning say, clear as day, "I declare, Rosie, I do believe you got a soft spot for that lad."

He sounded quite affronted by it, too.

And a laugh from Babbitt, a short bark of not being very amused. "Stubborn little bugger, aye. He'll come about, Drew, give him time, and a bit o' patience. Remember I've got a horse they reckoned couldn't be broke to bridle. I'm used to gentling stubborn buggers."

He wanted to be offended by that, he wanted to sit up and say that he wasn't a beast. No matter what they had said – what his sister had always called him, vicious animal, little cur, vile brute – he was a thinking, reasoning man, and would the colonel kindly speak of him as such. But it was a dream, and one of those dreams where his limbs wouldn't obey him, and he could only think it.

"He's going to be stiff as a board, come the morning," the dream-Venning said. "You like him, but you took his commission? God grant you don't conceive any great fondness for me, bor!"

"I like Lucey, and I still whipped him. And if you reckon being broke back to a plain trooper will keep that lad down, you're far off and away, mate. If I know that 'un, he'll make commander of the Army yet. Or dead, one or t'other. You see him up before I do, captain, tell him he's bloody stood down this night, and will remain on the sick and hurt list till he can walk ten yards without keeling over." Babbitt gave another humourless laugh. "And if he asks, I left my coat in here and he must have picked it up."

Which made no sense, until he felt something warm settle over him, something warm and redolent of wet wool and black powder and metal.

"Catch his bloody death, the silly young bugger," Hollie grumbled, startlingly close, and had his eyelids not been weighted with lead Russell might have started awake.

But he did not, and they said no more, and he slid back into sleep, with his head nestled in a mound of ragged straw, and a soldier's coat thrown over his shoulders, and a nervous, wall-eyed horse for company.

27

NO COMPROMISE

Made no difference at all, of course, and for the next few days the only real change was that Luce was the only person Gray didn't try and pick a fight with, Russell kept forgetting he wasn't an officer any more, and the new man took delight in baiting as many of Hollie's company as he could set hands to, and then complaining about when they bit.

(Literally, in Gray's case. Another day's stoppages.)

"It's not important," Luce said.

It sounded important. He sounded stiff and hurt – well, aye, he would be stiff, and hurt, for all Hollie had done to pull his blows – but also, like he wasn't going to talk about it.

"I'm sorry," Hollie said, for about the fiftieth time. "But Luce. Don't do that to me, brat. Don't put me in a corner."

"No," the brat said. He sat down, very gingerly, and still without looking at Hollie. It wasn't an ostentatious not looking, not like Russell, who'd jerk his head aside if he thought Hollie might catch his eye by accident. It was more a sort of withdrawing, like a lady pulling her skirt aside from something noxious in the gutter. Then he looked up. "No, colonel, I shouldn't. Because a cornered rat is the most vicious, no?"

"Aye. It is. And Luce, you were asking me to compromise –"

"Which you don't do. I am aware of that."

"Lucey!"

"Colonel?"

"It's not about you, Luce. It's about –"

"You, sir. As usual. That you can not, and will not, bend. I am well aware of that, colonel."

He wanted to get hold of his friend and give him a good shaking, because there were times when he wished to God the whimsical little bugger would stop thinking like a civilian, for once. And there were times when he wished he could think like a civilian himself, and not like a man who'd been a soldier for longer than Luce Pettitt had been drawing breath in this world. And oh yes, you did not do your friends any favours, when you were a soldier. Because today, they were your friends. Tomorrow, they might be your enemies, in a war like this one. When you took your commission, you lost the privilege of friendship. You couldn't expect to impose discipline on your men, if they didn't think you were fair about it. You couldn't play favourites. Couldn't *afford* to play favourites.

It didn't mean he didn't bloody want to, though.

"How is Gray?" he said, after a long pause. "He all right?"

"Yes, thank you."

"And, um, Russell?" Who scared him witless and worried him sick by turns, actually.

"Is fine. Thank you."

"Luce, I didn't want to –"

"But you had to. Yes. I understand, Can we not continue to discuss it, please, sir? I find my back is painful enough without I must sit and listen to your –" he paused. Said nothing. His eyes were very cool and very level. "Explanations," he finished, without actually using the word bullshit.

"You and Gray seem to be," what could he say? "Be careful, Luce," he finished, feebly. "It will help neither your position nor Gray's, if the men think you are. You know."

And a spark, a very small spark, of humour, lit the brat's eyes, an unwilling spark, as if he was laughing at some private joke that wasn't all that funny. "You have my word of honour. My tastes do not incline towards boys."

"You've been hell of a quiet, brat. Of late."

Wordlessly, Luce forgot himself sufficiently to push over his present epic. "Bloody hell, Luce," Hollie said, after a few minutes of quiet reflection. "That's just – bloody hell. With a bird? What, was she a bit – I mean, I've gone short myself, betimes, but – a *swan*?"

"It's metaphorical," Luce said.

"It's not physically possible, brat. That's just bloody perverse!
His feather'd pinions soft caress
Her shoulders, thighs, her snowy breast –
Lucey, I could just about bear you eyeing up boys, but not bloody ducks!"

And that, of course, was Lucey done for, because when all was said and done he was not so far out of the schoolroom, and he started giggling helplessly. "Stop it," he whimpered, "that hurts!"

"It's not *me* writing mucky poetry about women wi' no clothes on, going to bed wi' ducks!"

"Swans!" He pressed a hand to his bruised back, panting, flushed, but grinning like Venning's dog. "Oh, you are a bloody Philistine, Hollie. I swear. You are beyond redemption!"

"Dirty poems wi' water-fowl perpetrating acts of personal intrusion on lasses? And *I'm* beyond redemption? By God, brat, if I told Captain Chedglow you was writing lewd verse about some wench running round in nowt but her skin, he'd be praying for your salvation from here till forever!"

"Better than than imagining I'm after Gray's – bum," the brat said tartly. (He still couldn't swear. Two years with Hollie, who had a gob on him like a latrine floor when he put his mind to it, and Luce Pettitt still couldn't say arse.) "I take it I'll be leaving it with you, so you can read the rest of it?"

"Hoi! Cheeky bugger!" And grinning back at him, with a growing feeling of rightness, and things might not be as they were, but they were mending.

Luce was shaking his head, looking more indulgent than a junior officer ought to look. "Will you be joining the men for supper tonight, then? They would be pleased – you know –" he smiled, a little awkwardly. "There was some talk of music, tonight. Perhaps, you know, um, – companionship."

"Out of the baggage train? Lucey, if you come home with a dose, your mother will *kill* you."

"Oh, very funny!" And very embarrassing, so the possibility of a quick kiss and a cuddle round the back of the horse lines had evidently crossed the lad's mind, because he was scarlet to the ears. "It is intended as a very informal supper, with musical entertainment —"

"What, wi' that troop? Bloody Venning on the spoons, and you stood on the table talking about duck-fucking? What d'you do for an encore, Luce, recreate the siege at Newark, wi' cannons?"

"I *might* recite," the brat said stiffly, and then realised he was being teased, and his face relaxed a little. "Honestly, Hollie. They – we – I'd like it, if you could. I don't know, you've just been a bit – different, I suppose, a bit more formal, since you were made up." He shrugged. "Probably just me, being silly. I just thought. You know. Forgive and forget."

He wanted to. More than anything in the world, he wanted to. But he couldn't, because Russell's dereliction of duty had left him with a mounting stack of requisitions and warning orders and muster rolls, and so far as he could tell most of the allotted task of a colonel of horse was signing off bloody paperwork till his wrist ached. He looked up at Luce, with the brat blinking at him shyly, willing him to say yes. Ah, Christ, but he fancied it, though. (Even with the promise of company from the baggage train, God help us all, and the prospect of teasing Luce rotten in the morning about his sloping off with some rosy-cheeked laundress till all hours of the night.) Propping himself up against the wall in some noisy tavern where you had to shout at battle-order volume to make yourself heard, and you had to drink with your elbows tucked against your flank to avoid jogging your neighbour, packed like herrings in a barrel. Talking bollocks about horses, and wonders you'd seen in your travels, and – aye, well, talking of Het, and that eased his heart, just to talk of her, to say, casually, that he was a married man himself. Children. To laugh, and pass it off like the rest of them did, as if it were a thing of no account to have a daughter, but to talk of her at every turn anyway, because he liked the way the words felt, in his head. *My wife. My daughter.*

And then he shook his head, because he was expected, instead, at a more formal, more sober gathering, with Fairfax and the other senior officers. It would be quiet, and blameless, and respectable, and he would do nothing that he could not write and tell Het of, and doubtless she would be proud and happy that he was keeping such decent company. In bed before ten, doubtless, with the brat waking him up at gone midnight, giggling and reeking of the company of ladies of negotiable affection, equally doubtless. He wasn't going to spoil it for Luce. He looked at the papers on his desk, and moved them a little, tightening his lips.

"Not got time for that, Luce," he said briskly. "Dining with Fairfax this evening."

Not looking up, because he knew his friend would be a little hurt, but they didn't want a bloody officer stood there, blighting the proceedings. Venning, he'd get away with it. Luce had probably arranged it. They didn't want a *colonel* there, making it all stiff and formal and military.

He didn't look up until he heard the door close behind Luce, heard his boots thumping down the stairs.

Then Hollie sighed, and pulled the muster roll towards him, to note down who had fallen out sick that day.

Three lines in, he stopped, and sighed again.

"Bollocks to this," he said aloud. Took his pen again.

To my right well beloved girls

It has rained much this week, and I have been most grateful for the stout stockings you did send by the hand of Cpt. Venning who sends his regards as does Luce.

28

AN ACT OF MUTINY

Luce had not expected Gray's gratitude. Hadn't, actually, known why he'd done it, except that – well, it was how he'd been brought up, was all. He did not expect Gray to be grateful, or to understand, or to even talk of it.

He didn't *like* the little trooper. He admired anyone who was that indestructible – the only other person he knew who was that stiff-necked and sheer downright relentlessly pig-headed was Thankful Russell, and look where it had got him – but you couldn't like Gray. You could pity him, at the same time as knowing he brought it on himself, watching him sit mutinously at the table with a plate in front of him that Ward had just spat in. Wondering what stupid piece of ill-conceived vengeance he might come up with, and then wondering if you ought to turn a blind eye as he suddenly knocked the table with his elbow so that Ward's ale spilled into his lap, drenching his only pair of whole breeches.

"Break it up, gentlemen," Russell said, without looking up, and Trooper Wilding, fancying himself a wit, snorted contemptuously, grinning around him at his mates. "Can't tell us what to do, my buck. You ain't got an officer's sash no more, I think you'll find."

"In my head, I do," he said, still looking at his hands on the table. And then apparently without a pause for breath he was half across the table and Wilding was squealing like a stuck pig with Thankful Russell's eating-knife stuck through the web of his thumb, skewering his hand to the scarred wood.

Wilding wanted the former lieutenant disciplined, when he'd stopped squalling. He also wanted Luce to stitch the hole in his hand, rather than the usual suspect, fat Witless; claiming that Witless was not gentle and that Luce was tidier. Witless – who had been apprenticed to a barber-surgeon before the war and who was passing on what he knew to Luce, on grounds that many hands made light work – had told him, with some asperity, that he'd had worse paring his nails. Luce was getting used to that particular demand, and Cullis was getting used to not doing it, because Russell had been a plain trooper for something under a week and he was hating it, and the rest of the lads were hating him. They didn't mind a poacher turned gamekeeper, but a gamekeeper turned poacher they neither understood nor wanted. Well, all right, knifing one of your comrades went above and beyond Russell's normal sins of arrogance and insolence. "Report to Colonel Babbitt," Luce said, and he was getting used to giving that particular instruction, too, to one or other of them. The scarred young man gave him a look of utter loathing and slithered back into his place on the bench, the mobile side of his mouth set in a sullen droop. "No, Russell, now, not tomorrow, not when you've finished your supper – *now!*"

He did not know how Hollie did it. Had thought, actually, that he wouldn't be quite so casual, or scatological, or personally intimidating as his friend, were he left in command. As it happened, Luce was not the strictest disciplinarian at best, and it was as well that his remit was no further than maintaining order at mealtimes, presently. He found himself hoarse and flustered after any more than an hour in charge – making sure that no one spat in Gray's food, or that Russell didn't start a fight he couldn't handle, or that Eliot did not take more than his share and leave someone else with scant rations. All of which had happened in the last half hour. Calthorpe was still doggedly ploughing on with saying his interminable grace, and Moggy Davies, who'd been left with the dry heel of the bread, was protesting loud and long and unstoppably about it. Luce, in point of fact, had a headache.

"Shut up the bloody lot of you!"

And before God, they did. He suddenly had a room full of eighty very startled troopers all staring at him with eyes as round as cartwheels. Calthorpe had even stopped praying. Just about the only sound in the room was the noise of one of the troopers very carefully laying down his spoon, and even that was a sound that attracted the glowering censure of his immediate comrades.

"I will have order," Luce said, and he bloody well meant it, too. He had had enough. Quite enough. He was hungry, his head ached, and the healing scabs on his back itched like merry hell. "Trooper Russell, I gave you an order, now get your scabrous backside moving. Now. Trooper Gray, you are starting to get on my –" he couldn't say it –" nerves. Sit down and eat your meat."

"But he –" Gray began furiously, and Luce leaned on the board in front of the little trooper.

"And some have meat, and cannot eat. And may the Lord be thanked."

"God-damned bloody Covenanters," someone said, not quite quietly enough.

"Who. Said. That." – through gritted teeth.

Russell, not quite out of the door at a lope that bordered on the insubordinate, turned smartly on his heel. "Gentlemen," he said loudly, "you will form up on me, if you please."

And he sounded so much like his old, stiff self again, and not like a forlorn ghost, that a good dozen of the lads forgot it wasn't a formal command, and joined him in the passage. And there being a good quarter of the troop there, a few more of the undecided ones thought they'd better join in, and then as chairs started to scrape back, and the ones who wouldn't have took any notice of the former Lieutenant Russell thought that bucking Cornet Pettitt might be good for a giggle, filed past.

Leaving Luce, and Calthorpe, and fat Witless, blinking like a mole while he decided where he might be safer from the bullies, and Mattie Percey with his fists clenched because anyone who disobeyed Luce was disobeying Mattie's beloved Hollie, and Cullis, and the Weston brothers.

And Gray.

Gray took a step up to Luce's back, his head up, his hand on the hilt of his sword, battle-colours flying in his cheeks. "Where the fuck d'you think you're going, you scar-faced whelp?"

"Thank you, Gray," Luce said, very mildly. "Trooper Russell, you are aware, I trust, that this is an action of mutiny?"

Russell inclined his head. His eyes were very bright, and so far as anyone could tell, he was grinning. "I am saving you the trouble of disciplining us individually, sir. I thought perhaps the colonel could deal with us as a unit, rather than one at a time, given that we appear to be causing you some... unrest. I imagine the paperwork might be – onerous."

"Did you," Luce said, and it wasn't a question. "Fair enough. Order your ranks, then, gentlemen."

The only one who wasn't surprised was Russell. He had meant it, then. He really would have led the lot of them to discipline. And they'd have gone, too.

Gray slid into his customary place in the line, back marker, a head shorter than everyone else. Like a little sheepdog, Luce thought, and had to stifle a grin. He seemed to have acquired himself a sheepdog. To direct a pack of wolves.

Russell cocked an eyebrow. He was still grinning. Sideways, with all his teeth showing on one side and not the other, like a dog chasing a flea. "Shall I, then.... sir?"

"Lead off... *Trooper* Russell." The emphasis was intentional. A little reminder, though he wasn't sure whether it was a reminder to Russell to mind his place, or to himself not to underestimate that grim young man's ambition.

29

AN INCIDENT AT SUPPER

"You're keen," Hollie said, looking up as Luce opened the door. "I only just got the warning orders." And then, "Bloody hell, brat, we're not moving out quite yet, what d'you bring that lot for?"

He could, of course, lie. He could say that he had scented the thunder afar off, and was hot to engage the enemy. He wasn't sure which part of the enemy it might be, but if you guessed it was Prince Rupert, a man Hollie cordially despised, you couldn't go that far wrong. If Rupert hadn't actually done anything Hollie would still be keen to think the worst of him. "Ah," he said, trying to look stern and military. "When are we moving out, then, sir?"

"Um... day or so? Tomorrow, I reckon, provided them lazy arses in the foot can get mobilised?"

"Ah." Feeling a little as if the ground had opened underneath him again because every time Hollie had dispatches Luce had the forlorn hope that it might be word that it was all over, that they had come to some terms with the King. Preferably that they wouldn't all be hanged as rebels. That day was clearly not this one. "I – where?"

Hollie surreptitiously moved the very creased paper that was evidently not official correspondence, under the pile of much more formal and much less handled work. "Er, Lucey, lad, if you're not stood here all formed up and official because you're mad-keen to get up to Yorkshire and apply a little toe to Malignant arse…what are you stood there for? She's not sent me cake in the better part of a month." He grinned fondly. "Reckon the lass has been busy. With *my daughter*."

"No doubt. Sir. Um." If it were done when it were done... "There was an incident. Sir. At supper."

Hollie raised his eyes and sighed. "A Gray, sort of incident?"

"Little bit."

"Me and you are going to have a little chat about the matter of Gray, brat. There is talk. People putting two and two together – favourites, like." He wasn't at all comfortable with this conversation. You could tell, by the way he was shifting paper about. "He – er. I wouldn't mind if you –. Well. You know. I might. A bit. I mean, as long as you didn't –. Ah, Luce, you're not, are you? You're sure you're not inclining, um, you know? Grecian tastes?"

To which Luce could, perfectly honestly, say that he did not fancy the boy Gray. Not in the least, hand on heart, swearing on his mother's life, sure and certain. "No. And it wasn't, really, his fault."

"That's a first."

"Ward spat in Gray's supper. Eliot and Ward have been teasing him terribly since – well, since the morning Chedglow came. It's almost as if they're *trying* to get him into trouble."

Hollie looked up from his paper-pushing and his eyes were very gold in the candlelight, and his gaze was very level. "Brat, if you think you're helping him by making him your particular friend, you're not. Gray needs to stop pissing people off and stand on his own two feet, and if the lads think he's hiding behind your coats it will go the worse for him. Look at Russell. He's not an officer, and he's not a plain trooper – the lad's neither Arthur nor Martha at the minute, and nobody likes him for it."

"Well, it's funny you should say that, sir. You see, this incident. Things were getting a little out of hand at supper. What with Ward spitting, and Gray tipped his ale into his lap, and then Wilding cheeked Russell and Russell pinked him with his eating-knife, and it was all –"

"A bit much for you." Hollie sounded sad.

"A bit much," he agreed, because it was, and he was honest, if nothing else. Luce was not by nature a leader of men. "Russell, um, formed up the men to be disciplined."

"He did *what*?"

"He suggested it might save some time and administration were you to do the job, um, en masse. And to his credit, he was perfectly serious."

Hollie looked at the desk again, and his lips twitched. "Here – d'you think he's got the taste for being whipped, or summat? Because I can really do without having to paddle Russell's arse every time I want summat done."

"That is a frightening image, sir."

"I know. And it's not even you at the operational end. Next time, Cullis does it, I'm telling you that for nowt. I only done it myself last time to save your back."

There was a question Hollie was avoiding asking, and Luce knew it, but there was no answer that he was willing to give. Not until he knew himself. Because what could he say? It was something about Gray's eyes, and the set of his shoulders, and the way he bit his nails bloody. The way he'd take offence at anyone who got too close to him, picking fights with anyone who paid him attention, or showed him kindness. The loneliness of him, sitting apart, sleeping apart. Always alone. Not shy, but defiant, and wary.

No, Hollie wouldn't understand. Luce wasn't sure he did, until he'd seen Gray at supper that night, small and fragile and the loneliest figure in the world, in a room full of people.

Hollie would think Gray was miserably lonely. Hollie had been lonely, once, and it would tear at his heart to think of another living soul suffering so. He liked to pretend to be an unfeeling ruffian but under that spiky outer he was as soft as the kernel of a chestnut. He would think Gray was lonely, and unhappy, and because he was who he was, Hollie would want to make things all right for Gray.

And Gray was not lonely. Gray wanted, very much, to be left alone, unnoticed. Luce was increasingly sure of that. Had wondered, since he had first set eyes on the trooper, after the battle at Winceby, just what it was that was odd about a fat, spotty, plain boy. A fat boy with fragile wrists and ankles and a delicately-bony face, who ate alone and slept alone and wanted to be left alone. And now he was almost sure, but only almost, and so he would say nothing.

Hollie took a deep breath. "Right. Well. I suppose I'd better go and give that bloody lot their bollocking."

30

NOBODY IN THEIR RIGHT MINDS

It was short, sweet and to the point. A sufficient punishment that they were moving out in the morning, back to Yorkshire, and that a number of them weren't going to be coming back. He didn't say that last, but they knew.

"Rupert?" someone guessed, knowing Hollie's feelings on that head, and he said nothing again, but he thought his grin widened. Oh aye, Rupert. Rupert on the back foot, running from pillar to post because Fairfax had stolen a march on him.

Rupert with Hollie Babbitt and four troop of horse up his well-bred backside, harrying the ostentatious little bastard till he dropped. Didn't have brakes, they said about Rupert, and of all things, it was the one thing Hollie could do, stop that rabble of his. On a sixpence, if need be.

Hollie stood grinning, and oddly, it was Russell who grinned back, suddenly like a man with a purpose again.

"You want it back," he said, wonderingly. Because nobody in their right mind wanted to be an officer, with all the flannel and paperwork and protocol it involved. A *field* command, now, that was worth the having. Please your bloody self with a field command, and not have to keep people sweet and not swear in polite company, remembering who was in bed with whom and whether it was literally or not. "You want your sash back, don't you, Russell?"

The scarred young man looked as austere and impassive as ever. He was good at it. The marred side of his face didn't move easily, and he'd schooled the other half to give nothing away either. But he dropped his eyes, and the sudden flare of those fierce hawk-dark eyes gave it away, every time. He wanted it, all right. He wanted his command back. Well, well. There was blood in the boy yet. If he wanted his command more than he wanted drink or destruction, remained to be seen.

Hollie nodded. "Then you can fucking work for it, Russell. Show me you're worth it, and when I bring Rupert to bay – and I will, gentlemen, we've sat on our arses long enough this spring – you can have your commission back. But you will sweat for it, sir. You'll bloody earn it before I trust you again." And then he grinned back, because he couldn't help it. This time last year, this mutinous young rebel had had a hand in Hollie's courtship, and without him there would yet be no Mistress Babbitt. He might be as cracked as a pothouse jug but somewhere in there, was a decent lad. Somewhat plagued by misfortune, not all of which he brought on himself. "Won't you, Hapless?" he said.

31

A STILL SMALL VOICE OF CALM

It could not be said that Hollie ran away, exactly, but there was only so long he could bear in Russell's intense company before he started to feel somewhat uneasy. And besides, he had a letter to finish.

And he needed a drink, badly. It was bloody difficult stalking about on your dignity all day when what you really wanted to do was drag up a stool in the kitchen with a bridle in your hand, kick your boots off, and exchange idle pleasantry with the lads while you got on with mending a bit of harness. This damp played merry hell with the stitching on Tyburn's tack.

"Luce," he said, trying to sound casual, "fancy a bite of summat? I think I got a bit of that cheese left."

And Luce, who had known Hollie for the better part of two years now and was not in the least fooled, smiled with a degree of fond indulgence that gave him an uncanny resemblance to his Auntie Het, and shrugged. "I was going to have something to eat later. I've not much of an appetite, these days. But yes. Of course."

He hadn't, had he? He looked like a man, now, and not a boy, the bones of his face stark against his skin. Still a little bit tanned from last summer's campaigning, with a handful of freckles on his nose, and Hollie wondered, idly, if his own daughter might be slight and fair, after the Pettitt side of the family. (Het Pettitt. No wonder she'd married young, the darling girl. First Sutcliffe, and now Babbitt. He thought Henrietta Babbitt had a nice ring to it, mind.) The ends of the brat's hair were still sun-bleached, too. The lad hadn't trimmed his hair in over six months. Hollie touched his own thick russet ponytail. He was starting a fashion, God help us all, what with Luce and Russell both as long-haired as wenches. It was the slightness of him, though, that worried Hollie. He'd always been lean and elegant, but he was not yet twenty and he could have eaten a scabby horse without it touching the sides. Soldiering was not agreeing with Hollie's brat, for sure and certain.

"You all right, Luce?" he said, not at ease with gentleness, but unable to not ask. And Lucifer scratched his eyebrow and gave that somewhat wry, sweet smile. "Up to the elbows in paperwork, sir, and run ragged, but other than that – fine."

"If you've got owt to tell me, you know… "

And the brat's mist-grey eyes slid sideways, just the once, and they had never done that before, not to Hollie. And then he looked up, smiling again. "Oh, you know. Things. Nothing important. Shall I pour us a glass? I imagine it's the last time we'll see anything like civilisation for some months, if last summer was anything to go by."

He toyed with his glass, absently pushing it this way and that, making wet circles on the table. (On one of Fairfax's warning orders but that was all right, Hollie had that ingrained into his memory.) Saying little, smiling when he was spoken to, sitting looking at not a lot with that little crease between his eyebrows that made Hollie's brat look old before his years. "Well. Early night, I reckon. We'll be setting off about dawn –"

And there was a quick tap on the closed door.

"Who is it?" Hollie called.

"Gray. Sir. It's, um, Gray. Trooper Gray. I – "

"Oh Christ what's he done now?" Hollie muttered, extracting himself from behind the desk. "You'd better come in, then."

"Haven't done anything. Sir. This time." Gray's fierce eyes were uncomfortably downcast, and he was shifting from foot to foot. "Um. Sir. May I, uh, may I speak with you, um, with Cornet Pettitt, er, privately?"

"I don't believe we need to be any more private than this, trooper," Luce said stiffly.

"Oh, I don't mind," Hollie said, equally stiffly. "Little bastard probably wants to talk to you about summat personal, whelp. What with you being his most particular friend – and God knows he's not got many."

Gray's thin cheeks flushed, but he said nothing. Hollie stood up and brushed past the little trooper, whose head barely came to his shoulder, but who lifted his chin and glowered in what appeared to be quite involuntary dumb insolence. "I've an eye to you, Trooper Gray-with-no-other-name," he said over his shoulder. "Any silly business and I will snap you like a twig, do you understand me, boy? If you want me, brat, I'm in with Venning."

And to Luce's astonishment, Gray said nothing. Did not argue, did not glare, did not tense to spring, but merely drooped a little in the shoulders, like a wilting flower. Hollie nodded in satisfaction and slammed the door shut behind himself with a vengeful thump that rattled the plaster.

Luce, mind, did not like being alone with Trooper Gray. Not because he was afraid of the trooper, but because he was afraid of himself.

He swallowed hard. It gave him a very odd feeling somewhere under his ribs to see the lad so forlorn and wretched, so out of character. "Now," he said, trying to sound bracing. "What's amiss?"

Gray raised his eyes. They were wet and red. "Sit down," Luce said automatically. "I've some – no, that's not true, *the colonel* has left some wine concealed about the place. Captain Venning brought it, you see." He smiled, hoping to be reassuring. "Under his cloak, I understand, after dining with my lord Fairfax. He said it seemed to be surplus to requirement, and he, um, liberated it to be put to better use."

It was meant to amuse. It did not. "Gray – have you had bad news, trooper? Do you need leave of absence? I'm sure Hollie – I'm sure the colonel – I could speak to him, he'd not refuse you if I spoke to him on your behalf –"

"He will," Gray said dully, and Luce had not realised before what childish hands the little trooper had, clasped in front of him like a nervous schoolboy reciting a badly-learned lesson. "He would give me nothing, sir, and I would ask nothing from him. I – no – I have made a mistake in attending you, sir. I have wasted your time. I – may I have leave to go, sir?"

"Of course. Yes, of course. But –"

Gray turned to leave, but not before Luce had caught a glimpse of one single, solitary, precious tear that trembled on his lashes. Later, he would be astonished at his own daring. Then, he put his hand out without thinking and caught the lad's shoulder, spun him around. "Trooper Gray," he said sternly, and looked down into Gray's thin, tearstained, pointed little face, and something gave way inside him and he caught the lad in a fierce hug. "It will be all right, Gray, everything will be all right." And he wanted it to be. He wanted to make it all right. "Don't cry," he said, and for one dreadful, frightening moment he was almost about to put a hand to the boy's face and brush the tears from his cheeks.

And then he remembered who he was and what he was, and what Gray was, or was trying to be, and that this boy was a trooper under his authority: the knowledge of it, of what he had almost done, made him want to retch. He pushed Gray away, still feeling the hot, bony, fragility of the boy's shoulders under his fingers even when he was three feet away and staring at Luce with frightened eyes. Stormy, thundery-grey eyes, enormous in that blotched and woeful countenance, and Luce shook himself – this was wrong. This was – was – it was sinful, and abhorrent, and shocking, and the boy was frail and vulnerable and it was disgusting that Luce, who was his senior in both years and rank, should even be *thinking* of him in such a way.

He rubbed his hands on his breeches, trying to get the feel of Gray's birdlike bones off his skin. Apologised, for what pitiful little it was worth, in what he thought was almost his own voice. "Your distress moved me," he muttered awkwardly, and the boy shook his head.

"It is – it's not – it doesn't matter. Um. Sir."

He should not do this.

"Luce," he said, because the young trooper looked so forlorn and draggled, those dark eyes still drowned with tears and his lashes all spiked wet. "You might as well call me Luce. Off duty."

No more.

"Look. Er. Gray." It was like being possessed by some inner demon. Logic and reason told him to end this interview, end it now. Continue it with Hollie Babbitt's sardonic presence at his elbow, because he was sure and certain that Hollie's attendance at a further conversation would put a halt to any vile sentimentality on his part.

Or was Gray *trying* to sweetheart him? Was he mistaken in his suspicion, was that why –

"Gray sit down," he said firmly, and that inner voice of conscience almost died of an apoplexy. I'm trying to get to the bottom of this, he told it. Go away. Bugger off. "I think we need to sort this out. Because you can't go round like –" he flapped a hand vaguely. "That."

"I made a mistake. I should not have come. I thought you might help. I shouldn't have –"

"Gray."

The little trooper looked over his shoulder, one hand on the door handle.

"Out of interest," Luce said, "what is it short for?" He swallowed hard, and took that last step out into the void. "Is it, by chance – Grace?"

32

MORE ATTRACTIVE DROWNED RATS

"It's Gabrielle," she said, snapping the door closed. "And if you touch me, I'll cut your balls off."

"Believe me, madam, I have seen more attractive drowned rats fished out of sewers. What in God's name possessed you? To don breeches, and – dear God, woman, do you have a lover in this troop?" A horrible thought struck him. "It's not *Russell,* is it?"

She stared at him with her mouth open, and then shook her head, warily. "I don't like men!" she said irritably, and ran a hand through her comically short hair till it stuck up on end like a cockerel's crest, and he had to fight down a wild urge to giggle.

"No. Well. On the current showing with the rest of the troop, madam, the feeling is entirely mutual. What – why did you do it? Why *are* you doing it?"

"How did you know?" she said. Another habit of hers, of deflecting a question with a question.

"I wondered at Winceby," he said. "Your wrists and your face –"

"I am too pretty for a boy?"

"Er, no, Gray." She had spots, and an appalling haircut, and a pointed face like a cross fox. She was not pretty. "Hollie – the colonel – he commented that you seemed somewhat well-fed for a soldier that had been in Hull, on siege rations."

"Is he saying I'm *fat?*"

"Padded," he said, tactfully. "Padded. Gray – Gabrielle – you cannot stay dressed as a boy. You can't. It's – I almost – I mean, what would you have done, if Hollie – if the colonel – if he had had you whipped?"

"Squalled like a pig, I imagine." She scratched her jaw. Even knowing she was a – she was female – it was a mannish gesture. "You knew then, didn't you? That's why you – for me – well, I don't need your pity. Lucey. I could have –"

"Then why, madam, did you come slinking in here all teary-eyed asking me to help you?"

"Because I didn't think you'd take the piss!" she growled. "And I was wrong. So fine! Shove it up your arse!"

It took a lot to get Luce to lose his patience, but she was managing it. "I see. Actually, I see little point to continuing this conversation, madam. I can be of no assistance to you, and I think the most useful thing I could do is to go to the colonel with this piece of information and let *him* decide what to do with you."

"No!" she yelled, sounding so anguished that he stopped and blinked at her. "Lucey, please – please – hear me out? *Please?*"

Please wasn't a word he remembered hearing from Gray, ever, previously. "Is it so bad?"

"It's not great," she said forlornly.

He sighed, and cleared a chair of Hollie's paperwork. Since Russell's demotion, the troop's administration had become increasingly erratic. Hollie wouldn't mind. "Oh dear. I might not be the best person. I mean, if you are, you know," he didn't know quite how to put it, but waved a feeble hand in the direction of his belly, "in an interesting condition, I mean, I am personally unattached, but I, uh –"

"Pettitt!" she squawked, outraged. "I am *not* a bloody girl!"

And no, she was right, other than in the strictest biological sense, she wasn't a girl. She was a head shorter than he was and though she looked a ragged object of pity, in her shapeless too-big coat and breeches that were out at the knee, with her dirty hair and her dirtier face and her absolutely reproachable fingernails, he had a pretty good idea what would happen were he to point out as much.

He wondered how come Hollie hadn't noticed, because now she'd admitted it, it was obvious. She ran like a girl – the inelegant mince of someone mentally keeping a hampering skirt from tripping her up. That was what he'd noticed about her first, at Winceby. That, and the fact that she gave the impression of being a fat lad, and her wrists and her ankles and her face were as skinny as those of a drowned kitten. Which, when you looked, was the effect of shapeless clothing and sloping shoulders. "Gray – I have to ask – how the hell do you – you know, the other troopers, you know, stand up, how do you –?"

She gave him a furious glare. "You sit down for a shit, don't you?"

And when he'd finished choking on the wine that he'd just inhaled, he sat and tried to look stern at her, and couldn't help giggling. "How old *are* you, girl?"

It was also funny how quickly he got the idea, because as soon as the words were out of his mouth he took a quick step back and her fist just about grazed his cheek instead of knocking him over. "Fifteen!" she said indignantly, as if he'd just questioned her morality, and he sat down.

"Oh, dear Lord. Do your parents know where you are?"

"I haven't got any," she said. A little too quickly. And not very convincingly.

"Oh, dear Lord," he said again, with a sinking feeling somewhere in the region of the waistband of his breeches. "You're a runaway. You're not – you're not an heiress, or anything awful, are you?"

"You see too many plays. And it's not any of your business."

Well, he folded his arms, and leaned, casually, against Hollie's desk. "Gray, you came in here asking me for help. Now you can either be honest with me, and I will think about helping you – think about it, I said, because I will not aid you in any venture which is either illegal or immoral. So if you have conceived some unnatural lust for Captain Venning, or similar –"

It was intended to make her laugh. It did not.

33

THE BASTARDS ALWAYS CATCH UP WITH YOU

It had been one of those chilly, damp, bleak nights in early spring, with the smell of wet earth on the air and the branches still bare, though beginning to bud. Her feet were cold, and she could not sleep, in damp blankets, in the barn with the better part of eighty troopers snoring and farting around her.

– Gray did not like sleeping, anyway. It was boring.

She had meant to go out for a piss, it being one of the few times she could do it in privacy without fear of being overlooked. Her belly was rumbling, and she had also meant to pass by the dairy and see whether she could snatch a corner of cheese and make it look as if it had been nibbled by some creature. She did that often.

And she'd got up, and slipped out, and squatted in the ditch behind the barn, which stank even in the cold. And on her way back she had found her way blocked by Trooper Eliot.

"Well, well, well," he said, "fancy that – now then, Gray. Meeting a bird, eh? Late night assignation?"

Which, obviously, was not true, and she had said as much, and told him to mind his own business. (Possibly not quite so politely.)

Eliot had grinned at her, and Ward had loomed up out of the stinking dark behind him, because where one was the other was, as inevitable as your shadow. "Whasson, then?"

"Gray's wandering about in the dark," Eliot said. "Reckon he's a Malignant spy, meself."

"No, he ain't," Ward had said scornfully. "He ain't pretty enough for a Cavalier. He doesn't wash often enough." And he'd reached out and taken a handful of Gray's – admittedly not very clean – hair, and tugged it, hard. "See?"

And, you know, it was so unlike those two, to be friendly, even rough-friendly, that she was on her guard straightaway. They had been civil, and then somehow, she wasn't quite sure how, but there were a few of them, three or four of the lads, who were going to slip out for a little bit of a wet in a place a couple of miles up the road, some little place hardly better than a shed where they brewed their own and didn't ask too many questions about what decent godly Parliament men might be doing lifting the elbow quite so enthusiastically at coming on for dawn on a raw March morning. That had been the plan, anyway, and they had implied that a man who wouldn't join them for a few toasts to the Army was no man at all. (There might be girls, Eliot had said, smirking, but no promises. Sometimes there were girls. You know.)

Well, Gray had some pride, and she was touched on her mettle, that they implied she couldn't hold her liquor, and that she was less than a man. So she went.

She had no money, but they said that didn't matter, that they would lend her a few copper cash, and anyway, they'd teach her to play cards, and she could win herself a few coins. Beginners' luck. Bound to come away with her pockets jingling. And she had, that was the astonishing part! She had a facility with cards – she was quick, and deft, and her memory was good, and they said she was a natural, and she kept winning, and winning, until it was almost shameful. She almost pitied the poor locals she was fleecing.

"Gray," Luce broke in, seeing her shining eyes, "Gray, I said I would not help you to do anything that was either shameful or immoral. And so far as I can tell, to take money dishonestly from a poor man's pocket, is both."

She made a dismissive noise. "Bollocks, Lucey. They knew what they were doing."

"Of course," Luce said, quite mildly. "And presumably their families, who might want for bread, would be also so well-informed?"

"Oh, you are so stupid! You don't understand anything!"

"Possibly not. I have never been tempted to gamble, Gray, and nor do I choose to befriend any that do. I may assure you that neither myself, Captain Venning, nor Colonel Babbitt would hazard our livelihoods in such a wilful manner."

He hoped he was setting her a stern moral example. She eyed him consideringly. "Captain Venning is a turnip," she said, at length. "Rosie Babbitt is a full-on nutjob, and you've only just started shaving. I'd not trust the authority of any of you buggers, so don't be trying to put that one over on me. Just about the only one of you lot I'd take that line from is Russell, and he's normally flat on his back in the gutter, these days." She snorted. "Pretty pass, when the only one of you lot with any moral compass is a drunk with wandering hands."

"Yes. Well." He felt the back of his neck grow hot. "We are getting off the point, Gray, which is your gambling."

Her mouth twisted. "Yes. Well. Indeed. My luck changed."

"I am glad to hear it."

"I wasn't. I lost every penny." She swallowed, hard, and squeezed her hands together, and looked up at him, and there were tears welling up in her eyes even though she was trying to scowl. "I owe them two about three months' pay. And –" she licked her lips, and squirmed, "I lost my carbine, Luce."

"Well, so? We can reissue one."

"No, Luce." She spread her hands. "I lost the bloody lot. And the colonel's doing the paperwork himself. He would know."

"Well, what if he –" She was looking at him as if he was stupid. "Gray, if you don't wish to attract attention, perhaps you ought not to attempt to knee Trooper Wilding in the cods at supper. Just a thought?"

"You really don't understand, do you? Of course you can reissue me another carbine. I'm sure we could find me another sword, somewhere. I did have a pistol, but they just took that away from me, because they are bigger than I am, and there are more of them, and it was funny. We can carry on doing that forever, until the war ends, or until you tire of me and transfer me to another troop. Again." For the first time, Gray looked vulnerable, and tired. A breeze from the open window ruffled her short hair. "I can keep on running, Luce. Long as you like, I can keep on running. But the bastards always catch up with you in the end."

She sighed, and he wanted to do something, not because she was a girl, or smaller than he, or younger, but because it wasn't right that she would be so fragile and stubborn and hurt, and not have anyone to guard her back. The corner of her mouth curled up in a small, wry smile. "There. Now you know. If you tell anyone, I will kill you. You know that, don't you?"

"Have you killed a lot of men, Gray?" he said indulgently.

She blinked at him. "Three," she said. "Possibly four. Not sure about the last." And Luce closed his mouth and swallowed, hard, with a throat like sandpaper. He believed her, too.

34

THE SHE-WOLF OF AQUITAINE

"I'll go and take it back, then," Luce said firmly. "They can't refuse an order. I am their superior. And *then*, madam, back into skirts you go."

"Technically," Gray said, and he looked up at her, narrowing his eyes.

"*Technically*, Gray? *Moral compass*? Just a little girl of the streets with no particular birth or breeding, indeed – before I do you any favours you're going to tell me who your people are, mistress, and whether we are likely to have, I don't know, the Earl of Newcastle on the doorstep wanting his daughter back. Or something. I mean it."

"No one you know, Master Pettitt. I am of Aquitaine."

And he believed it, too. It was only the smallest lilt, almost imperceptible. Like Gray's womanhood – girlhood – invisible, unless you were looking. "The She-wolf of Aquitaine," he murmured, and she lifted her ragged head and glowered at him.

"Who are you calling a wolf-bitch?"

"This is not getting us anywhere. Gabrielle. We have, as I see it, three options. You put your skirts back on, and return to your family in Aquitaine. If Aquitaine is in fact where you came from. I'm sure we can provide you with a whip-round for passage. How you explain yourself is your own affair, madam, but that should be my preferred option. Or I turn you over to the colonel to deal with, which is also an appealing option –"

"On your honour, you said," she muttered, and if she had cried he'd have had no compunction about turning her over but she didn't, she grumbled like a sulky boy, and he had never mentioned honour. Which he told her.

"You don't understand!" she said, again, crossly.

"Indeed. *Je suis desolee, mademoiselle, mais* –"

"*Enculez-vous*," she snapped back, and oh yes, she was French all right. "I will not go back, sir, *I will not*. I do not care if you hang me, I will not leave this troop, I should rather die!"

"Well, without your weapons, Gray, it does look rather likely, doesn't it?"

– That was where she hit him, not hard, just hard enough to unbalance him and make him fall off his chair. And that made her laugh, and then she cried, like a girl this time, and he felt all of three inches tall.

"The bloody hell is going on in here, bor?"

Gray streaming tears and snot, scarlet in the face and near-hysterical, and Luce prone on the floorboards in a pile of paperwork and half a glass of spilled wine. Because what every crisis needed was a large and hard-of-thinking freckled Fenlander, not sure if he ought to be scowling or grinning. "Lucey, what you said to the lad? There ent no need for that, Gray!"

"Gray has come to me with a very serious disclosure," Luce said, with great dignity for a man whose backside was still smarting.

She caught her breath, and he saw her scrawny throat move, her eyes drop, her whole skinny little body tense up for flight. Her hand go to a sword that wasn't there. (Oh, Gray, not your sword as well, you foolish child.)

"Captain Venning, you do know that Trooper Gray is –" He meant to, it was his duty to, as a man, as a Christian, as an officer, and just for a second, the words teetered on the top of his tongue. And then he saw her face, as miserable and hunted as a little wild thing in a trap, behind Venning's shoulder. He sighed. "Being taken advantage of, by some of Colonel Babbitt's company?"

"Taken advantage of, how?" Venning said warily, eyeing Gray as if the little trooper might be some kind of dangerous incubus.

"Gray is not technically of an age to serve." It was perfectly true. *She* was not. "He has not yet attained the sense that comes with maturity," Luce said blandly, and Venning's sandy eyebrows rose. "D'ee reckon he'll live so long, bor?"

"He was tempted into gambling, it seems. And has been stripped of most of his weapons, by certain other members of the troop."

"That be Ward and Eliot, then?"

Gray shrugged. "I'm not saying."

"You're right," Venning said after a pause, not talking to the woeful little trooper. "He hasn't, has he?" He gave a sigh. "Don't hold with gambling, meself. Speaking as a man, and not an officer, I couldn't give a bugger what 'ee does in what spare hours the Army gives you, but I find once the lads start hazarding amongst themselves – ends in tears, I find. Always. There's always some smart-ass as wants more than what they has. You want to play, boy, you please yourself, but you do it as a bloody civilian, bor, for I won't have it in my troop."

Gray's mouth hung open. "You are – Puritan?"

"No, bor, I'm bloody pragmatical. You're sat here now snivelling because you lost, and there's many a young man would be plotting how best to win his gear back off of they two villains, whether above or below the board. D'ee reckon that'd be a comfortable company to command? Playing deeper and deeper, wi' they two leading you on, and any other bugger they can get as is stupid enough to play with them – it'll end in tears, trooper, or more like, it'll end in murder."

"May I ask, captain, might we just not make report of this to Colonel Babbitt?" Luce put in delicately, and Venning scowled.

"We might bloody not, cornet, no. I'll manage it myself. It'll go hard with Gray if it looks like he's running to senior officers every time one o' the lads looks at him badly, and it'll go hard wi' me if it looks like I can't discipline my own boys without Rosie holding my hand for me. You, you young whelp, are on curfew, as of now, as of my orders. Grounded, boy. You're not going out for so much as a tom-tit without a gate pass, signed by me, and prob'ly in triplicate."

"I'm not sure that will help," Luce said, "they pick on him."

"Thass not my problem, Lucey. Thass *his* problem. If he can stop hauling off and belting people with no provocation, he's going to find his days a whole heap easier."

"Yes, but –"

"No, not but, Luce. You're an officer, not a bloody wet-nurse. Gray might be the runt of the litter but it's about time he learned some manners, and you taking his punishments ain't going to teach him nawthen, Lucey!"

Gray raised a simmering gaze. "I have learned my lesson, Captain Venning. I give you my word of honour I will not gamble again."

"Glad to hear it, bor, and I don't care what 'ee does in private life, but under my command you're bloody right you won't." The freckled Fenlander grunted. "Glad we got that sorted out. Now, since we ent going to bother Rosie with this, since the big lad is up to the backsides in paperwork and is like to be teasy as a snake till we move off, any bright ideas as to how we are going to get your tackle back, trooper?" Luce began to grin. "I do, actually. We are going to win it back, captain. That was a splendid idea of yours."

"Count me out," Gray said quickly. "Count me out, sir," Venning corrected. "Thass got to be one of the daftest ideas I ever heard, cornet. Who the hell is going to play with them two, willing? Given that to my sure and certain knowledge the pair of 'em play crooked?"

"Someone they will never suspect of playing them at their own deceitful game, Drew." He grinned. "*Russell.*"

35

PIGS MIGHT WHISTLE

Russell was sitting by himself, by the window, watching the chaos of eighty troopers trying to find lost stockings, books, precious letters from home before they marched out in the morning.

Another man might have looked superior, having packed bags and baggage with care and organisation. Thankful Russell had a snapsack at his feet and the clothes he stood up in. He had nothing else, he had no books save his bible and he certainly had no letters from home.

"So the plan is, ply him with drink and turn him loose on them?" Gray said, at Luce's elbow. And that had been the plan, and now it wasn't. "I'll see what he says first," Luce said. "He might want to help."

"Pigs might whistle, but they've poor mouths for it," she said. "*Coward.*"

"Gray, he is a man, not a chess-piece. He deserves a choice."

"You're soft, Lucey." She strutted towards the scarred young man.

"And I am not sure you are kind, Gray," Luce said, almost inaudibly. "And I pray God that will change. It is most unwomanly."

The scarred lieutenant looked up as if his head hurt him. "Have you been drinking already?" she demanded, and Russell looked at her, and then, very deliberately, past her shoulder, and said nothing.

Venning looked contemptuous. "Been on the ale, has 'ee?"

Russell closed his eyes and even managed to look as if that pained him. "I suggest," he said, very carefully and distinctly, "that you take your solicitude and fuck off."

"I suggest a bucket o' cold water, before you take up anything like your duties, mate. Ach," Venning shook his head, sneering, "you are disgusting, Russell."

"If you came to tell me that, you wasted both my time and yours. I am well aware of it. Are you done with me?"

Venning would have been. Luce was not. "Hapless – ah, I mean, Thankful – I don't like to pry, but – does it hurt a lot?"

He opened one eye suspiciously. "I beg your pardon, cornet?"

"Well. I, um. You're not drunk, are you?" Luce glanced up at Venning, who was staring back at him as if he'd started speaking foreign. "So, given that you're sober, I thought – you know – what happened – I thought it must still hurt you. A lot. At times. And I just, " he shrugged, "wondered if I might be able to be of service. It's what friends do for each other, after all. You would do the same for me."

"Were I a little ray of sunshine, you mean? Well, Lucifer, I am not a little ray of sunshine –"

"More like a bloody raincloud," Venning muttered, "all right, I'm sorry I said 'ee was the worse for wear, but you got to admit it looks bad."

"Give a dog a bad name and," – and Russell's hand went quite inadvertently to his collar, as he remembered partway through that sentence where it ended. Where the rope scar was still visible enough to cause remark, if he wore his collar-strings loose.

"That an' all," Venning finished. "Aye. Well. Given that I made a bloody fool o'myself, the which I said I was sorry for, I d'reckon I owe you. What d'you ask?"

"That the pair of you leave me in peace," he said wearily. "Pettitt, you make my head ache the worse. It's like having a slightly bigger version of that benighted dog of yours slobbering all over me. Which reminds me, sir, where *is* that ill-governed mongrel?"

"What, Rosie?"

The lieutenant didn't intend to. His scarred face never displayed a flicker of emotion. But he laughed anyway, and then blinked as if he'd surprised himself.

Luce and Venning looked at each other. Venning raised his eyebrows. "Hapless," he said, settling himself on the settle next to the lieutenant. "Hapless, lad, can 'ee do that again?"

"Do – what?" Russell backed away an inch or so. "What are you asking?"

"Look – you know. Like that."

"I'm not looking like anything!"

"Ah," Venning said. "Thass the point, bor. Does 'ee play cards, at all?"

"I do not! I have never had dealings with the Devil's picture-books, sir! How dare you!"

"Scratch a bloody drunk and find a Puritan," Venning muttered, "might ha' known 'ee was bloody sober, if you're vicious."

"I –" Russell began furiously, and Luce put a hand on his shoulder.

"No, Captain Venning, this is not a matter for you. This is a matter between friends."

Venning looked briefly blank, and then nodded. "All right, Luce, thass how you want to play it, I'll leave you to it. Just outside if you need me." And he got up and left.

Russell blinked. "You will persist in calling me your friend, Pettitt, and I am not."

"What else should I call you?"

"A millstone," he said gloomily.

"Well, then, I shall burden you likewise, Thankful. Gray has had some property stolen from him. No, more than that. Gray is being bullied and hurt, and I would ask your help in making sure that it ceases. *Immediately.*"

"And why should I –"

"Because he is as hurt and lonely and angry as you are, sir, and I should expect some fellow-feeling from you!"

Russell's wry mouth twisted. "How remarkably astute of you, Pettitt."

"I want you to do something for me."

"I want a number of things, trooper." He tilted his head slightly. It was deliberate, Luce was sure of it. His scars seemed to look worse in the firelight, highlighted by a heavy growth of patchy silver-gilt stubble, and he knew it. "I do not expect to receive them. Now fuck off, and leave me alone."

"A friend?" Luce said gently. "For I think you need one."

"I think what I actually need is another drink, sir, because I find the present condescension a little hard to stomach. Sober." He stood up, and he was sober, and Gray caught her breath a little beside them because standing he was almost of a height with Luce, who was not considered short. And the two of them, tall and straight and fair, looked like a pair of rebel angels. "I am sorry," Luce said, and put his hand on Russell's arm.

"For what? Particularly?"

"That we troubled you. Come on, Gray. Let us leave the – leave Trooper Russell be."

That was the point where he was supposed to say – no, wait, come back, sit down. But it was Russell, and instead he shrugged, and pushed past Luce.

"You arsehole," Gray said furiously, "he's trying to be nice, and you –" Barely came up to his shoulder, so she took a wild swing at him anyway, her fist grazing his cheekbone. He took one delicate step aside, and the blow tipped his hat askew and no worse, and for a heartbeat Luce thought that would be all that would happen.

And then that elegant, proper young man, the former secretary to the Earl of Essex, the former company lieutenant – the failed suicide, the failed adulterer, the failed officer – whirled like a cat, with a half-empty jug of ale in his hand, and dashed the contents in Luce's eyes, and he would have shattered the heavy earthenware on the table corner and gone at him with the broken shards, but it would not break, though the table tipped and rolled crazily, and troopers scattered and swore.

Luce was useless, blinded and spluttering, and Gray was screaming. Like a boy, actually, rather than a girl: like a terrified boy who'd suddenly realised that the slow-worm he has by the tail is in fact a venomous and seriously disenchanted adder. Russell threw the empty jug to burst against the wall like a grenado and fled.

The room was chaos, ale-scented chaos, and that was as well, because in the commotion and the clearing-up, there was only Luce, really, who'd heard Russell go. And knew that as he pushed past, flinging out into the darkness – go and put a bullet in his bloody ear, the fucking madman, not fit to keep Christian company, possessed by black devils – that there was a limit to what any man could bear, alone.

Luce did wish Thankful Russell might acknowledge that fact, once in a while.

36

NOT TEMPERAMENTALLY INCLINED TOWARDS MODERATION

"I presume you come seeking an apology," Russell said frigidly.

For a man whose collar was soaked with his own tears, he was still remarkably unapproachable. Luce wasn't going to mention that, and so he said nothing.

"Retribution?"

"Actually, I came to see if you were all right. Having some history of, well, taking things a little personally."

"I am not temperamentally inclined towards moderation," Russell said. He meant it as a challenge.

"I know. We had noticed."

"Is he dead?" Gray wanted to know. "Or just sulking?"

"Why, Cornet Pettitt, you appear to have acquired a little dog."

"Why, Trooper Russell, you appear to have acquired a second arsehole, and you seem to be talking out of it," Gray mimicked unpleasantly.

"Come to drag me off to the colonel, have you? Fine. Hang me. See if I care. I have nothing else you can have off me, do I?"

"Oh, in God's name, Russell! I am hoping none of this will come to Hollie's ears, because really, he has enough on his plate at the moment anyway, given that the man who was *supposed* to be his bloody administrator is sulking in a midden!"

"I beg your pardon!"

"Sulking," Gray said, with relish. "In the midden. But then you're used to being in the shit, Russell, aren't you?"

"Don't you even think about it," Luce put in wearily. "Either of you. I'm a bit sick of the pair of you, to be honest. If we cannot be civil to each other, we are little better than animals."

"Hounds," Russell said, with his horrible twisted smile, and Luce shot out a hand and grabbed Gray's collar, yanking it tight enough to choke.

"He's baiting you. Don't bite. And Russell, stop being a – a "

"Prick," Gray said, with a feral grin of her own.

"Stop. It. Both of you. *Stop*. I came looking for you, Russell, because you seemed distressed, and *believe it or not*, there are some people in this world who are not able to turn their backs on a man in distress. I believe it's called *Christianity*, sir, and I believe you profess to call yourself a godly man."

"Do you plan to turn the other cheek indefinitely, cornet?"

"I hope and pray so, trooper."

"*Splendid*," Russell said, and slapped him, hard, flat-handed.

Luce took a deep, calming breath. And then he drew his pistol, "*I'm* armed, you ungrateful excrescence, and *you* are starting to try my patience." His cheek hurt. He hoped he sounded calm, because he didn't bloody well feel it. "Sit down and shut your mouth, or I swear, I shall put a hole clear through you –"

"And since you've got no mates anyway, no one would care," Gray added malevolently, and Luce rounded on her.

"And the same applies to *you*, mad-person! The pair of you! Hold your tongues!"

"Mad person?" Russell said quizzically. "What an interesting choice of epithet, cornet."

Luce put a bullet in the wall eighteen inches over his head, and he shut up after that. The horses tethered in the rest of the stalls did not, mind, and for a few moments afterwards there was screaming, whinnying, kicking cacophony, as thirty cavalry horses wondered where the battle was.

"Not sure you meant to do that, cornet."

"I can aim lower, Russell?" He took another deep breath, and ran a hand through his hair.

"Might want to put the pistol down first," Gray suggested.

"Will the pair of you *shut up*!"

There was an odd breathless, creaking sort of noise from the shadows of the empty stall. It took Luce a moment to realise that Russell was not, in fact, having a seizure, or an attack of some kind.

"Are you laughing?"

The noise stopped. "What's it to you?"

"I've never actually heard you laugh before."

"Well he's hardly had a lot to laugh about," Gray said, perfectly reasonably.

37

THE DEVIL'S PICTURE-BOOKS

He said he wouldn't. He was adamant that he wouldn't, especially when it was explained to him, slowly and clearly, that if Gray did not retrieve his weapons, Gray would as like as not end up with a musket ball through the head with a dawn coming very shortly.

"Captain Venning can explain it to you," Luce said. "At swordpoint, if necessary."

"Captain Venning is staying out of this," Venning muttered darkly. "'S got bad idea written all over it."

"All we need you to do, Russell, is play cards."

Of course, he would not compromise himself. Gray did not help at that point by yelping that the marred bastard was sufficient compromised already, was he not? – at which point Russell got up and walked out of the room, and had to be dragged back with promises of an apology and a second jug of wine.

"Spiced?" he'd said, with a glimmer of interest.

"*Warmed.*" Venning leaned across the table. "When you get back. With the kit."

"I have never touched the Devil's picture-books in my life."

Gray's eyes met Luce's across the table. He was weakening. "How you off for cake, Russell?" Venning said casually, as if the answer wasn't obvious from the fit of his coat.

"I am not so easily bought as that, sir."

"Sure enough. I seen more meat on bones that our Tinners buried a month back. I'm asking, trooper, because if you're like to spend all night gaming with that pack o' wastrels in God knows what poky hole, there's a good chance you're like to come home both half-cut and starved, and I'd rather not ride out to Yorkshire in the morning with you falling off that bloody knacker's-bait horse of yours every hundred yards for want of food."

"Doubtless delaying the advance of the Army by several hours," Russell said dryly. "What do I gain from this chicanery, may I ask? Where is to be the sting in all this honey?"

"Friendship, Russell," Luce said tartly, and was rewarded by a faint, sardonic lift of the other man's eyebrows.

"Of course. So I perjure myself, at some considerable personal discomfort –"

"I could maybe not kill you?" Gray muttered.

"*Considerable physical discomfort*," he repeated. "And danger. For what end?"

"A feeling of warmth," Luce snapped.

"If I wish to experience a feeling of warmth, cornet, I may gain as much by pissing my breeches."

Gray snorted helplessly and unless Luce was very mistaken, that scar-faced reprobate was beginning to enjoy this. "This is not a matter for levity, trooper."

"Indeed." He had almost regained his old coolness, his old air of imperturbable competence. His eyes were bright with a most unaccustomed humour, though. He brushed an imperceptible speck from his appalling linen. "I may be able to come to some agreement with you, cornet. For my recompense."

"Russell, you're not getting *paid* for this –"

"On the contrary, Cornet Pettitt. You may consider your slate opened."

He stood up, lithe and suddenly, weirdly, elegant, even in his stained shirt and drabbled breeches. Bowed. "Hold my place in the line, Trooper Gray. And I shall see you at dawn, God willing."

38

FIVE PENNIES AND A SHILLING

There were a number of advantages to being considered an unregenerate drunk, he thought. One of them was that if you were stiff and limping, still waiting for the bruises of a dozen lashes to fade from your back, people assumed you were staggering. If you happened not to have been to bed for the better part of thirty-six hours, either, due to the humour of one or two of your comrades who might have swapped their duty with you and neglected to mention till your sergeant kicked you out of your blankets – well, then, if your voice had an odd slur to it, that did no harm. Ward flinched, though, when he sat down.

(As well he might. Ward had been the bastard who'd swapped duty and seen Russell out on patrol for eighteen hours straight, straight in and straight out again, while Ward went sloping in for a warm fireside and his supper. Laughing.)

"I'm told you boys play," he said, and put his hand his pocket, and dumped a handful of coins on the table.

It was all he had in the world, and it scared him witless to do it, but he gave Ward his most amicable grin. "Teach me?"

Eliot came up behind and clapped him on the shoulder. That was deliberate, too. He caught his breath – it hurt – and then turned his head, dropping his eyes quickly before the bastard saw the intent there. "Good Puritan boy like you, Thankful? Don't think so."

"Fucking skint Puritan boy like me, trooper." It was astonishing how easily he could still do this, still slip back into his own homely Buckinghamshire burr, could swear and blaspheme and call on God to be his witness. He'd had a foot in both worlds, once. Prim and missish by day, under his sister's roof, and drinking and –

Well, he'd never gambled, to be honest. He'd only played the fiddle and kissed a few girls. "Could do with the money, t'be honest. Running out of people to buy me drinks."

"Want to behave yourself then, don't you?" Ward said disapprovingly.

Kettle, meet the pot. He nodded. "Can't seem to help myself, mate. You know what I reckon. I reckon when I took this –" he tapped his scarred cheek, "– I reckon it let half the sense out. I do, truly. I don't remember half what's said to me from day's end to day's end –" Going too far. He wasn't stupid, and they knew he wasn't. "What I tell that judas-haired bastard, anyway."

"Less o' that," Ward said. He was going to be the harder one to convince, then. Russell shrugged.

"See I've come to wrong place, gen'lmen. Didn't realise it was bloody Babbitt Appreciation Night. I'll –" he scooped his coins back, scattering them across the sticky table top, fighting down an urge to drop to his knees to hunt for the last pennies because that was all there was between him and indignity. Five pennies and a shilling in his pocket, and he could still tell himself he looked like a mendicant by choice. Russell, you're a ragged drunk with a rope scar round your neck and a ruined reputation. You *have* no dignity. He slid off the bench and grubbed in the greasy straw on the tavern floor, for those last coins.

Eliot's boot closed on his fingers, hard enough to hurt. "Lost summat, handsome?"

"Pretty much ever'thing, sir, pretty much ever'thing. What've you got?"

The boot moved. "Can't promise you nothing, mate. Like anything else in this life, you don't win 'em all."

He sighed, and crawled back out, and banged his head on the underneath of the table. That had not been an act. He was so tired he was hardly sure which way was upright. And, yes, he was more than a little cupshot. Little bit.

Ward's eyes were very bright, though, and he was watching Russell's face like an eager bridegroom. Wouldn't get much joy out of that, old son. Couldn't tell much from Russell's marred face, except that a man could be stupid enough to lose his hope and his beauty in one foul swoop and then come back to the Army for the King's men to finish the job. (Stop him. Stop the Great Whore of Rome, or die trying.) As a dog returneth to his vomit, so a fool returneth to his folly –

Ward put a cup into his hand and he sipped it absently, choked – it was not nice stuff, not at all, and it burned like the fires of hell all the way down his throat, and Ward laughed at him. "Thought you was used to taking it neat, Russell?"

Not that he could reply, because his eyes were streaming and he was doing his level best not to cough till he heaved, so Eliot chuckled instead, and moved up the bench for another truanting trooper. (Wilder? Wilding? Knew the face. The man knew his, too, and blushed, even in this dim light.)

"Now then, gentlemen, five shillings to start the pot, and I reckon you all know Lieutenant Russell –"

"He's not a lieutenant any more," Wilding said, wanting to be helpful, "he's one of us now."

"Well d'you know! Fancy me forgetting that! And there I was last week when he got broke for – well, whatever it was, it wasn't fair, was it, Russell?"

"Hm?" He'd been staring at the candle flame, letting it go in and out of focus as his gritty eyelids drooped. "What say?"

Eliot laughed. It was meant to sound friendly. Hit Russell in between the shoulderblades again, in another friendly gesture. Which hurt. "Don't you worry, young man. We'll take care of you. You know what they say, lucky in cards, unlucky in love?"

"Never played cards before. Devil's picture-books," he said gloomily, and one of the locals round the table got up and skulked away, muttering about not playing with preachers. Ward glowered at him.

"Wouldn't do it now if I didn't need the money," he added. "Got used to living on an officer's pay."

Take care of him, indeed. They lent him his stake – how kind, how very kind – and Eliot sat at his shoulder like a benign angel for the first few hands, telling him what was a good card, what was not. And they told him it was beginner's luck. Even so. He knew it was going to all suddenly turn about, but even so, the speed with which the pile of small coin before him grew made his belly feel hollow with fear. Sweet Lord Jesus Christ preserve him, no, not excitement. There were a number of things Russell craved in this world and excitement was not one of them, not any more. He was bloody terrified.

Ward said he wouldn't deal. "For surely," he said, "we want to start our lads off gently, don't we? Deal 'em, Wilding. Three cards apiece, on the table, there's a good boy. No – don't look, son, we play a straight hand here, we don't look at the cards before we play. Now. You're the bank. Now I'll look at my cards, see –" and then shook his head, slowly. "Aw, now. A two, a six, and a four. That's no good, is it?"

Russell grinned. (It hurt, but it had to be done.) "Me next! I got *two* sixes, look –"

Eliot patting him on the shoulder. "Calm down, calm down, go gently. Everybody takes it in turns, now. Round the table. One at a time is good fishing."

He lost. He lost heavily. (He breathed a sigh of relief, and hoped he did not smell as strongly of fear as he thought he might, because he did not want to win, not at all.) Wilding was as easy to read as a goodwife's receipt. His eyes went every which way, when he held a good hand, and when he held a really good hand he wouldn't look anywhere but at the table.

Eliot was harder, and not always predictable, and he had the habit of trying to distract by staring around him as if he was trying to assess everyone in the inn.

They all had their tricks. Russell's expressions were unreadable. He knew that. They all knew that. They thought they could read the rest of him and actually, twenty years of being punished by his sister for dumb insolence had broken him of most explicit expression, unless he chose to make it otherwise. And when you spent most of your waking time watching other men's expressions, trying to work out how to force the stiff, ragged muscle of your cheek to copy them, you noticed the little things. The dip of an eyelid, the way a man's eyes widened a little when he looked on a thing he coveted. Wilding studied him covertly in return, and, as the level in the jug dropped, not so covertly.

(Oh yes, Russell was as drunk as the rest – but he was used to that, now. Functioned as well drunk as sober. The pain in his head would have been unbearable, else, by now.)

"I'm out." One of the locals down. What frightened Russell was that the pile he had in front of him was about six month's pay, for a plain trooper, and the Lord alone knew what it was for a working man.

"Buy everyone a drink," he said firmly. "No, surely, everyone. You got to. Got to have a drink with me. 'M lucky – lucky tonight." And then went to stand up, couldn't. Actually couldn't, not feigned couldn't, he had been sitting cramped for so long at that undersized bench, all two yards of him twisted up and rigid in the corner. "You." He pointed at the local man. "You're up on y'r feet, go on, go get some drink. Take some coin. Ah, Devil take it, take all of it, leave me 'nough for another drink. And a girl."

Ward was staring at him, his mouth slightly ajar. "What? What's matter with you? Bloody staring at me –"

He could have easily taken the girl and the drink and the hell with this turnip who didn't deserve his losses to be made good. Wanted to, suddenly, with a pain that went through him like a knife in the guts, and the other man was afraid of him, took the sticky coins and went scuttling away into the fuggy darkness. Never, if he had any sense, to be seen again – or at least that was the intention. "Deal," he said grimly, and lost again, with care.

Started to play wildly, towards dawn, knowing that time grew short. Playing for trinkets, for promises. For a clean shirt. For the vengeful joy of watching Ward's dark features grow sharp with desire and greed, and to end by taking the man's precious things across the table. His wedding ring. His clean stockings. His Bible.

Eliot would play no more, was tugging on his friend's arm, hissing into his ear. Enough.

"Gray's harness," he said, quite clearly. "Three cards. Turn over."

"Worthless," Ward sneered, and Russell shook his head, very carefully, because it hurt, and little flares of pain ran up his temple from the badly-healed bone.

"Play."

Wilding dealt, stumbled with the cards, his fingers thick and red and shaking on the pasteboard.

Russell didn't know he was holding his breath till he felt his own heart beating in his ears.

Ward turned the cards, grinning. Two deuces. A knave.

No surprise. Russell had known about the deuces. He'd made the fingernail mark himself, on the corner of one.

He turned his own cards over, not daring to look. Two deuces. And a queen.

"Fuck. Me," Eliot said, and his eyes were round, and more than a little frightened, because that was sheer chance, sheer, wild, luck. That was not luck that should favour a marred, mad dupe with the cards stacked against him.

He was almost as frightened himself, at his own success. He hadn't expected it to work quite *that* well. But he forced himself to grin, in leering, drunken triumph, and to rake his profit into his snapsack, and to stand up and stagger outside and puke, till he thought he might die of it. Not with the sour wine, though that didn't help, but with fear, and if ever he had felt any desire to hazard, this night had broken it out of him.

He sat down in the spring mud by the inn door, with the first grey light of a grey dawn turning the trees skeletal, and he shook till he thought his bones would come apart, and then he stood up and went back inside.

He stank, dreadfully, of stale sweat and terror and bile, but that was all right, because he had a clean shirt in that snapsack. The first time he'd shifted his linen in a month, and he'd done it by his own wits, not another man's grudging charity. And whole stockings. Not especially new, and not especially clean, but whole.

He tipped his hat to the staring wench sitting bleary-eyed by the door. "Man said you'd paid for a girl," she mumbled, jerking her thumb at the darkness behind her and the stairs to her lodgings. "Up the stairs –"

He shook his head, just once. "Keep it." Best that she not be disturbed from her dreams to lie with a thing of nightmare, poor wench. Even a thing of nightmare in clean linen.

He hoisted Gray's carbine over his shoulder, and stumbled out into the dawn.

The bay horse lifted his head and whickered a drowsy greeting. Russell straightened the gelding's forelock, rubbed his muzzle – rubbed his own muzzle, not caring for a week's worth of bristle at all – and then slipped the two cards from up his sleeve.

"I do hope," he said aloud, "that neither of those two gentlemen has the presence of mind or the ability to count to more than fifty."

Palm him off a worthless hand, indeed. They must think he was blind, as well as stupid. Just as well he'd removed two of the deuces himself, not an hour before, for this very eventuality.

It was raining, a thin, cold, fine rain, and a cheerless cold morning, but – he lifted his head gingerly, and took a deep breath of the fresh air. Cold and raw, but he thought he might taste a faint promise of a distant spring.

39

RIOTOUS EATERS OF FLESH

They were a bloody bitter humiliation, the whole boiling lot of them. They were the last troop of Fairfax's horse out of Nantwich that bleak morning, with the sun coming up red as raw flesh over the Cheshire plain and black rags of cloud tossed on a rising wind, and every bloody judgmental eye in the Army on bloody Babbitt and his bloody dilatory rabble.

Fairfax himself was spitting. Reckoned it didn't look good – ill-disciplined, he said, and if Hollie couldn't keep four troop of horse in something like order he had no business as a colonel and he ought to just say as much. What kind of show did he think he'd put on, on a battlefield, if he couldn't get a little under four hundred men out of bed and upright with breeches on with seventy-two hours' notice.

Fairfax was very deliberately not mentioning the straggling arrival of several troopers missing at muster roll and presumed deserted, who had caught up after the body of the Army had moved off. Or, indeed, the appalling and disreputable appearance of same. Ward and Eliot looked like they'd both spent the night robbing graveyards. (For teeth, probably. He could never look at Ward's mossy, crooked fangs without being reminded of an ill-kept boneyard.) They always did, though, no matter how irreproachable their activity, but he doubted his commander was in the mood for lame excuses.

Lucey had been about as much use as pissing on a house-fire, dithering from pillar to post, forgetting where he'd left things, flapping, wailing. Taking limp poeting to its extremes, and there'd been several minutes when it had been touch and go if Hollie was going to haul off and punch him in the head. He was going to speak most sharply to that lad, just as soon as his own ears had stopped burning from the blistering he was getting from Fairfax.

He just didn't know what had been the matter with his officers this morning, at all. He did not know what had got into them. You'd have thought they were *trying* to keep everyone hanging about. Venning had been slow to the point of stupid, and Luce had been all of a-quiver.

Gray had looked sick, and he hoped that wasn't so, because he could do without being held responsible for spreading a contagion across the Army as well as being a malign influence of unpunctuality, ill-preparation and lack of respect. And Russell, well, Russell had turned up at a racketing gallop on that patchwork beast of his, stinking of drink and looking like he'd been rolled on an ale-house slopstone, thrust Gray's sword into the lad's hands and promptly fell off his horse. Black Tyburn hated waiting at the best of times, and had been in a foul mood all day, culminating in one of his interminable grating stallion's screaming matches with Fairfax's White Surrey. It was a horrible noise, with the two stallions yelling threats at each other across the lines at the sort of volume that made your ears ring.

He slouched back to their quarters. After all that – after he'd apparently delayed the entire Army of Parliament single-handed – they'd managed a good twenty miles, which wasn't bad going in hock-deep spring thaw and straggling along behind the artillery. It was hard to make someone two yards tall feel about the size of a thumbnail, but Fairfax seemed to have managed it. His temper was not improved by Venning's lolloping great dog, shoving his cold wet nose rudely into Hollie's hand.

Venning, however, seemed to have bucked his ideas up remarkable. "All right then, Ro –" he remembered they were dining in company, even if that company was only Chedglow and Webb. "Colonel Babbitt. Sir."

As quarters went, they were disturbingly elegant, and he couldn't even blame that on Lucey's influential friends and relations this time. Any house that was big enough to accomodate two companies of horse at a time, and then to facilitate feeding of same, even if it was only on bread and cheese and promises of anonymous stew – took some doing. Chedglow cleared his throat, preparing to say grace. He was a presumptuous whoreson, as well as a hypocritical one. Drew Venning met Hollie's eye with a bland smile and kicked the table so that Chedglow's wine-glass tipped into his lap, staining his hodden-gray breeches dark.

"It's a sign," Hollie said sweetly. "*Be not among winebibbers; among riotous eaters of flesh* – the Book of Proverbs, captain. The Lord does not favour your presence at table."

Chedglow's mouth worked, trying to think of a suitably godly retort.

"I reckon the Lord might intend you for officer of the watch, this night," Hollie went on, hoping he was keeping a straight face. "Because I surely do."

It was an interminable supper, generous and bland and not a patch on the food at White Notley, and he found himself looking round the house, wondering what Het might like. If she had to have an absentee husband, she might as well have one who tried to keep abreast of fashion, a little bit. (In Northwich?) Wondered if she'd welcome a twist of salt, for the novelty of it, given her closeness to the salt at Maldon at home. It went on. He'd half a letter to her, written in his head, and he longed for his bed and a pen and a bit of paper, but Webb had had a cup or two of wine too many and was in the mood to talk blusterous, of battles he'd won single-handed and great men who'd nodded to him in passing, and so Hollie sat, nodding in the right places and thinking of what anecdotes of troop life he might in all decency tell his wife, the better to amuse her and comfort her.

It was over, eventually, and he went yawning to his bed, intending to cast an eye at least over his own company before retiring, and reassure himself that he had not brought the hosts of Midian, no matter what Fairfax might imply.

Luce tagged at his heels. "They've not broke owt, then." Hollie said, with satisfaction.

"It appears not, no. I think Sergeant Cullis keeps them in order, while we're without –"

"A lieutenant," Hollie finished, "I know. It's all right, brat, you can say it. I don't take it as a slight on my judgement."

Luce smiled wanly. Russell did not seem an inspired choice for authority, presently. He had his head on his folded arms on the table, unconscious of the rowdy supper taking place around him. It was not the first time he'd been passed out cold with his head in his supper, and it would likely not be the last.

It was almost nothing. Gray leaned forward, and moved Russell's pale hair out of his supper. That was all.

Gray moved Russell's loose hair out of the congealing contents of his bowl. Gray, who cared for nothing and no-one.

Interesting.

40

HORSEMEN OF THE APOCALYPSE

"Rupert," Hollie said with grim satisfaction.

"Belasyse," Fairfax said, giving him a stern look, "you cannot blame Rupert for *everything*, Holofernes."

Someone elsewhere in the room snickered and Hollie, who could look bloody intimidating when he put his mind to it, lifted his head and glowered in the direction of the perpetrator. It being a better alternative than glowering at Fairfax, for giving away that of all the officers present at this briefing, there was only one with a conspicuously zealous upbringing.

"Rupert," Hollie went on, undiverted, "relieved the siege at Newark. And if he hadn't done that, we wouldn't be up to the ars –"

"Elbows," Henry Fowles said sweetly. (Fowles had served with Hollie at Fairfax's hand, the last time he was in Yorkshire. He was pleased to see him back, and he knew Hollie's absent-minded cursing of old.)

"There are some folk as can't tell the difference between the two anyway," Hollie said, and that easily-amused bugger at the back snorted again. "Whichever. We're up to 'em with Malignant cavalry who would not have been there if Rupert had not relieved the siege at Newark and freed 'em up to go pounding all over the countryside seeking for whom they may devour. So it *is* all his fault."

"It's raining," Venning pointed out. "How's that Rupert's fault?"

"Give us a minute, lad, and I'll work summat out," Hollie muttered darkly.

Colonel John Lambert had left Cheshire about a month before Fairfax, and had been making himself systematically unhelpful to the Malignants ever since. Having taken something of a hammering in the West Riding himself last year, Hollie did not envy anyone whose allotted task it was to hold Bradford as a garrison, given its somewhat indefensible nature. Bloody horrible place, it was. He'd never set eyes on Lambert, but he had heard great things about the man. Heard that he was not so much hot against the King but implacable against him. And, you know, Hollie was fond of Noll Cromwell, in a somewhat wary, little bit too much like his father for comfort, kind of way. Lambert, if he was what they said, Hollie thought he might understand. Brought up in one of those old-fashioned manors on the bleak edge of civilisation – piss-poor family hanging on to gentrification by the skin of their teeth, though Lambert's background was in wool and Hollie's in horses, and Hollie was pretty sure his own lot had never been in debt like the Lambert family had been. But then, that was wool for you, it was unpredictable, and the one thing you could guarantee in this world was that as long as there was trade somewhere men would need horses.

That, and Lambert was good at what he did, and Hollie was funny like that. Any man who could do a thing that Hollie had tried to do and failed, and do it well, commanded his respect. He had no good memory of Bradford or the West Riding, not a one, save as a place where he'd made a good friend in Black Tom. Though not always as good a friend in the official capacity of Sir Thomas Fairfax, and there was a difference. He was well aware of that. (And had met little Moll Fairfax, and she had been the first small girl-child he had ever made the personal acquaintance of. That was a bright blessing, one small brand from the burning – God bless and keep that dear little mite.)

Well, Lambert had kept his footing in Bradford, the stubborn terrier – what did they call them scraggy little dogs hereabouts, a tyke? Lambert in Bradford, and the King's man Belasyse stood off at Selby, another town Hollie had no kind memory of.

He wondered what it might feel like, being Lambert, at this time. Whether the man was afraid, or zealous, or anxious, or which, feeling the King's Army breathing down his neck but knowing Fairfax was on his way.

Whether it was a comfort, or if he was thinking – bloody get *on* with it, Thomas!

"You know they have been hard pressed at Bradford," Fairfax said smoothly, which was something of an understatement, Lambert had been more than hard pressed – the bugger had been practically flat.

"*Peine forte et dure*," Luce murmured at Hollie's elbow, and Fairfax twitched a little and gave the brat a brief, startled look of unqualified admiration. (There were times it was lovely to have your own personal Erasmus, Hollie thought smugly, watching a ripple of raised eyebrows around the room.)

"Summat like. Except that he wiggled out of it –"

"By the Lord's grace," Fairfax said sternly, and Hollie grinned.

"By the Lord's grace. And a deal of good luck and sheer brass neck on the part of the Colonel. We have been there, sir, we know exactly what it's like roughing it in Bradford running low on shot and with half the King's Army up –"

"Sir," Lucey said warningly, and Hollie, who knew exactly what he was about to say, carried straight on with a smooth, "- up the Calder Valley."

It had been touch and go for Lambert, almost overwhelmed by Belasyse and his backup come hot-foot from Newark in the guise of Major-General Porter's cavalry. He'd beaten them back, again and again, and then Hollie could only assume he'd got bored of being battered: regrouped, and broken out of the town intent on the serious business of giving Porter a taste of his own medicine. He bloody had, as well. Porter's cavalry had scattered to the four winds, clearly not liking to take it as much as they liked to give it. Porter himself had been sent back to Newark with his tail between his legs, deep in disgrace, and Belasyse had gone scuttling back into Selby and shut the door behind him.

"So, then, gentlemen," Fairfax said, with that rare, sweet smile. "That's where we are. I doubt very much if my lord Belasyse is just going to open up and hand us the keys, when we come knocking, after that. My guess is that the gentleman in question may be a little touchy on his honour, after Colonel Lambert bloodied his nose for him. Are we prepared for a fierce fight?"

"'S Rosie," Venning said comfortably. "It don't get much hotter than where our Rosie is."

"Bloody madman," Fowles muttered, sounding quite affectionate. "What do we do, then, sir? Not you, Rosie, I know what *you* mean to do. I've seen you do it."

"Frightening, ain't it?" Venning said. "And we're on the same side. God help the Malignants when they see that lunatic come barrelling down on 'em. And now we got Russell, just for the full set. Red horse, a black horse, and the Grim Reaper –"

"Well, I think we have ascertained Colonel Babbitt's campaign plan, then, provided he leaves anything for the rest of us to do?" Never sure with Fairfax whether he was offended or amused. He had that very dry sense of humour, and you had to look at his eyes to see if he was laughing or not, because the rest of his face was as blank as a stone wall, in company.

"*Colonel* Babbitt?" Fowles squawked. "When'd that happen?"

"About a month ago, while you lot were still squelching around in Cheshire stuffing your heads with cheese. *Some* of us was getting promoted."

"It was the only way to keep you out of any further trouble, Holofernes," Fairfax said sweetly. "And how *is* your unfortunate lieutenant these days? He does seem to have been somewhat quiet?"

Which made two of them: Fairfax knew damn well how Thankful Russell was, because he'd seen him only last week on the march down. He hadn't said a lot, but his eyebrows had raised, and he'd blinked a bit.

"Quiet. Aye," Hollie said uncomfortably, and refused to comment further. Such was gossip, and he didn't hold with tittle-tattle. Anyway, these last few days Russell seemed to be touching on his old self again, at times. He definitely had clean linen, even if it wasn't particularly good linen, he had shaved, his hair was combed. He had been known to smile, if he didn't think anyone was looking. He hadn't, precisely, turned over a new leaf, but so far as he could be predicted to be anywhere and doing anything, he tended to be somewhere near Gray, most of the time. An unlikely friendship, but so far, it was keeping Gray out of trouble and Russell alive, and you couldn't ask for much more.

He didn't know who either of their people were, but Christ, he'd had to write to his lads' families before now, and say that a man they'd known, a man they'd birthed, breeched, stood up in church and promised with, who'd sat at their table and laboured to put bread on it – wasn't a man any more, but a thing of clay, with not so much as a grave-marker to mind him by. And he wouldn't do it again, not when he had any power over it. (Someone would do it for him, one day. He was a soldier. He knew that.) Someone would write to Het one day, and tell her that he'd been a good man, and brave at the last, and that she should be proud. Be a thumping bloody lie, because he wasn't especially good, and if she knew the half of what he got up to, she'd not be proud at all, but that was what you wrote, kind lies. And you put money in with it, what you could afford, what was owing, and you hoped it made up for six lines on a ragged bit of paper, signed by a man with a stiff right hand whose writing wasn't always the best, whose name you didn't know.

Even Hapless bloody Russell had been birthed, though he might like to imply he'd been found, fully grown, under a gooseberry bush in the Earl of Essex's garden. Someone would miss the bugger, if some harm came to him. Gray, likewise. Someone would miss Gray. With luck, they might even come looking for him.

"I'll behave myself," he said gloomily.

"The Lord will make them as stubble to our swords," Chedglow added, and Hollie looked up at Venning and neither of them said a word, although Venning's expression was priceless.

Webb grunted, because that was what he did. "Sir," Hollie prompted, out of malice. "You are in a senior officer's company, Captain Webb. You will address your seniors with respect."

41

DREAM OF THE FLOOD

It rained. And it kept on raining, and the water kept rising, and they kept waiting. It felt like a hundred years, and Hollie was getting into a habit which he knew was starting to get on people's nerves – sending patrols out twice a day, looking. Looking for Lord Fairfax senior, who was on his way over from Hull. For Colonel Lambert, on his way from Bradford, and Sir John Meldrum from the Midlands. (He'd a lot of sympathy for Meldrum, too, who was too bloody old to be careering about the countryside with a pack of rebels, and had been honest enough to write an open letter to His Majesty telling him that after thirty-six years of loyal service, the most he'd got out of it was debts of over three thousand quid. Hollie could think of a number of better uses he'd have put three thousand pounds to, than supporting that arrogant Papist whelk.)

It wasn't the fact of his sending patrols out turn and turn about that was getting on his men's nerves, though, it was his humour of ordering them to look for gopher wood while they were about it, or bring back a breeding pair of Malignants. Luce got him back a proper one, right in front of everybody, by suggesting that if he was so keen on fetching a raven for this mythical Ark of his, perhaps someone ought to ride post back to Essex and fetch the company's own personal Elijah?

Chedglow didn't find it funny, not at all. Chedglow was out on as many patrols as Hollie could conceive, it being the only way he could think of to stop the horrible man from preaching from day's end to day's end, stirring up zeal amongst the ranks. Zeal was all very well, but zeal had a tendency to do stupid things on the field, in the hope of impressing the Lord with your fervour. Zeal was, pretty much, ungovernable. (Said Hollie, who was, pretty much, ungovernable himself, and who knew whereof he spoke.)

Lucey was in his element, bouncing about worse than Venning's dog, running messages up and down the lines all day. He had it in his head at the moment to write some kind of epic verse about Noah and the Flood, and there'd been a point round about noon where he had in fact asked Hollie whether he thought "the beasts were taken on in pairs" could be made to rhyme with "lions, doves, and hounds and bears".

Hollie had not screwed up his warning orders and shoved them down his cornet's throat with a pointed stick, but he had had to look sternly aside over the sullen grey expanse of the Ouse so as not to laugh out loud, which would have been both unkind and inappropriate.

The river was wide, and pewter-gray, and seething, silently, between its banks.

Not between its banks. *Over* its banks.

Hollie scratched his head irritably, then dismounted, looked around for that pointed stick he hadn't jammed Lucey's poetry down his neck with, and jammed it instead into the draggled grass at the lapping edge of the waterline. And then remounted Tyburn, and very carefully backed him up a length, and sat with his wrists folded on the black stallion's rain-pearled mane.

Luce was eyeing him as if he'd lost his wits, and he said nothing, but simply sat, in silence.

He was used to looking like a tit in company, and he didn't hardly count Luce as company, any more. Watching the river. Watching a duck, or a coot, or some damn' kind of benighted water-bird, paddle slowly into distant view in the slow-moving waters, and up-end itself.

"Are we waiting for something particular, Hollie?" Luce said patiently, and he nodded at the stick.

"Watch the stick, brat."

"It's a good stick, I'm sure, but –"

"All right, then, look for the broken branch, about three inches up. That little white notch, where the wood's split."

There was another long silence. "Hollie, um, have you gone poetical?

Because, you know, the broken branch as a metaphor, it's a good one, but – well, you know, it's kind of well-used. I'd look for something a little bit more, you know –"

"Submerged?" Hollie said, and Luce blinked at him.

"What?"

It had been a suspicion. It was still only a suspicion. It was a slightly wetter suspicion than it had been. There was a chilly little wind starting to get up, ruffling the water so that it lapped around the bottom of the stick. It was starting to lean, a little, as the water deepened.

"They've opened the fucking dam, Luce. They're flooding the fields. Clever little bastards. Fair enough. If they want to play silly buggers, me and you can play silly buggers right back at 'em." He jerked his head. "Pull the lads in. There's only Venning got webbed feet, out of our lot. And if you see Black Tom, tell him we're in for a wet night of it."

Tyburn tossed his head, harness chinking wetly, and gave a halfhearted rear. His forefeet came down into the mud with a sucking thud, and the black horse stepped abruptly backwards with his ears flattening. "I'm with Tib on this one," Hollie said. "Get the hell out, Luce. It's rising. And faster than it looks."

42

DAM FIELDS

It was difficult to imagine Drew Venning's freckled, pleasant face as anything other than cheerfully amused, but he hadn't been expecting Russell, and Russell hadn't been expecting him, and the pair of them stood gawping at each other in mutual shock for a second.

Venning was the first to recover his wits. "Trooper Russell," he said, in that crisp and accentless professional voice you only ever heard out of Venning when he was well and truly wrong-footed. "Was – was that you? Cackling like a – a setting hen half across Dam Fields?"

"*Me*? Do I strike you as a man much given to public hilarity, captain?"

Venning leaned in and sniffed, thoughtfully. "Not for another few jars, lad, no. What's 'ee up to, lad?"

"Are you implying that I am not entirely sober, sir?"

"Ent implying nawthen, bor, but it looks hell of a funny. Here's me, stood out here – pitched in to take sentry 'stead of Carew, lad can't stray too far from the privy today, poor bugger – stood here, scratching me backside and minding me business, looking out at fourteen square miles o' water." He shook his head absently. "Don't half remind me of home, all them drowned fields, just a few fence posts stuck up hither and yon, nawthen but frogs and ducks for bloody miles – anyways. There I am, enjoying me bit o' peace and solitude, and then all of a sudden there's you and Eliot of all people, plodgin' up the field looking purposeful. And you was cackling, Russell, you was cackling." He screwed one eye shut and squinted at Russell. "What's 'ee up to?"

"Home," Russell said, tucking a wisp of loose hair behind his ear and surveying the drowned landscape before him. A single raven flew across the face of the setting sun, croaking mournfully, and the air was beginning to grow chill. "Looks like home, you say." There was a long silence, broken only by the soft squelch of Venning's boots as he shifted his weight patiently in the sludge. "Do you know a great deal about boats, Captain Venning?"

"You what?"

Russell patiently outlined his plan.

"You *what*?" Eliot squawked, not having been previously aware of the half of it. "Are you out of your fucking tiny *mind*?"

"Less of your foul language in front of the captain, trooper," Russell said blithely. "It seems a remarkably simple plan to me, gentlemen. We take a small boat, and a barrel of powder. We row across the – fields – " he giggled again, and then pulled himself up, bright-eyed – "pop it outside the barricade, leave our little friends an incendiary calling-card, and, as our estimable commander would have it, we blow the fucker to bits. Simple. What's not to like?"

"Russell, you *are* out of your tiny mind."

"*Au contraire, mon brave.* Very much *in* my right mind, and tired of being bored out of it. Now. Either you can come – or you can tell me which end of a boat is which, captain, and I'll do it myself."

"We haven't *got* a boat, Russell."

"So make one. You're the expert."

It seemed ever so reasonable, looking at the neat, bright-eyed, enthusiastic Russell, bouncing, ever so slightly, with the wind blowing his hair in his eyes. Anybody'd think the lad wasn't mad as cheese, Venning thought. "Let me get this straight in my head here. So you want me to find you a spare barrel o' powder, and then you and this bright lad here are going to go paddling up the river, in a boat what you haven't found yet, and knock on the back door and ask Belasyse if he'd mind letting you in?"

"That's right, captain."

"Russell, you *are* a bloody nutjob, aren't you?"

"I imagine so, captain." He gave another one of his mad lopsided smiles. "Have I then your authority to draw powder?"

"No!" It came out rather louder than Venning had intended, more of a strangled yelp than an authoritarian bellow. "You can get back to your post and –"

"And?" A pause that bordered on the insubordinate. "...Sir?"

"Back to your post, trooper. And no more of this daft talk."

"Sir." And Russell wheeled about and went splashing back up the fields, whistling tunelessly to himself. He didn't, quite, have his hands in his pockets, but he was giving that impression, and he wasn't fooling Drew Venning for a minute.

"Trooper Eliot, you can just bloody well go after him, and – and that's an *order*, trooper. Tie the little bugger to a tree. Knock him on the head if you have to, and that's *not* an order, you understand me? But whatever cockeyed plot he's up to, stop him."

"You're *ordering* me to assault Trooper Russell, Captain Venning?"

"Thass right, lad. Off you go."

Eliot stood with his mouth open, revealing a row of unlovely stained yellow teeth. Then he saluted in a dazed manner and started to trail after Russell. "Best put a bit o' speed on, if 'ee wants to catch 'en up," Venning said helpfully, and then settled himself more comfortably to watch the sun set over the Ouse.

43

HIGHER GROUND

Hollie scratched under his ponytail thoughtfully. "Ousegate," he said.

"That's right, colonel. What are you doing?"

He was holding one hand up, fingers spread. "Checking for flippers, sir. Because last time I looked neither me nor four troop of horse had webbed feet. And it's about three foot high and rising out there."

"Indeed, colonel. And that's why it's your position – mine also, sir, I might remind you – to attack across the flooded fields."

"Aye, I know that. I understand that. With respect, sir, I appreciate the logic in what you're saying, but – uh, it's raining, sir?"

"You won't melt, Rosie," Fowles said with gentle malice, and Hollie gave him a stern look.

"I won't. Not being a bloody fish, Henry, I might struggle somewhat getting my horse, who as you may have noticed is a big old boy – even my Tib's going to be belly-deep coming across Dam Fields. It's not going to be a charge, sir, it's going to be a massacre. Nice bit of target practice for Belasyse, I'm sure."

Fairfax looked at him sadly. "Yes. Yes, I rather fear that it is, Holofernes. But no more so for us than it will be for Meldrum's men, or Needham's, on foot. You and I have fought those streets before, colonel. We know how hard it will be. We have no alternative."

He knew that. With the King dug in at York, there was no option, not if they wanted to clear him out, once and for all, like a nest of rats. Leave the shifty little bugger at York and next thing you'd have Rupert panting down the back of your neck, and then the North would be on fire again, and to be honest Hollie could do without it. He lived in Essex, now. Everybody he loved was out at Essex, if not precisely out of harm's way, then at least on higher ground.

– Grudgingly, he might admit that he was glad the old bastard was yet at White Notley. Because if it did all go down, if this was going to be the waterlogged end of days, at least she wouldn't be left unprotected. She'd have *someone*. Even if it was only him.

Rosie, thee grows maudlin.

Aye, but before, there had not been Het, there had not been the child, had she a name? did she yet *live*, even? There had not been anyone to care, before, and he sort of had it in his head that once he cared, some vengeful Old Testament God like his father's might take them as a hostage to his faith, like Abraham and Isaac in the Bible.

Thee will come about. Thee always does.

"Lose his foothold in York, and we can scour him out of the North," Fowles said softly. "Lose Selby, and His Majesty cannot hold York – no, not though the Robber Prince bring every single one of his troops to bear on us. Lose Selby, and he loses the river."

"Lose Selby," Fairfax said, equally softly, "and the North is lost. The King has not treated us well in the North Country, Holofernes. You know that. You know what we have suffered, with the poor price of wool, and taxation. How many good families have lost all, under His Majesty's misguided direction. Ask Lambert. He'll tell you."

"I'm not –" Not a North Countryman? Not in need of convincing? He shoved the sleeves of his buffcoat up his wrists like a man setting to do a dirty job, and realised what he was doing, and laughed awkwardly. "Not arguing," he finished, and ducked his head, because suddenly he was one of them again, and not doubting. Much.

"Makes a change," Fairfax muttered, and then gave him that rare, sweet, flashing grin. "We've all got families we care for, Rosie, you're not on your own. Trust in the Lord –"

"But keep your powder dry," someone muttered, that being the current joke amongst the common soldiery, and there was a ripple of laughter.

"Better hope it stops raining, then," Fairfax said, "hadn't we? Because we go in at dusk."

Dusk. Across waterlogged, treacherous fields, where a galloping horse might stumble and break a leg, or ditch a plated cavalryman to drown in the sluggish black Ouse. Fowles, for once, was the first to speak. "May I, sir – with respect, sir – are you out of your *mind*, sir?"

"No, Henry. Though I imagine it may come as a surprise to our friends within." He smiled, without much humour. "I hope, for the Lord knows we will need all the advantage we can get."

44

A GAME OF CHANCE

Out across the river, in the gathering darkness, Luce could see the first warm amber flares of campfires through the thin rain.

Campfires, and within the city, people were beginning to light candles. Sitting to their suppers, probably. Talking of the day, making children ready for bed, like his mam did at home, listening through the wall to her hearing Bab's prayers. Luce wondered if there was a little Yorkshire girl in one of those houses, kneeling beside the bed with her hair in bunchy bedtime braids. Whether she was frightened by all the soldiers, or if she was young enough to just shrug her shoulders like Bab did, it was just some funny humour of grown men to make themselves dislikeable.

Now I lay me down to sleep –

More important was supper. He could smell the woodsmoke, comfortable, homely. Like being back at his own home, like standing in the garden at Witham, a half-mile from the river. If he closed his eyes, and if he couldn't hear people talking in the funny, flat Yorkshire accent, he might almost be back at home, and any minute now Bab might come thumping out into the garden to tell him his supper was on the table and did he mean to stand there letting it go cold all night.

And instead, the Ouse was lapping, gently, at his boots and somewhere out in the dusk a horse whinnied, and there was a burst of laughter, and someone further away shouted a challenge or a greeting. And Luce was at war, and in Yorkshire, and he could still forget that, sometimes.

There were shapes, moving. A long, formless, shape, and a small, formless shape, and a squat, black one. He put his hand on his sword, automatically. "Who's there?"

One white face, in the cat's-light, jerking towards him. Thankful Russell might have covered his very distinctive barley-blonde hair with a greasy knitted cap, and he might be wearing neither plate nor boots, but that scar on his face was unmistakable. And Gray, barely standing shoulder-high to him, all eyes and dirty hair.

And Eliot, looking horrified.

"What," Luce said, carefully, "what do you think you're doing?"

"Nothing," Russell said, equally carefully. And Gray shook his – her – head, and Gray was a *rotten* liar. "Nothing," she said, wide-eyed.

"It's him," Eliot said, though. "He's bloody mad."

"Russell?"

"Nothing," he said, and, "Still nothing," Gray said, and Luce had to stifle a grin because of all things they *were* quite funny. But. He was still officer of the watch, and those two were as guilty as sin, though he wasn't sure of what.

"I suggest you two turn round, and go back to your unit, and stop messing about. And we'll say no more about this."

Eliot did, and Russell flung his head up and made to brush past Luce, who caught at his arm and was about to say something sharp. Before he had his mouth open suddenly found himself flat on his back in the mud with all the breath knocked out of him. Unhurt, but stunned, and wholly bemused.

He could see two pairs of scuffling feet out of the corner of his eye, though, and he was in possession of himself sufficient to roll out of the way when he heard the sharp slap of flesh on flesh, and struggled to his hands and knees to find Gray looking mad and mutinous, rubbing her hand-printed cheek.

"What did you do –"

"He hit me!" she squalled, and Russell cocked an eyebrow.

"I'm not the first, and I won't be the last. Striking a superior officer is a hanging offence, you witless child. Do you plan to stand here brangling all day?" And he was gone, sidestepping ankle-deep into the sodden grass, heading purposefully up the river.

"Russell you will return to your commanding officer and that is an order!"

"I shall not," he said over his shoulder.

"I will have you taken into custody and detained, trooper, if you carry on!"

Russell turned all the way round, and grinned his mad lopsided grin. "Detain me, cornet, and I may assure you I shall hang myself. And make a better job of it, this time."

Gray snarled like a little dog, a long, low, bubbling noise. (Most unmaidenly.) "He bloody well means it. Eliot – come *on*."

"What the hell are you thinking?" Luce yelped. "Are you *deserting*?"

"I bloody wish," Eliot muttered, "going up the bloody river, ent we. Smart lad here wants powder, and powder we shall bloody well have. He got some cockeyed idea in his head about lifting it off the Malignants and blowing the buggers sky-high with their own powder. Captain Venning wouldn't give him permission to do it, so he was going to go off anyway. Couldn't let the daft bugger do that, could I? Get his damn fool head shot off."

"Why, trooper, I begin to believe you may have a better nature after all," Russell muttered. "You're holding me up. Come, or do not come, but *get a bloody move on!*"

"No," Luce said, "no – wait – why?"

"Because if you think my idea's cockeyed, cornet, you didn't hear the orders as given to Ro- to the Colonel. We attack at nightfall, in the dark, over flooded fields. We go in the tradesman's entrance, Meldrum's coming in from the east, and Needham's coming in from the west. The left hand is not going to have the faintest idea what the right hand is doing. It will be carnage, cornet. I am merely doing my poor best to level the odds a little. Given my new facility at games of chance."

Luce blinked at him. "Thankful –"

"Not Trooper Russell?" he said, curiously, and Luce shook his head. "No. Not now. Thankful, you'll be killed."

He shrugged. "One way or another, we all die. In the Lord's grace, one hopes."

Luce took a deep breath, and put a hand on the sash at his waist. Warm, and smooth, and a little worn, now, a little darned at the point where it had rubbed on a tiny snag on his breastplate. He was proud of that sash. He was very fond of that sash. He wasn't the best officer in the world, but he did his own poor best to level the odds, and sometimes, he got it right. He fumbled a little with the knot that held it in place: his mind's way of telling him not to be so damnably stupid, he supposed. It almost slithered to the ground, and he caught it, the folds of three yards of silk tumbling through his fingers like a lass's hair.

"What are you doing, Lucey?" Gray said curiously.

"Give me a hand with my plate," he said. That inner voice that had assured him that Gray was trouble, that it'd all end in tears, was sniffing smugly. "I'm coming with you."

"You are –what?"

"Coming with you."

"For why?" she said, slightly muffled by having her head in the small of his back where she was fighting with a damp-stiff strap holding his plate in place.

He looked down at her, and back at Russell, who looked back, so far as Russell could be said to have any expression at all, with a look of incredulity. "The pleasure of your company, gentlemen," he said. "Eliot, would you be so good as to take my –" he wasn't that confident. His voice wobbled a little. "My harness, back to the colonel. You may, if you would be so good, give the colours to Matthew Percey."

Eliot's mouth was slightly ajar. "Oh. Aye. Sir."

"And – and Eliot. Tell him, if you would. Tell him. I am sorry, for any inconvenience this may cause. And that – that he has my mother's direction."

"You don't have to come," Russell said. He sounded rather oddly shy, like a child who'd been given a thing he coveted, but didn't yet know what to do with.

"Oh, I don't know." He tied his hair back with a bit of cord he'd found in his pocket. Shook his head to see if it stayed out of his eyes. (It did.) He had a strange, tickly bubble of excitement mixed with the fear in his belly. Of being off the leash, a little bit wild, a little bit dangerous. More than a little bit free. "I imagine it might be quite fun. Shall we?"

45

RAHAB IS LOOSE AMONGST US

"What are we going to do," Luce hissed, two miles up the riverbank and on foot and drenched to the knees, and Gray put her finger to her lips. Then he saw the Malignant sentry rise up twenty yards in front of them with his musket cocked, and then Russell hit him in the belly.

Choking and crowing for breath, curled round like a pillbug, all he could hear was the chilly, precise voice over his head saying, "Well, well, gentlemen, I appear to have found a rebel. Spying. What do you suggest I do with him?"

"You what?"

"A rebel spy. Take the stoppers from your ears."

"Who the bloody hell might you be, then?"

"Lieutenant Russell, sir," he said, and that cold voice sounded quite affronted that this imbecile sentry did not know who he was. "I thought I should have been one of the more distinctive members of my lord Belasyse's household?"

And, indeed, Luce did not know who he was, not any more, and he was suddenly afraid that he might have given himself willing into the hands of an unpredictable, black-brilliant man who might, or might not, feel himself hard done to by his commanding officer at being stripped of his own rank. And may, or may not, be prepared to exchange the life of an enemy officer for an officer's sash – be it royal blue or rebel tawny. "Russell, I don't think –" he began, in a tiny cracked voice he barely recognised as his own, and that strange, chilly Russell wheeled and kicked him full in the face.

"Shut up," he said, perfectly calmly, and while Luce was still writhing and bleeding and crying, Gray wound her hand in his hair and dragged him to his feet and wrenched his head back so that he stood choking on his own blood, mewing like a kitten.

"Well, then? Where is Sir John?" Russell said irritably, and it was being borne on Luce depressingly quickly that he would break, he would tell them anything, anything at all, if they only would not hurt him any more. He could barely see for blood and matted hair in his eyes, and the sentry was staring at all three of them.

"Here, you just stop that, you – you scar-faced whelp, you leave that boy be! You don't treat a man that like that!"

"Even if he is a spy?"

"He's a bloody prisoner of war, then, and you can treat him with some respect! Who do you think you are, boy, jumping up out of nowhere and ordering me about?"

"I told you, sir – Lieutenant Russell, out of Belasyse's household, and if you doubt me you can send a messenger to ask him – and hope that the rebels don't mount an attack while we're waiting, as this piece of scum admits they plan!"

He raised his hand, and he would have slapped Luce across his much-abused, bruised mouth again, if the sentry had not grabbed his arm. And then released Russell very quickly, as the scarred young man turned round with his mad lopsided grin. "Starting something with me, trooper? Give me Sir John's direction, and be quick about it, or I swear before God it will go hard for all of you."

He was shaking, and the muscle in his cheek was starting to twitch again, and Luce gave an involuntary little sob.

And very gently, Gray pressed her knuckles against his scalp, where the hair was beginning to tear loose under her fierce grip.

And he thought, he dared to hope, that it was meant to comfort, though he was not comforted, much.

"He's down at the Staith," the sentry said.

"Well, I thank God for it! We have a sufficiency of shot, I hope? That being what I hope he is doing?" Russell pushed officiously past the startled sentry. "They mean an assault," he flung over his shoulder. "Tonight. I did manage to extract so much from this dunghill cock."

"No," Luce whimpered, he had said nothing, he had not told anyone, had not said anything to Russell, even when the fair-haired young man drew his sword and rested the tip very gently in the hollow of Luce's throat, leaning just hard enough to restrict his breathing.

"He is a rebel," Russell said. "One less is no hardship, God knows. The godless vermin will be trying their best to breach us, come midnight. Take us in, trooper."

He didn't remember too much about the town of Selby from the last time, other than that there had been a garden wall with an overhanging climbing rose, and that as they rode underneath it Hollie Babbitt had broken a bloom from it and tucked it behind his ear, laughing, saying the red rose of Lancashire was a token that he hadn't got wholly native.

He thought they might have passed the same garden wall, because on foot, the thorns clawed at his eyes, and he whimpered a little again, under his breath this time because it didn't help. His wrists were bound before him with a length of linen torn roughly from the tail of his shirt, and Gray had her pistol in the base of his spine. And she was whistling. Somehow that was the more horrible, that as they passed knots of tense soldiers, all glaring at them, poised for the fight they knew was coming – Gray was whistling, perfectly casually. And Russell, striding along a length in front, nodding curtly at the occasional man, perfectly at his ease.

They passed the first of the barricades. "Spy," the sentry said.

"Going to hang him, then?"

"Prob'ly. But they're coming in tonight, lad here says. Might not need to." He sounded sad, and Luce wanted to weep again. Just in front of him, he saw Russell incline his head graciously.

"Midnight," he said. "They mean to catch us unawares, I conceive."

There was a mewling, whining note in Russell's voice that Luce did not like, as if he were a pettish child demanding reward. "Well," he said sulkily, "where is Belasyse? I need to see him!"

The sentry looked up at him with disgust. "I imagine he's got better things to do with his time than wait on your convenience. He's down the river, mate. Doing his job."

Russell twined his hand in Luce's hair and pulled his head up sharply, and Luce whimpered because he couldn't help it, he had not been expecting that, what with Gray's pistol in his ribs and Russell tearing his hair out by the roots –

"Will you stop doing that!" the sentry snapped, "he's not resisting, he's done nothing to you!"

"Do you know who this is?" Gray said curtly.

"She –" Luce began desperately, and Russell hit him again.

"Hold your tongue, spy. That, sir, is one of Fairfax's own personal company. Look at him. D'you not recognise him?"

He pulled Luce's head up a little bit further, and Luce went rigid.

"Chedglow," Russell said, quite coolly. "Sariel Chedglow, the canting puritanical bastard. Or Penitence, if you prefer. See? I've heard quite a lot from Captain Chedglow, in the last few hours. I believe he might tell me anything I chose to ask, now."

In the flaring torchlight by the makeshift barricade, Russell's lopsided smile was a thing of horror, all teeth and ridges of scarring, and the sentry winced involuntarily.

"Aye," he said, "I've heard of Chedglow, but he – he's dark, isn't he?"

"He washed," Gray said.

"Rahab is loose amongst us," Russell said ardently, and then said, "*Loose*," with an odd emphasis.

Rahab is loose amongst us. Loose.

Luce.

He looked up, blinking the blood out of his eyes, and behind him, Gray pushed something into the waistband of his breeches.

Her second pistol, by the feel of it.

"Take us in, then," Russell said again, and the sentry nodded, not taking his eyes off the scarred young man's face.

"You are a fucking nutter," he said again, starting to sound a little nervous, and Russell inclined his head.

"Not unlikely, I grant. I will stop at nothing, sir. Nothing. To see my cause victorious. March on."

They marched, or at the least, they staggered, with Luce prodded from behind by a scuttling Gray and dragged from the front by a stalking Russell, at the elbow of a sentry who couldn't bring himself to look at any of them.

Stopped at the inner barricades by another knot of soldiers, nervous, jittery, the torchlight glinting on cocked muskets and drawn swords and wide eyes.

"Oh for God's sake Paul! Tha's supposed to be stood by for action, not rounding up bloody – boys! What was they doing, helping theirselves to apples?"

Their sentry – his name was Paul, then. Paul who looked like someone's father, and had the beginnings of a paunch under his soldier's coat, and whose cuffs were black with powder – laughed uncomfortably, scratching under his hat, tipping it into his eyes.

"Aye, well, wish I could just leave 'em be, but this one here –" he jerked his head at Russell, "he reckons this one's a rebel spy, so he'd have him brought in for questioning. More questioning," he added, with a scowl at Russell.

"Oh aye? And where's he dropped off of? The moon? Don't recognise your face, boy, and the look of you, you're hard to mistake?"

"Belasyse's staff," Russell said coolly. "Been with him since Reading, in case you were too blind to notice. I was about ten yards behind him at Caversham Bridge, sir, and I could tell you what horse he rides and what suit he wore, should you misdoubt me? And this filth –" he shook Luce roughly by the hair again, "this damnable little scut was spying out the land, ready for an attack tonight. Midnight tonight, I say, they plan to attack by the dark of the moon and catch us unawares, and unless you let me pass with this traitor that's exactly what they will do!"

Paul blew his cheeks out. "The bugger of it is –"

"That he's right. Aye. I'd heard they was massing for the attack. If I hadn't know that…"

"Coming from up the river," Russell snarled, "I found this bastard lurking by Thorpe wood," and he would have aimed a kick at Luce had their own sentry not pulled him off-balance by the elbow.

"Shit."

"'s what I said, lad. Take 'em in, there's a good lad. I'm overdue coming off duty, me, I don't –"

"*Me?*" the guardian of the inner gates squawked, "I ain't going near Belasyse wi' that mess of bloody trouble. You can fetch 'em in, Paul, and I hope to God he promotes you for your pains!"

"Thanks!" Grumbling, he slouched through the gap in the makeshift barricade – "That's a bloody kitchen table, Bob Alliss, what you gone and put that there for?"

"Don't want none o' them bloody rebels getting in, that's what. Get 'em in and we'll never get 'em out. Took us nigh on four months to get the place straight after last time. Hey! Password, sunshine?"

"Oh, very funny –"

"Password, or you ain't coming in!"

"You know very well who I am, your brother's wife's sister is my Ellen's gossip!"

"We are wasting time, sir!" Russell hissed, and because it was Russell, and he looked like the wrath of God in the torchlight, Alliss flinched a little, but did not stand down.

"Aye. No doubt. But then if you're one of my lord Belasyse's staff, you won't mind giving me the watchword for the day, will you?"

"The watchword," Gray said, cocking her – other – pistol, "is we haven't got time for this shit. Let us pass. Now."

"Thief Lane," Paul said, "happy? Now let us go, will you!"

"With pleasure," Alliss said, giving them a mock bow. "Be nice to see a bit of action, it will. If you can lay hands to any spare shot, I'd be glad of it. Give them rebels a warm welcome, I reckon. We'll be ready for anything, come midnight."

46

AT THE ABBOT'S STAITH

He did not recognise Selby, though he could smell the river, off to his right. Paul had fallen silent, and a thin rain was falling again, so that their boots slapped on wet cobbles, thin slices of light showing through tight-shuttered windows, and Luce – confused and hurting and almost-hopeful Luce – wanted to cry, again.

"King's Staith's that way," Pzul said, "no?"

"Of course."

And he stopped, and turned round. "All right, you three. Game's over. There is no King's Staith in Selby town. What you up to?"

Gray made a questioning noise, a chirrup, like a little kitten – such a small, sweet, domesticated noise, for so feral a little person. Luce felt her pistol leave the small of his back, and she came flowing past him like a shadow, raising and sighting the weapon in one liquid motion. And he knew what she was about, and he could not allow it to happen, and so he threw himself sideways abruptly, not caring about the sudden agonising twist to his ankle or the handful of hair that tore free, and but her pistol fired anyway, echoing off the narrow walls overhanging the entry. "No!" he screamed, but it was too late.

None of them said anything for a long, a very long, heartbeat. But this was the town on the edge of war, and a single shot was nothing of report, and no one came. There were still voices, raised, questioning, answering, on the barricades. Horses. A little laughter, not a great deal. The tramp, tramp of boots, as men formed up. And then Luce breathed again, because there was yet no outcry.

"Hasty, Gray," Russell murmured. "Very hasty. Now what do you suggest we do with him?"

"He was kind," Luce said numbly. "He was *kind*. And you killed him."

"He was the enemy, Lucifer."

"He was not *my* enemy. Russell, what in God's name are you *doing*?"

Russell looked up from rifling the sentry's pockets, and the man stirred, moaned faintly. "Your aim, Gray, is reprehensible," he said, and his eyes were very bright in the slits of light from the shuttered houses, coal-black and mocking as a raven. "I do apologise for your mishandling, Lucifer. You may be adequately revenged on my person at a time and place of your choosing. May we now make some haste?"

"Wordy bastard," Gray muttered, "You all right? Luce?"

He thought he was. He thought he might have a tooth or two loose, and possibly his nose might be broken, but he could walk. Run. "Where are we going?"

"Exactly as we said, sir," Russell said happily. "To the Abbot's Staith. Where, God willing, Belasyse will be long gone, for he *will* recognise me from Reading, and then there will be hell to pay, and no pitch hot. I *do* know what horse he had, and I *could* tell you what his suit was. I was on the other side of the bridge to him, at Essex's shoulder. I may even have waved. No, gentlemen, if our gallant defenders intend to repel an assault at midnight," and he tossed his hair out of his eyes and grinned, with all his teeth showing on one side and not on the other, "they'll have a hard job without powder and shot."

Luce's much-abused mouth went dry. He swallowed, tasting blood. "Russell, you're a madman."

"I'm mad. *He* couldn't hit a barn door at thirty paces –" jerking his head at Gray, who scowled, "and that one down there, God willing, will be out cold till we're clear. Now. What are you going to be?"

"Scared witless," Luce said, honestly.

47

REAPING THE WHIRLWIND

Hollie didn't think he'd ever grow used to it: thought he might always feel slightly sick, and very shaky, and as if at any minute someone might discover him for the fraud he was. Promoted beyond endurance, as Fowles had once said gloomily. He tightened his hand on the slick rein, and Tyburn flung his head up, fractious as ever in the last minutes before battle.

The horse's shoulder was slippery with rain, but solid, and warm, and he pressed his free hand flat against the comforting reality of the black stallion's neck. The horse nickered softly, almost inaudibly, but Hollie felt the vibration run through the beast's tense body.

"You – keep your mind on your job," he said, and slapped the horse's shoulder gently. And then a movement at his elbow, and Tib tossed his head and side-stepped. "What time d'you call this, Lucifer? – Lucifer?"

But it wasn't Luce. It was Mattie Percey, his thin face anxious in the cat's light as he passed Luce's sash into Hollie's hands. Mattie was not the deftest, unless it was with horses. Hollie stared at him blankly, at the silk spilling out of Mattie's hands, spilling over his saddle bow, over his lap. "What –" he shook his head, "what's the meaning of this, Mattie?"

"I got the colours, sir. We –" He gulped, "he left me with 'em, sir. Him and Russell and Gray's gone on ahead. He said he'll see you in there."

He might have said something. But out of the corner of his eye he saw the ripple of White Surrey's mane, and the sudden splattering splash as Black Tom Fairfax's big white stallion bounded forward in what had to be the chanciest charge in the history of warfare, and he was in.

Hollie knew this place, or places like it, like the back of his hand, the narrow cobbled streets where a galloping horse could break a leg, or stumble and throw an incautious rider to break his neck; the echoing wet granite walls, muffling even the whine of ricocheting shot, the damp, earthy smell of wet stone and a stinking tidal river.

He hated this kind of fighting, when you might come skidding round the corner of a house and smash into a makeshift barricade manned by slab-faced weavers with billhooks mingled with professional, drilled fighting men with muskets. Or you might come clattering round in a shower of hoof-sparks and find yourself adrift in a cat's cradle of featureless walls and cobbles, with no way to know where you were but the smell of the river.

Percey had the colours, and Hollie thanked God for Calthorpe's distinctive patched black and white Delilah, and Cullis's square old white cob, that you could mark, because of all things the Lord had meant, He had not meant Mattie Percey for a cornet. The lad was trying to hold the colours up in one hand, all unbalanced, with the silk flapping like an old maid's washing in his face and his own horse spooked and shying at the snap and ripple of a square of fabric right down his earhole.

He kicked Tyburn up, and the black stallion flattened his ears and went from a controlled canter into a wild surge of a gallop, skittering up behind Percey, taking the colours up himself. Shoving them, with a grace that astonished him, into their proper place by the lad's knee, which did nothing for Percey's horse's equilibrium, but at least left Mattie's hands free.

He was guessing this was the outer barricade. He might be wrong. He might have got his inner map turned about, wheeling and doubling through the indistinguishable streets.

What he was bloody sure of, was that this was no place to go hand to hand with a man armed with what appeared to be a butcher's poleaxe, and there was no way of going forwards, and no way of going backwards with Drew Venning yammering like a god-damned goodwife, and

Venning's dog hurling itself at the barricades, and two troop of horse coming up on his tail. "As bad as fucking Rupert!" he yelled, at no one in particular, and caught the poleaxe on the blade of his sword in desperate fury before the Malignant son of a bitch took his head off with it, "And will you *fuck off* with that thing, before I take it off you and shove it up your arse!"

He did not do polearms. Yanking on that axe bloody well hurt, great red tingles all up his badly-healed wrist and across his shoulder. Its owner was wrenching at it, where it was hooked on the guard of Hollie's sword, and he was wrenching right back because as soon as that bugger worked loose he was like to find himself chopped in half, he or Tib.

Venning was yelling something incomprehensible down his ear, and he had a wonderful moment of clarity where he thought the freckled Fenlander was assuring him of reinforcements, but he bloody wasn't, he was apologising for the fact that his god-damned dog had gone through the barricade and was presently raising holy hell in the defences. Snarling and leaping and biting, which was marvellous, but indiscriminate, and then there was a single pistol shot and a wild yelp, and the growling stopped sharp.

Drew Venning said a word that no decent and godly young officer should have known, and gave his horse one vicious slash with the reins, and then he was gone, and his troop after him, not so much breaking through the barricades as trampling them to ruined splinters. There was a tiny gap, like the moment of calm stillness at the height of a storm, and Hollie – without his cornet, without his colours, without much of a plan – stood up in his stirrups and raised his bridle-gauntleted hand high above his head, that the torchlight might catch the blued metal at least and draw the eye. Stood up in his stirrups, and whistled, which was a deeply undignified thing to do, but he saw the cob's white head come up as Cullis jerked on the bridle, and knew that his old sergeant at least knew what he was about.

And went through the barricade himself, feeling the head of the poleaxe wrench against the guard of his sword, and jerk loose, and drag down the length of his forearm and across his flank, parting leather and squealing on steel. It would hurt later, he knew that, but for now he felt little more than a sting. Across Tyburn's quarters, and the stallion did feel it, kicking out with both lethal steel-shod hind feet, and someone screamed and fell, still howling.

Percey at his elbow. Cullis barrelling through behind, and Calthorpe, and one of the Westons: the three solidest horses in the troop, like a moving four-legged barricade in their own right.

Coming on like a storm of their own, tawny against blood-red, half a troop sliding through that narrowing gap, and then he heard a scream of pain and he knew the gap had closed, snapped shut on one of his lads. Hoped it wasn't permanent – or if it was permanent, God grant that it be quick. Tyburn's head came up with one of those disconcerting piglike grunts that the stallion was prone to, if you set your heels to him unexpected, and there was a sudden surge of black lightning under Hollie as the big horse put on speed.

And then the dog limping up alongside them, shoulder black with blood against the white coat, barely putting a paw to the ground, but running.

"You can keep up like the rest of us, or you can stop here, mutt," he said, though no one heard him. "Not carrying you on my bloody saddle."

Kicked the black horse up again, because a snail with the cramp was quicker than that ponderous flashy black of Venning's. "Dog's back there," he said, jerking his head, and Drew Venning would not have tears streaking his powder-black face, because he would not shed tears over a worthless bloody mutt of no particular birth or breeding, his eyes would not be wet and red at the thought of the loss of his lolloping shadow. "I'll take your lads on wi' me, and tha can catch us up. Shortly."

Venning gave a little gasp, and wheeled his horse.

"Might have to carry him," Hollie called, and someone sniggered, because when you'd just come clear of a fight, that few seconds of weightless joy when you realised you still had all your limbs and your heart was still beating, anything was funny.

"Like Prince Rupert," – he recognised Cullis's grim voice.

"Tosser," one of the Westons said, perfectly amiably, and the whole lot of them were giggling like gossipy maids.

It was a small, bright space, a tiny gap between the clash of swords and the scream of hurt men and horses, and all the time the thought at the back of his mind was beating like a sick headache that Luce was somewhere in these dark, featureless streets. With two of the most unpredictable men under Hollie's command, who might, or might not, consider themselves as friends, and whose loyalties might, or might not, lie on this side of the barricade. Parliament had given neither Russell nor Gray much cause to love it – Russell shamed and stripped of his commission, Gray bullied and hurt. Could argue they both had to learn discipline the hard way. Aye, and you could argue that particular school of hard knocks hadn't took with Hollie, either. He should have stepped in. Venning couldn't manage it by himself, and Luce was making a bloody bad fist of command, but then the lad had always wanted to be liked, too much to be an effective officer.

Hollie had had one truly efficient officer in his company, and he'd had him stripped of his commission and flogged, at the insistence of Captains Webb and Chedglow. Because he wanted to look like he knew what he was doing. Didn't want to be shown up, in front of officers with their own companies. Pride, Holofernes. Pride, and sinful vanity, and you are now reaping the whirlwind, you stupid, pig-headed, stubborn bastard.

He'd lost Russell, and there was a bloody good chance he was going to lose Luce, if he didn't take his head out of his fundament and think like himself, like an independent commander and not a bloody arse-licking lackey with no thought but for Fairfax to pat him on the head and tell him he was a good dog.

"Bollocks to this," he snapped at Mattie Percey, who blinked and looked taken aback. "Colours, Matthew?"

"Sir?"

Half of him was pitying Percey, who happened to be at his side when he was thinking aloud and hadn't a clue what he was on about, and once again he could have kicked himself because Luce would have known what he was on about, Would have probably come up with some cork-brained but apposite quotation. Would not have stared at Hollie with big, scared eyes and his mouth fallen open in bemusement. Hollie leaned out of the saddle and straightened the staff of the colours in Mattie's nerveless fingers, and then patted the lad's arm.

"Keep 'em up straight, Matthew, there's a good lad. What've we got this side, half a troop? If that?"

Chedglow was on the other side of the barricade, Chedglow and Webb.

Well, fuck 'em. They could deal with the hosts of Midian by themselves.

There was yet time. He might yet turn this around.

"Aye. Well. It'll have to do."

48

PLAYACTING

"Look to the river," Russell said wildly.

Anything was better than looking into the town, where there was a merry orange glow beginning to shine between the houses. Luce attempted a brief sprint, stumbled, and went to his knees hard enough to knock the breath out of his bruised ribs.

Gray helped him up. And that was kind.

"River?" he wheezed.

Russell stared at him, and then over his shoulder. "Patrol," he said. "Can't pull that stunt twice. Luce –"

Luce, straightening up, confused.

"Luce?" Russell prompted, and then shook his head. "Gray? Hit me."

Gray did not need to be asked twice. Gray cocked her head thoughtfully, eyed an opponent who was a head taller than she was, and kneed him smartly in the groin. Russell hadn't been expecting that, and he folded up with a rather pitiful yowl, and while he was curled up in a twitching ball in the mud she kicked him in the ribs for good measure. Whatever playacting he'd had in mind, he seemed to have stopped, in short order. He was presently neither lithe not graceful but he came out of the mud like a fighting demon and put her on her back, one hand knotted in her hair, hissing bloody murder.

Russell might have forgotten, or had never known, that Gray was a woman, but Luce had not, and she might have looked like the worst of scabrous street ruffians but he could not stand by and see a woman punched in the face.

"What the bloody hell-?"

Gray rolled over, shoved Russell off her, wriggled out from underneath Luce who was ineffectually belabouring both of them, and looked embarrassed. "Uh. Sir. Sorry. He was – it was him – he started it, sir."

"What the hell do you two think you're playing at, boy?" the Royalist officer said. He sounded bloody livid, so far as Luce could tell from flat on his belly with his face in the cobbles. "Brawling in the streets like some kind of –? The pair of you, you're on a bloody charge. Sergeant, I want these two desperadoes taking in and –"

Russell said, afterwards, that Luce had reared up out of the mud like some kind of besmottered revenant – he swore to it, hand on heart, and Russell did not hold with false oaths and so Luce had to take it on witness that he had, in fact, faced up to a patrol of a good two score of Royalist troopers, bristling with arms, and said, "I *beg* your pardon!" in tones of freezing disdain.

Russell said, afterwards, it was the kind of cork-brained thing that Luce would say, and Luce, unwillingly, had to agree. Luce and the Royalist captain stared at each other in mutual astonishment for a matter of what felt like years, and must have been at most a heartbeat, before the world burst apart in a roar of flame and noise, of trumpets sounding the alarms, of drums and shouting and horses whinnying and men screaming, and of hooves rattling in the narrow street like a carronade and a very distinctive voice yelling above the noise of it all, "*Lucey I am going to bloody well kill you!*"

Thankful Russell smiled his frightening lopsided grin. "I see the colonel is in fine voice this evening," he said, perfectly cheerfully. And then – he said, afterwards – as the first horses of Babbitt's ill-assorted troop came smashing into the back of a scattering company of very surprised Royalists, Luce had pulled Gray's pistol from where she had tucked it into the

waistband of his breeches, steadied it, and with a perfectly level hand shot the captain between the eyes.

Which was a thing Luce would never have done. Never. Shot a man in cold blood, and with an accurate aim? Never. The blood on his sleeve, afterwards, must have come from another place.

So he was standing in the middle of a deadly brawl in a Selby backstreet, staring and blinking while his commanding officer – his friend – hacked his way across the cobbles like an avenging fury towards them, swearing and cursing bloody vengeance on all Malignants. No more than a hundred yards separated them, no more than a hundred yards of cobbles that ran with blood and rain, glistening in the light of torches and gunfire –

"Lucey do you want to get your bloody fool head shot off?" Gray yelled at him, and suddenly he was back in his own body again, a not very comfortable body that was shaking so hard he almost sat down in the –

Luce suddenly realised what it was he had almost sat down in. It was leaking out of the enemy captain's shattered skull.

He had possibly less than a heartbeat to consider puking up his breakfast and supper before a pistol ball of their own went singing past his ear, and he fled, Gray at his heels like some happy panting terrier.

49

GOING IN UNDER A BLACK FLAG

It was a bloody lash-up, a street brawl lent a degree of credibility by the presence of plate and authority, and the decency and honour of his men of which Fairfax spoke so often, seemed to have been left the other side of Dam Fields. Too bloody fierce for that, with Venning using that four-legged blockade of his as a battering ram, and Hollie laying about him with the buckle end of his bridle if anyone came too close. Oh aye, they liked to make out the cavalry was the classy end of things, none of your raff and scaff on horseback, we are gentlemen, sir. As Hollie wheeled his own four-legged blockade to slam a good hundredweight of pissed-off stallion into a particularly vexatious defender, he did not feel much like a gentleman. Sweat was running into his eyes, stinging, and the long cut on his forearm was smarting like hell, and still the buggers kept on coming, pouring out of the alleys and the shadows like bloody ants.

Not fighting like a gentleman, now, not any more, as he brought his knee up into a musketeer's face with a crack of bone, whirled the horse to knock him aside. Even the indefatigable Tyburn was labouring now.

"Stop playing with 'en, Rosie, and get on!" Venning roared across a hundred yards of rain-slick Yorkshire stone, and Hollie shook his wet hair out of his eyes and smacked the big horse across the backside, racketing across the cobbles to Venning's side, and the freckled Fenlander grinned at him, panting. "Get in the abbey. Using it for arms store. Bloody heathens."

The abbey. It sounded so grand, so imposing, and Hollie shook his head because there was no way on God's earth they could take on an abbey – thirty of them, against a great monastic edifice – and then they were clattering out from between the houses and the thin moonlight showed a long green by the river, silvered out by night. "And the horses," Venning said, with a breathless cackle. "Arms an' mounts in there, bor. Could do with a few o' they."

In what was a good-sized church, actually, a fine, stone-built, noble silver building but it was still not much bigger than the church at White Notley, and they could still broach it.

(Maybe. With good luck and a following wind.)

"And they reckoned *you* was a bloody godless heathen, putting that black sod of yours in the chapel at Worcester," Venning sniffed.

Hollie sniffed back, reining the aforesaid black sod in for what breather he could catch, before another knot of Malignants stumbled across them in the dark streets. "Had to. Could do without that lackwitted red bitch of Luce's dropping a foal halfway through campaign." He leaned his hands on the black's solid muscled neck and took a deep breath. His ribs hurt like hellfires, as well. Damn that bloody man with the poleaxe –

"Heads up," Cullis panted, "getting too old for this." The sergeant's old cob gave a blubbery snort, as if Cullis had put a sharp spur into its well-padded ribs, and jerked into activity. "Buggers is stirring yonder."

Not half a mile hence, a sudden flurry of shot, not a full-on firefight, but as if someone had come across another someone all unexpected in the narrow streets. "Shit," Hollie said, because there was one very specific someone who might be somewhere unexpected, and he could well do without having to find him. "On me."

And how the hell he thought he might find one fight, in a town where they were breaking out in every flat space, with attackers and defenders almost indistinguishable one from another unless you knew their faces or their colours, the Lord alone knew.

But. There it was. "Needle in a fucking haystack," he muttered darkly, and Venning grinned, knowing exactly what he meant. And just to his side, Mattie Percey hefted the colours awkwardly again, and Hollie shook his head – no. "Going in under a black flag, Matthew."

Because for one, Percey was a bloody menace with those colours, and most importantly, they were *Lucey's* colours. That irresponsible little bugger was going to get them back before this night was finished, and be back at his duty instead of running round Selby with that bloody marred ranting nutjob, causing havoc.

They were distinctive. Two tall, lean, fair-haired lads, unarmoured, in a town under fire –

– *they'd be easy meat* –

They'd be no such bloody thing, they would be *distinctive*, he was being stupid, and giving the black stallion his head and setting him at a flat bolting gallop that sent sparks racketing from the cobbles, heading into the rat's nest of alleys that ran off the Gowthorpe down towards the river and the wharves and the water – that was just bloody stupid, Hollie. With Percey and his creaking old Windhover wheezing ten yards behind him, because where Hollie went Mattie went, and Cullis and Calthorpe and the Weston brothers hammering up a storm and sweeping up the rags of Venning's lads with them, with Venning yelling and cursing at the whole boiling lot of them because this was not their orders, they were supposed to be breaking the barricades for Fairfax, not rampaging all over town like hounds on a scent –

Stupid, Hollie. Stupid, and ill-conceived, and careless, and the sort of bloody cork-brained chivalric thing that Cornet Pettitt might come up with, and aye, he knew all of that, in his head, but it was Lucey.

Lucey who was incorrigibly nice, and who would be down there up to the backsides in Malignants and expecting it all to come right because Hollie wouldn't let him down. What were you supposed to do with a man like that – leave him to it?

And so he was cursing all Malignants, in his head, when he came skittering round the bend in the road that led own to the river, and almost straight into the back of the Royalist patrol. And if they hadn't been distracted it might have gone hard for Hollie's men.

As it was, not having eyes in the backs of their heads, the unfortunate Royalists had been somewhat occupied with the business of dealing with the suspicious characters rolling in the gutter biting chunks out of each other. Even without that appalling knitted hat dragged down over his barley-fair hair, even filthy and draggled and disguised, Hapless Russell was still conspicuous.

Bloody *Gray* was conspicuous, by being about three foot tall and looking like a drowned wharf-rat.

Tyburn went up on his hind legs with a squeal as Hollie's hand tightened on the rein and his heels closed on the black's sides at one and the same time in his surprise, and he didn't know what he might have done next had Lucey not erupted from the mud under the very noses of the Malignant troop and told them in his haughtiest tones that they were *severely mistaken*. And it was not well done of Hollie to laugh, but he wanted to, very badly, because in all the world there was no one like Lucey Pettitt, thank God. *Still* no one in the world like Luce, because Luce was still in it. He wanted to laugh, and he wanted to burst with pride and relief, and at the same time he would quite willingly have shot the daft little bugger for this, but instead Luce – Hollie's brat, his dreamy, unreasonable friend, who preferred to mend than break things – raised his pistol with a hand that was perfectly level and shot the Royalist captain in the face.

There was a very brief moment of absolute stillness, when the world held its breath. And then Hollie's lads went smashing into the back of the Malignant troop, and he was busy at his work: the bread-and butter work of not getting shot to bits, dragged off his horse and beaten, or run through.

Hard, bloody work, and the last thing he needed was a glimpse of those three damnable miscreants heading off towards the river at a flat run.

"Lucey," he yelled, pitching his voice to carry over the crack and whine of shot and the blare of futile orders, "Lucey, I am going to *bloody well kill you!*"

They were all unhurt, though. Didn't deserve to be, but were, all three of them, the lucky scapegrace bastards.

And he knew they were whole, because as they disappeared, into the dark, he saw Hapless Russell glance over his shoulder, and his teeth flash in that frightening one-sided grin.

And the marred bugger *saluted*.

50

SOME MADMAN ON A BLACK HORSE

"Well," Luce panted, "that was exciting. Can we *not* do it again?"

"Silly," Gray said, because that was all she had the breath for, and Russell, who had gone a very funny colour indeed and sounded as if every breath might be his last, said nothing at all, but jerked his head towards the docks instead.

"Keep," he wheezed, "going."

"No," Gray said. "Not till. You two. Start. Breathing."

"If I wasn't –" he caught his breath with a whoop, "breathing I'd be," another gasp, "dead."

"It can be *arranged*, Russell."

Russell hadn't the breath to laugh, so he sat on someone's back doorstep and dropped his head between his knees and his shoulders heaved silently. Luce could laugh, and did, and Gray glared at him.

"It's not funny!"

She dipped her hands in a puddle and splashed her face to cool it, pouring water from her cupped hands over her hair and her shoulders, and Russell – filthy, reeking of powder and splashed with dark stains of a nature better left unquestioned – bridled. "Gray, dogs might have pissed in that water!"

And then Gray laughed. And it was possibly the first time any of them had heard that particular sound. "You are a tit at times, Hapless," she said brusquely, and he cocked an eyebrow at her.

"Doubtless. God grant I remain a relatively fragrant one, though."

"You're worse than a bloody woman," she said, and Luce caught his breath, what he had of it, but she never even looked at him. "Come on. Let's get this finished."

And it was ridiculously easy, after that, because it was a distance of less than a quarter mile, and they could see the staithe from here, and because there was chaos all over the town already. And that was the trick of it, that was how they had got this far, they just behaved as if they belonged there and no one questioned: Gray limped, and Russell was filthy and bloodied, and when they presented themselves to the men standing sentry in this dilapidated state and made report that the town was attacked, and that they were relieved of duty –

"Thief Lane," Luce said wearily, having got the hang of this

– having been the last rags of one poor beleaguered troop, beaten back from the outer barricade by a vicious rebel assault from three directions at once, and now reduced to this desperate state of wretchedness. Useless, the three of them, and so they had been ordered to recruit fresh men from what places they could to man the inner barricades.

"On whose authority?"

"Hell do I know?" Russell wheezed, propped up against the rough bricks and panting with his mouth open. "It's bloody chaos out there. You just do what you're told, don't ask stupid questions. You going to stand here all day staring at me like a god-damn frog and let the bloody rebels overrun the place?"

The sentry spluttered a bit and bridled and said something about he wasn't taking his orders from no scar-faced puppy, at which point Russell opened the door and leaned against it with his arms folded, looking like one of the less forgiving fiery angels, while the sound of fighting in the town drifted to and fro, and the flare and glow of musket fire lit the houses a deceptively cheerful amber.

"Not in the mood," he said. "Hear that? Sounds like bloody Fairfaxes, bloody plural. In. There's lads getting killed out there. I would stop it, sir, if I could end this fight on the instant with no further blood shed I would do it. I have seen enough, this night. I would have no more blood spilled." And he slid down the door, quite abruptly, and sat on the floor with his head on his knees and sobbed like a man who had finally and rather horribly reached the end of his tether.

The sentry stared at him. "You're serious, aren't you?"

"Does he *look* like he's putting you on?" Gray said.

"Where –"

"Inner barricade. Up the Gowthorpe, about a hundred yards from the Abbey. We got set on by a troop of Fairfax's horse –" Gray eyed him narrowly, with a look that said he was going too far.

The sentry nodded. "Aye. You're right. You lot look fair done in. Well, good work, lads. There's a jug of ale behind the door."

"Aye, and the missus sent me off with a bite o' bread and cheese for me staybit," one of the other sentries said. An older man, not old, not young, but in his middle years: a thin, leathery man with faded blue eyes and a seamed face. An ordinary, weatherbeaten man that you might pass a hundred times and never look at twice. "It's in me snapsack, under the table. You'd be more'n welcome to it, lads. What? That 'un's only a nipper," he said indignantly, meaning Gray. "What kind of a bloody Christian'd I be, leaving these three sat here in the cold wi' nowt to eat? He's right. They done their bit. Time for us lot to go and do ours. We'll see you right, lads, don't you worry."

"Thank you," Luce said, feeling on the edge of tears. Any more of this kindness and he'd be on the floor with Russell.

The older man shrugged. "Don't thank me, lad. I hope anybody'd do it."

"I will not forget your kindness," Luce said, and meant it.

51

A THING OF PITY

They sat, awkwardly, after the Royalist sentries had moved off.

Gray sat cross-legged on the bare earth floor munching bread and cheese. Russell collapsed on the threshold still sobbing, which was uncomfortable. Luce not sure quite what to do, but busying himself as best he might tidying the table, pouring ale for them, straightening the ledgers. It smelt of damp, and the river, and the odd, slightly acrid smell of black powder, but it also smelt of old, musty flour, and wood. It was a warehouse. There was nothing military about it. It was a warehouse, that backed on to a river, and in a year – ten years – a hundred years, the Ouse would still be flowing behind the staithe, and ships would still dock and unload and store their wares in this plain, stone building, and men would buy them. Long after Luce was dead and buried, and this war was over, this place would return to its old occupation, of being a place of order and usefulness. It was an oddly comforting thought.

There was a watery sniff. "Are they gone?"

"You all right, Hapless?" Gray said, sounding oddly shy, and Russell sat up, wiping the back of his wrist under his nose.

"I'm getting good at this, aren't I?" he said smugly. "Did you leave any of that ale, Lucifer?"

Gray reached out and smacked him, flat-handed, round the back of the head. "You lousy bastard," she hissed, "you put that on! You *lied*!"

– and before Russell had lunged for her with his sword drawn, which was his clear intent, Luce had tripped him. Quite deftly, which surprised him, and the scarred young man went sprawling with his blade spinning away from him across the floor, and then Luce had to stop Gray from rejoining the assault. "He's a play-actor!" she bawled. "A deceiver!"

"A turd for your opinion, sir!" Russell yelled back at her.

"You tricked those men! They were good men, kind men, and you *lied* to them! You are no better than a fair-day mountebank, you – " And found herself looking cross-eyed down her nose at Russell's eating-knife, resting just under her chin.

"Unsay that."

"Russell," Luce began, because they had no time for this.

"You weep like a woman, you marred bastard! Like a bloody girl, to get what you want, rather than fight for it! Because you're not a man at all, are you? You are but *half* a man –"

"No, I'm not a man, Gray, am I? I am a *thing*, with no thoughts, or feelings. Not a man at all. God forbid the prospect of a thousand deaths on my conscience might trouble my sleep a'night, if I could have prevented it. I know what it is to be hurt, sir, and I should not wish such unhappiness on my worst enemy. Not even on *you*, Gray." He was shaking, and the point of his knife made a little bloody zigzag under her jaw. "Not even you, though God knows you would be improved by a little humanity. Sweet Christ! And they call *me* cold!"

Gray spluttered something, flushing.

"I apologise, Trooper Gray, if a reminder that I am not a thing causes you discomfort. Trust me, sir. I can think. I can feel. And remember. *You* can bleed."

He whirled away, tossing his ragged hair out of his eyes, and Luce felt a pang of pity for both of them. Neither of them would want it, or know what to do with it, but there it was. "Gray – apologise," he said firmly.

"I don't want his apology!"

"Thank you," Gray muttered instead, and Russell stood staring at her with his mouth open, looking as comically astonished as if she'd punched him in the belly.

"For –?"

"Getting my kit back for me. I never said thank you." And then she grinned, slyly, with the blood running down her throat and seeping into her collar. "For a feller that's neither a mountebank nor a shyster, that was a neat piece of sleight of hand. Now come on."

52

ONLY EACH OTHER, AT THE LAST

Back to the Abbey, then, because if they could break out the horses and leave a hundred or so panicked mounts running loose through the streets, not to say the weapons stored there, the Malignants would shatter like Venice glass.

"You all right, Rosie?"

He closed one eye and looked at Drew Venning. No, nothing ailed him. Not seriously. He was just bruised, and stiffening quickly, and getting too old for this. "I'm all right," Hollie said, "could do with a drink, but –"

"Couldn't we all, bor!"

"But one last push and the goddamn place is ours."

"Ah, and hope Lucey's got the common sense to be out of the way when it goes." A bloodied white muzzle emerged from the breast of Venning's buffcoat, and Tinners licked his master's bristly jaw with every sign of evident relish. "Wait for support?" the freckled Fenlander said hopefully, and Hollie shook his head.

"Be waiting a long old time, mate. Reckon we're about the only unit to be clear. Looks like it's us."

Only each other, at the last. A thing Het had said to him, sometimes, when it was just they two, alone in the dark, with the house settling about them. Only each other, at the last. He did need a drink, and not necessarily strong drink, for his mouth had gone dry as dust at that thought, and he could not swallow. What if –

It wasn't going to be. He forced himself to swallow, so hard that his ears popped, and met Venning's eyes with the best approximation of his old fierce grin he could manage. "We'll do."

The cobbles were shining in the gusts of thin rain off the river. It was cold. That was why he shivered, because he was cold, and wet, and a trickle of rainwater went down his back. "Form up. Where's Mattie?"

"Here." Still stiff and straight and so full of pride, sitting there on a horse that was older than he was, holding his borrowed colours at an awkward angle.

"Keep out o' trouble, Matthew. Luce'll bloody throttle you if you give him his colours back full of shot-holes."

Hearing the weird eerie clatter of approaching hooves coming on down the Gowthorpe, echoing off the overhanging houses. Voices, North Country voices, not that different to his own, shouting, giving orders, answering back, muffled, a little, by the clinging mist off the river. Drums, sounding the order to advance. Hollie found himself counting down the advance, working out in his head how long it might be before they would see the enemy troops. Whether surprise, and a full hit-and-run attack, might carry them through for long enough for Black Tom's own lads to win clear of the barricades and pile in.

How many there would be, and how long it might take for reinforcements to come, but he couldn't think like that. Because if he threw it all in now, if his poor half-troop of gallant bloody idiots was not enough and they died to a man on the cobbles in front of Selby Abbey, they would have bought enough time for Fairfax to get through the barricades without having this lot coming down the Gowthorpe up his backside.

He was cold. His hands were stiff and cold on the reins and he was frightened, suddenly, that he wouldn't be able to hold Tyburn. Clenching his fingers on the wet leather, trying to get some feeling back into them, while the black horse tossed his head and backed and reared, not liking it. He had never taken to an uncertain hand on the bridle, had Tib. Hesitation unsettled him like nothing else.

Five. Four. Three. Counting down in his head.

Mattie with the colours, wavering as even old Windhover sidled, his ears swivelling anxiously.

Two. Tyburn's forefeet came off the cobbles and he rocked backwards onto his quarters with an irritable grunt.

One.

And gone.

Bastards not expecting that, and Hollie bent low over the black's neck with his sword in his hand, and they came smashing down out of the shifting shadows like the wrath of God into the scattering middle of Belasyse's own troop. He wasn't hurt, he kept telling himself that, the numbness and the tingling in his right arm was the old hurt in his badly-healed wrist. Pushing, and pushing, because Tyburn was a hand's breadth taller than most of these scrubby light-bred beasts, and massive in the quarters, and he was a weapon in his own right. But there was nowhere else to go, in these narrow streets, no means to give way, and so it was push on or die in the fighting of it –

One of Venning's lads gone down, his mare screaming on the cobbles with a pistol ball in her somewhere, horrible sound, and Hollie was of half a mind to fall out and put a merciful shot in her himself, save that one of the Malignants had done it instead, and he looked up from his work and met the eyes of a man who was as miserable and frightened as he was himself, and somehow that unsettled him the more, for if he didn't want to be there, and the King's men didn't want to be there, what was the point of it, other than the whim of your betters?

He knew it was happening, that was the stupid thing. Both him and Tyburn, eyes moving over the ragged barricade because you will break, you bastards, looking for the gap, the weak link, and giving the order to charge and the black horse suddenly going up on his back legs with a squeal as if something had pricked him, and then they were springing forward, skating and skittering on the slick cobbles, with the purpose and intent of a missile.

Because moving in and out of the piled brush and the smashed furniture, through the defenders, with the flare of lit torches and the first spark and sing of musket fire, he could see those three buggers, scuttling like beetles.

Gray stooped over a bloody hand-cart, of all things, like a market-day apprentice with his master, and it looked so comical and so out of place that it might have been funny, except that Luce was looking harried and Russell was looking intent, and that was frightening. Hollie cursed under his breath, and pulled the black's head up, and turned him straight for those three miscreants – straight through the struggling knot of defenders at the barricade if he had to.

The defenders were about as astonished as he was, clearly had him down as some kind of death-or-glory boy, and just for one glorious moment he thought he was going to make it, he reckoned he'd get in just under the pike points while Belasyse's lads were all a-gape trying to work out what the bloody hell the mad bastard on the galloping horse was about, peeling off the rest of the troop and going hell for leather straight at the barricade for no discernible reason. Remembered thinking he'd make it, and wasn't it going to make a hell of a story, and then catching the eye of the Malignant sergeant and seeing his lips move in the words Hollie had been praying not to hear –

"Charge your pikes for horse!"

And shrugging to himself, he'd had a good run, he was rising forty, he had a wife and a daughter, not a bad life, he'd made his peace with his God: Tyburn's ears flickering – what the hell d'you think you're doing? – and then God knows where but that little bit of extra power under him, a sudden surge of black lightning, Hollie trying to find one face that was wavering, just one weak point if he had to go down.

The weight of his black smashing flank-on into the barricades, slewing on the cobbles, and someone on the other side going down screaming under the horse's hooves – something broke, but it wasn't bloody Lucey, thank God – the man screaming and the momentum of Tyburn's charge carrying him sliding sideways into the forest of points, the big horse unbalanced and panicked or even now Hollie would have had him out of there. Still trying, even at the last, to wrench the stallion's head round and get clear, and the big horse fighting him, and pretty much the last clear thing Hollie did remember was a stunning smack in the face from the crest of the horse's muscular neck as he reared, and then an appalling splintering sound.

And in the gap where he'd been the pike shot through, deadly, razor sharp. It would have speared Tyburn where he stood, gutted the stallion like a fish, had Hollie not glimpsed the flaring light on the lethal metal tip and yanked the black's head up, knowing how the stallion hated to have his mouth wrenched, knowing it made him unbiddable, and yet better that than with his guts spilling out on the cobbles. And it wasn't enough, the horse was quick, but the pikeman was quicker, and the metal went searing instead across the black stallion's chest, the black staggering and screaming like a woman in travail.

Another horse – a *lesser* horse – would have fallen.

Somewhere in the sprawl of struggling bodies around them, Cullis's old cob was squealing, in fear and panic. and yet after that first dreadful sound the black horse was silent, though his flanks heaved and trembled under Hollie. Then someone went smashing into them and Tyburn went down.

There was an odd, star-bright moment, when Hollie saw the paler flash of the stallion's girth-strap, the glint of harness in the flare of musket fire – the gleam of a shod hoof as the big horse went over, and it seemed to take an age before he hit the cobbles. Expecting it to hurt, and knowing there was nothing he could do about it, and yet, it did not. He felt it, though. Would have sworn, except that he had no breath with which to do it. An odd feeling, unable to move, unable to feel, unable to breathe, sprawled on the cobbles while a bloody fight to the death went on around him, so close he felt the clip of a skittering horse's hoof against his breastplate. Tyburn's outflung head across his legs, and the black stallion grunting piteously, the white roll of his eye catching the light as he struggled to get to his feet again, and could not.

"Get up, you sawny fule!"

"Tib –"

"*Bollocks* to the horse!" Venning yelled, yanking his own mount up onto its hind legs to punch his blade into a defender who'd forced his way in too close. "Hollie, get up!"

He didn't move quick enough, and Venning simply set his massive horse at the wounded defender, smashing him to the ground and grabbing Hollie by the shoulder. "Get on the bloody horse!"

It was chaos – bloody, brutal chaos, close work, hoping to God you weren't slaughtering your own men and trusting to your own height and vivid hair to be distinctive. He could feel Venning's horse starting to labour and as the freckled Fenlander wheeled again to push back into the fray, to rejoin his own embattled men, Hollie yanked his sword free and simply slid down the big horse's flank. Better his own two feet, than four failing ones, and better to die with a sword in his hand. And Fairfax had to come through soon. *Surely*.

He couldn't see his own lads, thought he might have seen big patched Delilah briefly, backing out and then piling in again.

A lanky, rawboned horse suddenly barging him aside, spinning him like an autumn leaf, its rider leaning from the saddle, and Hollie was tripping over his own feet to try and escape the man's vicious sideswipe that he knew must surely follow when the horse's loose rein flapped in his face and he snatched at it in protective reflex.

Snatched. Caught. Held, yanking the horse's head painfully to the side, and it went skittering round him in a stiff half-circle, and its dead rider slumped suddenly out of the saddle with a sudden gush of blood from his lolling mouth. Hollie dragged himself into the saddle (still warm under him, in this chill March night, and he tasted bile at the thought of it) – kicked the man's trapped boot out of the stirrup, and then dug his heels into the brute and sent it bounding across the cobbles, stumbling and side-stepping over the bodies.

"Venning!" he yelled, standing up in the stirrups, "hoi! To me!"

Not sure if he'd be heard, but Cullis heard him – twenty years of Hollie yelling his head off across battlefields over half of Europe, the sergeant's ear was tuned to Hollie's voice, raised a hand in salute. He heard Cullis giving the order to fall back, and they came like a wave of the sea, in a ragged but implacable order, swirling back around him. Percey with the colours still wagging in front of him, grinning fiercely through the bars of his helmet, strutting up to Hollie's side like he was the proudest man in the troop.

"One last push," Hollie said, and that was all he said.

Tib would have jumped the barricade and come at the Malignant bastards from the back.

Tib was dead on the cobbles, somewhere in this rain-washed nightmare, with his chest torn open, and Hollie had every intention of recompensing tribulation upon them that troubleth him. Burning for burning, wound for wound, stripe for stripe.

Aye. Well.

He forgot, for a second, what he was mounted on, and he touched his heels to the lanky misbegotten jade and the horse put its head down and lurched on a stride, and its sluggish willingness filled him with a sudden fury, because this was not Tyburn. Forced into a thing he'd never had to do with his own black horse, he sat down hard in the saddle and jabbed the benighted nag in the ribs, hard, with his spurs, and it plodded forward into a stumbling gallop, and that made him even more furious. This was no bloody warhorse, it was barely capable of keeping its own feet on the cobbles, and then he was engulfed in a blanket of shouting and struggling at the barricade again, kicking out and laying about him with fists and feet and buckle-end of the rein because it was too close for blade-work, all push and jostle. Shouting and cursing and swearing, and for once, that wasn't even coming from him, and it sounded odd to be hearing comfortable North Country voices calling foul abuse on each other.

There was a bastard with a half-pike trying to get at him, and he wasn't in the mood for any other buggers with pointy sticks. Caused enough bloody trouble, they had, and so as the razor point wavered towards him, jabbing, Hollie simply put the stupid horse into a gallop, straight for the pikeman. Who did not expect it, and whose eyes went comically wide in panic, but who stood his ground with his little stick. Right up to the point where, at a distance of less than a length and still coming, Hollie swapped his sword hand over and pulled the stupid horse wheeling skittering off to the right. Hacking down at the pikeman's exposed arm and shoulder left-handed because that, you fucker, *that* is for Tib: trying to force his way through a thicket of sudden swords and pikes and makeshift weapons, still chopping away at anything that came within his reach, hacking like a man scything standing corn –

"Rosie you lollopin' gret mawkin!"

Aye, well, hacking his way a bit too far, then, and realising he was all but cut off, with Venning forcing his way through the barricade behind swearing like a man pushed beyond mortal endurance, scarlet in the face with all his freckles standing out like spilled gunpowder. "I ent going to keep doing this, Rosie!" he roared.

"Got over, didn't we?"

"Oh, ah, and how we going to get back then, you silly bugger?"

"Fairfax'll see us right!" he yelled, laughing, suddenly borne up on the wings of the eagle. "Come on!"

And then they were streaming across the grass before the abbey, sticky turf and shot flying around them, strung out like a flight of wild geese across the moon. The nondescript nag had a stumbling turn of speed, on the flat, and there was one glorious moment when Hollie thought it was going to be all right.

Shortly afterwards, he realised that there was a troop of Belasyse's own cavalry coming up his arse, fit and well-rested and well-mounted, and that they were not happy boys. But by then it sort of didn't matter any more, because even stupid horse was getting the trick of it, and they wheeled about and prepared to engage again.

53

NO SENSE, AND NO FEELING

"Sir," Gray said, very meekly. "Taking supplies to the barricade on the Gowthorpe, sir. Getting light on powder, sir."

Three barrels of the stuff, in a hand-cart. No one with any sense would have believed that tale, Luce thought, with his most innocent expression. If they weren't almost indiscriminately filthy, somewhere between the outer and the inner barricade, with fire-fights breaking out in almost every alley in the town, no man of sense would have believed a word of it.

On the other hand, who'd believe that three good Parliament boys – two and a half good Parliament boys, not to miscount Gray – would break *in* to the town in the middle of a battle, steal barrels of powder from the magazine, and then –

"Thief Lane," Russell said out of the darkness, looming up with his hair in his eyes. They'd been giving the password quite indiscriminately for about an hour, to anyone who'd listen. "Can we go now?"

Wordlessly, the soldier who'd stopped them jerked his thumb towards the direction of the abbey. "Get on, then, lads."

"Cheers, mate," Gray said happily. She picked up the handles of the hand-cart and trotted along as if it weighed less than a handkerchief, with Russell sloping at her heels with his hands in his pockets and that awful hat pulled down over his bright hair. Nodding absently to soldiers as they passed, running through the almost-deserted streets to where the fighting was fiercest, and standing aside so as not to be ridden down by troops of cavalry.

And loose horses. It was, somehow, more shocking that there were horses in full harness, wild-eyed and panicked, running in the streets, their shod hooves sparking and clattering on the road, stirrups flapping empty against foam-streaked flanks. None Luce recognised, though, God be thanked. None of his company. Following the long straight run of Ousegate, running parallel with the river – a silver shifting light on the sullen water, coming on for high tide, glimpsed between the staithes –

"Ready, gentlemen?"

"Ready as I'll ever be, Hapless," she said, grinning up at him, and he did not grin back, but his raven-black eyes flared with a brief amusement.

"I think not, Gray. Luce?"

"I'm with you." And he was, suddenly and absolutely, he was with them. He was scared and he hurt but he was with them, with a feeling of absolute rightness, in a way that he had not been for some time. Not trying to be amongst them, for how could he – Hollie was right, he was an officer, he was set apart. But he could have friends. The oddly-assorted three of them: Gray who was neither a girl nor a boy, but her body was one and her heart was another, and Russell who was neither a lieutenant nor a plain trooper, but would always and ever be an officer in his head. And himself, with his head dictating that he might fight for liberty of thought and conscience, and his soft heart inclining more and more towards mending than fighting.

"If you're with us," Russell said, with that slightly mocking inflection to his voice, "any chance you can get on with it, rather than contemplating infinity?"

And Luce grinned at him, and muttered an apology, and took the cart handles from Gray, and they were off again, headed purposefully for where the fighting was thickest. Which sounded like the act of a madman, when you thought about it, and yet was the sanest thing in the world, that they might try and end this in as short a time as may be, with as little hurt. Gray almost skipping in her excitement, or perhaps taking two strides for every one of her two taller counterparts.

"Captain Venning," she said suddenly, standing on her tiptoe, and for a second when Luce saw the solid-muscled black hindquarters he thought no, it was Tyburn, that must be –

Must be Hollie Babbitt, conspicuous by the height and the thick horse-tail of hair down his back, distinctively coloured even in this light, dismounting with a most uncharacteristic grace from the back of Venning's four-legged black barricade and disappearing into the fray on his own two feet. "Shit," Russell said, which rather took Luce aback. "I had not realised they might be in so soon. I'm sorry, Luce. We may end up cutting our way in." And then he paused, with a wry smile. "Or, um, not."

No. Or, possibly, not. He felt a little sick, a little shaky, and yet there was no time for either, because he saw Hollie suddenly disappear, tangled with a mounted Malignant, and Luce simply stopped wavering.

Thought he might have shouted something. Found himself blocked by Gray, trying to force his way past her, and she was yelling in his face —

With Russell, smiling coldly sideways like a marred rebel angel, pushing past them both to stove a hole in one of the bottom barrels of powder with a musket butt. Tilting it, a little, that the powder began to run free in an acrid stink of rotten egg. "Stand clear, gentlemen," he said cheerfully. "Anyone know where Belasyse is?"

"What?"

"Run like hell, Lucifer. When I set a spark to this trail, Master Gunpowder is *not* your friend."

54

THE GENTLE RAIN FROM HEAVEN

He could see them, and then the buggers disappeared, and he was too embattled to keep looking, and could only pray God to keep them safe.

Aye, *them* – all three of them: Luce, who was his friend, and was dear to his wife, and had too much poeting to do yet to be dead in a Yorkshire ditch. And them two jonahs with him, who were sort of an acquired taste, like taking your wine unwatered, but who were yet – not precisely dear to Hollie, but he'd grown accustomed to having the two of them around, irritating the hell out of him. And God knows someone had to have an eye to Gray's preservation, because the choleric little bastard wouldn't look to it for himself – and Russell, Hollie had hardly had the keeping of the lad a month, people would start to pass remarks if he couldn't keep his own staff alive for more than four weeks –

And Hollie was tiring, and the stupid horse was tiring but too stupid to be anything other than willing, and Venning's black was lathered with sweat and dripping with foam –

Cullis's old cob staggering, blown, all but done –

They could not do this, they could not turn about and come again, and Hollie could scarce raise his sword arm for the numb weight of it and yet he had to, it was that or die. For all the glitter and the gallantry of it, it came to that: another man's reeking coppery bloody on your skin, a horse down on the cobbles shrieking in uncomprehending agony with a leg bent under it at an angle that the Lord had never intended.

That squint-eyed lad of Venning's – Lewis? the one who'd have bet on two flies walking down a wall? – his squint had been cured, in a terminal capacity, his wandering eye now a splintered shot hole that glistened bluish-black in the torchlight.

Hollie could bloody hear Fairfax, that was the worst of it, to know that hope was but a few yards away, and fighting as hard as he was himself but the length of a lane distant. Might as well have been a hundred miles, or the moon, for all the help it was. He wanted to cry, he was so tired he wanted to cry, he could barely breathe for the pain across his ribs and for sheer bloody weariness. He couldn't speak, his throat too dry and tight for any more than a horrible wheeze, so he lifted a hand so far as he could and hoped they'd see him give the order to go back in, again. And again, like some foul dream where you were condemned to repeat, over and again, the same action, the same blurred nightmare.

He could do nothing. He was done. And then, like a wave of the sea, he saw Captain Webb's company come crashing down on the barricades, finally – oh, thank God, thank God, Webb would come through, and sweep the defenders aside, and Hollie and what was left of his half-company would be relieved –

Another roar from the defenders, as they were swelled from the back by Belasyse's own company, pushing forward like a wave of their own. He saw Luce. Possibly Russell. One of them two, tall and fair and slight, distinctive, whichever of them, the torchlight spark off his bright hair between the dull blued metal of plate.

Saw him go down, whichever of them it was, suddenly and abruptly wrenched out of sight, and in all that seething torment it mattered, it mattered very much that one man whose name he knew should be saved, and he stood up in his stirrups and screamed till he tasted blood that Webb might look to him, that he might go to help that bright-haired lad, whichever he was – whoever he belonged to –

Webb looked straight at him. He knew the bastard had heard him. Saw the intelligence in the captain's face, such as there was. He looked at Hollie. Looked him in the eye.

Looked away.

Stood up in his stirrups as if he had not seen and roared and blustered and pointed to the river, harrying his men away from the fray. Away from Hollie. Away from Fairfax. To a place of greater safety.

Perhaps another man might not have noticed. Perhaps. Hollie knew, though. Hollie knew where the breaches in the barricade were, because God knows he had put them there, and at what cost they had been bought. Oh, it was noisy, and it looked ferocious enough, but the bastard was achieving nothing, all show and bluster. Worse, because he was sweeping the defenders towards Hollie's company, instead of away – veering his lads off towards the river, towards the warehouses, at a crashing gallop. Webb could have taken on the rear ranks. Could have caused havoc, if he'd come in, hard, from the back: Hollie pushing forwards from the barricade, and Webb harrying from the rear, it would have been bloody ruin.

Would have been, and was not, because Webb's brash gentlemen were scampering through the fleeing defenders, and heading most purposefully away from the fighting without so much as a shot being fired.

The sky was beginning to lighten.

"Webb!" he roared desperately, "here, you bugger, over this way!"

And the bastard kept on going.

He was *shy*.

The sudden knowledge of it fairly stunned Hollie mute, for a heartbeat. Thinking Webb must come about, must be planning some stunt, some perverse strategy – but he wasn't, he was skirting the fringes of the battle, like a fucking maiden pulling her skirts aside from a drunk in a gutter, picking off the halt and the lame if he had to, and he was deserting them, he was leaving them to fucking die like dogs while he bolted to hide up in the undefended warehouses.

"Son of a fucking bitch!" Hollie yelled, belting the stupid horse into life again, because that was a troop under his command and he was not bloody well having it left to be torn to bloody rags – "Get back here and *fight*, you lousy piece of shit!"

And he'd have gone after Webb himself, would have chased the mewling braggart through the gates of Hell if it came to it, and Webb knew it. Webb saw him coming, and his jowly face paled even from a distance of a hundred yards: his horse suddenly sprang into a clattering gallop, as if its rider had just rammed sharp spurs into its flanks, and he was gone, skidding into the shadows. And Hollie was yet half minded to hunt him down and make him eat his own braggadocio, except that he caught one bright flaring glimpse of the barley-haired lad again through the smoke, scrambling to his feet.

And then some bugger did open Hell's gates, in a great roaring wall of flame.

55

THANKFUL FOR HIS DELIVERANCE

And that had all but finished it, that sudden great exploding inferno, because it had come out of nowhere and died again almost as quickly. The stupid and the credulous of either army were afraid that it was God's punishing fire raining from heaven. The fierce were dazed and scorched, stumbling to their feet, blinking. Suddenly, in the flickering light of the dying flames of a barricade going to embers, the heart had gone out of all of them, a little. It was sufficient breathing space to realise that you were aching-tired, and blistered, and sore, and to set you apart from the fierce exaltation of battle and remind you that you were a man like other men, after all.

Dawn broke, as soft and grey as a pigeon's breast, and a pale misty light shone unforgiving on the wreckage of the Gowthorpe barricade. A thing that had looked like it might have been a kitchen table, once, its solid homely top cut about and scarred with the marks of some cook's cleaver, and a crack clear through the middle of it where the wood showed raw and new.

A thing that might have been a man, with most of the lower half of his face carried away by the blade of one of them bloody lethal pole-arms. He was not quite dead. Should be, and was not. Hollie sat on the wet cobbles with him until he was. It didn't take long, with the poor bastard bubbling and drowning in his own blood, clutching at Hollie's hand.

He hated the smell of burned wet wood, and spent powder. His head ached and his eyes stung and every bone in his stupid creaking too-old-for-this body protested.

His arm hurt and his ribs hurt and his heart hurt most of all.

His troop surgeon had stitched the long slash up his arm. Hollie had argued about it, though his heart hadn't been in it. Fat, stuttering, clumsy Witless had given him a stern look which wouldn't have disciplined a puppy, and Hollie was so miserable he'd just shut up and rolled his sleeve up. Being told off about the dirt clotting the edges of the shallow cut, and he had bucked himself up sufficient to say that it was nowt, it was a scratch. Witless had said it was a filthy scratch and if he didn't tend to it it'd get poisoned and he'd die so kindly hold your tongue Rosie.

Rosie, please note. He had fallen so low that Witless, bloody *Witless*, who'd managed to put a pistol ball through his own hat on one occasion in battle, was calling him that.

And actually, he didn't care. He limped down the horse lines, wondering if it might be an admission of age and defeat to not make his inspections. They wouldn't mind, the lads wouldn't –

Would turn out, what was left of them, the whole burned and ragged and dirty lot of them. Grubby, red-eyed with weariness, burned, bloodstained, each trooper of his own company standing at his horse's head all stiff with stubborn pride.

A pattering behind him and he turned round to see Venning's infernal dog trotting across the cobbles, tongue lolling like half a yard of pink ribbon. Pattering on three legs, the fourth paw tucked close to his besmottered chest, and Venning and his four-legged barricade pacing behind at the head of his own troop, their colours sagging and shot-holed but still flying.

"See 'ee's up and about, bor. Uh. Colonel Babbitt, sir."

"Haven't been to bed," he said. Didn't want to. Didn't want to sleep. More particularly, did not want to dream. "Go on, then. Let's hear it."

"The colonel means make your report, Captain Venning," the flat, grim tones of Sariel Chedglow at his most officious, because even having been put through one of the fiercest firefights in the war so far that zealous bastard believed in rendering unto Caesar the things that were Caesar's, which in Hollie's case meant addressing him in formal triplicate. And Hollie couldn't be arsed. His head was too muzzy to disentangle formal reporting.

"Piss off, Chedglow," he said without looking over his shoulder, and heard the affronted hiss of indrawn breath. "Drew?"

"Down about ten, I d'reckon. 'Bout another six hurt, couple not like to make it, most walking wounded. Have a look at 'en, I formed 'em up, see for yourself."

Hollie looked at them, since Venning was so proud of his lads.

Stout, unremarkable fen-slodgers almost to a man: plain, ordinary, and a long way from home. He nodded. "Aye. Good men." What could he do? What had he got to give, that might be of some worth to farm-lads and merchants' boys and working men, who'd walked away from homes and families and harvests to come up here, and maybe to die here? He couldn't give them peace, it wasn't within his gift. He couldn't even give them reassurance.

"Good lads," he said, and meant it. "You got some good lads there, Drew. D'you reckon an extra ration of ale might go some way to expressing the Army's, uh, gratitude?"

Venning considered. "Reckon it might, Rosie. Lads?" Smiles starting to break out on weary faces, not because it was a generous gift, because it wasn't, it was bugger-all. It was what he had, though, and he meant it.

"Captain Chedglow. Aye. You did well." Chedglow's sullen face almost lighting at the praise.

"By the Lord's grace," Hollie added, with his fingers crossed. He very much doubted the Lord had been overseeing Selby, last night. But Chedglow nodded grimly. "As stubble to our swords, colonel. Will you join us in thanks for our safe deliverance from the mouth of the dog?"

"Tinners wouldn't bite 'ee, bor, don't insult my dog's good taste," Venning muttered, wilfully misunderstanding.

Hollie gave him a stern look. "Drew. Shut up." Safe deliverance, though. Would he call it so, given – given what he had lost? He squeezed his eyes shut, because otherwise he might weep, at the thought of the gaps in his line.

Mattie Percey, standing with another man's colours bundled up under his arm.

Russell's wall-eyed bay, ungroomed, untacked, unkempt, rolling his mad blue eye at Calthorpe's big Delilah.

The raking clumsy beast that Hollie had acquired last night in the dark, half-grown and utterly charmless, shuffling at Mattie's side. Possibly the plainest brute he had ever clapped eyes on, and great raw patches on chest and shoulders and flank where the hair had been scorched away in the explosion, did not help. At some point in the battle someone – Hollie? maybe? – had yanked its bridle half over its head. The beast was so stupid it had not even protested. Somehow that was possibly the saddest thing he had ever seen, that homely brown horse with its bridle hanging over one ear and the bit hauled half through its mouth. It must have hurt –

Where there's no sense there's no feeling, Babbitt, the brute is too stupid to feel pain. Not like Tyburn with his tender ruined mouth, Tyburn who would not take a bit in his mouth after the way he'd been treated as a colt –

Even so. He found himself absently adjusting the bridle to fit the brown horse's clumsy head, to make it comfortable. Wondering who the hell had thrown tack on the bloody animal, and what plough-horse they'd stolen it off, for it to fit where it touched. For the brown horse to shyly touch its nose to Hollie's bloodied sleeve, as if it were relieved to at least see *someone* it recognised – he checked: not it, he, a gelding – and Hollie to rub the beast's muzzle. To find, with a lurch of the heart, that the brown horse's muzzle was as warm and soft as Tyburn's. His eyes prickled, stung and prickled, and he couldn't speak for a minute – so familiar, the velvet feel of a horse's whiskery chin on your hand, and yet so alien, so much clumsier than his Tib.

"Webb's in," Venning said gruffly, after a minute, and Hollie bit his lip till he tasted blood, and turned to face Captain Webb. Nodded at him, but did not greet him any further than that, despite the man's pleading eyes.

Webb's Adam's apple wobbled above his collar. "Got turned about in the fight, sir. Just as well I did, too, for we come across one of those warehouses by the river with the door broken open. Had to stop to secure it, sir. Powder store, sir. Couple of very desperate ruffians trying to supply the Malignants with replenishments, trying to run a cart up the Gowthorpe – we went behind to cut 'em off, sir –"

He deserved no praise. He had run. "That was Luce Pettitt," he said, very deliberately. "As you well know. And Hapless Russell. And Trooper Gray."

Webb stuttered something, flushing a dull purple.

"You left them, Webb." He wasn't in the mood for excuses. "You knew damn well who it was, and you knew they were in trouble. You must have passed within an arm's length of Lucey when you were *running away*. And Russell you could not have mistaken. You let my cornet die. An junior officer and two bloody brave troopers. You turned your back on them and you ran. You could have brought them clear and you did *nothing*."

"I –"

"Am a coward. Say it, captain. Good and clear so that no other fucker in my company is in any doubt. You are a coward. You are full of shit, and *Pettitt's blood is on your hands*." He was starting to frighten Webb, and he was glad of it, because the man was a liar and a bullshitter and he had no place in any troop that Hollie commanded. "Be assured, sir, Fairfax will not hear of this. Because you are not going to live long enough for it to be Fairfax's concern, you piece of shit. You are going to be in the van of every fucking charge I command, Webb, and I will harry your shameful carcass until you fucking break, because this is *your doing*."

"Sir. Yes, sir. I –"

"Am a worthless turd, Webb, say it." With the point of Hollie's sword under his bestubbled chin, raising a bead of blood on his bristly blue jowl. "Loud and clear, captain."

"I am a worthless," his throat worked, "I am a worthless turd."

"Correct, Captain Webb. You are a worthless turd and I would not trust you on latrine duties. You are unfit for command, sir."

"Sir."

He leaned into Webb's face, close enough to smell the man's stale breath. "I should rather have trusted the command of your troop to Pettitt, and *he* was a bloody poet."

"That's a bit harsh," Luce said, from less than a length behind them, and Hollie jerked upright with such astonishment that he nearly cut Webb's ear off, and the unfortunate captain pissed himself in fright. Not a thing recommended, in hodden gray breeches, and there was a ripple of unkind laughter from his own men as the dark patch spread over his crotch.

"*Alive?*" Webb squeaked, and Hollie could not stop himself from grinning.

"Looks it, no thanks to you."

"May the Lord be thanked, it's a miracle!"

"Well, no," Luce said, sounding deeply apologetic, "not a miracle, precisely, more that, well, we, Gray is what you might describe as, ah, unexpectedly fierce. And that Russell –" his bruised-looking mouth tightened briefly, "Russell does not perhaps know quite as much about powder as he thinks he does."

"Gray...*is?*"

The lad had acquired a stutter. Nerves, probably, or shock, or something, because he looked at Hollie with those big misty eyes – straight-on, for the first time in about a month, not sliding off to the side in guilt or awkwardness – and he said, "Gray's getting huh-*his* hand strapped up. I think he broke it, um, punching someone in the head on the barricade."

Webb's jaw hung open. "Both of you? Whole?" And to Hollie's utter embarrassment, the man dropped to his knees in the middle of the cobbles and began to offer fervent thanks to the Almighty.

"Well, Gray's broken his hand, and Russell – well, Russell took most of the charge, and I thank God for damp powder. He looks like the wrath of God, but then he always does, rather." Luce grinned at Hollie. "Let's just say that Thankful's temper has not improved overnight."

"What – what – Russell, too?" Tempted to join Webb in heartfelt gratitude on the wet stones, but instead Hollie contented himself with prodding Webb's ample thigh with the toe of his boot. "Get up, will you? Keep your bloody devotions to yourself!"

There was an odd, scraping, erratic, distant sound, echoing between the houses, and a growing murmuring from Hollie's company. And then Mattie Percey said, very low and very fierce, "Oh, *bravely* done, sir!"

"Leading this miscreant? I assure you, Percey, he is remarkably compliant."

Hollie's black horse should not be on his feet. Should not, in all probability, be alive. There was a great ragged flap of skin and muscle torn away from his chest, hanging like raw meat. His head hung almost to his knees, and each step was a shuffling agony, limping on three legs. With each erratic step the horse's shoulder bumped against Thankful Russell's flank, and the two of them picked their careful, painful way across the slippery cobbles one step at a time, pausing to rest too often. The black horse's flanks were heaving, and sweat was running down Russell's bruised face, but no one made to help them.

It would have seemed an insult, somehow, an affront to such dogged independence.

"Colonel Babbitt. Sir." There were bubbles of bloody froth at the corners of Russell's mouth, and his breath whistled in his chest, but he halted and straightened up. "Yours. I believe."

He put the reins into Hollie's hand and inclined his head stiffly. "May I stand down. Sir?"

The black horse staggered forward, just one more stride, and buried his head in the breast of Hollie's buffcoat. He'd done that since he was three years old, hurt and afraid in the fleshmarkets of Amsterdam, and Hollie had been the only other living being he'd trusted. Hollie who had been twenty-five, and hurt and afraid himself, after the death of his first wife. Eleven years of campaigning together, and it ended like this. Hollie put his hand on the horse's head, just behind the stallion's ear, where the pulse beat, fast and shaky. Where he'd rest the muzzle of the pistol, because he owed the horse that, if no more.

"Don't you dare," Thankful Russell said, so quiet that probably only Hollie heard. "If I can mend. *He* can mend."

The horse's flanks were heaving like a bellows, and long tremors were running through him. He could not survive that hurt. No beast could.

Even if he did – even if there was some fool daft enough to stitch the stallion like a quilt, and if the horse would stand quiet for it, and if the man was gentle-handed – he would never be sound again. Never fit for hard campaigning.

Russell's dark eyes were intent on Hollie's face. Hollie looked back, and did not look away. "Thee grows sentimental, Hapless," he said, equally softly, and the scarred young man lifted a shoulder as if he did not care. Or, rather, as if he did care, very much, and would rather it seemed as if he did not, for the show of it.

And without taking his eyes from Hapless, or his hand from the soft, beating tender place behind his horse's ear, Hollie called Luce to his side, for if there was any man he would trust to be gentle with Tyburn, it was the brat. And Luce would not think it a shameful vanity, to piece a horse back together, that he might live out his allotted span in some measure of peace. Nor would he think it shame that Hollie wept like a maid, for the loss of that last link to his youth.

"I think I can do it," Luce said eventually. "I can promise nothing, mind. He's not a young horse any more, Hollie." And then he smiled, rather wearily. "Will it keep an hour? I've to see to Gray's hand, and I really would like to look at Thankful's ribs."

It was the smell of burning that made Hollie's eyes water. That was all. He said nothing for a minute, but bit hard on his lip till he tasted blood again. "It will keep," he said. "But afterwards, I want all three of you buggers in my quarters. All *three* of you, Lucifer."

56

TAKING ORDERS FROM HOLLIE BABBITT

They reported at noon, or roundabout it, by which time Hollie had had about an hour's sleep and was feeling, if not kindly disposed, at least slightly more like a man and less like kindling.

"Well. Look at the bloody state of you three."

Luce's customary polished elegance was utterly destroyed by his apparently having been dragged backwards through a swamp and ridden over by a troop of horse. He looked delighted with it, though.

Gray was luminous with a fierce joy, bloody to the elbows, and stank of hot horse and burned wood. There was some as reckoned Hollie Babbitt was the fifth horseman of the Apocalypse, to which all he could say was, he might be in charge but for sheer unrestrained mental ferocity of biblical proportions he had nowt on Trooper Gray. That boy scared the hell out of Hollie, and they were on the same side.

And then there was Russell, and what could you say about Russell, except that he might still look austere but his eyes were alight with a rather disconcerting happiness.

"The lot of you. What the hell have you got to say for yourself?"

Luce looked as if he were about to laugh, and that was also new. The brat was keeping bad company, that was what it was. (The brat was growing up, and standing on his own two feet, and growing into his command. Damn it.) "If you are expecting an apology, sir, I think we did a rather good job. Actually."

A bead of sweat dripped from the end of his nose, which somewhat belied the dignified words. "And Tyburn is on his feet, and eating. Well, he took an apple from me earlier, with some condescension. I – it is early days, sir. Of course. But," and Luce smiled, and he smiled like a man who had done a thing of which he was quite unreasonably proud, "God willing, if the wound is kept clean, he will live."

Hollie nodded, as if he hadn't seen his horse's chest not half an hour after Luce had finished his work, with a row of stitches as neat as Het's mending and the raw edges of that horrible wound still seeping. "And the men?"

Gray held up his splinted hand wordlessly for inspection. Clean, and straight. He wasn't going to end up with a crooked little finger, the way Hollie had, after some overworked butcher had had at him after Edgehill.

Russell creaked like a well-worn buffcoat when he breathed, and he was surrounded by a vaguely exotic scent as of the still-room, but he seemed mostly intact. Somewhat black and blue, and redolent of burned hair, but intact.

"You going to enlighten me?" Hollie said, because he was, actually, curious.

"The intent was to lay a trail of gunpowder to the abbey doors as a fuse," Russell said primly, and Hollie raised his eyebrows.

"Whose daft idea was that? Because powder doesn't –"

"I am aware of that now, sir," the scarred young man said, without so much as a flicker of embarrassment.

"Foof!" Gray added, with a most expressive wave of his splinted hand. "That wasn't in the plan, was it – *Hapless*?"

"I note that you were as enthused by the idea as I, Master Gray," Russell said, and he sounded as cold and formal and contained as ever, but before God the lad was radiant with happiness.

"Russ – *Thankful*," Luce corrected himself, "Thankful was closest to the barrel that burst, and was consequently somewhat fuller of splinters than a hedgehog is of fleas. How is your side feeling, now?"

"Somewhat closer acquainted with the highway than a man's ribs ought to be."

Hollie snorted with unwilling amusement. "I think you ought to sit down before you fall down, Luce. Gray, shift a space on the desk. Move that, it's only papers. Or sit on it – not *me* that's got to deal with requisitions." Luce hooked the only other chair in the room underneath him and sat with a thump, and Gray parked one skinny buttock on the edge of the desk with an air of suspicion. And Russell remained bolt upright, not asking, stiff and quivering. Hollie shook his head. "In God's name, Hapless, I did not mean that *you* should stay stood there like a spare prick at a wedding. Find summat to sit on and bloody well sit down. Pettitt. Officer of the bloody watch. Allegedly. Finish making your bloody report. And can I have it plain, and not in blank verse – and preferably without interruption?"

"You ought to know what happened, sir. You were coming right in behind us. Sir," muttered Gray, and Hollie cocked an eyebrow.

"Was I talking to you? – Luce."

"Well, this powder, sir. Um. It was –"

"Requisitioned," Russell said smoothly. "It had been surplus to requirements."

There was a long pause. "Whose requirements?" Hollie said, equally delicately.

"Sir John Belasyse. I believe. Sir."

"You three were looting the Malignants? In the middle of a battle?"

"Pre-empting," Luce said. This language of diplomacy had a certain advantage all its own. "We merely anticipated a barrel or two, that was all."

"Anticipated."

"Sir."

There was another long pause. "Lucifer. How much of that stuff did you half-inch?"

"As much as we could carry away. Sir." Hollie said nothing, but folded his hands on the desk and looked encouraging. "About three barrels."

This time he said nothing because he actually couldn't. "Three."

"And a hand-cart," Gray added smugly.

"And a hand-cart."

"It seemed more expedient." Russell did not smirk, because it wasn't an expression he was capable of, but he had a trick of dropping his eyelashes and then looking back up, daring you to argue. If it had been a wench pulling that look Hollie would have called it flirtatious. With Russell, it was a challenge.

"You three bloody lunatics –"

"With half a troop of horse as backup," Luce pointed out –

"You three bloody lunatics piled into an embattled town, lifted a cartful of powder, and then decided to fetch up in the middle of the battle and set it off? All three of you are cracked!"

"We allowed safe egress for my lord Fairfax," Russell said defiantly.

"Hapless, you allowed safe egress for most of the Army of fucking Parliament, you bloody ranting nutjob! That barricade was spread across most of fucking Yorkshire! You are any number of things, you three, but what you are not is fucking artillery experts! Jesus Christ, Lucey, what the hell would my wife have said if I had to tell her you'd blown yourself to bloody bits?"

"Well, the road to York is clear, isn't it?" Gray on the attack, chin up and eyes blazing.

"I'm surprised there *is* still a road to York, not just a bloody smoking crater! What the bloody hell – "

Hollie stopped, shoved his hair behind his ears, and glared at the three of them, in turn. Luce looked sheepish, and the other two looked quite unrepentant. What the buggers did look like, mind, was a team. Gray stared back. "You covered us," he said flatly.

"Well, of course I bloody covered you – I'm married to his bloody auntie, I'm not hardly going to go home and tell her I've let him get shot to bits in defence of a cart full of bloody ill-gotten powder!"

"Did Fairfax not *mind*? – that you disobeyed an order, and came for us?"

"Docked a week's pay," Hollie muttered, and tugged some of his papers loose from under Gray's backside, scowling. "We're not talking about me, we're talking about you!"

"You lost a week's pay – for *us*?"

"Him. Don't get ideas, Gray." He straightened the requisition list. "I swear to God, this paperwork is a bloody state. I pity the poor sod as has to pick up my administration." And looked up again, staring out of the window thoughtfully. "Was a good fight, though. Job done, I believe. Straight on through to York, and nowt to stand in our way. We might not be the prettiest troop in the Army, but I don't reckon there's anyone can say we don't do a good job."

"We are about the Lord's work. Of course we do," Russell said primly, and Gray looked at him askance.

"You might be about the Lord's work, mate, but I take my orders from Rosie Babbitt. And no one else."

It was quiet, outside. It wasn't totally quiet, because someone in the city was demolishing a wall that had been rendered structurally unsafe by the combined efforts of Messrs Pettitt, Russell and Gray. Siege warfare was clearly not their forte. Hollie made a mental note to hunt down his old mate Black Shuck, if that ageing master gunner had survived Reading, and turn these three over to him for half a day, if they were going to make a habit of this kind of lunacy.

(They'd come back sweary and insubordinate, but with all their fingers. He could cope with that.)

There was a great rumbling crash about a mile away, and he looked back at the three of them with raised eyebrows. "Well, there went some goodwife's garden wall, gentlemen, I hope you're proud of yourselves."

Gray laughed. Luce, bless him, looked mortified.

"Joke," he added, before the brat burst into tears.

Linked his hands behind his back and stretched, because he'd been sat too long in a chair that was slightly too small for a man two yards high, and he was starting to get stiff. Something creaked. It was possibly the chair, and possibly not. "Do you three consider yourself appropriately disciplined?"

"No – stoppages?" Gray said warily, and Hollie considered.

"Oh, aye, stoppages. Glad you reminded me. You two are buying the ale, trooper, and Cornet Pettitt is buying supper. Providing that between you you managed to leave four walls of a decent inn standing, between here and York."

It was an odd thing with Gray – you got exactly what you saw, a scruffy foul-mouthed little ruffian who was almost perpetually in trouble and mostly filthy, but his eyes went rather touchingly round and shiny at the prospect of keeping such exalted company. His shoulders straightened up, and he almost strutted. "Gray," Luce hissed, not quite inaudibly, "tuck your shirt in."

Under a thin layer of grime and gunpowder, Gray flushed, and Hollie tried to look stern as the lad trotted past. At his master's heels, as ever.

He might take his orders from Hollie, but he took his lead from Luce, always. And that was good, because maybe, just maybe, there was the beginnings of a decent soldier under there, and a young man who might yet be made something of.

Provided he didn't get his damn-fool head shot off, obviously.

"Trooper Gray," he said mildly, and the little trooper's shoulders jerked.

"Good job, lad. Well done."

Which left Russell. As ever. A little of the joy faded from his face, staring woodenly at the wall. "Not done with you, Hapless," Hollie said. "Wait downstairs, please, Luce. Until I'm through dealing with Trooper Russell."

A little of the joy faded from Luce's, too, but he didn't argue, just shepherded Gray down the creaking stairs and engaged him in polite and very audible conversation, the better to not overhear Russell taking his lumps.

Bless the brat.

"You're getting docked another day's pay, Russell, for not being properly turned out. I do not expect to see my officers running around with the arse hanging out of their breeches, sir."

"Yes. Sir."

He'd learned. There was a twitching in his scarred cheek that spoke of a man biting his tongue, hard, but Russell said nothing that was not exactly as it should be. Respectful, submissive, and pig-livid. And not bloody listening, either.

Hollie nodded in satisfaction. "Nor do I expect any of my officers to be half-dressed on duty. Where's your sash, lieutenant?"

"You have it, sir," he said sulkily, and then realised what he'd just said, looking up with his dark eyes gone as starry as a maid's.

"Probably just as well you didn't have it yesterday, or it'd be all smothered wi' bloody powder and shot-holes, wouldn't it?" Hollie – whose own sash of office was a dreadful, faded, bloodstained rag of enormous sentimental value – rifled in his travelling-chest and unfolded the yards of tawny fabric. "I suppose you want it back?"

"More than anything else in the world. Sir." And that was an admission, from Hapless Russell. Hollie thought the occasion demanded some ceremony, some formal marking of its importance, and there wasn't a damn thing he could think of, other than to look out of the window as Russell tied it about his waist with hands that shook. And hand him a handkerchief, because it'd be a bloody shame if the scarred young man ended up blowing his nose on the lustrous silk, after all the trouble Hollie had gone keeping it intact, this last two months.

"Aye. Well. There is a bit of back-pay owing, lieutenant. Since I never actually took you off the muster roll as an officer. Due to me being bloody useless at figures and not having a competent administrator for a couple of months."

"I imagine you will be wanting the company accounts set in order, then," Russell said, with a happy sigh. Possibly the only man in the company who found his happiness in creating order from chaos, and not vice versa. "And, ah, finding some way of accounting for an additional three barrels of powder."

"Well you used most of them, didn't you?"

"There may be a little left over." He blushed. He actually *blushed*. And looked up and grinned, that dreadful one-sided grin with all his teeth showing on one side and none on the other. Fearsome, but happy. Frighteningly happy. "I should prefer them to remain official, sir. May I borrow your pen?"

"You may not." He put his hand flat between Russell's shoulders and steered him towards the door. "You know I mentioned the back-pay? Consider this your last night of freedom, Hapless. Tomorrow, you're back in harness."

"Sir?"

"Tonight, you're buying the drinks. March on."

EPILOGUE

Hollie Babbitt sat on the bed – which creaked, alarmingly, but there was no one in their quarters sufficiently conscious to care – and tugged at his boots.

Bloody lightweights. Lightweights, the lot of them. He had ten years on Luce and Hapless, and more like twenty on Gray, and he was *still* the last man standing.

Mind, they had been quite restrained. He reckoned the whole company had been restrained, and that it was mostly due to being stiff and shocked and still reeling from the fight. But game. Always game.

Gray had gone down first, which was no surprise, given that the more Hollie looked at Gray the more he thought the little bugger was barely weaned. Mind you, Gray couldn't half eat. Lucky they'd left the efficient Hapless in charge of the provisioning end of business. It was sort of oddly touching that Gray had been sat at the scarred, splintered table in the kitchen, his elbows touching Luce's and his spoon a veritable blur, wide-eyed with awe at his exalted company. He'd been sufficiently at ease halfway down the ale jug though, to point out that Drew Venning's boots smelt like summat had crawled in them and died. Venning checked, and it turned out that summat had. (Tinners had thumped his tail on the hearthstone and grinned at the cursing that had prompted. Half a baby rat could only come from one place.)

Anyway, Gray had been slipping slowly down in his seat, and Hollie had stood up to turn a piece of bread over on the fork and he turned round and the little bugger had pitched over sideways, all snuggled like a dormouse into Hollie's warm seat.

Luce had laughed, and put his own coat over the young lad where he slept. "I think he may be the only one amongst us who doesn't snore," he said. "He may stay."

Luce himself had politely made his excuses about midnight, and limped off up the stairs to seek a real bed. *Whistling.*

Leaving Hollie with Hapless Russell, who had remained as prim and self-contained as ever, bolt upright at the table working his way down a stack of toasted cheese at one elbow, their third jug of ale at the other, and the company accounts in front of him. It was actually fascinating to watch, truly it was. Conversation had lagged until finally, at coming on for dawn, Russell had looked up with a joyous grin that split his scarred face, shoved his hair out of his eyes, announced that the troop had finished this campaign twelve pounds in profit, and keeled over with a thump.

Hollie rescued the ink pot from underneath his lieutenant, and patted the lad's shoulder awkwardly. "Full on or backwards, the daft bugger," he said, aloud to the empty kitchen.

Gray murmured something from his comfortable spot in the settle by the fire, and Hollie looked up. Hollie had a daughter, now. He was training himself to look for signs of imminent peril to the young, like rolling off a settle and cracking your head open on the hearthstone. (Hollie had never set eyes on the child, and that grieved him, but he would. One day. Soon. They'd taken Selby, and shortly York would split like a wormy apple, and then surely to God the King was going to give it up as a bad job.)

Well. Gray was a lightweight, Luce was happy again, and Hapless would work till he dropped doing a thing he loved. Life was good. Hollie yawned, and scrubbed his hands through his hair, and rolled himself in his blankets. He only meant to shut his eyes a minute. They were stood down this night, on grounds of being somewhat wrecked; they had stout quarters, plainly provisioned, but amply. York was eleven miles up the road, and they had the Malignants on the run. The Army of Parliament could do without one plain colonel of horse, a little frayed, and so tired his bones hurt. Tomorrow –

No, an hour later, there was someone hammering on the door and yelling his name and he was out of bed with his boots on before he'd even opened his eyes, stumbling down the last four steps at once and hitting the wall at the bottom so hard with his shoulder that a chunk of plaster dropped loose. Dry-mouthed and sick and panicked, with Gray materialising at his elbow from his place on the settle and Russell coming awake so abruptly he tipped his chair over, surging across the kitchen flags with his sword drawn.

Bit of a disappointment, then, to realise it was only Elijah Babbitt, and that no one had run him through or shot him on the way down from Essex.

They'd let him through the bloody sentries because you only had to look at Lije to see whose sire he was – he had the same height and lanky build as his son, the same lamentably prominent nose and untidy thick hair. Lije was greyer than his boy, but in a bad light, they'd almost pass one for another, which was no bloody consolation at all, since Hollie had thought he'd left the appallingly godly old bastard back home in Essex. He was supposed to be looking to Hollie's wife – his wife, his new daughter, his home, all the things he held dear –

"She threw me out, boy," Lije said placidly, with an expression on his grim features that might have been described as self-satisfied on one of the Lord's less Elect.

"She – what?" Hollie said, gripping the age of the kitchen table hard, because otherwise he might puke or faint, and neither would do his dignity any good.

"She said I was sufficient mended to be more use to you than her. By, Holofernes, that lass knows where her duty lies! Aye, and she sent me with a packet of letters – where is thee going, boy? Will thee not join me in giving thanksgiving for my safe preservation?"

Hollie, worrying at the seal of his letters with his teeth, cocked an eyebrow at his father. "Aye. Probab– " Reading her words with the desperation of a drowning man, and then shaking his head, blinking. *"Thomazine?"*

Elijah's smirk widened. "Aye. Thee is Holofernes Thomas, no? Well, then. The child was christened Thomazine, to do thee honour. In thy *absence*, boy. I stood as godfather to her my own self, while thee was away smiting the heathen."

"Thomazine?" Hollie said again, feebly. "You called my little girl Thomazine? What the hell kind of a name is *Thomazine*?"

"Judith would have been worse," Luce said unhelpfully, from halfway down the stairs. "Good morning, Elijah. I am glad to see you in spirits. Thomazine is a fine Essex name, Hollie. If you will marry an Essex woman, you must be prepared for strange customs."

I was minded to call our daughter Jael, for a most unwomanlie desyre to drive a tent peg into the side of yr father's head like that most fiery lady in the Bible.

I did not think you would approve tho for I know how much you dislike being named Holofernes.

Tho as it is yr own dear self I do nott mind the writing of it so much.

I did nott think ember tart wd survive a journey so far and so I have sent a whole chese instead.

My dear love to Lucyfer and his mother sends hers also. Gabriel sends some munney and says Luceyfer is to spend it wisely and not buy sillies for his sisters, who have a suficiency of ribbons and laces and not to encourage their vannities further.

I have sent new linnen for Thankfull, the poor boy did seem ragged when last I saw him and stands in want of either a wife or a mother I do think.

And for yourself dear husband –

Hollie put his hand over the rest of the letter quickly, trying to look stern and righteous.

(She loved him. She loved him yet, and she missed him. And yes, he did remember that time he'd kissed her by the brook, in the early spring, two years back. Wasn't likely to forget. It had been raining, and there'd been a stormcock singing in the willow tree over his head, and from that day to this he did not know if that was how his heart sounded, happy, or if it truly had been a stormcock singing for joy fit to split his throat.)

Luce was looking at him with a very depressingly knowing glint in his eye. He knew bloody well what was in that letter, the little sod. Knew, and was as smug as hell about it.

Gray looked oddly disappointed that it hadn't turned out to be another shameless brawl.

Russell had a smear of ink on his forehead and three days' worth of beard and looked like he could do with going back to bed for another hour, but the chances of him doing it, even if was a direct order, were remote. Not while there was the sniff of action.

"Well," Hollie said, "since we're all up and about, gentlemen, shall we go and kick some arse?"

ABOUT THE AUTHOR

M J Logue is a trained archivist and literature graduate who lived in York overlooking the Ouse for five years, studying in the archives of York Minster by day and cleaning the school by night. Her interest in the seventeenth century began when she lived next door to a ruined manor on the edge of the Peak National Park, as a result of which she wrote her first novel aged 15. She now lives with her husband, son and three cats in West Cornwall.

"The Smoke of Her Burning" is the second of the Uncivil Wars books to feature Thomas Fairfax's Yorkshire campaign, beginning with "Command the Raven" (Bradford and Selby, 1643) and continuing in 2017 with "Babylon's Downfall" (Marston Moor, 1644)

Keep up with the adventures of the rebel rabble at
www.uncivilwars.blogspot.com

Printed in Great Britain
by Amazon